UNCHAINED BY A FORBIDDEN LOVE

ETERNAL MATES BOOK 15

FELICITY HEATON

THE ETERNAL MATES SERIES

CHAPTER 1

It was never a good day when he woke with the taste of blood on his tongue and no recollection of how it had got there.

Again.

Fuery stared up into the darkness, cold sweat trickling over his exposed chest and sticking the thin black bedclothes to his legs. He breathed hard, each heavy desperate exhalation shattering the silence, rasping in his ears together with his thundering heartbeat.

Icy claws gripped him, sinking into the blackened remains of his heart, attempting to pierce deep enough to reach whatever fragment of light remained in him.

He squeezed his eyes shut, dragged down a shuddering breath and held it, unwilling to let fear pull him into the darkness. He would not let it win. He couldn't. He exhaled slowly, a measured pace that created a sliver of calm, enough to give him the strength to shake the grip of his fear and allow him to extinguish that emotion.

Because fear was a weakness.

He did not feel such things.

He hadn't in a long time.

Not since he had hardened himself to the world.

Not since *that* night.

Fuery screwed his eyes shut even tighter, his lips drawing into a grimace that flashed his emerging fangs as the darkness welled again, pulling up memories from the abyss. They surged and fought for freedom, and he growled as he pushed back against them, battled and resisted them. The fight took longer this time, strained minutes in which the fear slithered back in and wrapped around him again, squeezing his lungs tight and hissing whispered taunts in his ear, words about the terrible sins he had committed that had the memories surging harder, almost breaking to the surface.

He gripped the sides of his head and squeezed hard as he snarled through his clenched fangs. Tears cut down his temples, hot against his chilled skin. He didn't want to remember, but he could never forget either.

He didn't want to go back into the darkness, refused to sink into oblivion again and do the vile bidding of the darkness that lived inside him. Not again.

He grappled with fear, wrestled with the darkness, and fought the tide of memories, and somehow, the gods only knew how, he managed to subdue them and vanquish the raw agony and the sheer terror that threatened to push him back over the edge.

He panted hard, body trembling from the exertion of overcoming the darkness and clawing his way back to the light.

Couldn't think about that night.

Never look back.

The past was pain.

A constant source of it that scoured his blackened soul.

No looking back.

He inhaled and exhaled, keeping them measured and deep, struggling for calm again as his past and his present churned inside him, rocking him and trying to keep him off balance, on the brink of teetering back into the abyss.

No looking back.

Fuery chanted it in his mind as he sought the calm—the quiet.

It was slow to come while the darkness roared inside him, drawn out by the fear that had paralyzed him, weakened him and opened him to it. Its inky tendrils snaked around his heart and squeezed it in his hollow chest.

Attempted to claim his soul.

Calm seemed an impossible dream while blood coated his tongue.

But gods, he wanted it, reached for it, desperate to shirk the grip of the fear and the darkness again.

They combined to overpower him and he could feel himself slipping again, skidding down that terrifying slope towards the cold forbidding darkness where it reached for him, beckoned him with promises of oblivion and an escape from the madness.

From the pain.

No looking back.

The past was a nightmare.

The past was pain.

Always pain.

He opened his eyes and stared up into the darkness as he forced himself to see where he was in a vain attempt to focus on the present. He was here, in the guild, in the free realm of Hell. He was far away from there. Leagues from the elf kingdom. Centuries away from his past.

Light streaked across the darkness and his eyes swiftly adjusted to the onslaught. A shadow made the slim vertical shaft flicker and then brightness exploded in the room, driving back the darkness entirely.

Just as the male on the threshold of his room drove it from his soul.

Hartt looked at him through sleep-filled eyes and murmured huskily in the elf tongue, "I felt you stir. Everything alright?"

Fuery went to nod, because any other response would leave him weak. Vulnerable. He stopped himself, paused and stared at Hartt where he stood dressed in only a loose pair of black cotton trousers and scrubbing a hand over his short sleep-mussed black-blue hair, yawning the whole time.

He didn't need to protect himself like that with this male.

Hartt knew the truth of him. Knew his secrets. His story.

Fuery slowly shook his head.

Hartt yawned again, smacked his lips together and rubbed sleep from his violet eyes as he stepped into the room. He quietly closed the door, descending the room back into darkness that lasted only a second. A soft glow burned in the glass lamp on the low round wooden table near the window to Fuery's left and gradually gained strength, driving back the shadows again and drawing some of the darkness out of the black plastered walls, softening the bleak colour.

Hartt's doing, because Fuery's own powers were unpredictable.

Unreliable since *that* night.

The male padded silently barefoot across the stone floor towards him and sat on the edge of the bed on his left, causing Fuery to roll towards him. The warm light chased over Hartt, throwing the left half of his face into shadow.

Hartt's violet eyes softened as they met his. "Tell me about it."

Fuery sank back into the double mattress on a sigh and averted his gaze, pinning it back on the wooden ceiling. Gods, he didn't want to speak about it. Everything in him screamed to protect himself by making the male go away, but that light Hartt always seemed to draw out of him emulated the lamp, fought to grow brighter and drive the darkness back.

He had to speak about it. Years of experience had taught him that. Holding it inside would only give the darkness a firmer hold on him, making it harder to shake it and increasing the risk of him sinking into that terrible oblivion again.

3

He didn't want to go there.

So he forced himself to speak.

"I woke…" His hands tensed against his bare stomach, fingers curling into fists, and he pushed onwards. "I woke with the taste of blood in my mouth."

He could still taste it now.

He dropped his gaze to his body. No trace of crimson on his torso. He uncurled his hands and lifted them, stared at his fingers and his callused palms, scouring them for a sign, some evidence that he had lost himself to the darkness and had killed.

There wasn't a single fleck of blood on him.

But it was there in his mouth.

Coppery. Vile.

"I think I did something terrible," he whispered and shook his head, numbness sweeping through him and bringing fear in its wake, a stronger wave this time, one that threatened to pull him under. Break him. "I don't remember. I can't recall how I got to my bed."

He shifted his gaze to land on Hartt.

The pity shining in Hartt's violet eyes drove shame through his heart like a spear and he quickly looked away.

"I put you here," Hartt said softly, his deep voice a bare whisper but one that soothed Fuery, easing his fear and the grip the darkness had on him. "You had an… *episode*… and I brought you home."

Relief bloomed inside him, sweet and warm, but the darkness still refused to release him and worry continued to slither inside him like a living thing, hissing in his ear that Hartt was lying, that he had killed and the male was covering it up.

Hartt seemed to see it, because he sighed and jerked his chin towards him. "Open your mouth."

Fuery didn't hesitate to do as he was ordered. The male leaned over, peered into his mouth and lifted his top lip with his left hand. When he prodded Fuery's tongue on the left side, sharp pain lanced the length of it and he flinched, almost biting Hartt's finger. The male was too fast for him though, reacted in a heartbeat and had his finger clear before Fuery's fangs could pierce his flesh.

"You must have bitten your tongue when you were thrashing around. That's all." Hartt eased back.

Gods, the relief that hit Fuery this time was like ambrosia. It poured through him, washing away his worry and easing the chill from his blood.

Hartt's lips tugged into a smile and he slowly shook his head. "For a male who makes a living taking lives, you are oddly affected by the idea of killing."

Fuery knew it was a paradox, that Hartt was right and he had no qualms about his life as an assassin.

But there was a vast difference between killing when he was in control and murder when he was lost to the darkness.

He had felt that way for many centuries.

He had felt it since *that* night.

Now he couldn't bear the idea he might kill someone innocent during one of his blackouts.

He looked to Hartt and saw in his eyes that he wouldn't tell him if he did. Hartt was noble in his desire to protect him from the pain of the things he did when the darkness was in control, but Fuery didn't want his friend to lie to him, to cover the truth and spare him like that.

He needed to know the things that he did. He had to know them. He could never atone, but he could bear his sins.

Because all that he had done, and all that he might do, paled in comparison to the sin he had committed.

That night.

CHAPTER 2

Shaia despised having to walk with the male beside her, hated the way he treated her as if she was fragile and liable to break. He never spoke to her as an equal, never entertained her when she tried to converse about things he believed she didn't need to know about purely because she was a female.

It annoyed her.

Almost as much as the ridiculous outdated traditions of elf society that had bred those opinions into him.

But he was necessary.

She had put off her family for so long that they had finally reached the end of their tether and were determined to marry her off at last.

They had found a suitable male for her, had negotiated with him, and now it was time to seal the deal.

She cursed elf society.

It treated her like a possession or an asset.

Not a living, breathing thing with free will.

Shaia scoffed under her breath at that. Free will?

She looked around the rolling green landscape bathed in light, at the fields that lined the worn earth road, and the males who toiled in them. Males. Ahead, in the village that nestled between one of the hills and the broad stream, the stalls of the market and the mills would produce the same results.

Males.

Not a single female ran a store or a mill. Not a single female toiled in the fields to turn the earth or harvest the crops, restricted to tasks like sowing seeds that society thought fitted their more delicate constitutions.

Not a single female fought in the ranks of the elf army.

Her heart plummeted in her chest and she pushed away from thoughts of the legions, but she wasn't quite quick enough to spare herself the pain that came whenever she thought of that noble duty or saw soldiers passing through the village.

She felt Eirwyn's eyes on her as a vile shudder over her skin and glanced across at him. Concern lit his violet eyes. Concern she could almost fool herself was real. Perhaps she was misreading him again, mistaking frustration for concern. He often became annoyed with her whenever she fell silent, drifting along in her own world and captured by her own thoughts rather than talking with him about whatever dull topic he had chosen and believed suited her feeble female mind.

Males.

Gods, she wished she had the strength and courage to stand up, tell her family that she would never marry and she was going to leave this small world behind and search for a meaning in life in the greater one beyond the borders of the elf kingdom.

Borders that had been her cage for her entire life, one she had never quite been able to break free from despite her best efforts.

She had travelled the length and breadth of the kingdom, had visited every region but the one around the palace, but not once had she managed to muster the bravery to do something her family would view as unforgivable.

Something society would view as disgraceful, and akin to committing a damned crime even though males could do it freely and without consequence or scorn.

She had never crossed the border.

She had reached it once, had stared down from a high mountain peak into the valley beyond, knowing it was part of the First Realm of the demons. She had gone back and forth for hours, fighting with the idea of setting foot in it and breaking with convention, flouting the rules of her family and society.

In the end, she had lacked the courage to take that step.

Her family were all she had, and although their relationship was strained by the things they had done, the thought of them turning their backs on her because she had done something society would view as disrespectful towards them, and unladylike of her, hurt too much for her to dare go through with it.

Even when her heart longed to see what lay beyond the elf kingdom in those shadowy lands she had surveyed from the peak.

She stared into Eirwyn's eyes, verging on speaking her mind and telling him that she hated what he represented, she despised that she was going to willingly leave one cage to enter another. The black slashes of his eyebrows dipped low and his lips thinned, a flare of irritation lighting his eyes as he slowed to a halt.

Could he see everything she wanted to tell him in her eyes? Could he see into her heart and see that it would never be his?

It belonged to another.

Gods damn convention and the slow pace of her species.

Other species in Hell had moved forward, their females given freedom and power, and a will of their own.

Why couldn't the elves move at that same pace?

Had anything really changed in the last forty-five centuries? The village was the same. The people in it hadn't changed. Even the larger towns had barely progressed. Her world was stagnant. Boring. She longed to shake things up, to do something that would alter her cage or perhaps break free of it.

Gods, she longed for that.

She had tasted true freedom once, so many centuries ago. It still felt like yesterday to her at times, when she allowed herself to think back to those halcyon days and managed to feel warmth from remembering them, hope and light, not cold and pain.

And darkness.

Four thousand five hundred years had passed since her birth, and what had truly changed in that time? Society had barely shuffled forwards a few steps. Females were growing stronger, beginning to gain more power and more respect, but it had taken her entire lifetime for it to happen and such power and respect was limited to the larger towns. In the villages, females were still treated like chattel, given to the male who offered the best payment to her family.

In her case, Eirwyn had offered both the highest bid and been the most persistent of her suitors.

Her family had caught her at a low point, when she had been depressed from the long months she had passed alone at her small home far from the village and her feet had carried her back to her family's house, a need to speak with others and see the faces of her kin dragging her back to them.

She had been weak, tired from fighting with them when she wanted to spend time with them in peace and happiness, wanted to relive the days that had come before she had matured and they had started looking for a suitor for her, an eligible male that filled their every need and desire.

She had regretted agreeing to it just seconds after the words had left her lips, but Eirwyn had been swift to swoop on her and announce their future marriage to the entire village, and now the deed was done.

She would marry him, and she would live with him.

But she would never love him.

She stifled another sigh and forced a smile for him. He was handsome enough, with his regal features and his long black hair tied into a neat ponytail at the nape of his neck, allowed to flow down his back to blend with his tailored black tunic that reached his knees and accentuated his fine figure, but she felt nothing for him.

Whenever she looked at him, she saw another. She saw a male who had lit a fire inside her, a spark that had burned in her heart and had given her strength, and more than ever she wanted to find the courage to stand on her own two feet and push back against tradition to claim the life she wanted for herself.

He began walking again, talking about the crops this year, as if he played any part in their success. He owned land, paid males to work it, and profited off their success.

Coin was the one thing she lacked, and the one thing it was impossible for her to come by without her parents, or a male. Eirwyn would at least provide that for her she supposed. No more scrounging for seed to grow her own vegetables and fruit, or relying on her parents to send her an allowance.

Hopefully, Eirwyn would allow her to continue working with nature in his garden, and she could lose herself in it for hours, filling her day with work and avoiding him as much as possible.

Shaia stared off into the distance where the windmills stood proud on top of several of the hills above the village, their blades rotating slowly in the gentle breeze that stirred the wheat fields surrounding them.

Her thoughts drifted as her eyes settled on one windmill in particular, set away from the village and high on a hill above the others.

She had met the son of that family several times in her youth, could remember how proud his family had been when he had joined the legions and had been chosen to serve under Prince Vail, and how relieved they had been when he had survived the battle near the borders of the free realm, a war begun by that prince when he had turned on his own men.

At the time, Shaia had cursed them, had wished it had been another male who had returned from that brutal battle and not their son.

The loss of that male, and the darkness of her desire for him to have survived and their son to have died instead, had propelled her into a deep depression that had consumed her for years, had clouded her heart and her mind, and had taken her decades to escape.

It was a depression that still consumed her from time to time.

"Shaia?" Eirwyn's bass voice penetrated her thoughts and she pulled herself away from her past and the pain that lived there and back to him. "You seem out of sorts today. Shall we not go back?"

She shook her head. "The walk will do me good. It will lift my spirits."

A lie, but one that came easily to her when the alternative was returning back to her family home while her parents were out. She didn't want to be alone with Eirwyn and he would insist on remaining with her until her parents returned. It was better to be out in the open, surrounded by others, tasting what little freedom she had.

What she really wanted was to convince him to walk the hills with her, or visit the stream so she could wade in its crisp waters and cool down, escaping the blistering heat of summer. Eirwyn would refuse though. He had made it clear that he thought it unladylike of her to want to do such things, and that her constitution would suffer.

She scoffed under her breath at that.

Females weren't as delicate as he believed.

Her eyes drifted back to the mill in the distance again. That family had a daughter too, one younger than she was and a female who was often the subject of rumours in the village. Shaia loved to hear the latest tales of her, pretended to be affronted and shocked, and even dismayed by the things she heard, while being envious and wishing she were in Iolanthe's boots.

Iolanthe roamed Hell, travelled far and wide, and even into the mortal realm at times, an independent female bent on doing things her way.

A strong female.

One who didn't allow anyone to stand in her way.

It inspired her, kept that fire burning inside her, but the flames fanned by whatever latest tale she heard soon died back, leaving only a feeble spark behind, one quickly constrained again and subdued.

Eirwyn gestured towards the hills on the other side of the stream, to the trees that blanketed several of the slopes, and she nodded and smiled, did her best to be congenial and please him.

Her family had caught her at a low point when she had come to visit them, had convinced her that if she married, she might be happy again.

She knew it was just another cage, but she was tired, and everything seemed so bleak now. Her life no longer had any meaning. What reason did she have to go on existing?

Gods, she hated how easily she slipped into these dark moments that felt as if they were going to consume her, her will stripped from her and a desperate need for company filling her, as if that would chase the cold emptiness from her heart.

It was after a particularly brutal bout of depression, when she had still lived at home with her family, that her parents had called in a doctor from the nearest town to tend to her.

Depression was a cage, but it had given her some freedom.

The doctor had spoken with her parents, stating that she needed a hobby or some space to help ease her mood. When her parents had asked her what she wanted, she had spoken from her heart, requesting that she be allowed a small home of her own to run, away from the village.

Her parents had been reluctant, but had eventually agreed when the doctor had pressed them. Her new home had lifted her spirits, and had given her a taste of freedom, allowing her to come and go as she pleased. She had buried herself in her garden, the long days flying past as she toiled from the moment it grew light until it became too dark to see.

But the loneliness, the solitude, got to her at times, especially during the longer winter nights, and her thoughts always turned to her past, and a time when her heart had been full and overflowing.

Then, the emptiness rose inside her to consume her again.

Driving her back home in an attempt to fill it.

"Shaia?" A male voice curled around her and she frowned and looked around as they entered the fringes of the village, seeking the source of it.

None of the males coming and going along the avenues between the thatched houses were familiar to her.

"Do you know that male?" Eirwyn said and she glanced up at him, catching him scowling in the direction of the village square as he smoothed his ponytail, his actions clipped and reeking of irritation.

Shaia looked there.

A handsome male strode towards them along the broad road between the grey stone two-storey buildings, his fitted black tunic detailed with elegant pale green embroidery around the edges of the two long panels at the front that reached his knees, the matching ones at the back, and around the cuffs. Tight black trousers hugged his lean muscular legs, tucked into polished black knee-high riding boots. Their silver clasps reflected the light, dazzling her as much as his wide smile and bright violet eyes.

Eirwyn pulled a face beside her, and she could understand why. While his own tunic and trousers were fine and tailored for him, they couldn't compare to the ones the male wore.

They bore symbols only those high in the court of Prince Loren could wear.

The male's smile became a grin and he waved, glanced over his shoulder and said something to someone behind him, and then picked up pace, heading towards Shaia.

She blinked as she finally recognised him.

The miller's son.

The last time she had seen Bleu, he had been a scrawny lad and had come home to the village to announce to his parents that he had been given the position of commander. His family had held a celebration in his honour, and Shaia had been invited, but had refused. The thought of seeing him in the finery of a commander and attending the celebration had been too much for her, and she had spiralled back into a depression.

Bleu had visited her the day after, and had apologised. He hadn't been the one to send the invitations to the entire village. She had been grateful when he had told her he wouldn't have invited her if he had and that he understood, and hoped it hadn't hurt her too deeply.

She had lied then too, telling him that it hadn't, when it had cut her deeper than any blade could have.

She moved forwards to meet him, pulling herself away from the past and managing to smile for him. This time, it felt genuine, warming her and chasing away some of the cold that seemed a permanent part of her now.

Her step faltered when a tall, beautiful female stepped out from behind Bleu, her violet-to-white hair matching her striking eyes. Those eyes darted around, taking everything in, not seeming to notice the way the males in the village looked at her, a mixture of admiration and fear in their eyes.

Shaia could understand their shock. It rippled through her too.

She had never seen a female dressed this way before.

Violet leather trousers hugged her long legs, paired with matching boots, and a white leather corset fitted snug to her torso, revealing a strip of toned stomach and a startling amount of cleavage.

Bleu glanced back at the female again, and then did the most shocking thing of all.

He snarled and flashed fangs at the males who were looking at the female, his pointed ears flaring back against his wild blue-black hair, and snapped in their native tongue, "Get your fucking eyes off my mate."

The males bolted, leaving the female looking around her with a confused crinkle to her brow.

"Bleu?" the female whispered, her incredible eyes landing on him, and continued in the mortal tongue, "I said it was not wise for me to dress in my usual manner."

"And I said I like you that way and people will deal with it. You don't have to be something you're not." He caught the female's wrist and tugged her into his arms, banding them around her in a way that caused a fierce sting in Shaia's heart. "I love you just the way you are."

The female blushed and pushed against Bleu's shoulders. "You are making a scene."

He shrugged and refused to release her. "Let them all stare. They're just jealous."

"That they might be, but I believe you are being rude to the elf female and her male looks displeased."

Shaia risked a glance at Eirwyn. He looked positively aghast.

She wished she couldn't understand why, because she wanted what Bleu and this female shared to be the accepted way of things, that such public displays of affection between a male and a female were not a faux pas or frowned upon by society.

That love in all its forms could be celebrated not scorned.

Bleu nuzzled the female's neck and then drew back, and Shaia ached as she saw the marks on the female's throat, twin scars that confirmed what Bleu had said. This female was his mate.

"I barely recognised you," Shaia said, hoping to pull Bleu away from his female, because Eirwyn was rapidly losing patience and she feared he would pull her away if Bleu didn't speak soon.

She wanted to know why Bleu had called out to her, and wanted to know more about the female, because she wasn't elf. She was something else. Something strong, and powerful, and independent.

Bleu finally pulled himself away from the female, but kept his arm locked tightly around her waist, pinning her against his side in a way that sparked envy in Shaia.

She had been held like that once.

Eirwyn placed his hand against the small of her back and a weight instantly descended on her, pressing down on her heart and making her want to twist free of his touch. While Bleu's grip on his female was possessive, it was born of love and a need of his female, a desire to be in contact with her at all times.

Eirwyn's touch was possession of another nature, a show of dominance over her, marking her as belonging to him.

Bleu's violet eyes narrowed on Eirwyn and he was silent for the longest time before he said, "I know your brother... Leif. He serves in my legion. I served your father, Commander Andon, once too. It was an honour."

"Your legion?" Eirwyn's tone held a trace of venom and a slight note of disbelief, and she had the sinking feeling that things were about to turn dire.

Before he could offend Bleu, Shaia stepped forwards and captured his focus. "Bleu is a commander, serving Prince Loren directly."

Eirwyn cast a glance over Bleu from head to toe and back again, and she was surprised he didn't curl his lip. "The same Bleu who was born to the mill on the outskirts of the village?"

"And now I see where Leif gets his lovely temperament and that lofty air. It clearly runs in the blood. I've had to beat it out of him a few times… so don't think I won't beat it out of you too." Bleu held his free hand out to Eirwyn. "You may call me Commander Bleu."

Shaia stifled the smile that wanted to curve her lips and schooled her features so Eirwyn wouldn't see her amusement. If she had thought he had looked aghast before, she had been mistaken. Now he looked aghast, his mouth hanging open and face reflecting his astonishment.

It had probably been centuries since someone had spoken to him with so little respect.

It had probably been longer than that since someone had pulled rank on him.

Bleu's steady gaze dropped to her as he lowered his hand. "Speaking of the legions… I have spent time with another male recently, one from the legions and one you know."

Shaia frowned at him. She didn't know anyone from the army but Bleu, and she barely knew him. She couldn't think who he was talking about.

"You must be mistaken," she said.

He cleared his throat and spoke very carefully, pressing each word home. "I believe you did know him once. I recall you telling me so in a town near the free realm. Do you not remember? It was forty-two centuries ago now so I can see why you have perhaps forgotten."

Her heart started a slow, hard thump against her ribs. It wasn't possible that he was talking about the one she thought he was, but she had only ventured near the free realm once in her lifetime, one reckless grief-fuelled moment four thousand two hundred years ago.

One moment where instinct had driven her there and she had come upon a battlefield, drenched in blood and scarred as deeply as her heart.

"Are you unwell?" Eirwyn's hand against her back pressed deeper into her spine and she fought for air, for the words that would make him leave her alone and give her space to breathe.

She managed to shake her head and muttered, "I will be fine."

14

Bleu watched her closely.

He was so different to how he had been that day, when she had gone looking for her love, desperate to find him alive even when she had known he was gone.

Bleu had told her then that the male she was looking for hadn't come in with the wounded, that he was dead.

Now he was telling her that male was alive?

It wasn't possible.

But what if it was true?

Gods, what if he really was alive and had been all this time?

Her throat closed as all her strength rushed out of her and she struggled to breathe, rasped as she sucked down shallow pants of air and her mind raced as quickly as her thundering heart.

She could feel Eirwyn's eyes on her, intent and focused, and could sense he was close to making another attempt to smother her. She had to speak.

"Would you introduce me?" Her voice shook and she quickly gestured to the female beside Bleu when he cocked an eyebrow, making it clear she hadn't meant the male he had spoken of but his mate.

Or had she?

Gods.

If she asked it of him, would he take her to that male?

Was it really possible that he was alive?

Everything in her screamed that it wasn't and Bleu was mistaken. Her heart had shattered when her love had died. She had felt it.

"This is Taryn, my mate." He beamed at her, male pride and a lot of love shining in his eyes.

"I am pleased to meet you, Taryn." Shaia turned to Taryn and focused on her to subdue the questions racing through her mind and give herself a moment to breathe.

The contrast between them struck her again. Suddenly, her green elven dress felt as if it was swamping her frame, designed to hide her body rather than make the most of it. The long sleeves had always irritated her when other females were allowed to wear dresses without them, and the fact it dragged on the floor was often highly impractical, but it was another elf tradition, and one she would dearly love to shatter.

She tried to picture herself dressed as Taryn was, wearing tight leather and a revealing corset, and failed dismally.

Her own corset sat over her dress, made of wrought silver swirls that felt as if they were crushing her ribs and her breasts rather than supporting her, cinched down the sides with ribbons. Some elf females dared to wear dresses that were lower cut, and corsets that revealed more bosom.

Shaia had tried that once, and had been banished to her room in her parents' home for one cycle of the moon.

She couldn't openly dress as she wanted, but she often did her best to break with convention when she could.

She always wore sturdier and cheaper clothing at her small home away from the village, a basic blouse paired with a long skirt. She would roll up the sleeves and open the buttons down the front to allow air across her skin as she worked, and sometimes lazed in the private garden with her skirt hitched up to reveal her legs as she soaked in the sunlight.

"Where do you come from?" Shaia couldn't even guess at what species Taryn was, but every instinct she possessed said that the female was strong, born of a breed with powers possibly more impressive than her elf mate's ones.

Taryn pointed north-east, to a place beyond Eirwyn and the high peaks on the horizon. "The land of dragons."

Shaia's mouth dropped open and she snapped it shut before anyone noticed. A dragon? Incredible. She had a thousand questions she wanted to ask Taryn, but Eirwyn was watching her closely again, seemingly waiting for her to break with convention.

She smiled and forced herself to respond with just a single word. "Fascinating."

It wasn't against society's rules for her to be fascinated by something. Eirwyn couldn't pick her up on it.

The pang of envy returned as Bleu tugged Taryn a little closer, gazed at her through adoring eyes and looked as if he would die if she asked it of him. Taryn stood tall beside him, her head high, and violet-to-white eyes leaping around, taking everything in again. She glanced at Bleu and then away again, and began speaking in another tongue.

Bleu responded, a smile in his eyes as he spoke with his mate.

Gods.

Shaia's heart beat painfully hard at the sight of them, at the way Bleu indulged her and the way Taryn stood at his side like an equal, commanding his attention and not held back by him. He didn't stop her when she broke away from him, turning in a slow circle, her eyes leaping back to him from time to time as she spoke. She pointed towards the mills and he turned, carefully caught her hand and swung it towards one in particular.

The one his family owned.

Her eyes lit up and she said something else.

Bleu smiled again, spoke to her and then looked back at Shaia.

"She's eager to meet the family. She's convinced she won't be accepted and until I get her there and she sees that they'll love her just as much as I do, she's going to keep slipping into the dragon tongue. Either that or she'll get so wound up she'll want to fly and people in these parts are jumpy enough about a stranger, let alone a dragon." He grinned, as if he actually liked the idea of Taryn shifting and terrifying everyone.

Shaia found she liked the idea too.

It would certainly brighten her day, if not her life and this dull little village.

Eirwyn pressed harder against her spine. "We should be going."

Panic lanced her and her eyes shot to Bleu, and she blurted, "How is our friend?"

Her voice shook as badly as her hands and she feared her intended would see it, but there was no way she could contain it, not when she was speaking about him. Her lost love.

Bleu's expression turned grave. "Unwell. The perils of being an assassin I suppose. It is dark work."

That terrified her as much as it delighted her. Bleu was trying to tell her everything she needed to know in a coded manner. He was giving her clues that she could follow. The male she had thought had died was alive, but terribly sick if she was interpreting Bleu's words correctly.

Tainted.

Gods, she needed to find him. She needed to scour every assassin's guild until she was with him again and could pull him back from the darkness.

That desire shattered when Eirwyn spoke, reminding her that she wasn't free to do as she pleased. "We must move on now."

Shaia's eyebrows furrowed and she looked to Bleu, desperate to learn more from him but aware that she couldn't remain any longer. Her purple eyes shifted to the dragon beside him, and courage bloomed, strength that she thought had died long ago with her male.

"Thank you," she said to Bleu as Eirwyn caught her wrist and pulled her away, her heart soaring as she looked back at him and his mate.

The dragon was free, powerful and independent. Bleu's sister lived her life that way too.

All it took was courage.

She could be independent too.

She could find the male she had thought she had lost.

She could find her mate.

CHAPTER 3

Eirwyn droned on about something. Shaia tried to pay attention to him as she re-tied her long wavy black hair with trembling fingers, gathering the twin braids that hung from near her temples and joining them in the silver clasp at the back of her head.

It became impossible as they entered the main semi-circular marketplace of the village and she whirled back through time, the mixture of two-storey thatched and tiled detached grey stone buildings that lined the curve of the square changing around her to grow sparser and the people transforming into those who had occupied the market that fateful day almost four thousand three hundred years ago.

The light of the portal beat down on her, making her dark blue dress uncomfortably hot. She tugged at the tight bronze metal corset as best she could while clinging to the heavy wicker basket she held tucked in her left arm. The fruits and vegetables she had purchased with her mother jostled back and forth, threatening to leap over the edge.

"Shaia," her mother called and she looked her way, nodded to let her know she was coming and hurried after her as she bustled down the lane in the busy market, disappearing into the throng as she moved from stall to stall.

The noise of the people rose around her, growing more animated, and snagging her attention.

She glanced up from wrestling with her dress as she walked, wanting to see what had caused the commotion.

A tall male dressed in the figure-hugging black uniform of the army filled her vision and she barely had time to gasp before he turned and collided with her, knocking the basket from her arms and sending its contents spilling across the dirt. She staggered backwards, the force of him slamming into her sending her off balance.

Her back hit a passing male before she could fall and the male who had knocked her muttered an apology and moved on with the rest of his group, laughing and pushing at each other as they weaved through the crowded lane. The male behind her righted her, grumbling about her being clumsy, and walked away without as much as a backward glance.

Shaia huffed, crouched and began picking up her scattered belongings before the people visiting the market began stepping on them. The last thing she needed was her mother discovering what had happened and finding her at fault. Things had been strained at home, her family's desire for her to make a good match wearing her down and putting her in a foul mood.

She was only two hundred. Who found the one they would spend the rest of their life with at such a tender age?

A shadow came over her and she covered her eyes with her right hand and looked up at the owner of it.

A male loomed before her, darkly handsome, his face set in a scowl and strands of his long black hair dancing in the breeze to caress his cheeks.

He smoothed it back into the ponytail with a huff and she half expected him to demand she move out of his way.

Shock rippled through her when he directed the full force of his anger over her head. His violet eyes were bright with it as his pointed ears flared back, and then he crouched in front of her and began helping her with her fruits and vegetables. She stared at him as he worked, carefully plucking each fallen item from the dirt, inspecting it for marks and dusting off the earth, and then placing it gently into her basket.

"Are you hurt?" he said, and her insides trembled, unfamiliar heat traveling along her limbs and curling in her chest as his deep voice sounded in her ears.

He lifted his violet eyes to meet hers and all the anger that had been in them was gone, drifted away like storm clouds in summer, leaving only warm light behind.

She couldn't find her voice to answer him.

He had stolen it together with her breath.

Gods.

He was gorgeous.

The banked heat simmering in his eyes seemed to echo the burning in her veins, a strange and unsettling sensation that lit her up and had the world around her falling away, leaving only the male before her. She stared at him, shaken by the force of the new feelings rushing through her, sensations that skittered over her skin and stirred her soul, awoke something inside her that had her growing increasingly aware of him as more than a person.

She grew aware of him as a male.

Raw. Masculine. Powerful. Handsome. Everything about him stoked the flames licking through her, had her breath coming faster as her pulse accelerated, drumming in her ears.

That heat in his eyes began to blaze.

Someone caught her arm and pulled her onto her feet, jerking her out of the spell he had placed her under and bringing the world crashing back down around her. She heard her mother speak, felt she should look at her but she couldn't tear her eyes away from the male.

He took hold of her basket, his face fixed in a placid expression that concealed whatever he was feeling, and rose to his full height so he towered over her again. He looked down at the basket, and then her, and for an agonising moment she thought he would speak with her again, but then he held it out to her.

She took it in trembling hands, still fighting to find her voice to tell him that she was fine. Better than fine. She felt wonderful.

Her mother pulled her away, into the crowd, and she glanced back over her shoulder to find the male watching her. Her eyes widened. A uniform. He wore the same clothes as the soldiers who had bumped her.

Disappointment flooded her, the light and airy feeling transforming into a cold sort of darkness as she realised he wasn't a resident of the village or any of those that surrounded it. He was a soldier, and he would pass through her small world and out of her life before she could even get to know him.

"Cursed soldiers. I do not see why we must entertain them by allowing them to stay near the village." Her mother's voice broke into the darkness, bringing light back into her heart, and hope welled inside her.

Hope that she would see him again, even when she knew her family would never approve of the match.

She drifted home with her mother, and kept on drifting, through days and the nights that followed, her concentration poor as the male played on her mind and a desire to venture into the village plagued her, tugging her towards it in the hope she would see him again.

Five days after their fateful meeting in the village, Shaia found herself sitting on a boulder on the bank of the stream struggling to focus on her task of washing clothes for her family.

One of the other maidens of the village spoke, but Shaia didn't listen to her as she stared across the broad swath of shallow water that rippled over the stony riverbed.

At the camp there.

Soldiers came and went from the round white tents, the volume of their voices rising and falling as they talked or teased each other. Sometimes, one would call across to her and her companions. The first time it had happened, one of the more delicate females had almost fainted and another had spouted vile things about how the males would snatch them and hurt them, almost causing a third to join the first in having a fainting fit.

Shaia took it all in her stride, unafraid of the males as they called or whistled, able to see they were simply flirting with them and were harmless. None of them had even set foot in the water. She presumed it marked a boundary, and they had orders to remain in the camp.

The males nearest the bank fell silent as a taller male passed through, his black uniform bearing a regal crest. A commander. She half expected him to make them go back to work, but he rolled his eyes and moved on, obviously uninterested in their exploits.

Were the soldiers here for rest?

Shaia scrubbed the last item of clothing on the ribbed piece of wood she had wedged against some rocks in the bottom of the stream, her focus on the camp more than what she was doing. Her knuckles were sore from repeatedly being banged against the ridges and she was sure she had broken more than one nail, but she didn't care. Her eyes scanned the tents and the faces of the males as they moved around.

The hope that had burst to life inside her when she had spotted the camp on the banks of the stream began to wane as she finished with the undershirt and rang it out before setting it down in her basket with her other clothes.

She unrolled the sleeves of her light green blouse and tied them at her wrists, rose to her feet and stepped out onto the pebbled bank, the damp hem of her skirt sticking to her ankles as she moved. The light warmed her bare feet, chasing the chill of the stream from them.

"Take the longer route, Shaia. You must avoid the soldiers." The youngest daughter of a noble family who lived close to hers looked terrified as she said that, as if she was picturing horrible things happening to her.

Shaia sighed and nodded to her, her older sister and the two other maidens, and turned away, heading along the bank rather than following the worn footpath towards the village. She had nothing to fear from the males.

And she hadn't seen him yet.

She held the heavy wicker basket in both hands, stumbling at times as her bare feet snagged on a rock or she stubbed her toe. She tried to keep her eyes away from the camp, but they disobeyed her and kept drifting back, heeding her heart and doing its bidding.

Was he not at the camp?

She followed a curve in the stream and her step faltered as a new area of the camp came into view.

Males sparred in a clearing, breathtaking as they battled with weapons or barehanded, a startling display of masculinity and strength that had her heart pounding in response.

She had never seen males fighting before.

Her eyes locked on the one who had caught her attention, stealing all of her focus away from the world and narrowing it down to only him.

He fought gracefully, bare feet kicking up dust into the thick hot air as he dodged and blocked each attack the other two males made with their blades, his bare hands swiftly knocking the sword arms of his foes, pushing their attack off course.

She gasped as he dropped to his knees and slammed his right hand up against the arm of the shorter male, stopping his blade at the last second, and his head slowly swivelled towards her.

Gods, *he* was breathtaking.

"Shaia?" A male voice penetrated her thoughts, shaking her hold on the past.

She tried to keep her grip on it but it began to slip, and despite her fierce struggle to stay in those days where the world had felt bright and beautiful, she came back to one that was dark and dreary.

Or one that had felt dark and dreary until only moments ago, until a ray of light had pierced the veil of darkness and brought warmth and hope back into her heart.

"Are you even listening to me?" Eirwyn snapped and she almost admitted that she wasn't, that he bored her and she hated him, and she would wish for him to go to Hell if they weren't already there.

Perhaps she could wish him into a more dangerous part of Hell.

"I am tired," she whispered and pressed her hand to her forehead, hoping to make him believe her.

He thought her a feeble thing, and if playing on that would keep him from suspecting she had been miles away, centuries ago and reliving a better time of her life, then she would do it. She had no qualms about it either.

Her mind attempted to delve back in time again, but Eirwyn huffed and kept her with him, holding her in the present as he moved closer to her and spoke.

"… Males in elevated positions above their standing speaking to me in such a disrespectful manner."

Shaia frowned in his direction, for a moment seeing her mother on a night over four thousand years ago, one where she had said almost the same thing about another male.

The only male dear to her heart.

"Bleu is the aide of our prince," she said without considering the consequences, "his top commander and a male who is respected by all."

Eirwyn turned a scowl on her, his purple eyes darker than she had ever seen them and filled with a silent reprimand. "Something is wrong with you today. You have been… different… since seeing that male. What is he to you?"

"He is no one to me," she said and his expression didn't lighten.

If anything, it grew darker, as if he could read her thoughts and knew that the one Bleu had spoken of meant everything to her though.

Instinct made her move a few inches away from him, a trickle of fear running through her that shocked her. As an elf, she possessed keen instincts, ones that could often warn her of danger before it presented itself, saving her from coming to harm.

Only once in her lifetime had she felt such an urge to move away from a male though, and then that male had meant to harm her, had ambushed and intended to rob her on the path between her home and the village one evening.

Did Eirwyn mean to harm her?

She steeled herself and steadied her heart. He wasn't like that, had never shown any sign of being the sort of male who would strike a female or even a male. She was just jittery because of everything that had happened and on edge because she feared he would discover why she had suddenly grown distant and would be upset enough that he informed her parents.

Her parents would probably respond by shutting her in her room for months on end and stopping her from being able to leave.

They had reacted that way after she had wandered to the borders of the free realm to find Fuery forty-two centuries ago, hiring a sorceress to place a barrier around her rooms that would prevent her from teleporting out of them.

At the time, she had been too distraught to think about leaving again.

This time, it would drive her mad.

She made polite conversation, not hearing her own words as her mind churned, formulating a plan that had her heart beating harder, a trickle of fear running through her veins but excitement too, mingled with hope that gave her courage and strength to do what she had wanted to for over four thousand years.

She was going to cross the border.

Because she needed to find Fuery.

She needed to see with her own eyes that he was alive.

CHAPTER 4

It had been the third time he had seen Prince Vail.

Fuery didn't remember much about their first meeting. Not how he had found Prince Vail's location, or his arrival at the small countryside cottage in rural England. He had only fragments of the time he had spent with his prince and commander, scattered pieces that felt more like a dream than memories.

Hartt had assured him the meeting had happened, and Fuery was inclined to believe him since he definitely recalled his friend coming to find him, and taking him back to the guild.

A lingering sense of warmth returned whenever he thought about seeing his prince again for the first time, a sensation that had built inside him during his time at the cottage. He had felt safe.

Home.

He hadn't experienced such a feeling in a long time, and it disturbed him now, because home was an impossible dream.

He couldn't turn back time to when he had been another male, one free of the darkness.

Untainted.

Prince Vail believed it possible though, and Hartt held on to that hope like a male possessed, or possibly obsessed, had spoken of it to Fuery more than once since that first meeting, encouraging him at every turn.

Fuery had no such hope, but he also didn't have the heart to tell his friend he was dreaming, and that reality was a far darker beast, one without mercy and light. There would be no saving himself.

He doubted Hartt would listen even if he did voice his thoughts.

His friend insisted he continued what he had started with Vail, allowing the male to assist him by attempting to bring him back into touch with nature in the hope it would lessen the burden on his soul and clear some of the darkness from it. Vail's connection to nature was strong. Despite the darkness he still held within his heart, Vail had a stronger connection to it than his brother, Prince Loren, the ruler of the elves.

Fuery's own connection to nature was so severely diminished by the darkness that it was almost non-existent. He couldn't remember how it had felt to be connected to it, to feel life flow through his veins and light fill his soul, and to take pleasure and comfort from being surrounded by pure, untainted nature in all her glory.

The garden of Vail's mate, the fair witch Rosalind, was beautiful, filled with colours that Fuery found dazzling, almost breathtaking, and Vail was convinced that it had helped him fight the darkness and claw his way back towards the light.

But Vail had retained his connection to that nature.

The same nature that had rejected Fuery, left him alone in a dark world without her light to guide him.

Hartt had taken him back to visit Prince Vail twice since that first meeting, convinced that it was doing him good and that it would help him as it had their prince, and eventually nature would begin to welcome him again, would open her arms to him once more.

Fuery wasn't so sure.

The sensation of home he had experienced during his first visit was fading with each subsequent one, like the light in him. It felt weaker with each trip to the cottage, and the calm and peace he had felt on first spending time with Vail in the garden surrounded by the trees and flowers, and the endless blue sky, was slipping away with it.

There would come a point when he would feel nothing again, when visiting his prince would give him no benefit.

Would Prince Vail and Hartt suffer when that happened? Would it pain them to know that there was nothing they could do for him?

Would they give up on him?

Like he had given up on himself.

Gods, he didn't want to disappoint them, even when he knew it was inevitable, so he went to see Prince Vail whenever Hartt wanted it, and he would continue to do so until they both realised there was no saving him.

It was no hardship for him.

The cottage was a beautiful place, nature condensed into a small area that made it feel like a bubble, a haven, a place removed from the world. He could see why Vail benefited from it, but he was sure it wasn't only that stunning pocket of nature that was restoring his prince's light.

It was the beautiful witch who lived there with him.

His prince's mate.

Mate.

Darkness stirred in his veins at that word and crawled through his soul at just the thought of her, and it whispered at him to stay away from Prince Vail and that cottage.

Stay away from her.

He didn't need to be around females who belonged to another, and didn't need a mate of his own either. He didn't want a female in his life, despised how other assassins at the guild brought them into his damned home and paraded them in front of him, or how Hartt would sometimes make him speak with female clients. He wanted nothing to do with them. Mates. Females.

He closed his eyes, drew down a shuddering breath and held it as he wrestled with his darker urges as they rushed through him, stirred to a frenzy by the path his thoughts were travelling.

Pain shredded his insides, anguish ripping at his heart. Memories flickered and his veins went as cold as ice. His claws lengthened, razor sharp and itching to tear into flesh, to spill blood and cleave bone as the darkness surged in response, a need to lash out flashing through him. He needed someone to take out this aggression on, to satisfy this terrible dark need to purge the pain from him.

Fair Rosalind danced into the black abyss of his mind and he snapped his eyes open as his breath gushed from him.

Never.

He would never hurt his prince's mate.

He would never harm a female. Not again.

Rosalind had been kind to him, sweet and caring. She had taken care of him whenever he had visited, knowing when to show herself and speak with him, and when to leave him alone with her mate as he struggled with his black urges, on the verge of losing himself to the darkness.

He had come close to losing his fight against it the last time and had left before Hartt was due to come for him, muttering some sort of excuse, although he didn't recall the exact words he had used. Scattered ones had filled his mind, a collision of excuses that had fought to be the one to leave his lips. He might have muddled them, because Prince Vail had looked confused in the heartbeat of time between him speaking to the male and somehow teleporting.

That teleport had drained him, left him weak and shaking, the black tendrils of the dark beast that lived inside him snaking over his vulnerable body and seeping into his heart.

It was always dangerous to attempt a teleport. All of his powers were unpredictable, but teleporting was the biggest drain on his strength, because he had to force it to happen. It had been a long time since he had been able to control a teleport too. The only time he managed to teleport, it was because he was desperate for some reason, driven by a base instinct to escape that ruled him.

If his powers failed during a teleport, there was a danger he would end up somewhere that might kill him, or worse, would be lost in the infinite darkness that waited in the space between disappearing and reappearing. That space was cold now, like ice, and stabbed at him with frozen needles that punctured his flesh and dug deep to chill him whenever he passed through it. It was tainted by the darkness inside him.

Darkness that was growing stronger by the day.

Nothing Vail did would change that.

He needed to stay away. Hartt would press him to return, and Prince Vail would be upset if he stopped visiting, because both of them wanted him to get better. Both of them needed to believe they could save him from the darkness before he was lost.

He couldn't risk it though.

As much as he wanted to be there, as fiercely and desperately as he wanted to believe they could save his black soul, he had to stay away.

He wouldn't be able to live with himself if he did something to Rosalind.

It would break him.

Every inch of him tensed and stilled as a sensation went through him, a feeling that something wasn't right and he needed to leave.

It was a feeling that often struck him now, and one he knew the root cause of even if he didn't want to acknowledge it.

He looked back in the direction of the guild, aware of where it was, always aware of it, no matter how far he travelled from it.

It was the same sensation he had whenever he was in that building now, one that stirred whenever Aya was staying with her mate, Harbin, in his quarters.

His home was beginning to feel like a prison.

A nightmare.

He shook it off and focused back on his work, scouting the lamp-lit black cobbled streets below him as he crouched on the dark pitched tiled roof of a two-storey inn in a large town near the borders of the free realm. Mountains rose beyond it, forming a steep barrier between the free realm and the land of the dragons. A final outpost for fae, travellers and mercenaries.

The last town.

Beyond the mountains, the valleys were deep and numerous, with only a handful of villages nestled in a few of them, none of which welcomed travellers or those outside the dragon species. Not unless they had gold anyway.

The sky glowed dim amber in that direction, the fires of the Devil's lands burning hot, and his sensitive ears picked up the distant sounds of the black earth cracking and splitting as the lava broke to the surface, forming new valleys and mountains.

Fuery chuckled low in his throat.

He had half a mind to venture there, to pit himself against the strongest male in Hell.

The chance of him winning was slim, but gods, it would be a glorious way to go. If by some miracle of the gods he won, he would take his place on the black throne and rule the strongest realm in Hell, legions of demons at his command.

A fitting role for a creature like him.

Whatever evil and darkness lived inside the Devil, it beat within him too, a drum that he marched to and embraced. He bent it to his will and wielded it like a weapon.

A blade more devastating than any made of metal.

Voices dragged him back to the town, ripped him from his fantasy of ruling Hell and bloodying claws and fangs on the battlefield as he swept across the lands like a black shadow with an army at his back, subjugating all who didn't fall to his blade.

He gritted his teeth and screwed his eyes shut, and fought back against the whispers in his mind, the ones that urged him to go through with it. Fight the Devil.

Rule Hell.

No.

He had been a protector once. He had fought to defend his homeland, and its people. He had been good.

He opened his eyes and stared at his hands, at the long black claws his armour formed over his fingers. They flickered between clean with the town people blurry beyond them, and drenched in blood, glistening against a gory backdrop of carnage.

He had been good.

He breathed through it, each inhale and exhale making the timing shift, so his claws were clean for longer, and the sight of them bloodied grew shorter, until it was only brief flickers and then faded completely.

His claws were clean.

But not for long.

He forced his focus back to the town again, watching the people coming and going along the street far below him, a wraith in the darkness. They were unaware of him, the oil lamps that jutted outwards from the haphazard black stone and plastered buildings on the main thoroughfare stealing their night vision, making it impossible for them to see him.

He scanned each male for a tattoo on their neck, one that would identify them as his mark.

When he had checked everyone present, he moved on, heading towards the main square. He leaped the gap between two buildings, landing silently on the sloping tiled roof, and kept low as he skulked across it. At the edge of the building, above the square, he squatted and waited, his eyes scanning the busy gathering below.

His mark would be here.

The intelligence given to Hartt said they always attended this gathering each lunar cycle to sell wares. He just needed to find the male, get them alone, and dispatch them.

A lone female dressed in a dark green ankle-length dress with gold detailing on the bodice crossed an opening in the square, a heavy basket tucked between her arms, her brown hair tied in a high ponytail that swayed with each step.

He tracked her, a memory threatening to stir, just beyond his reach.

His eyes dropped to her neck.

Widened.

A pentagram.

The mark.

Sickness washed through him and he stumbled backwards, landing on his bottom on the black tiles and almost rolling right down the pitched roof. He shoved his right hand out, bracing himself, his arm shaking as he stared at the female.

A *female?*

A collision of fear, agony, grief and self-loathing was swift to crash over him, transforming into a churning dark and malevolent tide that rose and consumed him before he could even think about trying to stop it. It dragged him down into its oily depths until he felt as if he was suffocating, about to drown.

He lifted his right hand from the roof and brought them both before him, his vision wobbling as he stared at his black armour. It flashed away to reveal pale skin marred with crimson. Blood that had crept beneath his claws. Stained them. He scrubbed at his hands, picked at his nails, but nothing he did made the blood go away. His breaths shortened, coming in sharp bursts as his heart rushed faster, sending his mind spinning as he sank deeper into the darkness.

He had to get the blood off his hands.

His head ached, throbbing madly as he rubbed his hands together. It wouldn't come off. The faster he tried to scrub it away, the thicker the blood grew and the more frantic he became. He shook his head as he shoved one hand over the other, despair engulfing him as it only smeared the blood and spread it, so it covered all his hands and began travelling up his wrists.

He watched in horror as it formed tendrils that crawled and writhed over his pale skin, consuming more of it, and the blood on his fingers turned black.

Darkness.

He snarled and pushed at it, shoving his hands down his arms towards his wrists, desperate to get it off him, to purge it somehow before it swallowed him.

Eyes landed on him, a sharp sensation that had his head whipping up and locking gazes with their owner.

The female.

He needed to kill her.

He growled, shook his head and scurried backwards on his hands and feet, forcing himself away from her. Broken memories overlaid onto the present, transforming her into another female.

A beautiful female.

Drenched in blood.

He twisted away from her, planted both hands to the tiles and retched, tasting metal as his body heaved violently, as if he could purge the darkness that way.

He couldn't let it take control.

Not a female.

Never a female.

His entire body shook, wracked by cold and pain that came in waves, each stronger than the last, crashing over him. Had to run. Had to leave. Couldn't let it take control. Never a female. He staggered onto his feet and into a fucked up teleport that had jagged black tendrils stuttering around him and ice chasing over his skin and ended with him landing hard on his side.

On the roof of the guild hall.

He grunted and rolled down the steep black pitched roof, hit the left tower that flanked the main entrance, and spun into a fall down the three-storey height of the building. He hit the cobbled street on his front with another grunt, fire sweeping through his trembling body, lancing his bones and threatening to steal consciousness from his grasp as it stole the air from his lungs.

Several of the people who had been walking along the main street of the small town gasped and stopped, and backed away from him when he vomited again.

He pushed himself up on shaking arms and stared at the puddle on the black stones.

Blood.

He swallowed hard, sweat beading on his skin, cold and sticky. More flashes of the female covered in crimson filled his mind, and he roared as he tried to shake them loose, tried to spare himself the pain. He muttered a prayer beneath his breath, a desperate plea to the gods to set him free of the torment, to make her go away. He pushed onto his feet and growled at the people staring at him, flashing his bloodied fangs.

They were quick to run.

Fuery clutched his side, grimacing as fire throbbed there, the pain pushing him deeper into the dark tendrils snaking around him and threatening to pull him into the black abyss.

He staggered towards the arched entrance of the guild, his chest heaving with each laboured breath as his heart beat hard and fast. He needed the dark of his room.

He needed the silence.

Each step took effort, every one more than the last, his progress slow as he fought to remain on his feet and not collapse again.

"What's wrong?" Hartt was suddenly before him, concern flashing in his violet eyes.

A growl curled up Fuery's throat and his eyes narrowed on the male.

"A fucking female?" Fuery bit out in the elf tongue, just saying the words enough to conjure images of his target and the female who haunted him, mingling them together to send him dangerously close to plummeting into the abyss. "The mark is a fucking female?"

Hartt paled. His eyes widened. "No. I did not know."

The horror in his friend's eyes, and his feelings, said that he truly hadn't known, and that he regretted what had happened.

Fuery tried to cling to that, desperate to use it to calm himself, but the darkness was too strong and he was slipping, weakening as it took its toll on him. The memories he had been fighting rose, his mind and body too tired to fight them too when it was losing a battle against the darkness that surged and writhed inside him like a living thing.

Never a female.

He tried to pass Hartt, but his friend stepped into his path. He stilled as Hartt's palms captured his cheeks, holding him gently, luring him into looking at him. He stared into the male's clear violet eyes, and managed to focus on them.

"You did nothing wrong," Hartt whispered softly in the elf tongue, keeping their conversation private.

A fact Fuery was thankful for considering the audience they had. Several members of the guild had stopped to watch, and a few stragglers from the crowd that had witnessed his fall outside were watching him too. None of them knew the elf language. His species had done their damnedest to keep it private to them, unknown by any other species.

"Listen to my voice, Fuery," Hartt continued, his eyes holding Fuery immobile.

He'd had eyes like that once. Clearest amethyst. Now they were almost black, only a sliver of violet remaining in them. Soon, that would be gone too.

Then, the red would start emerging.

"Fuery," Hartt murmured, shaking away that thought, and he forced himself to focus on his friend and his words, to listen to his voice and use it to ground himself.

He could feel the connection they shared as Hartt reinforced it, a blood bond they'd had for centuries now.

Blood.

He screwed his eyes shut as he saw the female again, staring at him in horror, her violet eyes wide and lined with tears.

"Fuery," Hartt whispered and he heard her voice.

Her sweet, sweet voice.

His eyes burned, his nose stung, and he growled through his clenched fangs as his heart splintered into a thousand fragments for the millionth time. Gods. He *missed* her.

"Fuery." Hands shook him, and that male voice pierced his mind, shattering the illusion.

33

He dragged himself back to the surface of the oily black water that churned around him and opened his eyes before he could drown in it.

Violet.

Could he ever have eyes like that again?

"You did not hurt a female. Remember that. You did not hurt her."

But he had.

Not the female in the square, but he had hurt the one before her.

One he never should have hurt.

He had been born to protect her.

Instead, he had killed her.

"Fuery, you are not listening." Hartt rattled him again, and he shot back to him, the darkness falling away enough that he could focus again, the suddenness of it releasing its hold on him almost sending him to his knees.

It lingered and lurked though, waiting like a shadow to strike again, to seize him if he let his guard down.

"Breathe through it." His friend had paled further, and sweat glistened on his brow as he breathed hard in time with him.

Their hearts laboured in unison.

"Breathe," Hartt urged.

Fuery sucked down one rasping shuddering breath, and then another, bringing the tempo of them into a match for the rhythm of Hartt's, strengthening the connection between them just as Hartt had in order to shake him from the grip of the darkness.

Black spots appeared in Hartt's violet irises.

Fuery shattered the connection between them and knocked Hartt's hands away from his face.

No. He wouldn't be responsible for Hartt's demise as well as his own. He wouldn't allow his only friend in this world to take the darkness from him. It was his burden to bear.

"I am fine now." He wasn't, he was far from it, but he needed to say something to convince Hartt that he no longer needed his help.

Hartt nodded, but the look in his eyes said that he didn't believe him, that he knew he was lying to protect him and he didn't like it.

The male's eyes dropped to his arm, and then he turned away and started walking along the arched entrance hall of the guild. Fuery silently thanked him for not taking it as he wanted. As unsteady as he was on his feet, he needed to walk in unaided, because he was damned if he was going to let the other members of the guild see him as weak.

34

He was tainted, almost lost to the darkness, but he was still stronger than all of them combined.

Hartt looked back over his shoulder at him as they passed the first set of thick columns that were set into the walls and supported the elegantly carved black stone roof of the entrance hall. "Will you be alright?"

Fuery nodded as he clawed back a little more control, enough that his legs stopped shaking and finally felt stronger beneath him, his steps surer as they reached the main foyer of the building, an enormous black room with a corridor off to his right and left, and a door in the far right corner of the room that led to the offices.

He bared fangs at a trio of young fae males lounging in the horseshoe of black velvet couches that encircled the monstrous marble fireplace to his left, all of them staring at him as if he had two heads. They quickly looked away.

"I will speak with the client about it." There was genuine regret in Hartt's smooth voice, and a note of anger that Fuery couldn't miss. "You are sure you will be fine?"

He nodded again, even though he wasn't, because he knew that while Hartt would speak with the client and give them hell for not mentioning that the mark was a female, he would still see the job fulfilled by another assassin for the guild.

He was far from fine with that.

Killing females was wrong.

They took the corridor to the right and he squinted whenever he passed one of the oil lamps on the black walls, his sensitive eyes hurting at the brightness of them. He needed the dark. The silence. Hartt led him deeper into the maze of corridors, right to the end of the long wing of the building, to a place where few ventured. It had been decades since Hartt had issued the order that this part of the guild was restricted, and only he and Fuery could go there. Fuery could understand why he had done it, even when it had stung a little at the time. His friend needed to protect the males he employed and felt responsible for.

From him.

He was the reason this area was off limits, and the reason Hartt had moved into the rooms opposite his, always on hand if he needed him.

Or on hand to stop him if he lost himself to the darkness.

When they reached his door, Hartt opened it for him.

"Try to sleep." Hartt smiled at him, but the concern in his eyes lingered, worry that cut at Fuery because he didn't want to be a burden on his friend.

The more Hartt drained himself worrying about him, and helping him, the weaker he was against the darkness that was stirring in him. Hartt denied it, but Fuery could see it. He could feel it. His friend was beginning to slip and fall, and it wouldn't be long before the light began to leave him and he lost himself to the black abyss.

He hesitated and then lifted his hand, grasped Hartt's shoulder and pulled him towards him. He pressed his forehead to Hartt's, but couldn't find the words to say what he needed to say to him, to warn him to be careful and to beg him to look after himself.

Hartt clutched him by the nape of his neck, pressing their brows harder together. "Rest, Fuery. I will check on you later."

He nodded, and released Hartt at the same time as the male's hand dropped from his neck. He watched Hartt leave, heading back along the corridor, the oil lamps sending warm light flickering over him. It hadn't slipped his notice that Hartt had come to him armed for war, his black armour in place, moulded to his body like a second skin.

He pulled down a deep breath, intending to sigh.

Stilled as a scent laced it and filled him.

He stared blankly at the other end of the black-walled corridor, ears ringing as numbness swept through him, swiftly followed by strange warmth.

He knew that smell.

Lavender and crisp morning dew.

His knees gave out, sending him slamming hard into the stone floor, but he didn't feel the fiery lightning as it shot through his bones.

What fresh hell was this?

Tears filled his eyes as he drew another shuddering breath, convinced he was mistaken, and caught the scent again, stronger this time. It couldn't be. He focused, but the darkness pushing inside him made it difficult. He gritted his teeth and growled as he shoved back against it, desperate to catch the scent again.

This time, it was a feeling that hit him, a sensation that he hadn't experienced in what felt like forever.

It wasn't possible.

He snarled as he clawed at the flagstones, tipped his head back and growled at the gods, silently begging them to have mercy on him because this was too cruel.

He couldn't bear it.

The visions of her that overlaid onto the present and the nightmares that haunted him each time he closed his eyes were torment enough. They didn't need to do this to him. It was too much. He could already feel himself spiralling into the abyss, pulled down by the scent of her in his lungs, and the desperate need it birthed inside him, one he knew would never be fulfilled.

He couldn't see her again.

Because she was gone.

He shoved his fingers through his hair, tugging the long lengths out of the clasp at the back of his head as he dug his claws into his scalp. The scent of his own blood joined the sweet fragrance that lingered in the air, tormenting him.

Gods, he was losing his fucking mind.

He could smell her.

Feel her.

His mate.

The female he had killed.

CHAPTER 5

Shaia shifted foot to foot in the dark-walled corridor, her thick brown leather boots silent on the polished black flagstones beneath her feet. She drew down one breath and then another, trying to settle her racing heart as she waited. She licked her lips and rubbed her damp palms on her trousers, and blew out another breath.

It had taken her almost half a lunar cycle to reach this point, and she was tired, and a little afraid.

More than a little afraid.

Was this truly the place where Fuery now lived?

Was he really alive?

The thought of seeing him again had her trembling, her nerves threatening to get the better of her and stirring thoughts of leaving. She had done so on her first attempt to uncover whether Fuery resided in the monstrous black gothic building in the middle of a town in the central region of the free realm. She hadn't even reached the imposing arched entrance before she had lost her nerve and had scurried back to her small room at an inn at the other end of the bustling town.

She flexed her fingers and shook them, trying to stop them from trembling, and sucked down another breath.

This had to be the place.

The shifter in charge of the first assassin guild she had found in the free realm had been swift to usher her out and point her in the direction of this one when she had revealed the reason she had wanted to meet with him.

Apparently, just the mention of Fuery's name was enough to have a grown male, and powerful hellcat shifter, blanching and sweating.

He had look terrified.

What terrible things had Fuery been doing in their time apart to build himself such a fearsome reputation?

She took to pacing the broad corridor, working off some energy as she waited. Gods, she had been here for hours now, surely? The male she had meant to be meeting, the leader of this guild, had exited the room at the end of the hallway to her left in a hurry, the loud slam of the door hitting the wall as it opened startling her.

That had been almost fifteen minutes ago now.

Maybe he wasn't coming back.

Just as she thought that, the male appeared at the end of the corridor and she finally got a good look at him.

An elf.

Her heart beat harder, faster, and her nerves rose again, undoing all of her hard work.

If an elf led this guild, perhaps this was the place after all.

Was Fuery here?

The male muttered things under his breath as he stormed towards her, pushing long fingers through his short blue-black hair, ploughing furrows in it as a black tunic, trousers and boots materialised over his slender body to replace the armour he wore.

Had he rushed from his office to fight someone?

Had someone come to harm his assassins?

The thought that she might have been in danger sent a surge of adrenaline through her veins and she looked towards the end of the corridor beyond him, a vision of a battle forming in her mind.

Gods.

It was all a little exciting.

And perhaps a touch terrifying.

When the male neared, she carefully smoothed her hair back beneath the black hood of her cloak, making sure the length of it remained hidden. She had tied it back, and she was sure some males had long hair like hers, but she didn't want to give this male any reason to turn her away before speaking with her.

In order to move easily, and unmolested, through the free realm, she had strapped down her breasts with bandages before dressing in a drab dark grey tunic and pair of tan trousers that she had stolen from one of the male servants of her parents' household. She had paired them with her black travelling cloak, and had managed to make it across the free realm, and even through the interview with the hellcat, without rousing suspicion.

Her disguise was amazing.

No one suspected she was female.

The elf male lifted his violet eyes and they widened, as if he had only just noticed her.

"This is no place for a female... not right now. Leave," he barked in a mortal language and strode past her, leaving her standing in the corridor staring in shock at the other end of it.

She looked down at herself.

Or at least she had thought her disguise was amazing.

"Wait," she said and slipped into the office before he could slam the door in her face.

He huffed, narrowed his eyes on her and muttered in the elf tongue, "Your funeral."

"Why?" she responded in the same tongue, and he swiftly turned to face her, his eyes narrowing further.

"What the hell is an elf female doing away from the kingdom?" He was quick to shut the door behind her, and she didn't miss the way he peered into the corridor to check it before he closed it.

Was he worried someone would see her?

"I am looking for someone." She pushed her hood back, and his expression only blackened.

"Go home. We deal in death here, not the lost." He jerked his chin towards the door, rounded the large ebony desk in the centre of his office, and slumped into the black leather chair on the other side, a sigh escaping him as he sank into it.

He looked frazzled, worn down, and pale.

What had happened in the span of time between him leaving his office and returning? Whatever it had been, it had clearly drained his strength. His hand shook as he tugged a drawer on the right side of his desk open, fumbled around and pulled out a metal canister.

Blood.

He unscrewed the cap and the air filled with the tinny tempting scent of it as he drank deep from it. She had taken blood a few times, when it had been called for, needing it to replenish her strength. Her stomach rumbled, the hunger she had been denying over the past few days rising back to the fore. A sip of blood would be enough to restore her lost strength, and would achieve it far quicker than consuming food.

But the taste of blood reminded her of that day millennia ago, when it had been Fuery's on her tongue, slipping down her throat, replenishing that which he was taking from her, forming an eternal cycle between them.

And it hurt, the pain so intense she always felt as if she couldn't breathe, as if it would kill her.

When the male lowered the canister from his lips, he·sighed again and leaned back in his chair.

His violet eyes slid towards her. "You're still here?"

She nodded, hesitated for only a heartbeat, and then stepped towards him, approaching the desk as she pushed away her painful memories and forced herself to focus on the future. On Fuery.

"You say you do not deal in the lost, but I have heard differently." She resisted the temptation to twist her hands together in front of her, determined not to make herself appear weak in front of this male.

His eyes narrowed again.

She cleared her parched throat, and did her best not to fidget as her nerves rose, her heart slamming against her ribs.

"I have heard the someone I am seeking is here." She weathered his glare as he sat up and slammed the canister down on the surface of his desk.

"So go and find them, and stop bothering me," he growled.

"I will… if you would be so kind as to point me in his direction." Her voice warbled and she cleared her throat again, afraid he might view her nerves as a weakness and use it against her in some way. "His name is… Fuery."

His handsome face darkened.

"No. *Leave.*" He slammed his palms into his desk, causing the canister to topple and roll towards the edge of the dark wooden surface, and shot to his feet.

She jumped, her heart leaping into her throat, and swallowed hard as she staggered back a step.

So Fuery was here, and this male didn't want her to see him. Why?

Was he that dangerous?

She focused on the building, on everyone in it, trying to find Fuery among the males she could scent. When she couldn't feel him, she pressed her hands to her chest and focused on the connection they had once shared, expecting to feel something.

Nothing.

Tears lined her eyes as a voice in her heart whispered the male she longed to see again wasn't here after all.

No.

He had to be here.

She studied the male opposite her, and caught the flicker of concern in his violet eyes, an emotion that told her that Fuery *was* here, somewhere in this hellish place, and the male knew him well.

Was worried about him.

"You cannot see him. I do not know what business a female has with Fuery, but I do know that it will not end well for him... so you will leave." His tone, so dark and menacing, left little room for her to argue.

She did it anyway.

"No. I am not leaving without seeing him. I will not be told what to do... not anymore. I have spent four thousand years mourning Fuery... believing him dead." Her strength wavered and her voice grew quiet as emotions bombarded her, feelings that had been tormenting her from the moment Bleu had told her Fuery was alive. She stared down at the desk, lost and adrift in those emotions. "I do not understand how that came to be... I should have been able to feel he was alive through our bond."

The male went deathly still.

"Bond?" His deep voice was low, cautious.

She risked a glance at him, and found him staring at her, his eyes wide and lips parted, surprise painted across his face.

She nodded slowly. "Fuery is my fated one. My mate."

Gods, when was the last time she had said those words?

She stared at the male before her, numb to her bones as she let them sink in, together with the fact this male clearly knew Fuery, confirming what Bleu had told her.

Her mate was alive.

Her knees trembled, feeling suddenly weak as it swept over her, and she had to lock them to stop them from giving out and sending her to the stone floor.

Gods, he was alive.

Tears burned her eyes, pain blazed in her soul, and she reached for the connection that should have existed between her and her love.

But it wasn't there.

"Your name?" the male said, his tone hard and unyielding. A command.

"Shaia," she breathed, and the way his eyes widened again said that he knew that name. Her name.

He paled further, swallowed hard as he glanced at the door behind her, and then set his jaw. "Leave."

Why?

His eyes leaped between her and the door, and she detected his fear. It was buried but there, running through him and slowly growing stronger together with other feelings. Worry. Anger.

His violet gaze finally settled on her again, and his eyes danced between hers, searching them as he stood silently on the other side of the desk, gripped by whatever thoughts were running through his mind.

Thoughts about Fuery?

"Please?" she whispered and inched towards him. If he could feel her feelings as she could feel his, then he had to know that she needed to see Fuery. She needed to know her mate was alive, even if he was unwell. "I have trekked for days… I am tired and I will not believe Fuery lives until I see him with my own eyes. I *need* to see him."

"No," he bit out and rounded the desk. He didn't stop until he was toe-to-toe with her and towering over her, his face dark as he glared down at her. "Fuery is alive. You will have to take my word for it though. He is not strong enough to see you right now. It is best you return to the elf kingdom. I will send for you when I feel Fuery might be ready."

No. She wasn't going to accept that as an answer.

"I told you… I will not be ordered around, not anymore. I will see Fuery. He is my mate and you cannot keep me from him." She stood her ground when he growled at her, flashing short fangs, even though she wanted to back off a step and place herself out of harm's way.

This male wasn't like the ones she was used to dealing with—refined and noble, one who strictly adhered to the rules of society and the laws of their kind, unlikely to strike her or hurt her because of them.

He was a killer.

She could see it in his eyes as they narrowed, could feel it in the fierce drumming of her heart behind her breastbone and the instincts that he awakened that whispered to her, warning her to run now, while she still could.

"And I told you, I will *not* let you see him," he hissed in a low voice, one that sent a cold shiver through her. He paused and regarded her with icy, clinical eyes, and then a tight smile curled his lips and a chill skated down her spine. "If you want to see him, track him with your bond."

She frowned at him as hurt lanced her, a fiery brand that seared her soul and marked it.

His cruel smile widened. "Bound and young, no doubt… uneducated about how a connection between mates works."

She glared at him now, but he didn't relent or apologise. He remained cold and distant, intent on wounding her when she was already bleeding.

"If you wish to see Fuery, prove to me you understand the power of a bond." He stepped closer to her, forcing her to tip her head back to keep her eyes locked with his, stoking the urge to flee that was rising inside her together with shame that felt as if it might swallow her. He sneered down at her. "Tell me where you went wrong with Fuery, and prove to me you will not make the same mistake again…"

His tone darkened, turned so glacial that another chill swept through her, this one freezing her soul.

"Because your mistake has cost Fuery greatly."

She staggered back a step from that blow, blinked and stared at him as tears blurred her vision and she felt that strike cleave her heart in two and cut clean down to her soul. She didn't understand, but some part of her knew it was the truth. His words clawed at her, shredding her insides, and she struggled for the words she wanted to say, her voice failing her as she fought to deny it.

His violet eyes brightened.

His lips flattened.

The aura of darkness he emanated grew blacker, warning her away as her senses screamed that she was in danger here. He meant to hurt her.

He did.

But with more words that lashed at her.

"*Leave*," he ground out, little more than a growl as his ears flared back, the tips growing more pointed as anger swept across his features and laced his scent. "And do not come back until you can tell me all of that, because from where I am standing, it looks as if my bond with Fuery has more meaning and purpose than yours ever did."

Shaia stumbled back another step towards the door, a shiver rushing over her arms and down her back, shock sending her mind and heart reeling, and tears spilling onto her cheeks.

The male grabbed her arm in a bruising grip before she could respond, yanked the door open and marched her along the corridor. She staggered along behind him, her ears ringing as she struggled to take in everything that had just happened and pull herself together.

When she had finally managed to gather herself, she was stood outside the guild, the doors closed in front of her, and the people passing by were staring at her, whispering things about her.

Shaia stared blankly at the arched wooden doors, the male's words swimming around her mind, and the truth in them tearing at her heart.

Together with his anger.

He blamed her for Fuery's condition.

She hadn't been prepared for that, had come here believing she would see Fuery again and somehow everything would work out and he would welcome her back into his life.

Instead, she had been kicked out.

Told to return when she knew where she had gone wrong.

Had she gone wrong somewhere?

Her stomach squirmed as she considered that question, and the undeniable answer that immediately sprang into her mind.

She had.

She had felt something through the bond, and then it had gone silent, and she had assumed Fuery was gone, taken from her too soon. She had mourned him for centuries, had thought about him constantly, yet their bond had always remained empty, a hollow space inside her that had ripped at her every day of her life.

Shaia took a hard step towards the door as the shock of being turned away so cruelly faded and anger rose to take its place, and stopped herself before she could raise a hand to bang on the wood and demand entrance.

The male was right.

She had believed Fuery dead because something had happened to their bond.

Something that the male believed should have been obvious to her.

If she had known more about bonds, and how they worked, as the male clearly did, she might have been able to find Fuery four thousand years ago.

She might have been able to stop him from becoming lost.

The male's words echoing in her head grew more vicious, taunting her with her failings, until an ache started in her chest, and it birthed a need to find out where she had gone wrong. She hadn't abandoned Fuery as the male clearly thought, but she had condemned him because of her lack of knowledge.

He was right about that.

But she would learn, somehow, and she would return and tell him where she had gone wrong, and assure him it would never happen again.

And he would let her see Fuery.

CHAPTER 6

Hartt was acting strange. Stranger than usual anyway.

Fuery stared at him where he sat on the other side of his huge ebony desk in his black-walled office, speaking with a male. One of their assassins. Fuery leaned against the black wall near the door, standing guard as he always did whenever Hartt met with a new client or one of their recruits, his skin-tight black armour in place, and his arms folded across his chest and the sole of his right boot pressing into the plaster behind him.

He didn't like how closed off Hartt had been the past two days. Something was up and it nagged at him, setting him on edge. Hartt wasn't normally so distant from him, rarely blocked him through their bond, and never passed a day without speaking to him.

That had happened yesterday.

He hadn't spoken to Fuery from the moment he had left his quarters, feeling able to face the world again, until the time he had decided to retire. Hartt had led him to the guild's library on the upper floor, and had left him there.

At first, Fuery had thought him too busy with meetings to speak with him.

When dinner time had rolled around, and Fuery had headed to the cafeteria in search of some fruit and vegetables to appease his appetite and keep his strength up, it had been blindingly apparent that Hartt was avoiding him.

The male had chosen to sit not in their usual place, but at a table of young recruits, and had spent his entire meal speaking with them. Fuery had watched him closely, becoming increasingly on edge as Hartt failed to smile and the sombre edge to his violet eyes didn't lift. The second he had taken his eyes off his friend, Hartt had disappeared.

Definitely avoiding him.

Or at least he had been.

This morning, Hartt had come to his quarters and had asked him to sit in on the mornings meetings.

He hadn't spoken a word to him since then.

Had he done something wrong?

Fuery pushed that fear aside and focused on his breathing to soothe the darkness as it tried to use his momentary weakness against him to seize hold of him.

It was likely guilt eating away at his friend, and a touch of anger by the feel of the emotions he could finally sense trickling through their blood bond.

Hartt was furious that he had sent Fuery after a female mark.

Female.

Fuery screwed his eyes shut and pushed that out of his head too, afraid that if he thought about it that it would dredge up memories he wasn't strong enough to face right now. He was still shaken and weak from his fight against the darkness. It had been stronger this time, had swept him under swiftly when his mind had tricked him into believing he had smelled her.

Felt her.

His darker side snarled that Hartt should feel guilty, that he deserved to writhe in it for sending him after a female. The rest of him felt guilty instead, the root cause of his problem with hunting females rearing its ugly head again to torment him.

He drew down a slow breath, hoping to find some calm in it and some strength, enough to purge the darkness that was beginning to well up inside him again.

He tensed as he caught a female scent.

Aya.

The darkness was quick to seize him the moment his guard dropped, stripped from him by the smell of Harbin's snow leopard mate as it swept through the building.

Fuery snarled and fought against it, struggling as black tendrils wrapped around his soul and burrowed into his flesh, and teased the edges of his mind. He shook his head, shoved his fingers into his shoulder-length blue-black hair and clawed it back as he ground his teeth and growled.

"No."

He knew what came next, dreaded it but wasn't strong enough to stop it.

An image flickered in his mind, a beautiful female drenched in crimson.

Ripped apart by his claws.

Those claws formed over his hands as his armour responded to the imagery and they cut into his scalp, sending fire streaking over his skull and filling the stifling air with the heavy scent of blood.

Blood. Female.

His female.

He tore trembling hands away from his head, cracked his eyes open and stared at them.

Blood glistened on them.

"Fuery," Hartt whispered, and hands gently claimed his shoulders, fingertips pressing in and making Fuery aware of him where he now stood just inches from him.

The bond they shared opened to him, Hartt's worry coming through it loud and clear, together with affection and a touch of fear.

Gods, he was too tired to fight.

He sagged in Hartt's grip, aching for the male to take away his pain and stop his suffering, and then rallied and pushed away from his friend. It was hard to take that step back, to sever the connection between them, but he had to do it. He was tired. Soul-deep tired. In his current condition, it was too easy for him to lose his focus and allow the darkness to seize him.

If he couldn't control it, Hartt would try to aid him.

It was bad enough that he had been responsible for one death.

He hated being responsible for another's demise too.

"Look at me." Warm palms framed Fuery's face and he obeyed Hartt, opening his eyes and lifting them to meet his.

There was still hope in Hartt's eyes.

Ridiculous hope.

Every day, Fuery slid closer to the abyss. It was only a matter of time before he fell into it. There was no redemption for him now. He was tainted beyond saving, and that was something he had lived with for a long time. Accepted.

Only his blood bond with Hartt was preventing him from slipping under the oily tide of darkness inside him. Without the bond Hartt had imposed on him, he would have been lost long ago.

That bond had saved him countless times, pulling him back from the maws of evil.

Gods, he had hated it when Hartt had forced it upon him centuries ago, because it had tied Hartt's demise to his, tainting him too, but now he cherished it fiercely. He had done nothing to deserve it, or the depth of the affection Hartt felt for him, a friendship that meant the world to him.

One that had almost filled that black void in his heart where love had once been.

The large black-haired male sitting on the chair beyond Hartt turned curious cerulean eyes their way and rose to his feet, his black boots scuffing the polished stone floor. Tight black jeans and a matching t-shirt moulded over his heavy build, clinging to each muscle like a second skin that reminded Fuery of his own armour and how it hugged his slighter frame. The male ran an assessing gaze over him, and his lip curled slightly, relaying his feelings loud and clear together with the hint of disgust that laced his eyes.

Because he thought him weak.

Unfit to help run a guild of deadly assassins.

Fuery wanted to bear fangs at the shifter, but turned to Hartt instead.

"I am fine. Stop coddling," he growled in the elf tongue, keeping his words private between them.

Hartt sighed. "I know you hate it when I do it in front of others, but the episodes are becoming more frequent... and it is growing difficult to help you in private."

"Stop helping me then," Fuery snapped.

Regretted the fuck out of it when Hartt's violet eyes widened slightly before he recovered and Fuery felt the hurt that went through him.

Hartt had sacrificed so much for his sake, and he was a bastard for not appreciating that, and speaking of letting him drop into the black abyss so casually when Hartt's life was also on the line, tied to his.

"You guys need some alone time?" the hellcat drawled, a quirk to his mouth and twinkle in his eyes that said he had found his own words amusing as he insinuated he and Hartt were having a moment.

Fuery felt like making him eat them.

Together with his fist.

"You want to rethink that question?" Hartt snapped, and the male backed down, taking his seat again, but didn't apologise.

Fuery didn't like him, and he didn't trust him.

Fane was secretive and detached, more so than Fuery had ever been. Fuery didn't like to leave Hartt alone with him, because he recognised a feral bastard when he saw one.

Hartt flicked a glance at Fuery, looked as if he wanted to sigh, and strolled back around his desk to resume his place on the other side. He pressed two fingers to a black folder and slid it towards the hellcat male.

"This den has all the hallmarks of the one you are hunting so this will be strictly off the books. Covert. Understood?" Hartt didn't release the folder from his grip when the male tried to take it. He kept hold of it until Fane nodded.

When Hartt surrendered the file, Fane flipped it open and Fuery peered over his shoulder at the white pages.

There were markings etched on them in red ink, symbols that reeked of witchcraft.

He lifted his gaze to the hellcat's when he felt Fane's eyes on him and glared right back at him. He refused to back down when Fane continued to stare at him, his blue eyes glowing brighter. In a fight, Fane wouldn't stand a chance. The bastard knew it, but it still took him long seconds before he finally backed down and stopped challenging Fuery.

Fane snatched the file and stormed from the room.

Hartt stared after him. "Why do you push him so hard? You know he's a feline shifter and he finds it difficult to back down from any challenge issued to him."

Fuery shrugged and kicked the door closed. "The male is a feline shifter and should know about prides, and therefore he should know his place in this one and not challenge me."

Hartt leaned back in his leather chair and sighed, and then his eyes slid back to the door and he quietly said, "I do not think Fane understands anything relating to such things anymore... not since his family sold him into slavery."

Before Fuery could respond, Hartt spoke again.

"Enter."

His friend looked weary now, but Fuery didn't tell him to take a break. Hartt wouldn't like it. They were similar in that respect. Hartt hated being coddled as much as he did. It was late though, and Hartt had been handing out new orders, receiving reports, and meeting with clients for over twelve hours.

At the very least, Fuery needed to convince him to eat.

A big gruff brunet shifter stomped in, as packed with muscle beneath his fitted black t-shirt and combat trousers as he was in his bear form.

Klay was their newest recruit.

He had done two missions for them so far, barely enough to prove himself. Fuery had been the one to question him when he had applied to join the guild, and when he had asked why Klay wanted to become an assassin, the big bear had almost bitten his head off.

It turned out the male didn't like explaining himself.

Was that a bear trait?

Fuery had thought so at first, but no longer. Klay was here for a reason, just as everyone else was.

He tuned out the bear's discussion with Hartt as he was assigned another minor mission and given a report on how Hartt thought he was progressing, and tuned back into Hartt's feelings. His friend was tired. After he was done with Klay, Fuery was going to force him to head to the mess hall with him to get something to eat.

Klay conducted his business quickly as usual, and was out of the door in less than five minutes. Fuery respected that about him. The male knew how to be expedient, possibly because he was always eager to take down his next mark and work his way up the ladder. For what purpose, Fuery didn't know, but he would be keeping an eye on the bear.

Just in case.

"We are going to leave your office and eat something," Fuery growled and kicked away from the wall, crossing the room to Hartt as he slumped into his chair and blew out a long sigh. "Or I will go up to the cafeteria and eat someone."

Hartt slid him a black look, one that screamed how unimpressed he was, and bored of hearing that threat. Fuery made it every time Hartt refused to take a break. It hadn't failed to get his friend moving yet, even when Hartt knew it was meant as a joke.

"Fine." Hartt pressed his hands into his desk, pushed back and stood. "I have nothing left on my schedule anyway."

That wasn't as satisfying as making Hartt take a break when he was busy, but Fuery would take the small victory.

He opened the door for his friend and waited for Hartt to pass him before he followed him into the black corridor. The oil lamps at intervals on the wall lent a soft light to the hallway that he found soothing, and the scent of them drowned out the other smells in the guild. Including Aya.

He quickly shoved her out of his head before his mind could latch onto the female and strode beside Hartt, keeping pace with him as he yawned and trudged towards the main reception room.

They were barely two steps across it when he smelled someone unfamiliar.

"I need to meet with someone," a male with tawny hair laced with gold threads hollered, getting everyone's attention, including Hartt's.

Fuery growled at the newcomer, and not only because he was about to stop Hartt from getting some much-needed sustenance and rest.

The male was strong, powerful, and a potential threat to his friend, and him.

"You the boss?" The male jerked his chin towards him.

Hartt stepped past him and moved in front of him, blocking the incubus's path to him. He folded his arms across his chest, causing his black knee-length tunic to tighten across his back and over his arms.

"I would be the male in charge here," Hartt said, capturing the male's attention.

His green eyes, flecked with gold and blue, shifted to Hartt and something that looked like relief flitted across them as he moved towards them.

As he drew closer, Fuery caught his scent more clearly, and an image leaped into his mind, one of white cells splashed with red blood.

"I know you," Hartt said at the same time as that feeling went through Fuery. "You were there the night we broke Harbin out of the hunter facility."

The memory crystallised in Fuery's mind, and he saw a replay of his fight against the mortals, cutting them down with his blade as Hartt worked to free Harbin. They had broken a dragon out too, one Harbin had wanted Hartt to bring with them, and one they had met again in a building.

One where he had crossed paths with someone he hadn't seen in millennia.

Bleu.

Gods. The male had been a skinny youth barely strong enough to lift a damned sword when Fuery had known him, and had protected him in a fierce battle.

A battle that seemed fragmented now, twisted in his mind, some of the pieces not quite fitting. When he had ended up at Prince Vail's cottage in the mortal realm, that male had warned him that the darkness had a way of distorting their memories, bending them into new shapes that satisfied it and made it easier for it to steal control of them, and that was the reason pieces of the battle no longer fit and seemed out of place.

"Archangel," the incubus whispered, a lost look in his green eyes as the gold and blue swirled, a sign of his shifting emotions. "My mate now works for them... and I need to get her away from that wretched place. It's poisoning her mind and making it impossible for me to make her see the truth."

"The truth?" Hartt frowned.

"That she isn't mortal." The incubus raked fingers through his scruffy hair. "I just need to get her away from them, but her partner has too tight a hold on her... the whole damned organisation has brainwashed her on top of the spell she's already under."

Fuery could feel Hartt softening, and while he wanted to tell Hartt they already had too many jobs open, he held his tongue, aware it was pointless trying to argue with him.

Although he led a guild of dangerous assassins, dealt in death and had killed hundreds in his years of service, Hartt had a gentle side, one that often led to him taking on jobs out of pity and a need to help rather than the coin it would gain him and the guild.

"Your name?" Hartt said and moved a step closer to the male.

"Fenix." The male offered his hand.

Hartt took it and gave it a hard shake. "We will help you, Fenix."

Fuery couldn't help but wonder whether it was because Hartt wanted another shot at Archangel, or whether he was hoping that someone would show up again to defend the mortals there as he had last time.

Someone neither of them should want to see.

Thinking of Prince Loren and his intervention when they had been at Archangel to rescue Harbin brought memories of Bleu back with him, and from there he ended up thinking about Prince Vail.

He was alive.

That knowledge still rocked Fuery to his soul.

Still seemed impossible, a dream, even when he had spent time with the male.

Vail.

A male he had served under, the one he would follow into the very pit of Hell and march beside to the fortress of the Devil himself if he asked it of him, was alive.

Not dead.

Gods, he had thought Vail was lost forever.

Now that he knew Vail was alive, Fuery wasn't sure what had made him think he was dead. It was muddled. A product of the darkness, just as Vail had warned him when he had mentioned pieces of the battle ·they had been in didn't fit?

Even now, when he knew that Vail was alive, part of him still believed that he was dead.

It was strange, unsettling, a weird sensation that often left him lost and adrift, staring into space as he tried to figure out what was real and what was an illusion created by the darkness.

It was so fucked up.

It had left him doubting his mind, and had left him feeling he had lost it and had gone insane.

If Vail was alive, was it possible his other memories were wrong too?

It hurt too much to think that, so he shut down that line of thought, ending it before it could seize him and only drive him deeper into despair. It wasn't possible, and thinking in such a way would only torment him, giving the darkness a tighter hold on him.

The memories he wanted to be a lie were real.

He was a killer.

With his own hands, he had killed his beautiful mate.

CHAPTER 7

Sweat rolled down his pale skin, tracing lines over taut muscles that shifted with each hard breath he took and stirred wicked heat in her veins. His mouth moved silently, the words he said to his sparring companions in the sun-drenched camp beyond her reach, those firm lips fascinating her and setting her heart racing.

Shaia swallowed hard when he rose onto his feet and turned towards her in a single fluid move that caused his body to come alive in a symphony of power, muscles bunching and stretching, drawing her eyes back down to his bare chest.

She had to move.

Her hands shook against the wicker basket of wet clothes, and her feet refused to obey when she issued them a command, a demand that she break away from the stream and the alluring male on the other side.

She didn't want to leave.

It seemed he didn't want it either, because he said something else to the males and then jogged towards the bank. He didn't hesitate as he reached it. He plunged into the stream, splashing water everywhere as he waded through the knee-deep river barefoot, not slowing as he headed straight for her.

Shaia looked around her at the green valley, part of her afraid another member of the village would see him coming to speak with her and would report it back to her parents, or worse.

They would create a scandal out of it.

The rest of her rebelled against everything that had been bred into her, screamed that she had come here wanting to see him and now she could, and she had to take this opportunity.

She needed to speak with him, needed to see him again and bask in his masculine beauty, needed to understand what it was about him that had entranced her so deeply, affected her so swiftly, making him all she could think about.

He stopped when he was barely two metres from her, ankle-deep in the water. "Were you hurt?"

He breathed hard, distracting her, drawing her mischievous gaze back down to his bare chest. Water glistened on it, catching the light. A single bead broke away and tracked over his abdomen, luring her eyes with it as it cascaded over chiselled perfection. She swallowed hard again, desperate to wet her parched throat as her eyes caught on his black trousers that rode low on his hips.

They were wet, moulding the material to his thighs and other places.

Shaia stifled the blush that threatened to scald her cheeks and pulled her eyes back up to his face, ashamed at herself. She had never stared so openly at a male before. She had seen males in the fields with their chests bare, ones larger and more muscled than he was, but none of them had affected her in the way he did, setting her heart pounding and blood burning.

He looked down at himself, grumbled a rather wicked and shocking curse, and bent towards the water. She could only stare as he scooped it up in his hands and washed his chest, sweeping away all the sweat and the dust.

Making him even more tempting.

"You must think me a ruffian or a peasant," he muttered and pushed his hands down his chest and then his arms, clearing the water from his skin.

"Not at all." It left her lips before she could stop it, before she could consider the consequences of responding so quickly to him and how he might interpret her words.

He froze halfway through pushing his long black hair from his face and stared at her, his fingers tangled in the wet ribbons and body deliciously tensed.

Gods, she had never spoken so out of turn in front of a male before, so careless and free with her words that she had been in danger of revealing everything to him.

She liked him.

Her thought back in the village just moments before she had met him haunted her.

Perhaps it was possible for a female of barely two hundred years to find a male she wanted to spend the rest of her life with after all.

But her heart had chosen a male far different from the one her family wanted for her.

One who was still staring at her in silence, his clear violet eyes a little wider than usual, relaying his surprise.

"Thank you for your concern." She struggled to keep the tremble of nerves from her voice and to stick with a more appropriate set of responses, ones her family would approve of and deem correct for the given situation. Ones she didn't like at all, not when her heart spoke different ones, things she wanted to tell him and couldn't stop herself from tacking on. She managed to do it in what she hoped society would think an appropriate way. "Though there is no need for you to be concerned, as I was not hurt."

His tempting lips curved into a smile. The brightness of it stole her breath. It made him even more handsome. She hadn't thought that possible.

"I am glad... although I think I hurt the reputation of the squad. Your mother seemed rather disgusted by us."

"Mother is disgusted by most things."

Her eyes widened and her hand would have flown to cover her mouth if she hadn't been holding the basket. Had she just said that out loud? Her heart stuttered, and then thumped harder against her chest. She stared at the male, unable to believe she had spoken of her own family that way around a stranger and afraid of what he would think of her.

His smile was slow this time, and a little wicked and teasing, as if he liked the way she had spoken so openly, so not the way she should have been speaking around him.

"I am sorry," she whispered, although she wasn't sure who she was apologising to—him or her family.

"Don't." His smile held, bewitching her and relaxing her at the same time. "You did nothing wrong."

She felt as if she had though. What world did he come from where speaking so harshly of a family member was acceptable?

A world a million leagues away from her one, that was for sure.

A soldier on the other side of the bank shouted a name and he twisted at the waist, causing his muscles to ripple with strength, and the ridge that arced over his hip tensed.

"I'll be back soon," he hollered and the soldier moved on.

Shaia stared at him.

Fuery.

Was he as violent and tempestuous as that name suggested?

As rough and forceful?

Before she could stop herself, she fell into imagining it, entertaining wicked things that heated her cheeks and would give her mother a heart attack if she knew.

Fuery said something else to the male, his deep voice curling around her and drawing her back to him, making her imagine him whispering into her ear, his breath warm on her throat.

He turned back to her and his left eyebrow rose. "Are you unwell?"

Shaia quickly shook her head, dislodging the fantasy but not the flames scalding her face. If anything they grew worse, roused by the fact he had obviously caught her daydreaming about him.

He looked her over and a little colour touched his cheeks too, reached his eyes and made them darker as he met hers and stared into them. Her breath lodged in her throat, heart racing there, and her hands shook against the basket again.

She had to say something, but her voice felt weak. Lost to her.

A male had never looked at her the way he was, with hunger in his eyes, blatant desire that stoked hers and made it burn hot and fierce, sending an achy shiver over her skin and rousing feelings that she had never experienced before.

She had to say something.

Her mouth moved automatically, her words distant to her own ears. "Where are you going?"

He blinked, a flicker of confusion chasing some of the heat from his eyes.

"You said you would return soon." Implying he was going somewhere.

Was he leaving the village?

A sharp pain pierced her chest in response to that thought and she wanted to take hold of him and make him stay, something shockingly powerful inside her demanding she not let him go.

Demanding she make him his.

What wicked need was this?

He smiled again, stepped towards her and took her basket from her hands. She shook as his fingers brushed hers, his skin hot and sending electric tingles arcing up her arms.

"I am taking you home. People will start talking if I stand here staring at you much longer."

Oh.

Not a good idea at all.

As much as she wanted to remain near him, as much as the thought of him walking her home delighted her, she couldn't allow it.

Shaia reached for the basket. "People will start talking if they see me walking with you."

Hurt danced in his eyes but he vanquished it a second later. It didn't stop her from feeling that pain echoing in her chest, wrapped in shame and guilt. She blamed her upbringing. Walking alone with a male at her age was considered a very bad thing to do, something that would bring dishonour to her entire family.

But she wanted to walk with him.

She wanted to walk the opposite way, away from her family, and not stop walking until she was free.

Free to be with this male.

Fuery.

"People won't see us," he whispered, tempting her into surrendering to him. "I know a secret way."

"To my home?" She couldn't hide her shock on hearing that, but managed to conceal the thrill that chased through her at the thought he had wanted to see her again too.

He nodded.

"How do you know where I live?" She studied his face, searching for the answer there, afraid he wouldn't give it up easily even though he had been nothing but open with her.

Completely unguarded.

It struck her that she had been behaving the same way, that she felt as if she could be herself around him and didn't have to hold anything back, because it was the way things should be between them.

"I am a scout." He looked off into the distance, giving her his profile. Such a noble one. He looked as if he belonged to a strong lineage, one elevated in society, but she hazarded a guess that it was quite the opposite. "The commander charged me with mapping the entire area for three leagues around the camp. I spotted you in the garden of a large stone dwelling... and you seemed at home there."

"And?" She had the feeling there was something he wasn't saying.

A touch of rose coloured his cheeks again.

His violet eyes began to darken, his pupils dilating to devour his irises, and his deep voice was low and rough as he murmured, "And I watched you."

"For how long?" She supposed the correct reaction given the situation should be shock, but she felt more fascinated than horrified. Thrilled. Excited.

His violet eyes slid towards her. "Until you went inside."

A long time if he had caught her at the start of her walk. She had been spending a quarter of her day in the garden recently.

Shaia started walking and didn't miss the glimmer of satisfaction that danced in his eyes as he followed her, her large basket of sodden clothes held tucked against his bare chest, wrapped in his strong arms.

She forced her eyes and her thoughts away from them before she could imagine him holding her like that. "When was this?"

"Three days ago." The look in his amethyst eyes as he glanced at her again told her that he had been back since, watching her while she was unaware of him.

While she had been thinking about him.

She blushed at that.

Part of her knew she should tell him to stop, tell him that it wasn't appropriate and neither was him escorting her home, but she couldn't bring herself to say it, because he had only been doing the exact thing she had wanted to do.

She had wanted to see him again too.

They broke away from the stream and headed up a grassy hill towards a sparse green forest that crowned it. Her heart thumped against her chest, a heavy beat that dragged her down and slowed her steps. She took her time in the woods, dragging her heels as she picked her way along the dirt path, a sense of dread building inside her with each step.

The edge of the forest came too quickly despite her best efforts, and she paused under the shadow of a leafy tree laced with violet blooms.

Fuery stared off down the long sloping meadow that stretched before them, forming a barrier between them and a two-storey stone building nestled in the bottom of the valley. Smoke rose lazily from the tall chimneys set into the tiled gently sloping roof at the kitchen end to the left and several of the tall rectangular windows had been opened to allow air into the rooms.

Her home.

He was still, his eyes fixed on that house, distant from her, and she wanted him to speak, needed him to tell her what was on his mind and ached to know if he felt the same keen pain in his chest as she did, the thought of parting from him disturbing her very soul.

Shaia glanced down at the grey stone building, loathing it more than ever because it represented a barrier between her and Fuery, a cage in which her parents expected to keep her until they found a male they believed suitable for her.

She looked back at Fuery and saw the male she wanted for herself, needed more than anything despite only knowing him a short time. Her need for him was woven into her being, stitched into her soul, like a ribbon that tied them together and had been gradually shrinking, drawing them to each other.

He closed his eyes, drew down a slow breath and sighed it out as he turned towards her. Long black lashes shuttered his beautiful eyes as he stared down at the basket in his arms and then he lifted them to meet hers. She ached deeper, fiercer than ever at the sight of them and the regret she could read in them.

He held the basket out to her.

She placed her hands on the thick rim of it, close to his, and forced herself to take it even though she didn't want to.

He refused to release it. His grip on it tightened, knuckles burning from the force of his hold, and he stared at the damp clothes again, his struggle written plainly across his face for her to see.

She knew what he couldn't say, because she burned with the same need.

She didn't want to part from him yet either.

It felt too soon. She hadn't had enough time with him yet. She didn't think she ever would, even if they had eternity.

"There is a rumour in the camp that we will be moving on soon," he whispered, each word lancing her heart and sending sharp pain echoing through her body.

She wasn't sure what to say.

He slowly lifted his head and met her gaze, and husked, "I know it is wrong... you can say no and put me in my place... but I want to see you again."

It was wrong.

Or at least that was what her family would believe.

But her family weren't the ones standing in the shadow of the trees with him, heart racing and blood pounding, feeling alive for the very first time.

She was the one here, and to her it felt right.

So she swallowed her fear and pushed out the words she wanted to say, not the ones society dictated she should say.

"Next wash day."

The clouds that had been gathering in his eyes parted.

His lips curled into a faint smile.

He nodded and stepped back, his motions stiff and relaying how hard it had been for him to place that small distance between them.

"Next wash day," he whispered, and turned away.

Shaia watched him go, not feeling the weight of the basket in her hands as her eyes tracked him. Everything felt light and bright. Wonderful. It was as if she was floating.

Warmth spread through her, a sort of lingering heat she knew would never fade.

For the first time in her life, she felt truly happy.

But happiness was fleeting.

CHAPTER 8

Shaia fluttered her eyes open, a sigh escaping her lips as she rose up from the dream and reluctantly left it behind. She lifted a hand and scrubbed her eyes, wiping away the tears that tracked down her temples and soaked into her dark hair and the pillow beneath her head.

She pushed back the covers, rose from the single bed and padded across the room. She glanced at the dark wooden wardrobe to the left of the door to the living room, and then away again, fixing her gaze on the masculine clothes she had draped over the back of a wooden chair in the right corner of her small bedroom. It was better to remain in disguise. She didn't want anyone recognising her.

She dressed quickly, donned her black travelling cloak and headed through her cramped living room to the door of her home. It creaked as she pulled it open, and she stilled as she stopped on the doorstep.

Endless inky blue sky stretched above her but she saw a reflection of how it had been that bright summer's day when she had met Fuery at the stream and had learned his name, and had discovered the need she had been experiencing had been running through him too, as unstoppable as that river.

Gods, she loved him.

She loved him with all of her heart, so deeply she ached whenever she thought about him, and cursed herself whenever she considered the assassin's words and that Fuery's condition might be her fault. If she had known more about bonds, could she have stopped him from becoming tainted?

Lost?

She gathered her heavy black cloak around her to keep the morning chill off. The fire in her bedroom had gone out in the night and her fingers were stiff, cold to the bone, her hands pale in the slim light. She fixed her gaze on the distance, waiting.

The sky lightened, the portal glowing bright orange and spilling pink across the vault of Hell, as close to a sunrise as she had ever witnessed. It bathed the elf kingdom in gold, gilding the pockets of trees that dotted the sweeping valley below her and the mountains in the distance across the plains. Her eyes tracked the light as it caught on a stream that snaked through the rolling hills, leading her gaze towards a small village nestled close to one of the forests, far below her. The village began to shine as the light streaked over the blades of the windmills and traced over the thatched and pitched roofs of the mixture of pale and dark stone buildings.

Home.

But not her home. Not anymore. Not for a long time.

Fuery had become her home, and when she had lost him, this small house had become her refuge, and had grown dear to her. The village was the place where she had grown up, but this was the place where she had grown into the female she wanted to be.

She wanted to avoid the village now, but it tugged at her, her connection to Fuery and her memories of their time there pulling her towards it. She needed that connection again, needed the comfort of her memories more than ever.

She wanted to head down to the river, to retrace their steps and find the tree near its banks where they had spent time together.

Where Fuery had carved their initials and had told her that their love would be eternal.

She stared at the distant village, her eyes lazily tracking the gently turning windmill blades as her thoughts began to weigh her down again.

Where had she gone wrong with Fuery?

The male she had met with, one she now remembered someone calling Hartt as he had forcibly evicted her from the guild, had mentioned he had a bond with Fuery, and that it meant more than hers with him ever had.

She knew what he had meant by that.

His bond had saved Fuery somehow.

Hers had damned him.

She shook her head, refusing to think that way, to allow Hartt to rattle her with his words. She had returned to the elf kingdom not to lick her wounds, or give up. She had returned to find out more about bonds between mates so she could go back to Hartt and tell him what he had demanded to know, and then she would make him let her see Fuery.

Shaia focused on her body and willed her portal to open, and stepped through the darkness to appear closer to the village, a short teleport that left her legs unsteady. She had almost collapsed after teleporting to her home from the assassin's guild in the free realm, the distance of the leap taking its toll on her.

She needed to rest, but she couldn't. Not yet. Not until she had seen Fuery.

She trudged down the grassy hill towards the village, her nerves rising with each step, and chanted in her head that no one in the small gathering of houses would recognise her with her disguise back in place, her hood obscuring her face.

Besides, she wasn't heading into the village anyway.

She was heading for a windmill on the hill above it.

One where she hoped to find an answer to the question plaguing her.

Where had she gone wrong with Fuery and their bond?

It wasn't something she could ask her family, and not only because they would be furious with her for disappearing without a word when she was meant to be marrying Eirwyn and would employ a be-spelled talisman to keep her locked in her room, unable to teleport.

No, she couldn't ask them because no one in her family were fated mates.

Her parents' marriage had been arranged.

She reached the windmill, and breathed a sigh of relief when she spotted Bleu's mother in a field near it.

Ciana was as beautiful as Shaia remembered, graceful and elegant even though she wore working clothes of a dark brown pinafore over her deep blue dress and her long black hair had been tied back into a tight bun to keep it from her eyes as she tended her crop.

The female looked up and a warm smile reached her eyes as Shaia pushed the hood of her black cloak back, making their amethyst depths shine. Shaia's nerves disappeared as she basked in that warm light, wishing her own mother was as kind and gentle, and accepting, as Bleu's was. This was a female who had embraced her daughter's desire for independence, and had defended her more than once, and worked the fields even though the village scowled at her for doing a male's work. Gods, Shaia would have given anything to have such a female on her side.

"Is Bleu here?" Shaia said when she was close enough.

Ciana moved out of the wheat field and came to the pale grey stone wall that enclosed it. "He was here. He returned to the castle yesterday with his mate. My... she is wonderful. A little odd, but Bleu clearly loves her, and I am so happy to see him happy."

She beamed at Shaia, that happiness shining in her eyes and making her positively glow.

Damn. Shaia had missed him.

Her nerves returned, the thought of having to travel to the royal palace terrifying her a little. She had never been there, only knew about it from stories people in the village had told her. Even her parents had never been invited there. It was a place reserved for either the elite of society or soldiers.

Soldiers like Fuery.

She swallowed hard and tried to stifle the ache that started behind her breastbone as she thought about him, pictured him in his uniform of a crisp black tunic and tight trousers, and black riding boots. He had looked so handsome, his face lit up with his smile and pride in his violet eyes, his hand resting on the blade that had hung at his side. One fit for a commander.

"Child, what is wrong?" Ciana asked, shaking her from the memory of seeing him that night thousands of years ago.

Gods, she had been so proud of him.

And she had hated how society had scorned him still, because he hadn't been born into the echelons of it.

Because he had earned his position.

Just as Bleu had.

They had both worked hard to rise from little into a revered position within the legions.

Shaia shook her head. "It is nothing. I have been travelling too much and I am weary. I was hoping to catch Bleu here so I could speak with him."

"You are free to go to the castle, Shaia. All are welcome there," she said with another warm smile, and glanced at Shaia's cloak. "This matter is obviously of great importance to you... enough that you have clearly travelled a long way."

In disguise.

Ciana didn't say it, but it was there in her gentle eyes.

The female reached over the wall, took Shaia's hand and squeezed it.

"Do not let convention stand between you and that which you desire. If Bleu had done that, he would have been working these fields instead of me. If Iolanthe had done so, she would be here with me, complaining every hour of the day about how males were free to come and go as they pleased." She chuckled, the sound rich and warm, and full of love. "Bleu was always a bad influence on her... go and let him be a bad influence on you too."

Shaia nodded, her heart buoyed by his mother's kind words, and the support that shone in them, telling Shaia that she knew her fear, and what she desired, and told her to go out there and not let convention stop her.

She released the female's hand, pulled her hood up and focused on the furthest point she had been in the kingdom, and teleported. When she landed on the deep grass that reached up her calves, her eyes immediately settled on the palace in the distance. High walls surrounded it, made of the same mixture of pale and dark grey stone as the castle it protected. Beyond it, mountains rose, a fitting backdrop for the tall towers with their conical roofs that reached towards the sky from the sprawling main building.

Shaia drew down a deep breath to prepare herself for what came next. Even at this distance, she could sense the power that hummed around the castle in the air, and knew the tales she had heard were true. Teleporting into the proximity of the castle would see her pulled to one central portal in the courtyard, a precaution that was necessary to protect the prince from intruders.

She willed the teleport, felt the power shimmer over her skin beneath her clothing, and disappeared.

Her pulse quickened the moment she appeared in the courtyard, on a circle of flagstones in the middle of a beautiful orchard. Paths cut the grass beneath the trees into sections, leading off in different directions, the one before her heading towards the grand arched entrance of the castle.

Gods, it was far larger than she had anticipated.

Imposing.

A little terrifying.

A few of the guards positioned at the end of the avenues that led from the portal landing point glanced at her, some arching an eyebrow as they looked her over. She probably looked like a beggar in her cloak and worn trousers and top.

Or suspicious.

She pushed her hood back, not wanting the guards to get the wrong idea about her. She wasn't here to hurt the prince they protected.

Where would Bleu be?

She looked around her. To her right, the path led towards an open gate that revealed the countryside beyond it. To her left, it cut through the orchard in the direction of an archway in the wall that intersected the castle grounds, one that gave her a peek at buildings and a congregation of soldiers.

Would Bleu be there, overseeing those males?

Her heart gave a hard, painful kick and she brought her hand up, pressed it to her chest, and rubbed it in an attempt to soothe the pain just the thought of seeing males of the legion, dressed in their finery, birthed in her.

Fuery.

She swallowed her fear, for his sake. He needed her, and she needed him, but Hartt would keep turning her away unless she could give him an answer. As little as she wanted to see soldiers of the legion, as much as it would hurt her to look upon them, she needed to go there and see if she could find Bleu in that place.

Shaia hesitated.

Someone hollered an order, and another joined it, and she froze as an entire legion of soldiers marched through the archway towards the castle, past a beautiful fountain, and banked around the orchard and out of the gate that led into the countryside.

Some of the males spoke of manoeuvres.

If the soldiers were training, it stood to reason that Bleu would be leading them as their commander.

Which meant he was busy.

While she knew Bleu, she couldn't say that she was close to him, definitely wasn't close enough that he would find time for her in his schedule if he was in charge of the soldiers heading out to practice their drills.

One of the guards turned her way and frowned at her.

Instinct pushed her to leave, to find another way to discover more about bonds, before the guards decided she was a threat and threw her in the cells. She would be no use to Fuery there.

She was too tired to teleport though, weary from her travels and unused to using that particular ability. It would be a while before she could teleport again, but she couldn't stand here waiting for her strength to return. She ducked her head and took the path to her right, following the soldiers out into the countryside.

They had all banked left, heading up the hill.

Shaia hesitated, torn between still trying to find Bleu and finding another source of information about bonds.

When the two legions of soldiers gathered on the hill broke apart and formed ranks facing each other, she dragged herself away and headed down the hill to her right instead.

The sound of running water captured her focus and drew her towards it, making her lift her eyes in search of the source.

Gods, this end of her small world was beautiful.

Endless green stretched from the mountains on her right to the ones on her left, hills undulating between them, as far as her eyes could see. A brook followed the curves of some of the hills, snaking between them and catching the light from the portal. Along its bank, the grass was long, swaying in the breeze together with the rushes.

Shaia drifted towards the water, her mind filling with a vision of a different stream, one that was shallow and broad, with a pebbled bottom. One where she had passed stolen hours with the male who had captured her heart, and still held it in his hands, despite their years apart.

She would see Fuery again.

She would learn where she had gone wrong.

Somehow.

She removed her cloak, draped it over the grass on the bank of the brook, and sat on it.

The castle towered a short distance away, stunning in the warm light, seeming to sparkle. She had never seen it this close, so close she could pick out all the details and see the green vines that covered some of the balconies, their blue flowers filling her with an itch to see them closer. She had never seen such blooms before either.

She had never set foot in this end of the kingdom.

Had never left the kingdom.

Never travelled to the free realm.

She had done all those things now. It sank in fast and she needed a moment to take that in. She had broken with convention in so many ways. A smile touched her lips. Fuery always had had a way of making her go against society.

Her thoughts flitted between memories of him as she stared at the castle, not really seeing it. She saw Fuery as he had been four thousand years ago, a young male full of hope and love. A strong male who had moved Hell to be close to her, to be good enough for her.

Gods, he had always been good enough for her, even when he hadn't seen it.

She didn't need a male of status to make her happy.

She only needed Fuery.

"Are you unwell?" The deep baritone rolled over her, sweeping her thoughts away, and she looked up at its owner, her eyes widening a little when she realised it was getting dark.

How long had she been sitting here, daydreaming of Fuery?

She looked off to her right, to the hill where the soldiers had been. They were gone.

She had wasted hours, time in which she should have been seeking a way to see Fuery so she could help him.

"Did you come to the palace for something?" The elegant male pulled her focus back to him.

He had a kind face, with twinkling violet eyes that spoke of intelligence and maybe a keen wit, and held himself well with an almost regal bearing that made him look as if he had been born to wear such a fine tailored tunic. There were dragons and elves on the two long tabs at the front of it that reached down to his knees, stitched beautifully in hues of blue and green.

She wasn't normally in the habit of speaking to strangers, but something about the male soothed her and had words bubbling up before she could stop them.

"I came to see someone, but changed my mind… and I meant to leave but it was so beautiful." She looked around her at the green hills, the babbling stream, the castle and the mountains.

"And you needed the connection to nature to soothe you. Why?" The male crouched before her, resting his elbows on his knees.

He was astute too.

She hadn't even realised that was the reason she had come out to the meadow and the stream.

But he was right.

She had needed nature to soothe her.

All elves had a connection to it, one that kept light burning in their souls and allowed them to temper the seed of darkness that lived within their hearts—darkness that elves tapped into whenever they needed a boost in strength. Fuery had told her once that the soldiers were trained in methods of harnessing the darkness, using it as a weapon to aid them in their battles. It had sounded dangerous to her.

Now that she knew what had happened to him, she wanted to blame his training. It had taught him to awaken the darkness, but it was a volatile thing, easily able to overpower even the strongest male. He had been playing with fire, and in the end it had not only burned him, but had consumed him, pushing out the light.

Gods, she wanted to help him find that light within himself again and pull him from the darkness.

The male beside her preened his short blue-black hair back as he waited for her to find her voice to answer him, and she spotted the black and silver bands around his wrists. Armour. She had seen Fuery's a few times, and he had even shown her how it looked when he called upon it and the black scales rippled over his body like magic, flowing from the bands.

Was this male another commander?

Bleu had worn such fine clothing when she had met him in the village. Maybe this male could help her find him.

"The person I came to see… he told me that someone I believed I had lost was in fact alive." She picked at the grass, her eyes on the blades, avoiding his keen gaze.

"You seem upset by this, and not relieved," he said and moved to sit beside her. He planted the soles of his polished black riding boots to the grass and rested his forearms on his bent knees, leaning forwards slightly so he could keep his eyes on her face.

Shaia shrugged.

"I tried to find him, and was turned away by another male, one who is bound to him. He told me not to return until I understand where I went wrong." She squeezed her eyes shut and hung her head. "I cannot feel him."

"The male bound to him?" When those soft words left his lips, a note of confusion in them, she lifted her head and looked at him. His eyes were as soft as his voice, soothing and coaxing her into speaking and telling him more.

What was it about this male that made it so easy for her to speak with him?

She should have already made her excuses and left, or asked him to take her to see Bleu. Yet here she was, talking openly with a male she didn't know, one who didn't seem shocked that she was flouting society's rules and not behaving at all as a female should.

Shaia shook her head.

A flicker of understanding dawned in his eyes.

"Ah." He nodded, a smile teasing his lips, one that was somehow solemn. "The lost male is your mate."

A trickle of cold went through her and she wanted to deny it, afraid that this male was a noble and word would get back to her family, but then she remembered that Fuery was her everything. He was all that mattered.

She would forsake her family just to be with him.

Had intended to do just that when he returned from his assignment.

Only he had never returned.

She nodded, plucked another blade of grass and studied it. "I believed him dead in the battle four-thousand-two-hundred years ago."

The male beside her tensed, and her eyes leaped to his face in time to catch the way his expression shifted towards something akin to wariness for a heartbeat before it softened again.

Or pain.

Had she pained him?

She studied him, the blade of grass forgotten as she tried to judge his age, worried that he might be one of the survivors of the war she had mentioned. He appeared around the same age as Bleu, as her, but could easily be older by centuries or more. Elves aged so slowly after maturing that it was difficult to tell, but it was certainly possible he had been involved in the war. She made a mental note not to mention it again.

When he relaxed again, she did too, returning her gaze to the grass and then the stream. Her thoughts drifted back to Fuery.

"How could I believe him dead if I am bound to him?" she whispered to herself, seeking the answer from her heart because it seemed no one else would give it to her.

Her heart sounded decidedly masculine.

"The answer to that is simple. The bond between you became weak when the male you had formed it with became tainted."

Tainted.

Shaia wanted to squeeze her eyes shut on hearing that word, but she forced herself to look at the male to her right instead. "I fear Fuery would be lost if not for the male who has bound himself to him."

She swore the male tensed again, but he appeared as relaxed as ever, his expression gentle and soft still, and no trace of darkness in his eyes.

"I know a little about bonds," he said, "and the tainted."

She feared she had said too much. "Please don't tell anyone at the castle. I'm afraid they will send soldiers after him. I know what the prince does to the tainted."

"I will not tell a soul." There was that flicker in his eyes again, as if she had hurt him. "I share a bond with a female myself, and a bond with a male, and both are complex things. It is easy for a bond to feel broken when the person at the other end draws away from the light. Our bonds are forged by nature, and nature does not like the darkness. It thrives in the light. So when darkness invades the heart of a bonded elf, it drives out the nature that forged the connection between that elf and another, and it is easy for that person to believe the bond broken."

Was it really that simple?

Was her bond with Fuery still there, only muted by his darkness because nature feared it as strongly as the elves?

"There have been times when my bond with another became so weak I thought it broken." He looked off into the distance, beyond the castle, his expression turning solemn, and then he looked at her, his gaze filled with a mixture of pain and hope. "If you focus on it, you should still be able to feel it is there, and it always has been."

Shaia slowly blocked out the world around her, her focus turning inwards, towards the bond she shared with Fuery and that slender ribbon that connected them.

But no matter how hard she focused, she couldn't feel Fuery.

She couldn't feel their bond.

"Was Bleu lying?" she whispered to her knees and fought the tears that wanted to rise and burn her eyes, refusing to let them come. Refusing to lose hope even when it all seemed so impossible.

Hartt had made it clear that Fuery was alive. She clung to that, using it to hold together the tattered shreds of her hope.

The male beside her smiled. "Bleu is not in the habit of lying. He is often painfully truthful."

Her eyes widened. "You know Bleu?"

It would stand to reason that he would if he were a commander of the legions, but it still surprised her, and had that hope growing stronger.

"I do." He didn't look as if he would expand on that, and before she could ask how he knew Bleu, he spoke again. "Close your eyes and focus on your bond, both with your mate and with nature."

Shaia did as he had instructed, and tensed as his hand came down on the back of her neck, cool against her skin.

He palmed it. "Relax. I am only trying to assist you."

Her connection with nature flooded open, stronger than she had ever felt it, sending a chill sweeping over her skin. Gods, it was magical. She felt one with it in a way she never had before, as if nature was the life that flowed through her veins, was each beat of her heart and breath of air in her lungs.

"You are doing well," he murmured. "Your connection is naturally strong. Very strong for a female. Focus on your bond now."

She tried.

But nothing happened.

"I am... I'm not sure how," she whispered, ashamed to admit that and feeling like a fool as it hit her that she knew so little about bonds.

There was a smile in his voice as he spoke. "You simply have to focus on the one at the other end of it. Call him into your mind, and invite him into your heart."

She could do that.

She conjured an image of Fuery, which wasn't difficult. He sprang quickly into her mind, dressed in only his black trousers, his chest bare and glistening with water as it had been the day they had met at the river. His violet eyes sparkled at her, bright with his smile as he spoke with her.

Warmth flowed into her, light and life that had her feeling as if she was soaring, able to touch the sky. Her heartbeat slowed, falling into rhythm with his, and she reached for him.

Opened herself to him.

Darkness flooded her, oily and thick.

Choking her.

The male snatched his hand away from her neck on a muttered curse and the connection shattered.

Shaia breathed hard, tears stinging her eyes and her body awash with crippling pain that tore at her, felt as if it was ripping her apart molecule by molecule.

The male beside her panted too, struggling as fiercely as she was. She cracked her eyes open and looked at him as she clutched at the grass on either side of her hips, desperate to feel nature, cool and clean, surrounding her.

Anything but that vile darkness.

"I… I'm sorry," she murmured, fighting for air to ease the pain still ricocheting around inside her. "I'm not sure what happened."

He sucked down a deep shuddering breath. "It was not your doing, not your fault. I am responsible. I should have considered the consequences of using my powers to forge a stronger connection between you and a male who is not only tainted."

Shaia swallowed as her heart plummeted.

"He is *lost*." He stood and she grabbed his left hand, held on tightly and refused to let him go.

"Please… do not tell anyone. *Please*?" She clung to him, images of the legion tracking down Fuery and hurting him rushing through her mind, tormenting her.

The male looked down at her, his eyes colder now. "You believe you are capable of taming such a beast?"

She nodded. "I... I can. No... I am not sure, but I must try, because his sickness is my fault. If I had known how to feel the bond between us, he might not have fallen into the darkness."

The male took a step back, slipping from her grasp, and she shot to her feet, her heart thundering as fear flooded her veins.

"Please, don't tell the prince." She reached for him but he evaded her, shifting his arm behind him and beyond her reach. Desperation lanced her, drove her to seize him again and not let him go until he swore he wouldn't tell anyone what she had told him. She shook as she reached for him, fear at the helm, filling her mind with horrific images. "The prince will kill him."

He stilled, his face going slack, all emotion draining from it. "You honestly believe that?"

She bent her head, fought the shame that swept through her again, born of the terrible thing she had said about their prince, and then lifted her chin and nodded. "I know what the prince does to the tainted and the lost."

His eyes darkened again. "Do you honestly believe me capable of killing the tainted and the lost when my own flesh and blood is among them?"

Shaia's knees almost gave out.

She stared at the male, growing painfully aware of who she was speaking to and increasingly horrified by the things she had said to him.

Prince Loren.

Gods.

She bowed her head, clutched the front of her trousers and cursed herself. "I am sorry. I only know what I hear."

He huffed. "That is the crux of your problem, is it not? You know only what you are told, and do not seek the knowledge for yourself."

She wanted to say that the crux of her problem was society in that case, and it was responsible for her mistake. It was hard for a female to educate herself, to rise above the position tradition wanted for her and go against everything it believed she should be, and should do. She had fought against it and her parents for centuries, had grown up stealing books from her father's library and hiding them until she had finished reading them, learning all she could about the world.

Tradition wanted her restricted to knowledge suitable for a lady.

No tales of wars and great battles, or stories about the other species who also called Hell their home, and legends about the Devil and the terrible things he had done.

It wanted her to know about sewing and crafting, about tending to flowers and fruits and vegetables, and other ridiculous pastimes that she had grown to despise over the years because they represented everything that was wrong with elf society.

She wanted to say all that to him, to the prince who ruled this realm and had the power to make sweeping changes to their traditions, freeing females and allowing them to enjoy the same pursuits as the males of their kind.

Only she wasn't brave enough.

Because she had already wounded him with her careless words.

She felt wretched when he touched her left cheek, slid his fingers down to under her jaw and lifted her chin, and she saw the hurt in his eyes.

"Do you believe I will punish you too?"

She quickly shook her head. It was the truth. He had been nothing but kind to her, had helped her immeasurably, because even now she could feel an echo of Fuery within her. The bond to him was frightening, because it was so dark, like staring into a cold vast abyss, but gods, it was a relief to feel it there again and know that he was really alive.

"I owe you everything," she whispered to Prince Loren, and then pulled her courage up from her boots and found some strength to put into her voice. "I cannot thank you enough... and I feel terrible that I said those things about you... but I need to protect Fuery."

He regarded her for a few seconds, and then nodded. "I understand, because I too feel such a need. I constantly lie to my council, telling them I do not know where Vail resides, because I cannot bring myself to surrender my brother to them. I would do anything to protect him."

She could see in his soft violet eyes that he truly did understand her desire to protect Fuery from the legion responsible for hunting the tainted.

"If I wanted all the tainted and lost dead, I would have sent the legion after Fuery the second I met the male in the mortal realm four lunar cycles ago."

It took Shaia a moment to take in those words. They swam in her head, shock making them ripple and distort, slow to come into order and sink in.

When they did, they knocked her hard, had her wobbling on her feet as she stared at Prince Loren.

"You... you have seen him?" Her voice shook as much as her legs.

He nodded.

Relief swept through her, powerful and potent, making the hope in her heart grow stronger because she was sure Prince Loren would never lie to anyone, and she believed him when he said he wouldn't send anyone after Fuery.

She could save him.

Prince Loren shattered that relief and shook her hope when he spoke again.

"I saw enough to know that if you do not move swiftly, you will not save your mate from the darkness. He will be lost forever."

CHAPTER 9

A bolt of white lightning suddenly shot through Fuery, driving back the darkness that was his constant companion and bringing him to his knees. The black gravel bit into his shins as he breathed hard, struggling as an onslaught of emotions rushed through him, clashing hard within him and tearing him apart.

He growled as the light pulsed brighter, sending sharp pain sweeping through him, a collision of feelings dredged up from his past and condensed into one searing blast that felt as if it would shatter him.

He couldn't breathe.

Fuery grasped his throat, tugging at the scales of his black armour, fighting for air.

Something was wrong with him. Terribly wrong. Cold prickles swept over his skin beneath his armour, tightened his chest and chilled his blood. He needed to return to the guild. He needed to speak with Hartt. Hartt would know what was happening to him.

He wanted to teleport there, but he couldn't, didn't have the strength and couldn't focus through the sensations detonating inside him, bombarding him and leaving him quaking. He would have to find the nearest public portal. He could make it. He needed help.

One of the demons chuckled low, reminding him that he wasn't alone. Another joined him.

That had his mind sharpening even as pain wracked his body. Danger. He was in danger, open to attack as he was now. He needed to purge the pain. The light. Light part of him wanted to cling to even as the rest of him screamed to extinguish it.

He gritted his teeth and focused, fighting to subdue his muddled emotions and the agony they caused.

As the pain began to ease and he finally got his emotions back under control, the darkness pushed back against the light, more vicious than it had ever been. It swamped him, gripped him fiercely and pressed down on him, squeezing the light back out of him.

Stealing control.

He reached for the light, the reaction an instinct he had no power over and didn't understand. It slipped through his fingers as the darkness responded to the need that went through him, rising to swallow him and seemingly determined to shut out the light again, as if it feared it might lose its grip on him entirely.

Gods, Fuery wanted that light back.

He wasn't sure where it had come from, but it felt familiar.

Like coming home.

A roar rushed through him, screaming up his throat, and the darkness seized hold of him, squeezing him in sharp claws that penetrated deep enough into his soul that it shook the light from him.

He sank into it.

The first demon didn't know what had hit him as Fuery launched to his feet, a blur in the low light. His long black claws met the large male's throat and then blood spilled over his bare chest, thick and dark, and the male gargled as he went down.

The second demon, the one who had laughed at him, was quick to move out of his path, distancing himself from the dead male as he dropped to the black earth near the fire of their camp.

Fuery didn't hesitate to shift his aim to the nearest male, a young demon who was now fumbling with an enormous sword, the firelight shimmering over his tight bronze leathers that hugged his thick legs as he spread them in a fighting stance. He had been a last minute addition to Fuery's client's list of marks, a mercenary in training. Unfortunately for the male, the first job the demons had taken after welcoming him into their team had been kidnapping a fae female for sale on the black market.

Her father was paying handsomely for her return, and the death of everyone involved in what had happened to her.

The young pale-haired demon swung the blade at him, a clumsy blow that Fuery easily dodged. He pivoted around to behind the male, faster than the brute because of his size. Demons were strong, but they were at a disadvantage when faced with one of Fuery's kind. They were heavy-set with bulging muscles that gave them power but at the cost of speed.

Elves tended to err towards a lighter build, with compact muscles that gave them both power, and agility. Fuery had long ago honed that speed, learning to use it to his advantage against any foe.

He was behind the male in a flash as the young demon spun on his heel to face him, leaving him turning this way and that, hunting for him. He grinned and raked long black claws down the male's bare back, tearing a satisfying bellow from his lips. The male arched forwards, staggering a step, blood swiftly rolling down his back from the four long slashes.

The second demon, the one Fuery had decided led the team, landed a hard blow on Fuery's left cheek, sending him swaying to his right. He rocked back onto his toes and slowly turned his head towards the male.

The big black-haired male's equally as dark eyes widened slightly as Fuery remained standing, a momentary show of fear that Fuery relished.

On a snarl, Fuery kicked off towards him. He ploughed into the demon's bare chest and stilled for a heartbeat as he felt the fiery cut of the male's blade across his left side.

Not possible.

He shoved the demon hard, sending him staggering backwards, gaining some space. His eyes darted to the blade the male gripped in front of his obsidian leathers. A black dagger.

Made from the metal mined in the elf kingdom.

The same metal as his armour.

Fuery slowly lowered his head, his eyes dropping to the wound on his side, a long gash in his armour that seeped crimson.

The only metal that could pierce his armour.

The demon palmed the blade, a sure grin stretching his lips to flash his fangs, and his black horns curled further around the curve of his ears, the sharp points flaring forwards in a show of aggression.

Fuery eased his hand down, feeling nothing as he stared at the blood flowing from him. He pressed his fingers against the thick glossy trail and then pulled them away, brought his hand in front of him and stared at it.

Blood.

On his hands.

Inky darkness bubbled up, chasing out the last remnants of the light as he sank deep into his memories and drowned in them.

He threw his head back and roared as that darkness consumed him.

Crimson burned across his vision.

And then everything went black.

Pain was the first thing he grew aware of as the darkness began to lift and he was pulled up from its depths, a battered and broken thing, soul-deep weary and hollowed out.

Gods, he hurt.

It felt as if someone had scoured his insides, clawed them all out and shattered every bone in his body in the process.

His vision came back, slow to focus but when it did, he saw black earth and something fuzzy beyond it. He frowned and shifted his gaze there, his breathing shallow as he struggled against the tangled threads of darkness that refused to release him, clung to him as if they feared they would die if he shattered their hold on him.

He feared he would die if he didn't.

The world beyond the patch of earth beneath his cheek came into focus. A village of tents made from the hide of the beasts of Hell. A dying fire in the middle of the circle of five tents. A smoking heavy iron pot suspended above it. The air filled with the acrid stench of whatever was in it burning.

And blood.

He froze as his gaze caught on something else.

Bodies.

Six males. Demons. They had been ripped apart, limbs scattered and flesh shredded. The one nearest him had his face caved in and his horns broken, torn from his skull and left on the black earth near him. That earth had been churned up, revealing how brutal the fight had been.

A battle.

He pushed his hands into the dirt, his arms trembling as he eased off his chest and into a sitting position on his knees.

His whole body ached, fire consuming it, racing in lines over his arms and sides, his thighs and back. His head.

He shook it as his vision lost focus again and it came back, sharper than before.

Revealing something else.

A fae female lay prone in the dirt just a few feet from him. Her clothes torn. Delicate body broken.

Covered in blood.

Fuery looked down at his stained claws.

No.

He roared out his agony and stilted darkness swept over him and dragged him down into it, but the cold of it kept him grounded this time, because this darkness wasn't the one that lived in his soul and tormented him.

It was a teleport.

He fought to focus as his mind screamed that he had killed a female, an innocent, desperately trying to direct the teleport so he wouldn't land on the roof of the guild this time. His battered body wouldn't be able to take the fall. It would break him.

Mercifully, he landed in the street.

People shrieked and scattered, and he staggered onto his feet and lumbered towards the arched entrance of the guild.

Hartt.

He needed to see Hartt.

He stumbled into the guild, his legs weakening with each step, wobbling beneath him as the pain rose back to the fore, the agony of his injuries tearing at his control. He breathed deep and fast, fighting the darkness as it tried to rise again, roused by his weakness and what he had done.

He had killed another female.

Her blood was on his hands.

Relief so sweet that it brought tears to his eyes hit him as he caught Hartt's scent and sensed the male ahead of him.

He reached for their bond, needing the strength it gave him to shatter the fragile hold the darkness had on him so it couldn't drag him back down into it.

He rounded the corner and Hartt loomed ahead of him in the enormous reception room.

"Hartt," he croaked and reached his right hand out to the male.

Hartt turned and Fuery's eyes widened as he saw someone beyond him.

A female.

Her violet eyes widened as she spotted him, her soft pink lips parting in shock he swore he felt ripple through him.

What fresh Hell was this?

He stared at her as his knees gave out, sending him down hard on the polished black stone floor.

"Shaia?"

CHAPTER 10

There was a ghost standing before him. Come to haunt him. Torment him.

His ki'ara.

His sweet Shaia.

Fuery knelt on the stone floor of the guild reception room staring at her as she stared at him, her violet eyes as bright and beautiful as he remembered, and her sleek fall of wavy blue-black hair warmed by the oil lamps that lit the expansive space. Those lamps warmed her skin too, giving it a golden hint that reminded him of when they had met that summer over four thousand years ago.

Before he had killed her.

Had he passed out and this was nothing but another dream of her? She haunted his sleep, so it was possible. Whenever he closed his eyes, he didn't find rest—he found her.

There were the twisted, torturous dreams where he saw himself destroying her, completely ruining her—killing her—and then there were the more wicked dreams of her. In those dreams, he was the male he had used to be, the one before the darkness had engulfed him. Sometimes, those dreams pained him more than the ones of killing her.

Dreaming of what might have been, and what had been, killed him.

He stared at her.

She wasn't real. He wanted her to be, but she wasn't. It wasn't Shaia stood there staring at him with tears shimmering on her lashes. She was gone, had departed this world and it was darker for it. *He* was darker for it.

His breathing quickened, heart accelerating as his throat closed. Tears stung his eyes and he clawed at the black stone beneath him, aching to rip through it and bury his hands in the earth, to sink deep into it and somehow restore his connection to nature. He needed the comfort, but she would reject him, as she always did.

She loathed the darkness inside him.

That made two of them.

He hated it too, but he couldn't shake it. He wasn't strong enough. Gods, he wanted to be strong again, but it was hard to overpower the darkness crawling and slithering inside him, infecting his mind and his body, and destroying his soul little by little.

It was easier to give in to it.

He looked down at his hands, at his body.

At all the blood on him.

Not only his.

He lifted his hands from the floor and turned them palm up before him and stared at them. It was the fae female's blood too. He chuckled mirthlessly, a hollow bitter sound in the strained silence. He had killed her.

That was the only reason he was seeing Shaia now.

He had killed another female and the darkness had conjured her to torment him.

It wanted to break him.

He hesitated, fear washing through him, battering his strength. The desire that ran through him was stronger than fear though, and he found the courage to lift his eyes from his hands.

He settled them on the vision beyond Hartt.

Gods, she was beautiful.

He had forgotten how beautiful she had been.

Every instinct he had as her mate burst to life inside his battered body and screamed at him to rise back onto his feet, cross the short span of stone tiles to her, and gather her into his arms. He needed to hold her again. He needed to feel her nestled close to him, her warmth seeping into his skin, and her scent swirling in his lungs, comforting him. He needed it more than anything. More than life in his veins. Air in his lungs.

A beat in his chest.

He needed her.

Tears blurred his vision as he stared at her and he blinked them away, desperate to keep her in focus, afraid she would disappear on him if he didn't.

"I never wanted to hurt you," he whispered to himself in the elf tongue, to her, even though he was sure she was only a figment of his imagination and he was aware everyone in the room with him, Hartt included, would think he had completely lost his mind. "I am sorry… I am sorry…"

Gods, he *had* lost his mind.

Who was he kidding?

He was seeing ghosts of his past, and the torture of it was too much. The urge to stagger onto his feet drove through him again, pushing him to obey it. He tried, but his broken body ached so fiercely that it sent him back to his knees, the pain stealing his breath and sending his limbs trembling. He could only kneel and gaze up at her. His love. His everything.

His Shaia.

"I missed you so much," he murmured, voice strained as his throat closed tighter. "I am sorry... so sorry... that I killed you."

Hartt moved, coming to him and easing into a crouch before him. The ghost stayed where she was, her steady violet gaze locked on him, looking right into his eyes and holding him captive.

He couldn't tear his eyes away from her, even as guilt and shame ate away at him, stealing more pieces of his soul and feeding it to the darkness. He wanted to look into those eyes forever, because she was looking at him as she had used to, back in those halcyon days, when all of her love for him had shone in her eyes and bathed him in warmth and light.

He lowered his head and growled through his clenched fangs, his lips peeling back off them in a grimace.

He couldn't take it.

He didn't deserve her looking at him now. He was a monster. A fiend. He had failed as her mate.

Hartt pulled him onto his feet and Fuery couldn't stop himself from reaching for her as fear of being parted from her again crashed over him, battering him.

Shock swept through him when she reached for him too, stretching out a slender hand towards him.

A clean, perfect little hand.

A stark contrast to his bloodied black claws.

Fuery snatched his hand away, afraid she might touch it and he might taint her.

"Do not move," Hartt said, and at first Fuery thought he was speaking to him, but when he looked at the male, he was looking in the direction of the ghost that hovered before him.

A beautiful phantom and a terrible nightmare.

She shrank back a step, as if she had heard Hartt, and lowered her head.

Fuery laughed at himself and the ridiculous hope building inside him.

She wasn't real.

She only responded because she was a figment of his tired mind, under his control, and he had heard Hartt's words.

She had reacted because he had ached for her to do so.

Her lips parted, soft pink and tempting, and gods, he wanted to take those lips with his, to taste her and drown in her as he used to, spending hours worshipping them and stealing every kiss she would give him.

"Fuery," she whispered.

Too much.

He growled and struggled against Hartt, the agonised sound echoing around the room to mock him. Hartt's grip on him tightened, the pain of it a strange sort of comfort that he clung to, desperate to ground himself again.

The bond between them grew in intensity, offering more comfort to his weary soul, easing some of the pain in his heart.

Stripping away his defences.

What he had done came rushing back in to swamp him and the darkness seized it like a weapon, used it to weaken him as he fought to wrest control from it again.

"I woke in a village," he whispered in the elf tongue as Hartt dragged him towards the corridor, his eyes locked on the ghost of Shaia. Desperation edged his words as he tried to purge the darkness growing inside him by spilling his sin as quickly as he could manage, confessing all to Hartt in the hope it would help as it had many times before. "I had killed many… I killed another female just as I killed you."

Gods, he wasn't confessing to Hartt.

He was confessing to her.

"Do not talk any more, Fuery," Hartt murmured. "Save your strength."

They reached the corridor and Fuery lost sight of his ghost, but he could still see the horrified expression that had settled on her beautiful face as he had confessed his sins.

"I am sorry." Fuery stumbled along behind Hartt, his voice hitching as tears filled his eyes and his heart blazed, each step agony as his wounds stretched and felt as if they would burst open, and his bones burned and grated beneath his skin.

"Do not worry about it." Hartt pulled him closer, turning him to face forwards and wrapping an arm around his side beneath his arms to support his weight. "I will go to the village. I am sure there is an explanation and that you did not kill a female."

"*Again*," Fuery said. "I did not kill a female again."

Hartt muttered, "If you did, it would be the first female you have killed."

Which made no sense to Fuery.

Hartt knew his black past, knew his sins and what he had done to the beautiful apparition they had left behind in the guild entrance hall.

They reached Fuery's quarters and Hartt opened the door and led him inside. Light flickered to life in the oil lamp on the small table on the right of the room near the window, chasing back the darkness as Hartt moved forwards towards the double bed.

Fuery eased down onto the dark covers, his eyes not leaving Hartt as he tried to make sense of everything that had happened.

Hartt's deep voice was soft, laced with affection and concern. "There is blood in the cooler. Drink some. You need it to heal. Swear you will remain in the room while I deal with a few things."

Fuery nodded.

"Rest," Hartt said softly.

He caught Hartt's wrist when the male turned to leave, and Hartt looked back at him, the concern that had been in his voice shining in his violet eyes.

"I cannot," Fuery whispered and clutched Hartt's arm, unwilling to let him leave when there was more he needed to tell him. He needed to unburden his heart before he could rest. He needed to hear Hartt tell him that there was nothing wrong with him. Nothing more than usual anyway. "There was a light in me, Hartt. A flash of sunshine... and it blinded me. I keep seeing it wink in the darkness... an echo... but it is still there. I can feel it, Hartt. Someone put a light inside me."

Hartt leaned over and smoothed his hair back with his free hand. "You are just tired. You need to rest."

"I will try." Even though he knew it was impossible because if he focused, that odd light was still there, casting shadows in his heart.

Hartt slipped out of his grip and headed for the door, and Fuery tracked him, part of him wishing his friend would stay and the rest needing him gone so he could have silence in which to think. To feel. He wanted to nurture that light that lingered inside him, needed to come to understand it somehow and learn where it had come from.

"Where are you going?" he rasped, his thoughts flitting between the strange light and the demons he had slaughtered, the two blurring together and rousing the darkness that now slumbered inside him, the pain echoing through his body keeping it at bay, rendering him too weak to fight as it always wanted him to.

It would leave him be now until he was healed, stronger, able to do its vile bidding. He had starved himself the first time he had realised it lost interest when he was weak. It had been a mistake, and one he had never repeated. When he had passed out from hunger, he had come around surrounded by a bloody scene and with his belly full.

Hartt looked back at him from the door, stopping halfway through closing it, and smiled at him. "I am going to look into some business for you, remember?"

Yes, he remembered.

He nodded. "The other female I killed."

It had slipped his mind for a moment, but it came back in a flash, a brutal blast that tore at him and had him trembling again, sick to his stomach. The light that echoed inside him seemed to grow a little stronger in response, pulsing brighter, but still faintly.

It comforted him.

Even as it drove the darkness wild, made it bash against the cage he tried to keep it locked in and push to break free.

Hartt muttered something as he closed the door, but Fuery caught the words.

"The only female you killed."

CHAPTER 11

A bolt went down Shaia's spine, lighting her up inside, and she tensed, her gaze leaping towards the entrance of the guild building and her argument dying on her lips. Before her, Hartt went rigid, his eyes sliding to his left, telling her she hadn't imagined the feeling that had arrowed through her.

Fuery was here.

"Leave," Hartt growled, his voice blacker than she had ever heard it, and reached out to grab her arm.

To teleport her away?

"No." She evaded his hand, refusing to let him order her around or make her do something against her will. "I know where I went wrong now, and you said I could see Fuery if that happened. I want to see Fuery."

"Believe me, you don't want to see Fuery. Not as he is now. It will be too much for you, Shaia. He is not the male you knew. It will be too much for him."

That almost had her doing as he wanted and leaving, but the need to see Fuery with her own eyes and know he was alive was too strong, easily suppressing her desire to go and spare Fuery the pain of seeing her.

"I need this," she whispered, and then with more conviction added, "You cannot make me leave this time."

Hartt's violet eyes leaped from the entrance hall to her, and the emotions that flickered in them warned her that he wasn't embellishing things, that he honestly believed this meeting between her and Fuery would prove too much for both of them.

He pressed a hand to the breast of his black tunic. "He is not well. Something is wrong."

She could feel it too. It was the same feeling she'd had when speaking with Prince Loren, when he had helped her open the link between her and Fuery. Darkness. Pure darkness.

And pain.

So much pain that it stole her breath.

She ached to take that pain away, to ease it and Fuery's suffering, to bring light back into his soul somehow and save him.

The sensation grew stronger, sliding down her spine, wrapping around her limbs and tightening its hold on her.

He was coming.

"Last chance," Hartt muttered, an edge to his tone that told her to take the out he was giving her for her own sake.

She shook her head even though he couldn't see it. She wouldn't leave now, not when she was on the brink of seeing Fuery again, not even when she feared what he would look like now.

When Hartt turned and she caught sight of Fuery at the entrance to the black-walled reception room, her breath left her in a rush and her legs weakened.

But it was Fuery who fell to his knees on the black flagstones the moment his eyes landed on her.

He was more beautiful than she remembered, more breathtaking, and the pain of missing him swept through her, so intense that she couldn't breathe, couldn't think, was left shaking and wrecked.

He was a mess, his eyes appearing black and his pale skin covered in blood, his armour torn in places to reveal vicious wounds, but gods, he was still *her* Fuery.

Her ki'aro.

She had mourned him for millennia, and now she wasn't sure how to process the fact that he was still alive, but sick. Terribly sick. She could see it in his eyes as he stared at her as though she was an apparition sent to haunt him or torment him. She could feel his pain, his fear, his suffering through their weakened bond. Pain that had nothing to do with his injuries. It pulled at her, and she needed to do something for him.

But she could only stand and stare, too shell-shocked by the sight of him to move and act, reeling from every emotion that flooded her, both her own and Fuery's.

"Shaia?" he breathed, and her knees almost gave way, a chilling sort of weakness sweeping through her that brought tears to her eyes as she heard his voice again, her name on his lips for the first time in four thousand years.

His breathing quickened, becoming laboured, and he raked claws over the obsidian stone tiles as he stared at her, his black eyes shimmering with unshed tears.

And then he lifted his hands from the floor, turned them palm up, and stared down at them, his eyes wide. Pain flooded her, so intense her breath lodged in her throat together with her heart.

His pain.

She didn't hear a word he said as he lifted his head again, his lips moving silently as her ears rang and she fought the fierce onslaught of his emotions, the terrible darkness that pushed at her, trying to seep through their connection. She held it open despite the danger, refused to close it when Fuery needed her.

Hartt moved to him, and she stared as he pulled Fuery onto his feet.

Her Fuery.

He was as tall as she remembered, his build slender but powerful, slimmer than Hartt's. He kept looking at her, the disbelief mingled with pain in his eyes tugging at her, together with the injuries he bore. He needed her. She needed to take care of her male.

He reached for her.

His armour still formed sharp obsidian claws over his fingers, but she wouldn't hesitate to place her hand into his as he wanted, because she knew he would never hurt her.

When she reached for him, the pain that flowed from him into her grew stronger, and he lowered his hand, a flicker of something like guilt crossing his handsome face.

"Do not move," Hartt said, his violet eyes dark and his tone brooking no argument.

She moved back a step, showing him that she would do as he wanted, because now she could see that he had been right.

Seeing her again had been too much for Fuery.

He was slipping. She could feel the darkness rising inside him, and knew if she went after him as she wanted that she wouldn't be helping him. She would be helping that darkness take hold of him.

"Fuery," she whispered, filled with a need to go to him and desperately fighting it for his sake.

He needed time to recover from his wounds, and to calm his mind.

But it was hard to remain where she was as Fuery growled, the agony in it tearing at her as he fought Hartt's hold on him. Hartt's knuckles blazed white as he tightened his grip on Fuery and pulled him towards the corridor.

Fuery's eyes turned wild.

"I woke in a village," he whispered in the elf tongue as Hartt dragged him away. His eyes locked on her, and his deep voice was as wild and desperate as his expression. "I had killed many... I killed another female just as I killed you."

Killed her?

"Do not talk any more, Fuery," Hartt murmured. "Save your strength."

Fuery fell silent, and she jerked forwards as he disappeared from view, a new need rushing through her.

She needed to know what he had meant by that.

The pain she could feel in their bond grew, and she couldn't bear it. She closed her eyes and reached for him, no longer caring that the darkness might try to seep into her. It was there waiting, oily and choking, but she pushed past it, strengthening her connection to Fuery in a desperate attempt to help him.

She needed to comfort him.

He was distraught and he needed her.

He grew distant on her senses, and she wanted to follow, but remained where she was, aware that if she dared to go after Fuery that Hartt would be angry with her and would kick her out again, and she needed to speak with him.

She needed to tell him that she knew where she had gone wrong.

Because she hoped that Hartt would help her with Fuery.

It killed her a little that Fuery would never be the same, and that Hartt had been there for him when he had needed someone the most.

It should have been her.

She had failed him, her beautiful warrior.

Now he suffered because of it, and was in danger of slipping into an abyss and never coming back.

Her heart bled for him as she stood alone in the grim black reception room, his words and his pain ringing in her mind and her soul.

Movement off to her left drew her gaze there.

Hartt.

He rubbed his right hand over his mouth, his expression drawn and solemn as he moved silently across the stone floor towards her, his boots making no sound.

She took a step towards him.

He lifted troubled violet eyes to her.

They quickly narrowed into thin, dark slits and he shifted course, heading straight for her. A cold wave rolled off him and crashed over her, and her instincts blared a warning.

"You have done enough damage," he snapped. "It is time you left."

"No." She stood her ground on trembling legs. "I came here to see Fuery."

Hartt growled in her face. "You have. Now you will go."

Shaia shook her head. His expression darkened further and the threat of violence as the pointed tips of his ears flared back against his tousled short blue-black hair unnerved her, but somehow she managed to hold her ground.

"I have not seen Fuery yet," she whispered, and the menacing edge to his expression and his body language softened a little. "I have seen another male… one akin to my fated one… but one who is not my ki'aro."

Hartt's voice dropped to a bare whisper. "That male died centuries ago. He doesn't exist anymore."

She looked beyond him, towards the corridor, her senses reaching out to Fuery and finding him not far away. He felt calmer now, and she took comfort from that.

"I believe he does." She brought her gaze back to Hartt. "Somewhere in there. I need another chance to draw him to the surface."

"No." All of the warmth and softness instantly evaporated from Hartt. "It's too dangerous for Fuery."

Shaia closed her eyes, breathed deep and then looked at him. "I know. I do not want to hurt Fuery, but I cannot leave."

He looked over his shoulder again, and this time when he looked back at her, the softness was in his eyes again, mingled with hope. He was going to change his mind. She knew it. He was going to let her remain and help Fuery.

"You want to help Fuery… you can start by explaining what the *fuck* you did to him." Hartt snapped his gaze back to her, and his tone lashed at her, drilling an accusation into her heart that left her shaken. "Because he said someone put a light in him… and that was why he lost it."

Gods no.

All the pain she had felt in him, all the fear and the distress. It was all her fault.

Hartt grabbed her arm and she jerked as he yanked her in the opposite direction to Fuery, viciously pulling her down the corridor towards his office. She stumbled along behind him, ears ringing as she struggled to make it sink in.

The more it did, the fiercer the pain in her heart grew.

The door slamming shut startled her back into the room and she stared at Hartt as he shoved her down into a chair and rounded his ebony desk. Rather than sinking into his chair, he paced the length of the wall, his strides clipped and screaming of the agitation and anger she could sense in him.

"You told me to find out where I had gone wrong," she said, unwilling to take all the blame for what had happened to Fuery. "I went to speak about it to someone I know and who is also recently mated, but when I reached the castle I lost my nerve. I rested near a stream outside it and a kind stranger came to check on me. I talked with him about it… and he helped me open the connection again by strengthening my one with nature."

Hartt froze.

Slowly shifted his head towards her.

His wide violet eyes landed on hers.

"Do *not* tell me that you told Prince Loren about Fuery… do not tell me you chose the one male in the damned kingdom with the power to hurt Fuery… to sentence him to death." Hartt rounded on her and slammed his hands down on the desk, causing her to jump. "Don't you *dare* fucking tell me that you just told the male in charge of a death squad that Fuery is tainted."

Before she could say anything in her defence, he threw his hands up in the air and growled, flashing long white daggers as his ears grew more pointed.

"Why not just kill Fuery yourself? It would be fucking kinder!" Hartt growled and shoved his fingers through the longer lengths of his black hair, tugging on it and ploughing furrows in it as he started pacing again. Quicker this time. "I don't fucking believe you."

She flinched again.

"You told me to learn where I went wrong," she said, her voice smaller than she would have liked.

It shrank to a squeak at the end when he turned on her again.

"I didn't fucking tell you to bring a death squad down on Fuery!"

She rallied and growled at him. "Prince Loren swears he will not tell the council. He lies to them about his own brother. He already knew Fuery was tainted and did not send the squad after him."

Hartt slowed to a halt and muttered, "I suppose that is true. And just who do you know at the castle anyway?"

"A male, we grew up in the same village. His name is Bleu."

Hartt's violet eyes shot wide again. "Bleu? Commander fucking Bleu? The high almighty son of a bitch who idolises Fuery while he wants my fucking head on a spike?"

She wasn't aware of that. "He knew Fuery when I knew him, back when he served in the legions."

"I fucking know that," Hartt interjected. "Fuery has a soft spot for him. Gods only know why. Bleu has no love for the tainted."

"If you would let me finish," she snapped and her own eyes widened at the tone of her voice, at the venom that had been in it. If anyone in the elf kingdom heard her talking to a male like that, she would be ostracised. She softened her tone. "Bleu is the one who told me Fuery wasn't dead."

"Fuck me." Hartt slumped into his tall-backed black leather chair, as if all his strength had suddenly left him. He pinched the bridge of his nose and sighed as he closed his eyes.

He looked pale again.

Drained.

"Is something wrong?" she said, keeping her tone soft and low, hoping to calm him.

He ground his teeth, the muscles in his jaw popping, and grimaced. "It is Fuery and our bond. Whenever he gets like this, it… it just makes me a little tired and testy."

That was an understatement.

"It does more than that. It pushes you towards the darkness too." She waited for him to deny it.

He didn't.

She couldn't help but wonder what damage he had done to himself with the blood bond between him and Fuery, and she also couldn't thank him enough, because she wasn't as stupid as he thought her. She knew that without the bond between him and Hartt, she would have lost Fuery long ago.

"You are not alone now." She leaned forwards and placed her right hand on his ebony desk, stretching it towards him. "I will use my bond to help bring Fuery back and give him peace so he can begin to heal, and you can too."

Hartt's eyes narrowed again. "It was your bond to Fuery that drove him into this state. Fuery felt you reopen it and forge a stronger one between you."

The guilt she had felt on suspecting as much flooded her again, a torrent that was stronger this time and threatened to carry her with it. She clung to the slender thread of hope that had kept her going over the past few weeks.

But even as she clung to it, hope began to leach from her.

What hope was there when her attempt to reconnect with Fuery had driven him mad and hurled him deeper into the darkness?

Hartt breathed a deep sigh, tipped his head back against the rear of his leather seat and closed his eyes.

"Give him time," he murmured, sounding as tired as he looked. "A few days and he will be settled again, and maybe then you can see him… although I am not sure it will do much good."

There was something he wasn't telling her.

He opened his eyes and slid her a look that told her not to ask, and warned her he wouldn't answer if she did.

But she needed to know.

"What is it you are hiding from me about Fuery?" Whatever it was, it felt as if knowing it was vital if she wanted to help her mate.

"We are done for now." Hartt stood, his regal tone and cold air making it clear he meant it and she wasn't going to get anything else out of him. He rounded the desk, caught her arm and pulled her out of the chair. He marched her to the door, opened it and pulled her along the corridor, not slowing his pace until he reached the entrance of the guild and pushed her through it. "I need to go somewhere and you cannot be here."

"I will return in a few days." Surprise danced through her when he didn't tell her to leave, or not return, or push her away.

He just nodded, pivoted on his heel and strode back into the imposing black building.

Shaia took a few steps backwards, her eyes roaming up the height of it to the third floor where the façade rose in a steep triangle to meet in a point above a stunning circular stained-glass window that sat above the arched doorway. The towers that flanked the entrance rose higher still, spearing the dark vault of Hell, their conical tiled roofs reminding her of the castle in the elf kingdom.

She wasn't sure she would be able to wait a few days before the need to see Fuery overwhelmed her, driving her to return to the guild.

She wasn't sure she could go further than a few steps from this very spot, not without hurting herself. She needed to be close to Fuery. Her instincts had awoken at the same time as the connection they shared, and they pushed her to stay near to her mate, in case he needed her.

Because he needed her.

She looked around at the broad cobbled street that curved along the front of the guild, and the dark stone buildings that lined the other side, facing it. Some were private residences by the looks of them, large and regal affairs that were two or three storeys in height and had fine carving on their stone walls. A few were stores, the bottom level being the shop with large glass windows that displayed goods, and the second level having smaller windows, most likely used as the home of the shopkeeper.

One was an inn.

It was off to her left, a few buildings down, placing it closer to the side of the guild where Fuery's quarters were, and one of the rooms at the front of the top two storeys would give her a good view of the entrance of the guild.

She strode towards it.

She would give Fuery a few days.

And then she would see him again.

CHAPTER 12

Fuery's heart hitched at the sight of her as she appeared over the brow of the hill, the strong sunlight threading her long dark wavy hair with gold highlights that matched the colour of her fine dress. He couldn't help but notice she had chosen not to wear her sturdy work clothes today.

The gauzy layers of fabric swayed around her slender legs as she walked, teasing him with glimpses of their forms, stirring his blood, and light glinted off the elaborate wrought silver swirls that formed a corset over her torso.

Her stunning violet eyes widened as they landed on where the camp had been on the flat ground at a bend in the river, and he swore he felt her pain as she dropped the wash basket she clutched in her arms.

He pushed away from the tree as he willed his portal and purple-blue light traced over him. He stepped into the teleport, coming out of it right in front of her.

The pain that had been in her, the darkness, turned to light, illuminating her face and shining in her eyes.

"You did not think I would stand you up, did you?" He stooped and picked up the basket for her, when all he really wanted to do was gather her into his arms and never let her go.

When he straightened and smiled for her, her pain seemed forgotten, the light in her eyes glowing brighter as her soft pink lips curved into a gentle smile of her own.

"I do not have long." He cursed himself when all that light drained from her beautiful face, and stepped towards her. The basket he held bumped into her, a barrier between them that he had forgotten. He quickly set it down beside him and straightened again. He reached for her hands and she didn't deny him, and she didn't hesitate to place her delicate ones into his either. "We will be back this way soon. I swear it. I will come back. Would you... will you... wait for me?"

Gods.

Would she?

There was a vast difference in their standing, and it was a miracle that she had spoken to him last time, and had come back to meet with him again in secret. Would she bend the rules further to wait for him? Or would she return to her world, one where he didn't belong?

She surprised him by squeezing his hands and nodding.

He lifted her right hand to his lips and pressed them to it, stealing a kiss and breathing her in, memorising her scent so she would be with him whenever he needed her. Her pulse ticked against his lips, a quick rhythm that had his racing faster. He closed his eyes and tried to place her scent.

Blood.

Tinny and revolting, even as it was tempting.

Fuery snapped his eyes open and stared at the crimson that glistened on his razor-sharp black claws.

Endless darkness surrounded him, black lands that were grim and desolate. The wide valley rose in the distance around him into jagged peaks that towered high into the dim sky. He looked down at his feet.

At the scattered bodies that littered the churned dark earth.

The scent of death hung heavy in the thick air.

Blood that he had spilled.

He closed his eyes and pushed away from the nightmarish sight, back towards the light, because he needed to see more of his beautiful mate.

Even when he knew it would only pain him.

The darkness resisted and then parted to reveal the warmth of candlelight, hundreds of them burning in gilded chandeliers, illuminating an enormous rectangular room with high arched windows set into the pale stone walls.

A ball.

Nerves shot through him as people jostled him, their scents swirling around him into a blur that made it impossible to distinguish one from the next. He wiped his palms on the front two long sections of his formal jacket and swallowed hard as his eyes leaped around, scanning the faces of the attendees.

Eight lunar cycles.

He had been away for eight lunar cycles.

Had she waited for him?

Gods, he feared his beautiful female was gone, slipped from his grasp, or perhaps she had been a mere figment of his imagination.

He had dreamed of her so much that she seemed born of that unearthly world now rather than reality.

Eight lunar cycles and he finally had a reason to return to the village where he had left her.

He paced a few steps back and forth, feeling as if the nervous energy buzzing in his veins would overwhelm him if he didn't keep moving.

Just days ago, his commander, a highborn male, had pulled him into a meeting in his office in the garrison at the castle and had announced he was hosting a party—a grand ball—at his dwelling near the village and that many of the noble families were due to attend.

Fuery had wanted to lash out verbally at Andon for rubbing his nose in the fact he was free to come and go from the castle as he pleased, and able to return to the village Fuery longed to see again.

Liable to see the female he was dying to return to as promised.

Until his commander had told him that he would be coming with him, because he believed they should celebrate his achievement too.

Fuery had been working hard, had near-exhausted himself in order to rise within the ranks. Half a lunar cycle ago, he had achieved the position of assistant to the second commander, who had also been invited to the ball.

He had done it all for her.

For his beautiful female.

He wanted her family to approve of him, despite the differences in their breeding, because he had also come to realise something else.

She was his fated one.

His ki'ara.

It had only taken him a few weeks after leaving her to realise the reason behind why he couldn't stop dreaming of her, why he felt compelled to return to her every hour of the day and needed to see her again and see she was safe.

It had been hard to stay away and resist that need to be close to her, and had been sheer torture to keep his distance until he was ready. Now he felt good enough to approach her and her family and make it known to them that he was her fated male.

It didn't ease the hold his nerves had on him though.

If anything, the thought of approaching the female and her family, and presenting himself to them, made his nerves worse. They were gradually fraying his sanity, and he feared that if he didn't see her soon, he would go mad.

Fuery stilled right down to his soul when he caught her scent.

Lavender and sweet dew.

His head turned, gaze zipping to her as she entered the room on the arm of an older male dressed in an elegant tailored tunic and trousers that put his own formal clothing to shame.

Gods, she was beautiful.

He could only stare as she turned heads in the room, her lilac dress hugging her shapely figure and flowing down her arms from her shoulders, held over her torso by a fine silver metal corset. Her blue-black hair had been pulled back from her face, pinned at the back of her head and allowed to tumble down from there in a cascade of waves and curls that bounced with each light step.

The soft pink lips he had been dreaming of for eight long cycles had been painted a darker shade, luring his eyes down to them, but they couldn't hold his gaze.

It slid lower, to the smooth column of her exposed throat and the stunning silver choker she wore wrapped around it, threaded with crystals that twinkled in the candlelight as brightly as her beautiful violet eyes.

Those eyes landed on him.

Widened.

He saw the shock go through her, felt it run through him too, followed by something he could easily fool himself into believing was happiness.

Gods, he wanted to go to her.

He wanted to know her name.

He had been an idiot, so flustered by being in her presence the few times they had met that he had kept forgetting to ask.

His heart picked up pace, beginning a hard drumming against his chest and in his ears as the male escorting her spotted his commander and steered her his way.

Hell, he was going to have a hard time stopping himself from killing the male if it turned out he was something to her.

Something Fuery wanted to be.

He did his best to act casually as the male glanced his way, holding his position next to his commander, and somehow resisted staring at the female as she halted close to him.

"Commander Andon. It is a pleasure to see you again." The elegant male had a way of speaking that dripped with power born of standing in society, a regal air that had Fuery itching to do something, only he wasn't sure what it was he wanted to do. Beat the male into a pulp? It would be a start. That need instantly dissipated when the male continued. "May I introduce my daughter, Shaia?"

Daughter.

Shaia.

Gods. She suited her name so perfectly, had the beauty to match it.

Shaia glanced at him and then her gaze leaped back to the commander and she dipped in a curtsy. "It is a pleasure to meet you."

"And who is this young gentleman?" Her father nodded towards Fuery.

"Lieutenant Fuery of my legion. Recently promoted. We have high hopes for him. I thought since he will no doubt be taking command of his own legion soon that he could see how things work on this side of society." Andon's words were meant kindly, but all the light that had been building inside Fuery slowly drained from him as the male spoke.

Revealing something that had the older female beside Shaia scowling at him.

Her mother.

He recalled her from the first time he had seen Shaia, and the look she was now giving him said that she remembered him too.

And she still looked down on him.

He ignored her when Shaia moved a step to her right, coming back into view, and smiled at him.

"You have been moving up the ranks quickly since we last met." Her smile was so bright it blinded him, purged the darkness gathering in his heart and had his nerves fading.

He nodded. "Commander Andon has been kind enough to say he has never had a soldier rise so swiftly from scout to lieutenant."

Andon slapped him on the back, jerking him forwards. "Because I have not. It takes mettle to do what you have done, Fuery... strength and heart that is rare these days. Not one in twenty thousand soldiers display the fortitude and dedication you have."

He was not going to blush at that praise. Not in front of Shaia.

The small trio of musicians stationed at the other end of the room began to warm up and the crowd parted, forming a space in the centre of the grand room. A few of the attendees partnered up and stepped onto the dance floor.

"Would you do me the honour?" He held a hand out to Shaia and focused so it didn't shake and reveal his nerves.

Shaia didn't hesitate to reach for him.

Until her mother spoke.

"I am afraid our daughter will not be dancing with you." She placed a hand on Shaia's arm and pulled it back, and then turned her cheek to him and addressed the nobles that had gathered around them. "How is it we are expected to entertain those born of lowly stock simply because the kingdom takes pity on them and gives them a position above their station? I remember a time when only nobles could be granted such positions."

A few of the males and females nodded in agreement.

Pity? Given? He had earned his position. He had fought for it, broken bones for it.

He had *killed* for it.

His blood started a slow burn in his veins as he glared at her mother, catching the contempt in her gaze as she laughed with the other nobles, the expensive jewels and gold that covered her wrists and her fingers catching the light as she lifted her hand to her face to delicately cover her vicious mouth.

He fisted his hands at his sides.

Those who were given things were the nobles, not elves born with nothing as he had been.

His nails dug into his palms.

But what hurt him worse than her mother's cruel words and condemnation, was the fact Shaia stood there and said nothing as her own flesh and blood insulted him.

Fuery didn't bother to make his excuses.

He pivoted on his heel and pushed through the crowd, heading towards one of the open doors that lined the side of the long room and allowed cool air into it. He needed that air. He couldn't breathe. He tugged at the collar of his ridiculously tight jacket, unhooking the two sides of it and then twisting the first two buttons on his chest free of their loops. He pulled at the damned thing as he strode out into the darkness.

Wanted to rip it right off his back and toss it to the ground.

He growled and stormed down one of the paths into the garden, not caring where he was going as long as it was away from the ball and the bastards attending it.

Gods.

It hit him hard that everything he had been through the past eight lunar cycles hadn't been worth it because it had changed nothing, and nothing he did could change it either.

He could be crowned prince and he would still never have the approval of her family.

He couldn't win.

Tradition dictated that he needed permission from her family even if she was his fated one.

It was how things were.

He couldn't see that changing either.

The bastard nobles would fight to keep that tradition in place in order to protect their precious children from those they viewed as beneath them.

Lowly.

He snarled through his emerging fangs and twisted another button free, so cool air washed over his bare chest. His steps finally slowed as he reached a sea of roses, some of which grew over stone arches placed along the paths. Pale blue flowers laced between them, glowing in the darkness like stars.

Fuery stared at them and drew down a deep breath, pulling the mingled scents of the flowers into his lungs and feeling the comforting touch of nature as she reached out to him. He sank into it, needing her warmth tonight, because he felt as if he was breaking.

Liable to fall apart.

His beautiful Shaia would never be his.

How was he meant to cope with that?

How was he meant to go on with this burning in his chest, this blazing fire inside his heart and his soul that screamed she belonged to him? She had been made for him. She had started that fire in him and it had burned throughout the time they had been apart, consuming him and driving him, filling him with a need to see her again and be with her.

It was a fire that would never die.

Eternal.

He frowned.

It was a fire that was growing stronger by the second.

"Congratulations." Her soft voice came from behind him, a breathless word followed by a pant for air, and then another.

She had followed him, quickly by the sounds of things, going against convention and the rules he despised so much now.

"Thank you," he said gruffly, refusing to face her while he still seethed with anger over what her mother had said and done, and burned with hurt at the thought she would never be his.

She might have followed him, but it changed nothing.

She lingered behind him, the air between them thick and heavy, pressing down on him. Did it press down on her too?

He tried to resist, but the need to see her was too strong, overwhelming him, and he tilted his head to his right so he could look over his shoulder at her.

The slender blue light of the flowers bathed her skin, making it almost white, and darkened her eyes so they were near-black. It drained the colour from her lilac dress too.

Gods, it hurt to look at her and know she would never be his.

It hurt to look at her and know she was destined for someone else.

When she had been made for him.

"You must have worked very hard, as Commander Andon said, because you have only been gone a short time."

A short time? It had felt like an eternity to him.

He finally turned to face her, and caught the sombre edge to her expression, one that told him that she felt that way too, but she was trying to be polite, behaving as society expected of her.

He shrugged. "It does not seem worth it now."

Her face fell. "Why?"

He averted his gaze, settling it on the rose bushes that lined the path to his left. "Because I did it for my fated one."

Her soft gasp shook him and he felt her anger flow through him, her belief that he spoke of another female and the hurt she felt because of it. Hurt that gave him courage.

He heaved a long sigh. "It turns out I am still not good enough for her... and I never will be. According to her mother, lowborn males will never be good enough for her daughter."

She stilled.

Fuery glanced at her.

Shock shone in her eyes.

He couldn't bear it any longer.

He was done playing around, through with society and convention and everything that stood in his way. He was done with it all.

He seized her left wrist and dragged her deeper into the garden, following the path that ran beneath the stone arches and the glowing blue flowers.

"It's killing me," he husked, voice thick and dark. "You are my ki'ara... so how can you not be mine?"

Her arm trembled in his grip. "Are you sure?"

He spun her in front of him as he reached a high stone wall and backed her into it. "As sure as there is blood in my veins and a soul in my chest that is tied to yours."

She whispered, "Gods... I feel it too. I thought I was imagining it, but I feel it too, Fuery."

He claimed her lips on a low growl, couldn't stop himself as her words rang in his mind and his name spoken in her soft voice seared itself on his soul, marking him forever. She shook harder as she grasped his shoulders in trembling hands and for a crushing moment, he feared she would push him away, but then she was kissing him back, her lips clashing clumsily with his, her nerves racing through him to merge with his own.

His heart pounded, hands shaking as he pressed them to the wall and then found the courage to claim her hips. The feel of the soft curves of her waist beneath his palms, and the way her flesh gave beneath his fingers as he gripped her, tore a moan from his lips and he kissed her harder.

She moaned as he fisted her dress in both hands and clung to her, pinning her to the wall with his body as it ached for her, stirred by the feel of her kiss and the taste of her. Her little fangs scratched at his lower lip as she gave herself over to her passion and need, and he tried to keep his from her, afraid he would cut her with them and hurt her.

"Gods, Fuery," she breathed against his lips and he groaned and shuddered, held her tighter as he pressed his body against hers, the need to feel every inch of her too fierce to deny.

She skimmed her hands down his shoulders, a desperate jerky movement that spoke of the need he could feel in her, told him that her passion was stealing control of her just as his stole control of him.

He kissed her deeper, his tongue breaching the barrier of her teeth as he grew more confident, and less clumsy, becoming accustomed to kissing.

She rattled his confidence by meeting his tongue with her own, and the softness and warmth of it almost undid him. He trembled, electricity arcing through him as he absorbed the pleasure of her caress. It stoked the need in him, had him pressing harder against her, near-mindless with the urges running rampant through him.

Her hands reached his chest.

Her fingers dipped into the open V of his jacket.

The first brush of her fingertips across his bare skin seared him, had him growling into her mouth and clutching her tighter, dragging her against him. She moaned, a breathless little sound that made him burn hotter for her, and touched him again. It was more confident this time, accompanied by a light raking of her long nails that had him grunting and kissing her harder again.

He lowered his left hand to her hip, palmed it through her dress and shook at the supple feel of her thigh. She moved into his touch and surprised him by lifting her leg. He groaned as his hand slipped beneath her thigh, close to her buttocks, and her knee pressed against his hip, caging him against her.

His cock ached, painfully hard in his trousers, and he couldn't stop himself from pressing it against her belly.

Rather than being disgusted and shoving him away, she moaned and slid one hand around the back of his neck, pulling him closer.

He rubbed against her, the pleasure that rolled through him with each stroke of his hips stealing control of him piece by piece, driving him to do more.

Fuery dropped her leg and fought his nerves as he eased his hips back. He pressed a trembling hand against her mound, and swallowed her gasp and the following moan as she arched towards his touch, her eagerness flooding him with need.

She surprised him again by dropping her hands to her dress and pulling her skirts up, her actions rough and swift, speaking of the desperation he could feel flowing through her.

He groaned as she revealed her thighs, and shuddered and growled as she caught his hand and pressed it back against her, over her undergarments.

She was damp against his fingers.

Hot and moist.

He kissed her again, caging her against the wall with his body as he fumbled with her delicate mound and fought the urge to rip at her clothes and seat himself inside her.

Fought the urge to claim her.

She tensed when he slipped his hand inside her undergarments and moaned at the same time as he did when he found her centre and slipped his fingers into her moist folds.

Sweet gods.

He pressed his forehead to hers, panting against her lips in time with her as he touched her.

Explored her.

She was so soft, far more so than he had imagined, but her tiny bead was tight and hard, begging for his touch as he swept the pads of his fingers over her, taking in all of her. When he dipped his hand lower and found the entrance of her sheath, she quaked in his arms and moaned.

"Fuery." She clutched his shoulders, nails pressing in hard, and rose on her toes.

Her breath washed over his lips as she panted in response to his touch.

He pressed his forehead harder against hers and lifted his hand higher again, to her tight bundle of nerves. He fondled it, using her breathless little moans as his guide together with the pleasure he could feel building inside her.

He wanted to be inside her slick heat, wanted to know all of her, but he wanted to savour her and this shared first experience too, wanted to draw it out and make it last forever.

"Oh, gods," she whispered and rolled her hips, her actions desperate and wild, as if she had lost control.

He claimed her lips again, swallowing her murmured words as he touched her, stroked and teased her, rubbing his fingers back and forth over her quivering nub, determined to bring her to a shattering first release.

She rose higher on her toes, seeking his touch, urging him on.

Fuery dropped his mouth from her lips to her throat, and she wrapped her arms around his shoulders and head and held him to her as he kissed and licked it, and teased it with his teeth.

She was close.

It drummed in him.

He lowered his hand again and groaned against her skin as he found her entrance, discovering it was wetter now, slick with arousal. He fought the urge but it was too strong, the need to feel her easily overpowering him. He hesitated for only a second before pressing the tip of a finger inside.

Sweet gods, she was tight and hot around them.

He barely reached his first knuckle when she jerked against him, crying softly into his ear. The feel of her body flexing around his finger and the hot wetness that flowed down it drew a startling, and humiliating, reaction from him.

A blinding release of his own crashed over him before he could do anything to stop it, had his cock pulsing in his trousers, throbbing madly as he spilled.

He withdrew his finger from her and settled against her, feeling her frantic heart hammering against his chest as she held him, beating discordantly to his own. He wanted to growl as he wrapped his arms around her, needed to roar in victory as he held her close to him and felt the bliss rolling through her, pleasure he had given her.

She was his now.

"Fuery," she whispered, and he lifted his head to look at her, sensing her need to see him.

Voices in the distance had her tensing.

He quickly helped her cover herself, heat scalding his cheeks as he thought about how he had brought her to climax. She was his first, and he swore she would be his only.

If she would have him.

"I will meet you again."

Five words that offered the sweetest balm to his heart as they rang in his ears, her soft voice laced with heat and tenderness, and determination. He nodded and she pulled him to her for a quick kiss that seared his soul before hurrying away towards the grand house.

Fuery sighed, twisted and sagged against the wall.

He looked down at his hand, the one that had touched her intimately.

Saw bloodstained black claws.

He stared at them, watching the blood drip from them and spill to the ground, a constant flow, as if he was bleeding.

He was inside.

He had killed her.

His beloved Shaia.

His ki'ara.

He squeezed his eyes shut and pushed away from the memories that tried to surge to the surface, refusing to let them sweep over him, and clung to this happier moment, when everything had been bright and beautiful, exactly as he had wanted it to be forever.

But he had ruined it, and he couldn't escape that, not in reality and definitely not here in his dreams.

He looked at the house, and her retreating figure.

He didn't kill her now. He didn't kill her yet.

But it would happen soon.

CHAPTER 13

Shaia had tried to be patient, as Hartt had asked, but it had been difficult. After securing a room at the front of the inn, she had passed most of her days sitting at the sash window of the small, grim room, watching the entrance of the guild.

All manner of people had come and gone in that time. Some had been easy to spot as either a client or an assassin, while others had left her guessing.

Not once had she seen Fuery.

Hartt had come and gone a few times, and each time she had seen him he had looked brighter, with more colour in his cheeks and light in his eyes, telling her that Fuery was recovering.

Males weren't the only people to come and go from the imposing black building though.

She had seen females dressed in provocative clothing enter on several occasions, staying no more than an hour at most. When they left, they were looking in their coin purse, seeming satisfied with what they saw.

Shaia had tried not to think about Fuery with those females.

Tried and failed.

He had promised himself to her, but when he had looked at her, it had been as if he had seen a ghost, as if he didn't know her.

What if he had been with other females in their time apart?

She didn't want to entertain the idea, because it hurt, but she also refused to be foolish enough to think that he had been faithful to her, because it would only cause her deeper pain if she made herself believe that only to discover she had been wrong.

She sighed and looked back into her room, wriggling on the hard wooden window seat as she glanced around it. It was hardly luxurious. The double bed was worn and dipped badly in the centre of the mattress, as if some of the supports were broken, and the sheets and covers had been so frayed and filthy that she had teleported her own pale blue ones to her from her home in the elf kingdom. She had never been so thankful that her powers allowed her to teleport anything she owned regardless of distance.

The only other items of furniture were a dresser with woodworm that stood against the wall near the door opposite her, beyond the bed, and a small round table to her right, tucked into the corner there together with two wooden chairs.

Neither of which had seat cushions.

The fireplace smoked so badly she didn't dare to light it to provide some illumination in the dark room, and the candles on the mantelpiece were so dusty she feared they might go up entirely if she brought a flame near them.

When the innkeeper, a round male of questionable fae origin, had shown her to the room, he had promised to get the fire working for her and had then offered to bring her meals.

Shaia had politely refused.

If the room was this bad, she didn't want to see what the food was like.

She looked back out of the window.

Froze.

Fuery stood on the threshold of the guild, dressed in a black knee-length jacket, riding boots and trousers that were a poor echo of the ones he had worn as an officer in the legions. He looked brighter, the dark arcs beneath his eyes paler now and his face less gaunt, and infinitely less bloodstained.

When he spoke, she glanced at the person with him.

And saw red.

A beautiful female with burgundy hair dressed in a long deep gold robe that was secured at her waist with a tall band of gold filigree that cinched in her curves and accentuated them stood close to him, talking animatedly with him.

Had he come out with the female, or had he met her there?

Her heart pounded, stomach squirming as a hiss sounded in her ears and in her heart.

She didn't look like a whore, wore far too much clothing compared with the others Shaia had seen, but looks could be deceiving.

The hiss grew louder, setting her blood aflame, when Fuery handed the female a small leather pouch that looked an awful lot like the coin purses the whores had touted on leaving the guild.

Shaia was out of the door before she could stop herself, her anger sweeping her down the hall and then the stairs, and straight past the innkeeper as he greeted her. She slammed the flat of her palm against the heavy wooden arched door and growled low in her throat as she stormed out onto the street.

The female was gone.

And so was Fuery.

She growled louder now and felt her pointed ears flaring as her anger burned hotter. No damned way he was going to escape her.

She crossed the distance to the guild in the blink of an eye as she teleported, and landed just on the other side of the tall arched doors.

Fuery's shoulders tensed beneath his black tunic the second she appeared, his steps slowing as he walked towards the reception room.

"Who was that female?" she snapped, all the fires of Hell raging in her blood, driving her to confront him and not back down until she had an answer.

He slowly turned to face her, his eyes enormous and wild.

And very black.

Sorrow swept through her, washing away her anger in an instant, and she whispered, "Gods, Fuery... your eyes."

They had looked bad when she had seen him just a few days ago, but she had fooled herself into seeing some violet in them, enough that it kept the hope alive in her heart, the dream that she could somehow redeem him.

That hope threatened to fade and die as she stared into them and saw the truth.

There was barely a glimmer of violet around his pupils.

He averted them and she felt his shame through their bond as it raked him.

She took one step towards him, and then another, drawn to him by her need to comfort him and tell him they would fix this, somehow. It didn't matter that his eyes were more corrupted than she had thought, revealing just how fiercely the darkness that lived within all elves gripped him now.

They *would* fix this.

"Look at me, Fuery," she murmured softly, hoping to encourage him, to coax him into looking at her and seeing that she would help him somehow. He kept his head bent, eyes hidden from her, and she risked another step towards him. "Fuery... look at me."

Pity washed through her, sorrow that had her venturing another step closer, her eyebrows furrowing as she monitored the feelings going through him and felt the shame growing stronger.

She was about to ask him again to look at her when he lifted his head.

Revealing silver-blue eyes.

Tears lined hers, born of hurt that he would hide something from her, using a trick all elves could to blend into their environment, when they had always been open with each other.

His jaw tensed as black emerged around the edges of his irises and it disappeared again, driven out by him as he struggled to hold the silver-blue colour.

She shook her head, weathering the pain and the devastation that threatened to tear her apart as he continued his charade, pretending nothing was wrong with him, lying to her.

"Don't hide from me," she whispered, voice breaking as the hurt grew stronger, beating fiercely in her heart.

The black pushed again, together with a flicker of violet, and he growled as he looked away from her just as the silver-blue fled his irises, the pain in that snarl pulling at her because she knew it stemmed from his love for her—love that had him wanting to conceal the extent of his corruption from her because he couldn't bear her seeing it.

"Fuery." She held her hand out to him, desperate to comfort him.

He snapped his head up and hissed at her, his pointed ears flattening against the sides of his head as he bared long white daggers at her.

Shaia stopped dead, halted in her tracks by his show of aggression, and then withdrew a step when she felt the conflict in him, the fear colliding with fury. She didn't want to push him, hadn't meant to upset him. She had only wanted to comfort him.

The black in his eyes began to spread, devouring the remaining corona of violet, warning her that she was on the verge of losing him to the darkness.

"You had such beautiful eyes," she murmured, unable to stop herself even when part of her was aware it would hurt him. "Flecked with pale lilac."

He bared his fangs at her again as his face crumpled, his pain staggering as he stumbled backwards as if she had physically struck him. He slammed into the wall on the right of the broad corridor, his left shoulder striking the black stone hard and sagged against it.

"Do you not remember me?" She slowly stretched her hands out towards him, afraid of frightening him or driving him deeper into the hold the darkness had on him. "Is this your life now... killing and sleeping with other females?"

He snarled at her. "I do not kill females. Hartt said I did not kill the fae... it was the demons... and I killed them."

Her heart bled for him. He had muddled her words. She opened her mouth to unravel them for him.

He spoke first.

"I am sorry I killed you."

Shock struck her hard and fast, his pain blazing in her heart and stealing her breath as she stared at him and realised he believed what he was saying.

The things he had said when she had last seen him came rushing back, rocking her harder. He had said something similar then.

He thought he had killed her.

Shaia shook her head and risked a step towards him. "You never did such a thing, Fuery. I am not dead."

Pain flitted across his handsome face and then he growled, shoved his fingers through his shoulder-length hair and tugged at it, pulling it free from the clasp that held it tied back. He tipped his head back, his lips peeling off his teeth in a grimace as he snarled again, the pain in it tearing at her, driving her to take another step forwards.

To comfort him.

He suddenly dropped his chin and stared at her, tears in his eyes as he clutched his head in both hands.

"I wish that was true," he croaked, his black eyebrows furrowing.

Shaia crossed the span of black flagstones between them in a heartbeat and placed her hands on his arms, drawing his hands away from his head before he hurt himself.

He stared at her, his eyes growing wider, disbelief echoing in them as they dropped to his arms and her hands where she touched him.

His single whispered word tore at her.

"Impossible."

CHAPTER 14

Fuery stared at her hands where they clutched his wrists.

He had truly lost his mind.

It was warm where she touched him, and his armour peeled back beneath his jacket, his need to feel her delicate hands on his flesh making it clear his wrists before he had even issued a mental command.

He trembled as her skin met his, the sensation overload of feeling her warmth on him, the soft press of her fingers, too much for him to take. It felt too good.

But it wasn't real.

Gods, this was the worst form of torture.

He had been beaten, ripped apart and left balanced on the brink of dying, injuries so extensive it had taken him months to heal his broken body, but the torture and pain he had felt then was nothing compared with the agony that pulsed through him in waves that radiated outwards from the points beneath her hands.

He couldn't take it.

He hissed and jerked his hands away from her, stumbling backwards until his back hit one of the columns in the entrance hall. He sagged against it and stared at her through eyes rapidly growing blurred.

"You are not real," he whispered, his throat raw and heart burning. "I wish that you were. I prayed so hard to reverse what I had done so you were not dead, but the gods would not listen to me."

Tears filled her beautiful amethyst eyes, put there by him because she was a figment of his wretched imagination, and it was his pain reflected in her.

She reached for him again. "Fuery, I am not dead."

She had said that more than once now.

It was a lie, his mind playing tricks on him, because he wanted her to be alive. He wanted his prayers to be answered.

"I *am* alive."

Those three words struck him hard, stripped him of his strength and turned his knees to rubber beneath him, and he hissed at her. Desperate to escape her, he turned and pushed away from the wall, and darkness swallowed him, jagged and freezing, chilling his flesh. He landed hard in the reception room just metres from where he had been, stumbled a few steps forwards and grasped the back of the black velvet couch to stop himself from collapsing.

He breathed hard, the agony of seeing the ghost and hearing her sweet voice colliding with the sharp drain on his strength from the teleport.

When he heard footsteps ringing in the corridor behind him, he broke away from the couches and staggered across the large room towards the hallway in the right wall, the one that would lead him to his quarters.

He glanced back over his shoulder when he was halfway there.

Shaia charged around the corner, a wild look in her violet eyes.

"No." Hartt's barked words echoed around the room. "You said you would wait. Leave."

He looked at Hartt, confused for a moment. Wait? Leave? His confusion only increased when he discovered Hartt wasn't even looking at him. He was looking at Shaia, as if he was speaking to her.

Which made fuck all sense to Fuery.

She was a ghost.

Unless she could make herself visible to others too.

He laughed, low and vicious.

Or he had completely lost his fucking mind and was imagining the whole thing.

Shaia's gaze swung his way and she started towards him, but she didn't make it far. Fuery could only stare as Hartt swept into her path and did something incredible.

He grabbed her shoulders to hold her back.

Said something Fuery didn't hear.

Because the second Hartt's hands touched her, a red veil descended and rage boiled through him.

Stupid, considering she wasn't really there, and this whole thing was just his fucked up mind playing tricks on him.

She wasn't real, because he had killed her.

Yet he turned on a pinhead and roared as he launched himself at Hartt, unable to stop himself as the unmated male laid hands on his female.

His female.

He would kill the bastard for touching her, for trying to take her from him, when she was his everything—his world.

His beautiful mate.

Hartt grunted as he slammed into him, lost his grip on Shaia and went down hard with Fuery on top of him.

Fuery snarled, gripped his shoulder and pulled him onto his back beneath him on the flagstones. He grinned as he punched Hartt in the face. Once. Twice. A third time. A sickening crunch was his reward as Hartt's nose broke. The male growled and bucked up, launching a hand at his face. He shoved Fuery under his chin, tipping him backwards and off balance, and teleported from beneath him.

Fuery shot to his feet and turned in a fast circle, his eyes scanning the room and his heart pounding, his senses on high alert as he waited for Hartt to reappear.

The air shimmered off to his left.

He roared and kicked off in that direction.

Hartt hit him in the back, and Fuery growled in frustration, cursing himself for falling for that trick when he had seen Hartt use it countless times on a foe. He spun on his heel and blocked Hartt's attempt to grab him, caught him around the back of his neck and pulled him towards him at the same time as he lunged forwards. His forehead cracked against Hartt's, ripping a pained grunt from the male, and sending lightning spider-webbing across his own skull.

He released Hartt as the male staggered backwards, and shook his head, trying to clear it.

The second the pain ebbed, he growled and attacked again, landing punches on Hartt's face and side, determined to make the male pay for daring to touch his beautiful, sweet mate. Hartt finally fought back, his eyes bright violet as he bared fangs at him and blocked his blows, and landed some of his own.

"If you will not bloody listen to me, I will beat you down until you do." Hartt growled, managed to grab him by the throat, and the world twirled around him as the male tipped him off balance and slammed him onto his back on the polished stone floor, knocking the air from his lungs.

The male had been speaking to him?

Fuery recalled his lips moving, but he had heard no words above the thunderous rush of his blood, and the rage that burned in it.

Hartt backed off, breathing hard and almost tripping over his own feet. Blood streamed over his lips from his nose and from a cut beneath his right eye.

Fuery's rage burned hotter, the violent clash and Hartt's resulting injuries not nearly enough to satisfy it. He wanted to paint the black walls crimson with Hartt's blood and entrails.

He flipped onto his feet and kicked off, a grin stretching his lips, put there by the pleasing images and the thought of making them real.

Shaia appeared between him and Hartt.

Fuery skidded to a halt, his fist stopping close to striking her. It began to tremble in the air between them as he stared at her, his eyes slowly widening as what she had done swept through him like a violent rush of ice in his veins, extinguishing the fire.

He dropped his hand and shook his head as he backed away, confusion colliding with conflict and pain so intense he felt sure a part of him was dying.

She had defended Hartt.

She had protected him.

A low feral growl curled from his lips as the fire swept back in and he quaked with the need to rip the male apart so his female would look at only him.

But at the same time, a thought went through him, unwelcomed and unwanted, one that cut him to his soul, plunging the blade in deep and causing him agony the depth of which he had never experienced before.

She deserved a decent male like Hartt.

Not a tainted bastard like him.

He stumbled backwards, still shaking his head, his eyebrows furrowing as he looked at the pair of them and saw them as a couple, the two people he loved most, needed most, turned against him and leaving him bereft, alone in a world he wanted no part of without them at his side.

"This is not real." His voice hitched. "Please... I cannot take this torment."

His left knee gave out, striking the black stone tiles hard, but he picked himself up again. When he straightened, Shaia had moved.

She stood mere inches from him.

He shook his head again and tried to back away.

She caught his wrists, and when he attempted to break free this time, she didn't let him. She tightened her grip.

Gods, the pressure around his wrists felt real enough.

He stared at her hands and then lifted his head and met her gaze.

She whispered, "You did not kill me."

"I did." He remembered it vividly, because he saw it every night, every time he closed his eyes.

He had seen it happen in a thousand different ways and all of them had destroyed him.

She gently shook her head, her mane of wavy black hair brushing slender shoulders that were shaking. He could feel her trembling. She was afraid. Of him?

"You remember wrongly," she murmured softly. "You are just muddled, Fuery. The darkness has mixed your memories up."

Vail had said something similar. That was the only reason she was saying it now, because someone else had told him that and at the time he had wanted to believe it might apply to what he had done to her too—that he might not have killed her.

"If I was a ghost, as you believe, why would I be dressed like this?"

He looked at her clothing—a pair of worn tan trousers, old brown boots, and a washed out grey tunic.

"Because I cannot bear to see you as you were." He was sure that was the reason she was wearing male clothing and not the beautiful dresses she had worn in all the times he had seen her in the past.

Before he had killed her.

She sighed, the sound light and melodic, but holding a weight of hurt and a dash of frustration. "My poor, beautiful warrior."

He growled at her, despising the way she said that, as if she pitied him. *Pity*. It sent him spinning back to that night he had been dreaming of, to the grand ball where they had first kissed and first touched. He didn't want anything given to him out of pity.

He wanted to earn everything, including her heart.

He had earned it, hadn't he?

Before he had killed her.

He tried to break free of her again, but she refused to let him go, and he stilled again as her thumbs brushed his flesh on the inside of his wrists, a soothing touch that had his fight flowing out of him.

"I am mad... not muddled," he whispered to himself, feeling it as he looked at her, as he felt her hands on his skin, squeezing his bones.

He had finally lost his mind.

"You are muddled, not mad," she countered. "I am not dead, Fuery."

His throat closed, and he couldn't squeeze air past it as he considered the possibility that she really wasn't dead. It was too much. He had lived for millennia believing he had killed her.

Hartt adjusted his torn black tunic, frowning down at it, catching Fuery's attention. When Fuery looked at him, he lifted his head, locking eyes with him. Fuery wasn't strong enough to say the words, to ask the question balanced on the tip of his tongue, because he feared that if he put it out there, it would build hope in his heart that would kill him if Hartt told him the wrong answer.

Was this really Shaia before him, alive and not dead?

Hartt nodded, and softly said, "She is real, Fuery. I wanted her to stay away until you were stronger. The light you felt inside you... it was Shaia reaching to you through your bond."

Fuery's breath left him in a rush and he sank to his knees, dragging her hands down with him.

It wasn't possible.

He stared up at her and tried to believe that Hartt was telling him the truth and that it really was her standing before him, gazing down at him with soft eyes filled with understanding and concern.

He reached for the connection they had once shared, the one that had died when she had, or maybe before then. Something inside him had snapped the night he had first lost himself to the darkness.

His connection to her?

It had felt as if all the light had flooded out of him, and the darkness had swept in to replace it.

Light that had sparked to life inside him only a few days ago.

A light that Hartt said she had put there by opening her connection to him.

He focused on that connection, fostered it as he stared at her, deep into her eyes.

Light flickered inside him.

The darkness rushed to swamp it and extinguish it, and he growled as he broke free of her grip, shoved to his feet and staggered away from her, slamming the connection shut again. His hands shook as he gripped his head and snarled through his fangs, fighting the darkness as it writhed inside him, pushing him towards the edge, stirred into a dangerous frenzy by that echo of light.

By her.

He looked back at her and she lowered her gaze away from him, pinning it on the floor. Gods, she couldn't even bring herself to look at him, to see what he had become. He needed her to look at him, ached with a desperate desire to have her eyes on him again, looking into his and telling him that all was not lost. She refused though, keeping her violet ones turned away from him, and he growled as pain so fierce it shattered him speared his chest.

His eyebrows furrowed as a need to escape surged through him, a desperate need to distance himself.

To spare himself.

She couldn't be real.

And even if she was, it wouldn't change a thing.

She would never be his.

He only wanted her to be his. That was all he had ever wanted. His only dream. One that had slipped through his grasp and was so disgusted by him that she refused to look at him.

Because he was tainted. Evil. Darkness made flesh.

He deserved her scorn.

He growled and squeezed his head, his claws forming over his fingers as his armour completed itself to protect him from the threat he felt, one it could never shield him from, because it came from inside him.

The darkness.

He sank into the despair that was now his old friend, a constant companion that had been with him for longer than he could remember. It had been born inside him when he had stepped into the darkness and embraced it, and had realised that he would live forever, until the darkness consumed him or he was killed.

It had become part of him when it had hit him that she was gone and he no longer had a reason to live.

He had doomed himself to an eternity alone, a shallow existence that slowly ate away at him.

When Hartt had given him a new path, he had taken it, his despair driving him to take on any foe, regardless of their strength, in the hope one of them would end his misery.

Because he wasn't strong enough to do it himself.

How many times had he asked himself why he was still breathing? How many times had he asked himself why he fought back against his enemies, rather than let them end him? Why, when he was injured and in danger of being killed by his foe, did the need to live surge through him, driving him to fight harder?

To survive.

There was no reason for him to live, yet there was a piece of him that clung to hope—to life—unwilling to let him die.

Why?

He stared at Shaia.

Because that part of him had always known she was alive?

A shiver chased over his flesh beneath his armour and clothes, and gods, he wanted to believe that, ached to believe that she was standing before him, but fear was slowly building inside him, whispered words that had him backing away from her, distancing himself when he wanted to move closer to her.

She despised him, would only look upon him with hatred and disgust if she did raise her beautiful eyes to his face.

He was tainted.

Damned.

The darkness was strong in him and he had embraced it, desiring oblivion, wanting an end. He had tried fighting it, but there had been times when he had coaxed it, had needed to feel it washing through him. He was no longer the male he had been when she had loved him.

He was a ghastly shadow of that male. A wraith. A monster.

He might have been good enough for her once, but no longer.

He would never be good enough for her again.

There was no coming back from the evil that lived inside him.

As his despair mounted to a crescendo he felt sure would break him, the darkness so intense that no drop of light remained, and he wanted to sink into it and lose himself, never to return, she finally raised her eyes to meet his.

There was no scorn in them. No disgust. No trace of the feelings he felt sure beat in her heart—ones all elves felt towards the tainted and the lost.

Shaia lifted her hand and held it out to him, and gods, he wanted to take it, but he couldn't, and it killed him.

He couldn't taint her too.

He backed away from her, and when she took a step towards him, Hartt moved and placed a hand on her shoulder, holding her back.

That single action reignited Fuery's rage but made it hit home at the same time.

She was real, alive, and as beautiful and pure as he remembered.

And gods, maybe he was wrong, maybe she didn't despise him, because she was looking at him with love in her eyes.

It was too much. The room closed in on him, the emotions that rushed through him causing a torrent that threatened to sweep him under and left him feeling as if he was drowning. He needed space and air, both to stop himself from attacking his only friend again, the only one who had stuck by him through the long and weary centuries, and to process the reality that she was alive.

His beautiful ki'ara was alive.

He took one last look at her and then drew on his strength, called on all of his power, and focused on his body. Dark jagged lines chased over his arms and the world around him disappeared as he managed to teleport.

But he still saw Shaia.

He saw her hurt as she realised what he was doing, and felt her pain go through him.

And he couldn't bring himself to go far away from her, to a place where she couldn't reach him.

She was his mate, and she needed him.

He landed in his quarters and dropped back to his knees.

He hadn't been there for her though. He had left her alone for centuries, his connection to her closed, believing her dead when the truth was so much worse.

She had been alive all this time, *alone*, believing him dead.

All this time she had been out there, and now he knew the part of him that had pushed him to live had been aware of it, aware of her and that she needed him.

His heart.

He pressed his left hand to his chest and breathed through the pain that beat in it. His pain. Her pain. They mingled together to steal his breath and burn his soul to ashes.

He had thought her beyond his reach once, but she had stepped within it, had believed him worthy of her.

But he had been mistaken back then.

Now she was beyond his reach, the darkness inside him a gulf between them he could never cross.

And nothing he did would ever make him worthy of her again.

CHAPTER 15

Shaia lowered her eyes away from Fuery as he fought with himself, his body trembling violently and eyes on the verge of becoming pitch black. Gods. She knew he would hate for her to see him like this—a warrior weakened and rendered vulnerable. A shadow of the male she had known four millennia ago.

It was hard to keep her gaze off him as he struggled, an echo of his emotions ringing in her blood as he waged war against whatever darkness gripped him. She wanted to know, wanted to lift her eyes, close the distance between them and take him into her arms and hold him until the battle had passed and he was on even ground again. Then, she would ask him what it felt like whenever the darkness gripped him, would make him tell her so she could understand and find a way to aid him.

She wanted to shake its hold on him forever.

She wanted to guide him back to the light.

She hadn't been there for him when he had needed her, had left him alone in this world to face the darkness without anyone there to support him, to help him hold it at bay and vanquish it.

Hartt moved, a slight shift of his weight but enough to remind her of his presence in the huge black-walled room with her and Fuery. It reminded her of something else too. Fuery hadn't been alone, or at least he hadn't been alone through every year of the four thousand she had been apart from him.

Hartt had been there for him, had been the guide drawing him back to the light in her place, had bonded himself to her mate in an attempt to save him.

It should have been her.

She felt wretched as she thought that, as she felt it in every drop of her blood and fibre of her being.

She had failed her beloved.

Now, she stood with her head bent, her eyes locked on the black stone tiles beneath her boots, failing him again.

Hartt hadn't taken his eyes off Fuery.

The elf male offered support to him as he fought, made it clear that he was there if Fuery needed him, silently showing him that he only needed to ask for his assistance and he would give it to him, regardless of the danger to himself. He would fight to bring him back from the darkness once again, even if it attached itself to him in the process.

Gods, she had thought she was sparing Fuery by keeping her eyes away from him, but the hurt in him was mounting, a sense of desperation that made it blindingly clear she had been wrong.

Her actions hadn't spared him.

They had wounded him.

They had allowed the darkness he had been fighting to grip him harder, because she had weakened him by refusing to look at him, had stirred black thoughts and feelings that beat in her chest—in her heart.

He was wrong.

She lifted her head and held her hand out to him, desperate to show him that she hadn't meant her actions in the way he thought, that she had only wanted to spare him because she had known he would hate her seeing him like this.

She hadn't meant to hurt him.

He hesitated, and for a heart-stopping moment she thought he would take her hand, and then jagged black tendrils snaked over his body and he disappeared.

She lunged forwards, desperation driving her to seize him before she lost him again, and her hand cut through the shimmering air where he had been.

Her senses reached out, seeking him as her heart throbbed, pain pulsing in it as she cursed herself for doing everything wrong. Her fear and her pain settled as she found him nearby, still inside the guild.

In his quarters?

The tension drained from her shoulders and she sagged as she eased back onto her heels and stared towards the direction she could feel him in, a desire to follow him rising swiftly inside her and urging her to go to him.

To make everything right.

Somehow.

"Stay where you are this time," Hartt muttered and took swift steps across the polished stone floor before she could respond.

He disappeared down the corridor off to her right, and she shifted foot to foot as she waited, growing aware of the fact she was alone in the grim reception room of a guild of assassins.

Loud footfalls echoed behind her.

Her head whipped around, gaze leaping over her right shoulder. One of those assassins strolled in, his face a black mask as he rubbed at his shoulder through a tight black short-sleeved garment, and muttered something beneath his breath. He huffed and pushed his wild silver hair out of his face, and a deep sigh escaped him as his silver eyes closed.

He drew down another breath.

Stopped dead a few feet from her.

Those bright silver eyes flicked back open, locking straight on her.

"Anyone told you it isn't wise to wander into a guild of assassins, Little Female? Especially this one." His voice was a deep rumble, but there was a note of warmth in it she hadn't expected, one that seemed at odds with his cold expression and lethal air.

"I-I am waiting for Hartt." She wanted to curse herself for stammering, making herself appear weak in front of the male.

English was not her first language, but she had tutored herself in it during her years in her small home, together with a smattering of other languages, ones her parents would never have allowed her to learn. In society's eyes, females of her species had no need to know anything other than the elf tongue.

He eased back onto his heels and looked her over, taking in her masculine clothing with an arched eyebrow. "You don't look like a whore, and last I checked Hartt wasn't interested in that sort of 'business' anyway."

Her cheeks blazed, and her temper caught fire with them. "I am not a whore!"

"Good thing." He casually cocked his head to his left and ran another assessing glance over her. "You're not a patch on Iolanthe and I figure he's got a pretty big crush on his ex-fiancée."

She frowned, her anger deflating as curiosity seized her.

"Bleu's sister? I heard she had been promised to a male." She looked back towards the corridor, and tried to imagine Hartt with Iolanthe.

Iolanthe was adventurous, a match for him in a way, but Shaia doubted she ever would have married a male against her wishes. It was tradition though. If an elf female failed to find their fated one before their thousandth birthday, they were married to a male of the family's choosing.

126

Thinking about that had Eirwyn popping into her head, and how she was promised to him, and would have married him if Bleu hadn't come to her and told her that Fuery was alive.

Shaia shoved Eirwyn out again, together with the shame that swept through her. She might have been strong enough to refuse her parents before the wedding had taken place. She might have been brave enough to stand him up, as Iolanthe had with Hartt.

The male was saying something to her.

She looked at him, and blinked, feeling awful as he scowled at her, obviously displeased that she hadn't been listening.

"You know Bleu?" The male tried again, and she nodded. He blew out his breath on a low whistle. "I bet that went down well with Hartt."

He jerked his left thumb towards the door in the corner of the room that led to the offices, winced, and rubbed at his shoulder again. "I'm guessing he's not in, since you're stood here brightening the room?"

Brightening it?

He had an odd way of speaking, and she doubted his clothing came from Hell. She had never seen so many pockets on trousers, or boots with such strange soles. They weren't made of leather or wood. He looked down at his feet, his silvery eyebrows dipped low, and then he raised his eyes back to her.

"I can get you a pair if you want... the, uh, clothing thing... you into cross-dressing or just find it comfortable? I mean, a lot of females in the mortal world wear trousers and shit, but I haven't seen many down here dressing like that." He ran a finger through the air, up and down, and then his frown melted away into a grin that lit up his eyes. "Aya loves tight jeans and t-shirts. Fuck... the way they hug her arse makes me want to growl and grab it every fucking time I see it."

Shaia presumed Aya was this male's mate. "I thought the guild did not allow females here. Hartt said—"

"Hartt's cool with it," he spoke over her and then added, "It's Fuery who loses his shit. I have to keep an eye on the mad bastard when Aya visits."

She growled and flashed fangs at him, her pointed ears flaring back against the sides of her head as fury rippled through her on hearing him speak of her mate in such a vicious, cruel way. His eyes widened, shock sweeping across his face.

A gasp left her as she realised what she had done and she lifted her hands to her mouth, her eyes growing round. "I am sorry... I..."

"Have a thing for Fuery," he said in a low, slow way that made her feel he was peeling back her layers, seeking the truth inside her, and he wasn't going to stop until he knew it.

She didn't want him prying into her personal life, and she refused to allow him to fluster her into saying things she wanted to keep private, so she put it out there before he could speak again.

"Fuery is my mate."

His eyes widened further.

"Well, fuck... my condolences." He closed the gap between them and slapped a heavy hand down on her shoulder, a twinkle in his eyes that said he wasn't being serious but didn't stop her from growling at him.

Her growl sounded deeper than normal, and very dangerous judging by the way the male paled and eased his hand away from her.

"I would suggest it is unwise to lay a hand on the female, Harbin," Hartt snarled and stepped around her, coming to stand between her and the male. "Unless you want Fuery swinging you around this room by your tail?"

Harbin swallowed and blanched further, and then shrugged stiffly. "I was just playing."

Hartt's expression remain cold and hard. "I am not sure Fuery would see it that way. Shaia is his mate... and you know how a mated male would view what you have just done. Next time, before you act or speak to Shaia, think about how you would feel if someone spoke or acted towards Aya that way, and then multiply whatever black desire you feel by a thousand, and that is what Fuery will do to you in response."

The edge to Harbin's eyes said it didn't really bear thinking about.

He ran a glance over Hartt's ruined tunic, looked as if he wanted to mention it and ask whether Fuery was responsible for his appearance, and then bent his head. "Noted. I'll file my report later."

Hartt nodded, but caught the male's arm before he could pass him, and glanced across at him. "Shower... because if Fuery smells her on you, it's your funeral."

Harbin swallowed hard again and hurried away. Was Fuery that terrifying?

She looked to Hartt for the answer, and saw it in his grim expression as he turned towards her, his violet eyes troubled and laced with concern, worry for his friend.

"Is he... well?" She wasn't sure that was the right word to use, because she wasn't sure he would ever be well again.

Even if she could drive the darkness from his soul, he would still be vulnerable to it. It would never truly leave him. He would always be in danger of falling into it again.

Hartt sighed, rubbed the back of his neck and stared at her, conflict shining in his eyes as he studied her in silence. The minutes dragged by as she waited for him to speak, her fear growing, whispering to her that he was going to make her leave again when she desperately needed to stay.

"As well as can be expected," Hartt finally said but the tension building inside her didn't dissipate.

She waited for him to continue, feared the words she knew he would say next, and was ready to rebel against his wishes and fight him on it. His violet eyes flicked towards the hallway that led to Fuery, and then leaped back to her, and she braced herself.

"You want to see him?"

Those five words hit her hard, struck her dumb, and she could only stare at the male as they pinged around her head.

The complete opposite to what she had expected him to say.

He sighed when she just stared at him, her mouth gaping open and eyebrows pinned high on her forehead.

"No need to look at me like that," he grumbled in the elf tongue. "I am starting to feel that Fuery needs to see you. He will not settle. Perhaps you can achieve that."

He turned away from her and strode back the way he had come, heading into the corridor and disappearing from view. She hurried after him, heart picking up pace as she neared the doorway and doubling in speed again when she took her first step into the black-walled hallway. Oil lamps flickered at intervals along it, lending warmth to the dark walls, chasing over her as she sped after Hartt.

When she reached him, he slowed his strides and she fell in behind him, her steps silent on the stone tiles beneath her boots.

She followed him through the maze of corridors, tensing whenever she passed a door and sensed someone on the other side. Some were powerful, sparking her instinct to protect herself, and she moved closer to Hartt whenever it happened. He glanced at her a few times, his face an unreadable mask that gave nothing away.

When she tried to sense his emotions, she found nothing. No trace of feeling in him. She could catch his scent, could feel him near her, and could hear his heart beating steadily and slowly, but she couldn't detect a hint of what he was feeling. He had shut her out.

Why?

Because he was worried about Fuery?

He had no reason to hide that from her, because she had seen it in him when he had returned from attempting to get her mate to settle, and had witnessed it back in the reception room when Fuery had been there, battling with himself.

She glanced at a door as they passed it. Had he closed himself off because of the occupants of the rooms around them, wanting to keep his emotions hidden from his assassins?

That made more sense to Shaia.

Hartt didn't want them feeling his concern for Fuery, because he wanted to protect her mate. He didn't want his assassins to know that Fuery was struggling.

Because he was a danger to them?

She knew of the darkness. All elves were warned about it from an early age. The darkness could make an elf view a friend as a foe, and there were many tales about elves who had lost themselves to the darkness and had attacked their own kin.

The cautionary tale of Prince Vail was one of them.

That male had turned on his own legion and had attacked them. He had attacked Fuery, and the two had been close at the time, more than commander and subordinate.

They had been friends.

Thinking about that battle dredged up the pain she had felt then, hurt that she had carried through the centuries and had never really faded or left her. It had remained in her heart, burned in her soul still, even though the male she had mourned was alive and she was on her way to see him.

To soothe him.

Hartt stopped outside one of the dark wooden doors, steeled himself and looked at her. "I will be just across the hall."

She nodded, the nerves that had been swift to rise inside her when she had halted and had felt Fuery close to her abating a little as he gestured to the door behind him. She focused her senses, and her heart went out to Fuery when she felt his pain and something else.

All of the rooms at this end of the guild were empty. Unoccupied.

A precaution to protect the assassins from Fuery?

Sorrow welled up inside her as she thought about that, and imagined how her beautiful warrior felt as he passed his hours in his quarters, aware that he was alone, and aware of the reason for it. Gods, it had to tear at him.

Hartt was there, the only one brave enough to sleep within Fuery's immediate reach, and it touched her, warmed her heart and chased some of the chill from it. She turned to him, wanting to thank him for caring deeply enough about Fuery to remain close to him when all others had distanced themselves.

He nodded before she could utter a word, turned away and opened the door to his own room. Before he could disappear on the other side, she caught the edge to his expression, the shimmer of something in his eyes that gave away his feelings at last.

He was more than worried.

He feared for his friend.

Shaia turned her head towards Fuery's door, and resolve flowed into her heart, buoyed her courage and had her nerves settling.

She would alleviate that fear for Hartt.

She would do all in her power to ease Fuery and release him from the grip of his darkness.

She reached for the door handle and froze as Hartt's door opened again and he poked his head around it.

"Be wary of Fuery's mood... it can change in an instant." His violet eyes held hers, cold and sharp, sending a shiver through her that threatened to stir her nerves again.

She nodded, and he eased his door closed, leaving her alone in the corridor.

She swallowed hard, blew out her breath to settle her nerves, and told herself that Fuery wouldn't hurt her. She knew it in her heart. No matter how fiercely the darkness seized him, no matter how vicious it turned him, he wouldn't hurt her.

He loved her.

She grasped the handle, twisted it and pushed the door open.

"Hartt, I need to see..." Fuery trailed off as he turned towards her, his words dying on his lips as his eyes settled on her.

She wanted to weep when she saw the violet in them.

A bare thread of it around his pupils.

She reached out to him through their bond, focusing on the connection between them, and that need to cry grew stronger, had her throat closing and tears welling, when she sensed the darkness was receding, freeing him of its vile and wretched grasp.

It continued to fade as he stared at her, a large double bed with black covers standing between them. The lamp on the small table beside the head of it on his side flickered, sending golden light shimmering across his bare chest and over the window at his back.

It struggled to warm the space that felt cold to her, sparse with only the bed and the side table in the room, more like a cell than a home.

She frowned as she looked closer at the bed and saw deep scratches on the wooden frame and headboard, long grooves that looked as if they had been made with Fuery's claws, and matched marks on the black walls too. Were those marks the product of him losing himself to the darkness?

His shame swept through her and she dragged her gaze away from them, not wanting to upset him, and settled her eyes back on him.

They dropped to his bare chest.

His eyes fell there too and he suddenly moved, reaching for the jacket he had discarded on the bed.

"You have so many scars," she whispered, eyes charting them all, and he froze mid-reach, leaning forwards with his hand almost on his jacket, and lifted his eyes back to her.

He blinked and swallowed, and she felt the conflict flow through him, tearing him apart, and saw in his eyes that he wasn't sure what to say.

"I am sorry, Fuery," she husked, her voice tight as she gazed at all the scars, and imagined all the battles he had fought and how often he must have danced close to death, stepping within its reach. "If I had known more about bonds… I should have known more… I should not have believed you gone so easily… I should have done something."

He slowly eased forwards, wrapped his long fingers around his tunic, and equally as slowly straightened and put it on, never taking his eyes off her, not even when he buttoned it, covering his chest.

Stealing the scars from view.

When he was done, he flicked a glance at the door behind her and then back at her.

"Are you real?" he rasped.

She nodded. "I am."

Shaia reached her hands out to him and edged around the foot of the bed, towards him. When he tensed, she slowed, moving more cautiously, her senses monitoring him and Hartt's words ringing in her mind.

She tried to shake them away.

Fuery wouldn't hurt her.

She slowly closed the distance between them, and her heart hitched when she was within a few feet and could feel his heat. His masculine scent of spice and earth wrapped around her, transporting her back to better days, ones where she had lazed in his arms in their secret spot on the bank of the river.

The tears she wanted to keep back rose into her eyes again.

Fuery's black eyebrows furrowed as he saw them, and he looked as if he wanted to reach for her.

She wanted that too.

But she knew he was still fighting the memories he believed real, the ones where she no longer lived, and feared that if he touched her, she would reveal herself as nothing more than a figment of his imagination, his fingers ghosting through her.

Her poor, beautiful, warrior.

He feared touching her, but she didn't fear touching him. She would give him the comfort he desired, and the contact he needed.

She gently placed her hands on his wrists, over the cuffs of his jacket, and carefully raised his arms, and then let her hands slip towards his. The first brush of their skin drew a sharp intake of breath from him, and his eyes darted from hers to their hands.

His were trembling.

"You are dead," he whispered and his throat worked on a hard swallow. "I killed you."

When his corrupted eyes leaped up to hers, she shook her head.

"No. You are just confused." She offered him a smile, one she hoped would comfort him and reassure him that she spoke the truth. "The bond confused us both. I thought you were dead too. When you lost yourself to the darkness the first time... I felt the connection shatter... and I thought you were dead."

He looked back down at their hands, the black slashes of his eyebrows pinned high on his forehead.

Gods, he looked so lost.

She could feel him clearer now, could pick apart the emotions that shimmered in their growing connection as it slowly restored itself, reinforced by both of them. He still feared she was a ghost, a vision sent to torment him, but he was beginning to believe she was real.

He was silent and still for long seconds that felt like an eternity, his eyes never leaving their joined hands, and then he whipped his head up and his eyebrows furrowed, a hint of fang showing between his lips as he spoke.

"You thought I had slept with another... that I would ever do that to you..." His face crumpled again and his deep voice dropped to a low whisper that carried all the pain she could feel in him. "When you are everything to me."

Gods, that made her want to cry.

"I am sorry," she whispered, despising herself for hurting him, but rejoicing at the same time, because it had pushed him into revealing that he still loved her, and that he had never been with another. "I saw you with that female…"

"A client. She changed her mind about a job and Hartt had me return her down payment."

Relief blasted through her, so sweet and sharp that it stole her breath. In its wake, came another feeling, and then another. She felt like an idiot for flying into a rage and presuming the female had been a whore, and then she felt terrible for not trusting Fuery and for believing he would ever be with another female.

When he had promised to be hers and hers alone forever.

"The past few weeks have been difficult… and they have taken their toll on me." She hated that it sounded like an excuse in her ears, and hoped he wouldn't hold it against her. It wasn't the first jealous outburst she'd had in their time together, and she recalled they had pleased him once, because they had revealed the depth of her love for him. She studied his eyes and his feelings, trying to see if it still pleased him now, and ached all over again as it hit her that it was her Fuery standing before her. Her beautiful Fuery. She still couldn't believe it. "I have mourned you for forty-two centuries, and then suddenly you were alive, and you had been living your life without me."

He dropped his gaze again and his hands tensed against hers, his shoulders going rigid. "I am sorry… I thought I had killed you. I did kill you, didn't I? You are just a ghost… yet I can touch you."

He lifted his left hand, hesitated, and then edged it forwards and placed it against her cheek.

That ridiculous need to weep arrowed through her again but she held it back and focused on the feel of his palm on her face. Warm. Strong. Gods, it comforted her more than he could ever know. It made the long centuries alone worth it.

She would have waited forever to feel this again.

"You are so warm," he murmured, and the tears she had been fighting slipped onto her cheeks. His eyebrows furrowed again as he tracked one with his gaze, and then he brushed it away with the pad of his thumb, bringing more as her heart ached in response to his tenderness. "Life has been so cold without you."

Shaia lifted her hand and placed it over his, pinning it to her cheek. "I am here now."

"You are not going anywhere?" His eyes darted between hers.

She shook her head.

His gaze locked with hers, and his mood shifted. She could feel it changing, but she didn't let it frighten her, stood her ground and waited for whatever emotion had gripped him to reveal itself to her.

His pupils dilated.

His eyes fell to her lips.

He murmured throatily, "I dreamed of you the other night... I dreamed of the ball."

A blush climbed her cheeks, scalding them, and her heart missed a beat as she remembered that night and how she had wanted so much more than his kisses and that fumbled moment.

He drew down a deep breath, and growled. "You *need*."

She flushed all over, startled that he could sense her rising desire, even when she knew it happened between mates. Her pulse picked up when he stepped towards her, anticipation swirling inside her, pushing her to the edge of begging him to take her into his arms and kiss her because he was right and she needed him. She needed him now. It felt as if she might die if he didn't touch her, didn't re-enact that night with her against the wall of his room.

He stilled, and moved back, and she wanted to growl at him.

"You do not want me." He lowered his hand from her face, slipping it free of hers, and cold swept through her, confusion at the crest of it. She frowned at him, unsure why his mood had suddenly changed and what had given him the impression she didn't want him, when she was burning for him. He looked away from her, towards the window to his left. "You couldn't bring yourself to look at me."

Her confusion mounted, clouding her mind. When had she made him feel that way?

The clouds scattered as she remembered the moment in the reception room, when she had felt the same hurt go through him.

When he had lost himself to the darkness and had been fighting it, tormented by it, and she had looked away from him.

"No, Fuery." She shook her head and seized his hands again, refusing to let him distance himself from her when he was wrong. "I knew you would not want me to see you like that... I thought I was sparing you."

She stepped towards him, closing the gap between them, narrowing it further this time, so his heat embraced her and he was all she knew.

She lifted her eyes to meet his, held them as they darkened again, and opened herself to him. She would never hide anything from him. She would never hold anything back. Even when confessing such things had her nerves rising, palms sweating and pulse pounding.

"I want you, Fuery... I wanted you from the moment we met and I have never stopped wanting you."

CHAPTER 16

Those words struck Fuery as fiercely as his instincts as her mate, almost sending him to his knees on the dark stone floor. He swallowed hard and fought to hold himself together, to keep his boots planted to the tiles and resist the urges that went through him.

Some of them terrifying.

Gods, he didn't want to hurt her.

He knew he would if he surrendered to the need running rampant inside him, a startling combination of hunger and darkness, a pressing desire to claim the delicate female standing before him and stamp his mark all over her.

His fangs itched at the thought of penetrating her pale perfect flesh and mouth watered at the hazy memory of how sweet her blood tasted, and how good it had made him feel as he had drunk from her vein, pulling all of her into him. It had felt as if he had been joining their souls, mingling a part of hers with his.

He trembled, on fire with the hunger to surrender to his blacker urges and fulfil his needs.

And hers.

He balled his hands into fists as the claws of his armour formed over his fingers, and gritted his teeth as they sliced through the scales to cut deep into his flesh, filling the tense air with the sickly scent of his own blood.

He couldn't.

He forced himself to look at her. To see her.

She was delicate. Beautiful. A rare bloom that deserved tenderness from him, and one he would likely crush if he wasn't gentle with her.

He didn't want to ruin her.

If he surrendered to the dark needs running through him, he would do just that.

The males of the guild feared him for a reason, and while he no longer remembered the things he did when the darkness pulled him under, when he lost himself to it, he knew from the way they avoided him and the looks they cast him that he was dangerous in that state, vicious and cruel, and revelled in the sick things he did while under the influence of the darkness.

He couldn't count the number of people he had hurt when lost to that darkness. They were too numerous.

He couldn't count the number he had killed.

When he lost himself, he had no awareness and therefore he couldn't stop himself from doing terrible things.

If he lost himself when Shaia was around him, if the darkness seized him, born of his desperate need to stake a new claim on her as his fated one, he would hurt her. He was sure of it.

As sure of it as he was the fact that he wouldn't be able to live with himself in the aftermath.

It was a miracle that she was standing before him, flesh and blood, not dead.

Not killed by him.

If he surrendered to his need, he might kill her.

She had been living without him for four thousand years, and that had torn at him just moments ago, but as the darkness pushed inside him, driving him to stake that claim on her, he wished she had never discovered he was alive.

It killed him, ripped at the fragile remains of his soul, but he wished it regardless.

She had mourned him by her own admission, but she had been safe from him. She had been living her life and looked well for it.

"Fuery... say something," she whispered and her hands twitched, as if she wanted to reach for him again.

He shook his head, warning her not to do it. He wasn't strong enough right now. The darkness was growing stronger, rising to wrap inky tendrils around his heart and whisper wicked tempting things in his mind.

Shaia blinked and looked down at her feet, and he could see her withdrawing into herself, pulling away from him, and it hurt so much he couldn't breathe, wanted to seize her and make her come back to him.

He stood firm somehow, holding himself at a distance, and forced himself again to look at her. His beautiful mate. She was alive, and she had meant those words she had said to him, offering them as a balm she had thought would soothe him.

Words that tormented him worse than the nightmares of killing her.

He could feel how much she needed him as she stood close to him, could feel how much she loved him still.

Gods.

He didn't deserve it. He didn't deserve her.

But he couldn't stop himself from taking a step towards her, driven by his need of her.

She lifted her eyes, bringing them to meet his, and he faltered, fear swift to rise and rock him as it crashed over him, taunting him with images of the things he might do to her, a thousand terrible memories of waking to find himself surrounded by death, carnage he had wrought while lost to the darkness.

He stilled again, heart labouring as he battled with himself, torn between going to her and satisfying the need he could feel in her, obeying his instincts as her mate, and telling her to leave.

The desire, the deep need of her he had always felt, had never faded. If anything, it felt stronger now than ever. But it was sheer torment. He might have been worthy of her when they had mated all those centuries ago, but he was unworthy of her now, and it was only a matter of time before she saw it with her own eyes.

He was tainted, not only by the darkness but by the terrible things he had done as an assassin.

He couldn't touch her, not even when he felt as if he would die without that physical contact between them.

He couldn't taint her.

The longer he stared at her, the stronger that feeling grew.

He was unworthy.

The need to maim and kill, to spill blood, both his own and his enemy's, constantly beat inside him, never relenting. Even now, in her presence, he hungered to bloody his claws, the darkness pressing him to lash out and fight, desiring it so he would sink deeper into its hold.

Such a beautiful female didn't deserve a beast like him.

He needed to protect her.

But, sweet gods, he couldn't bear the thought of making her leave.

His instincts as her mate and the need to possess her was strong, crushing, overwhelming him as he breathed in her scent and watched her, saw her desire flickering in her stunning violet eyes and felt it beating in his veins.

He needed her fiercely too, felt he might finally die if he didn't touch her soon. The small distance between them was too much. He needed her closer.

In his arms.

He needed to feel her in them, against him, her skin warming his.

He needed it so much he couldn't breathe, but fear of hurting her held him back, kept him at a distance as his mind filled with images of him harming her while lost to his passion.

Killing her.

"Fuery." She finally found the courage to raise her hands and hold them out to him.

He drew down a deep shuddering breath and stared at them, tempted to take them and draw her into his arms where he needed her.

He studied her instead, and as she slowly lowered her hands to her thighs, his gaze followed them. It was strange seeing her in masculine clothing. The dull brown trousers and drab tunic covered her from neck to toe, but revealed the shapely forms of her legs at the same time, making him want to growl, grab something and wrap it around her so no other male could gaze at them. His thoughts travelled down another route as he stared at them, transporting him back to the river and the trees, and the time he had taken her against one and she had wrapped those slender legs around his waist.

He did growl now.

She tensed on his senses, and a flicker of her emotions ran through him. Embarrassment mingled with need, desire so strong that he felt sure she had heard his thoughts and had remembered the same moment he had.

He lifted his eyes back to hers, and wanted to ask if she had, but other words left his lips.

"You are real?" He wasn't sure how many times he needed to ask that before he finally accepted that it really was his Shaia stood before him.

It seemed so impossible.

He could feel her though, a connection that tied them together, his heart to hers, and entwined their souls.

A connection that had been closed to him for what felt like forever but was wide open again now.

That blast of light that had rocked him had been because of her.

She had done something to reawaken their bond.

Fuery wrestled with his words, aware that he needed to say something to break the heavy silence, but unsure what to say. That he needed her too? That he loved her still? What use would such words be to him? They would only wound him in the end, when she turned her back on him or when he found the strength to make her leave.

The sensations running through him, emotions he thought dead long ago, were relentless, pushing him to go to her and touch her, to say something that would charm her or ease her, to do whatever it took to make her love him forever.

They were overwhelming, a force he struggled to tame and control as he fought with himself and tried to make himself believe she was real.

Gods, she was real.

The more he looked at her, the more a single feeling grew, one that had beat in him centuries ago and had never died.

He would do anything for her.

He would break every bone in his body, endure any pain, for eternity.

But being near her was torture.

It killed him because he wanted her so desperately, but he couldn't trust himself with her.

She was delicate, fragile, and he told himself that on repeat, desperate to make it sink in. He no longer knew how to be gentle. He couldn't treat her the way she deserved to be treated, no matter how fiercely he wanted to do that.

No matter how fiercely he wanted to be the only male for her.

She was everything to him, and he wanted to be everything for her, but he hadn't deserved her back then, and he really didn't deserve her now.

Shaia stared at him, her feelings growing increasingly tumultuous as she waited for him to speak. She toyed with the frayed hem of her grey tunic, slender fingers tugging at the loose threads, and he sensed her rising nerves.

Her desire to say something.

To make him speak.

He pushed words out.

"You asked me about females… have you been with…" He couldn't bring himself to finish that sentence as fury clawed at his heart and rage burned in his soul, just the thought of her with another male enough to have him sinking into the darkness, reaching for it so he could use its strength to slay any male who stood between him and Shaia.

She gently shook her head.

Light filled him, driving back the darkness, freeing him of its grip.

"There has only been you," she whispered in a low, soft voice, her gaze as gentle as her tone, and her steady feelings telling him she spoke the truth.

He clung to that.

He sank his bloodstained claws into it and seized it hard, wanted to drag it down to him and hold it to his chest, to the black and battered heart that beat for only her.

The look in her eyes implored him to take her hand when she reached for him again, her fingers trembling in the air between them.

He wanted to do it.

Wavered on the brink of accepting her hand and her touch.

He was weak though, tired from fighting the darkness that had seized him in the reception room, darkness that continued to push and might grasp him again at any moment. He couldn't control it, couldn't hold it back right now. The thought of hurting her, tainting her, tormented him and gave the darkness strength, making it impossible to vanquish no matter how fiercely he wanted to subdue it so he could touch her again.

"There has only been you in my heart, Fuery."

He clenched his jaw and growled in response to that and the need that struck him as her words rang in his ears, making him want her more than ever, stirring a desire to seize her hand and pull her against him, to clutch her against his black and battered heart and force her to love him again, to be his again.

Fuery forced himself to move back a step, placing more distance between them.

It was too dangerous.

"Take my hand, Fuery," she whispered, a temptress that seemed to know his every thought, could read the things he wanted to keep hidden from her. She stretched it towards him, her steady violet gaze locked with his, her heart keeping a slow gentle rhythm that was at odds with his own thundering pulse.

She had to know what she was asking of him. She had to know. If she could feel him, could read him, then she had to know his darkest thoughts, and his deepest desires.

She had to know how dangerous it was for her to tempt him with her touch.

He would ruin her.

He would be her downfall.

The way she looked at him, reached for him, said that she didn't know what she was dealing with. She didn't know the danger she was in.

He would spell it out for her.

Fuery held his hands out in front of him and waited for her to look at them. When her eyes dropped, he flexed his razor-sharp claws, and goaded the darkness a little, courted it just enough that she would feel it in their bond as he narrowed his gaze on her.

"You want these hands on you?" He growled and curled his fingers into his palms, didn't flinch as his claws sliced into his flesh and spilled his blood. He stretched his fingers again and pushed his hands towards her, and her gasp broke the silence, her need to come to him and tend to his wounds running through him. He snarled at her, stopping her from moving, the feral sound loud in the still air. "There is blood on my hands, Shaia. I might not have killed you... but I have killed others. Hundreds. *Thousands*."

He heard her heart hitch, her sharp intake of breath as she tensed, and felt her eyes leap to his face and then back down to his hands.

"I paint my black claws red each day, spill blood and split flesh, sever bone, and cut life from the breast of whoever stands in my path." He narrowed his eyes on his claws, slick with his own blood, and growled low. "I paint my black claws red... and I like it. I enjoy it. I *hunger* for it."

He lifted his eyes to her.

"Even now."

Her eyes leaped up to his and widened, and her pulse picked up.

"I want to kill even now... while you are before me. I want to bloody my claws... I want to feel the pain as my foe lands a blow... I ache to battle and be the victor, to be the one left standing. It is all I know." He paused and looked down at his claws. "It is all I love."

He lowered his hands to his sides, and lifted his head again, locking gazes with her. She paled, and he knew why. The darkness within him was surging forwards, corrupting his irises.

His pupils.

He could almost feel them as they fought to change, switching between round and stretching into a point at the top and bottom, turning elliptical.

It happened easily now, a sign that the darkness had almost secured its hold on him and he was balanced on the razor's edge, a step away from the abyss and freeing the monster that lived inside him.

"You thought me dead... what a blessing you must feel that thought was as you gaze upon me now. I am not dead... I am something worse. I am the monster all elves fear. I am the beast males whisper of in fear, dreading the day I will come for them." He moved past her, opened the door and drew down a deep breath, one that dragged her scent down into his lungs and soothed him even as pain tore at him, the thought of what he was about to do ripping him to pieces and hollowing out his insides. He glared over his shoulder at her. "Leave, Shaia... leave and do not look back. The male you loved, he is dead, just as you thought. I am not that male... and I never will be again."

She blinked again, her eyes flickering between him and the corridor, her pain shredding his heart as fiercely as his own was.

He felt her urge to speak, knew the words she wanted to say, and he couldn't bear it.

He seized her arm in a brutal grip, one that tore a pained gasp from her lips and had tears welling in her eyes, and pulled her past him, shoving her into the corridor. Her right shoulder hit the wall opposite his door and her pain went through him, both the physical and emotional. A need to apologise rushed through him, a desire to soothe her pain and steal it away riding hard on its heels, but he forced himself to remain where he was.

Because he needed her gone.

Not for his sake.

But for hers.

He needed to protect her, and this was the only way he knew how.

"Leave," he snarled. "I never want to see you again."

The tears lining her violet eyes trembled on the brink of falling. He focused on his connection to her and slammed it shut before she could feel his pain, the agony caused by his need to comfort her, to make her stay.

The door across the hall from his opened and Hartt stood there, giving him a look that called him a bastard. As if he didn't already feel that in his heart. He was a bastard for hurting her, but it was better than killing her.

She glanced at Hartt, and then bowed her head and hurried along the corridor.

Fuery gripped the doorframe, digging his claws into the wood, anchoring himself to it to stop himself from going after her. He willed her to look back at him.

To come back to him.

The strength drained from him as she kept walking away, the distance between them becoming unbearable, tearing at him and pushing him to go after her. When she disappeared from view, the light inside him winked out of existence, and he sagged to his knees, his claws raking down the doorframe, leaving deep grooves in the wood.

"Why did you do that?" Hartt said, his voice soft and low, and came to crouch in front of him.

Fuery stared at the male's feet. "You know why."

Hartt's sigh said that he did, was aware of his desire to protect Shaia, and he thought him a fool for pushing her away instead of drawing her closer. His friend's gaze left him, and he wanted to growl when he realised the male was looking in the direction Shaia had gone and was thinking about her. He bit it back and told himself that it was better this way.

She would return to her life, and would continue without him, safe from the darkness that infested him, and from the monster he had become.

"She might have saved you," Hartt whispered and rose onto his feet.

Fuery knew that.

He knew the words Hartt wouldn't say too, ones that ate at him and had his stomach squirming, and his heart aching.

She might have saved them both.

CHAPTER 17

Shaia had half a mind to turn on her heel, storm back through the building and give Fuery hell for pushing her away. The other half was aware of his pain though, and the fear that had been a constant inside him from the moment she had stepped into his room.

Back into his life.

She had pushed him hard enough for one day.

She hated the way he felt, and the way he thought. She hated the way he pushed her away, seemingly determined to keep his distance from her and not allow her back into his life.

She hated the way he had closed himself off, shutting down their fragile connection.

She hated it all, but she understood why he had done it, and why he was acting the way he was.

When he had been fighting with himself after her confession, she had taken the time to attempt to place herself in his boots, to decipher and understand the feelings she could sense in him through their bond. She had considered how mated males worked, and how he had behaved around her in their brief time together before he had disappeared.

It had led her to one conclusion.

He wanted to protect her.

He had always been fiercely protective of her, had loved her deeply, the sort of love no amount of time apart or together could change. It was a love that burned in her too, as fiercely today as it had the day they had met. No. It had grown stronger over the time they had spent together, and the years they had been apart, forged by the things that had happened into a stronger love, one that was unbreakable.

That same love burned in him. She knew it, had seen it in his corrupted eyes and had felt it in his heart. He loved her.

That love made him scared.

He feared hurting her when the madness seized him.

He feared the way she might look at him when he was gripped by the darkness.

He feared he would break her love for him and she would leave him.

So he had pushed her away.

It hurt.

It cut her deeper than any blade, and she was bleeding inside.

But she understood his reasons.

"Shaia." Hartt's deep voice coming from behind her slowed her steps as she reached the grim reception room, and she stopped and looked back at him.

Sorrow shone in his violet eyes.

She looked away from him, because she didn't want his pity.

Her fight wasn't over yet.

Fuery hadn't won.

She wouldn't give up on him.

She was going to patch up her heart, give him time to loosen the hold his darkness had over him, and then she would be back to fight for him all over again.

She pulled the hood of her cloak up over her hair and bent her head as she started walking again. She didn't tense as she passed some males in the arched corridor, no longer afraid of them or any at the guild. Fuery pushed her away, but he would fight for her if anyone dared to touch her, and he would kill any who hurt her.

She believed that.

She believed in him.

No matter how fierce the darkness was, no matter how violent it made him, he would never hurt her.

She would find a way to prove that to him.

She ducked out of the arched wooden double doors and quickly crossed the cobbled street to the inn, and hurried past the males lingering in the small tavern area on the ground floor. She swiftly took the steps and didn't slow until she was closing the door to her room, shutting the world out. She pulled at the ties of her cloak, pooled it into her arms and dropped it on the end of her bed as she passed it, heading for the window.

She settled there, her eyes locking on the wall of the guild, on the point where she knew Fuery's room was located.

She could feel him.

The connection was weak, but it was there if she pushed, still within her reach, and she knew she could open it again if she wanted. She resisted the temptation. Fuery needed time to come to terms with the fact she was alive, and their reinstated bond.

Hartt was right about that.

Feeling their bond reawaken had triggered an episode in Fuery, giving the darkness power over him, and it was going to take him time to learn how to deal with it and the way his sickness reacted to it. She would give him that time.

It was difficult though.

Minutes trickled past as she sat by the window and stared at the guild, trying to formulate a plan and decide what step to take next. Every second of each minute, she could feel an echo of Fuery's pain, a glimmer of it through their bond.

Gods, it was hard to remain where she was knowing that Fuery was alone in that damned cell-like room, suffering because of her.

Again.

She brought her knees up, wrapped her arms around them and held them to her chest.

How was she meant to help Fuery when just reawakening their bond had been enough to tip him over the edge and into the darkness?

How was she meant to make Fuery see that he could be with her without fear of hurting her when there was a tiny part of her that feared such a thing happening?

Gods.

She threw her head back and screamed out her frustration, not caring if anyone heard her because she needed to get it all out of her. It was tying her in knots, pulling her in too many directions at once, and she couldn't take it.

When her voice gave out, she buried her face in her knees.

Deep in her heart, her bond to Fuery flickered, a weak thing that felt as if it might fade away at any moment.

She clung to it, nurtured it in the way Prince Loren had taught her, just enough that it remained, because she needed to feel it, needed the comfort of it to carry her through the dark hours ahead of her.

She needed Fuery.

She turned her head to her right, rested her left cheek on her knees and sighed as she stared at the imposing guild building.

Pain burned in her heart, pulsing stronger with each beat. Her pain. Born of a feeling she couldn't shake.

Jealousy.

The only reason Fuery was still a part of this world was because he shared a bond with Hartt. That bond ran deeper than the one she shared with her beautiful dark warrior.

Hartt had the bond she wanted with Fuery.

Her ears pricked when a noise came from her left, a soft swishing sound that had her looking towards the door beyond the bed.

She frowned at the small white folded piece of parchment on her floor, uncurled and padded across the room to the door. She bent and picked it up, and unfolded the note.

There was a single sentence on it, written by a neat and elegant hand.

Do not give up on him.

She lowered her gaze and stared at Hartt's signature, and felt the gravity in those words. They stirred her soul, soothed her aching heart, and gave her strength as they fortified her resolve.

She wouldn't.

Hartt hadn't given up on Fuery, and he had been there during Fuery's darkest times. The male wanted to save his friend.

She wanted to save her mate.

She had been approaching Fuery all wrong. She wasn't alone in this fight. Hartt was there with her. If they worked together, they could save Fuery. She was sure of it.

Somehow, they would pull Fuery back from the darkness and weaken its hold on him.

Starting with showing him that he wouldn't hurt her, not even in his blackest rages. She could temper the darkness for him, could be the light he needed.

Proving that to him was going to be easier said than done.

She would need to get Fuery to lower the barriers around his heart and let her in.

Her heart threatened to sink at that.

It was going to take a miracle.

CHAPTER 18

Shaia was improving with the blade, her swipes more precise now, elegant almost as her hand fluidly glided through the air at chest height and forced him to lean back to avoid her blow. She tossed the dagger to her left hand, a move that would have given her an advantage, an opportunity to strike at him again while he was off balance, if she hadn't broadcasted her intent to him.

Fuery shot his hand out and snatched the blade as it passed in front of her chest, his eyes tracking it as it spun end over end, so he struck at just the right moment to grab the curved hilt. The black leather was warm beneath his palm and fingers, sending a hot shiver through him at the same time as her surprised gasp.

Her amethyst eyes leaped to his and she blinked.

"You were too obvious." He shrugged, flipped the black dagger in his hand, catching the blade between his fingers, and held it out to her.

She snatched it back and glared at him. "You are too skilled."

"Too obvious," he countered, and gods, he had missed their easy playful banter and the way she spoke to him, a little bite in her words that showed him how at ease she was around him.

Her frown knit harder, narrowing her eyes and compressing those lips he wanted to kiss.

When was the last time he had kissed her?

It felt like months ago, but it might have been only a few weeks.

Gaining the rank of commander, and a position serving directly under Prince Loren, had afforded him a little freedom, and he was making damned good use of it. He was free to come and go from the castle as he pleased as long as his duties were done, and he returned each night.

When he had returned four lunar cycles ago to tell Shaia about his promotion, she had been excited for him, and he had seen in her eyes and felt in her that she was also excited about what it meant for her. That alone had brought him back to her most days when he wasn't on duty, meeting her in secret at a spot near the stream, where hills formed on one side to create a steep cliff that curved with the river, granting them some privacy.

The woods were thick beneath it on their side of the river, and another hill rose up, the trees blanketing it. The carpenters and craftsmen often visited the woods, but never ventured as deep as their secret spot, the density of the trees making it hard for them to haul their lumber out. They stayed close to the fringes of the forest.

Shaia shifted foot to foot, bare feet silent on the sandy bank of the river.

She palmed the dagger.

He had given it to her on his second visit after becoming a commander, a gift to show her that he had thought about her request and was happy to fulfil it.

Her eyes had lit up at the sight of it, and she had kissed him. Hard. Gods, she would have stolen his heart with that kiss, if it hadn't already been hers.

Every visit since then, he had spent most of it teaching her how to fight.

She wanted to know how to handle herself, and he wanted it too, with a ferocity that had shaken him when he had made his decision.

He needed to teach her, because he needed to know she would be safe when he wasn't with her, when he was leagues away and unable to protect her.

He stared at her, feeling that need bubbling beneath the surface of his skin, deep in his heart. He wanted to be with her always, to stand at her side and never move from it, but it wasn't possible. He still had work to do if he was going to achieve the dream they shared—convincing her parents that he was a suitable male for her.

There were days when he didn't want to wait though, when the call of his instincts was too strong and he found it hard to deny them.

She was his fated one.

The female he loved with all his heart.

He wanted her to be his mate.

She slowly lowered her hand to her sides, so the dagger brushed the layers of her sky-blue dress, and her eyes locked with his, her lips parting.

The dagger fell to the dirt with a thud.

Her mouth claimed his, tearing a moan from his throat.

He tunnelled his left hand beneath her fall of black wavy hair, grasped the back of her neck and kissed her hard. His right hand seized her hip and he slid it to the small of her back and hauled her up against him, so her body pressed against his and he could feel her heart thundering, hammering against his, speaking of the need he could feel running through her.

Need that matched his own.

She moaned, a quiet little sound that stirred his blood into an inferno, and he lifted her from the ground and carried her into the shade of the trees, out of the open. He set her down and she didn't resist him as he backed her against the broad trunk of one, his lips dancing over hers, her taste flooding him with warmth, heat that had him trembling right down to his soul.

He tugged her close and kissed her deeper, tangling his tongue with hers, tearing another teasing moan from her lips that he swallowed and savoured. She grasped his bare shoulders, her touch sending a hot thrill through him, a bolt that lit him up and had him pressing against her, desperate and wild with a need to feel her soft curves cushioning his body.

Nerves threatened to rise but he pushed them down, managing to subdue them and focus on his task rather than allowing his mind to leap ahead. This wouldn't be the first time they had touched each other. There was no reason for him to be nervous.

Unless.

Unless it became more than touching.

His heart pounded faster at just the thought, the nerves he had managed to gain control over threatening to burst free and run rampant through him. He broke the kiss and pressed his forehead to hers, breathing hard as he fought the urges rushing through him, need that he had battled more than once in their times together and would quell this time too.

Gods, he wanted to make love to her though.

He wanted to feel her warm body gloving his, and hear her cry his name as he brought her to a shattering climax.

"Fuery," she breathed, a plea that dragged him back to her and told him that he wasn't alone.

He could feel her desperation too, could see it in her eyes as he drew back. They were wide, wild, her pupils devouring the amethyst as she gripped his shoulders and pushed forwards, so the metal swirls of her corset pressed against his torso.

She trembled beneath his hands, her breath coming faster, and teased her lower lip with one tiny fang.

She pushed her hips forwards.

Against his.

Too much.

Not enough.

Fuery growled, grasped her waist and pressed forwards, pinning her to the rough trunk of the tree. She moaned as his rigid cock met her soft flesh and kissed him again, her tongue pushing past his lips to tease his fangs. He groaned and shuddered as she teased them, drawing them down, filling his head with wicked, dangerous thoughts.

Ones about biting her.

Her left hand skimmed over his shoulder, up his neck, and his groan became a damned whimper as she stroked the curve of his ear and feathered her fingers up to the pointed tip. Shivers tripped through him, each one hotter than the last, stirring his need to dizzying new heights, and he couldn't stop himself from moaning and rocking against her, showing her just how mad with need she was making him.

How much he wanted her.

When she caught his jaw, turned his head to his right, and leaned towards him to stroke her tongue from his lobe to the pointed tip of his ear, his restraint shattered. On a low growl, he grabbed her backside with both hands, lifted her and pressed between her thighs. She responded by wrapping her legs around his waist, and he groaned and shuddered as she pressed against him, all heat and temptation.

Her tongue stroked his ear again, flicking the tip, her breathless little sigh of pleasure as he ground his cock against her soft heat tearing a moan from his lips and driving him to obey the need he could feel building inside her.

Need that matched his own.

"Shaia," he whispered, on the brink of falling and needing to let her know just what she was doing to him, how she was pushing him too close to the edge.

She only moaned in response, and grazed her teeth down the curve of his ear to the lobe. She caught it between her small fangs, ripping another low groan from him as he shuddered against her and couldn't stop himself from rubbing between her thighs. She trembled and gasped with each one, and surprised him by pressing her hips closer at the same time as she tightened her legs around him.

"Fuery."

He had never heard his name said in such a passion-drenched and lost way, and gods, he wanted to hear her say it that way again, needed to experience the blast of sheer pleasure that had gone through him on hearing what he did to her.

That she wanted him. Needed him. Only him.

He growled and seized her mouth again, kissing her hard, unable to hold himself back as his mind leaped forwards, his body growing painfully hard at the thought of finally making love to her. She moaned and dropped her hands away from him, and he wanted to growl at her, but when he broke the kiss and looked down, he couldn't breathe.

She pulled at her sky-blue skirts, parting the layers, exposing her thighs to him.

Sweet gods, the sight of the aching bulge in his black trousers so close to her had his mind emptying and his ears ringing.

She only made the ringing grow louder as she placed a trembling hand over that bulge.

Fuery groaned and pressed against her soft palm, shook all over as she tentatively rubbed him through his trousers. Too much. Not nearly enough. He needed more.

She was way ahead of him.

Her nimble fingers tugged at the lacing on his trousers, and part of him wanted to grin when she loosed a frustrated little noise as her trembling made it hard work. Before he could help her, she had torn the laces from the holes, and cool air washed over his exposed cock.

And then heat.

Incredible heat.

He groaned and pressed his forehead against hers as she touched him, his balls growing tight and his cock feeling as if it might burst. Sweet gods. He felt sure he might die.

She thumbed the tip and he caught her hand and pulled it away, breathing hard as he fought to subdue the pressing need to climax that had swept through him in response to that innocent touch.

"Fuery," she whispered.

He slowly lifted his head and met her gaze.

It was dark, filled with need that he could sense in her, a hunger that ran through him too, lighting up his blood and pushing him to satisfy it.

She blinked, a flicker of nerves crossing her beautiful face, and worried her lower lip with her fangs.

And then she moved.

Raised the hem of her dress to reveal her cream undergarments.

Ran her fingers over their silky material and upwards, to the cinched waist.

Pushed them down, exposing the soft flat plane of her belly.

Fuery growled, dropped her feet to the leaf litter and fell to his knees before her. She gasped as he placed his hands over hers and moved them with his, drawing her underwear down. His heart pounded in time with hers, a fast beat that drummed in his ears and throbbed in his mind as he tugged the silk down and revealed her dark curls.

Sweet gods, he wanted to kiss her there.

He wanted to taste her on his tongue, wanted her nectar coating it as he drank down her moans.

But more than that, he wanted to sheath himself in her.

He reached her ankles and she stepped out of her underwear, and he glanced up at her face.

No trace of nerves lined her delicate features. There was only determination and need, a hunger that called to him and had his instincts pushing him forwards even as his nerves spiralled out of control.

She reached her hand out to him and brushed her palm across his cheek, her violet eyes telling him she was ready and she wanted to do this.

Too much.

He shot to his feet, claimed her backside and wrapped her legs around his hips again. She shook in his arms, but it wasn't only nerves that had her trembling. It was need. She pressed forwards, bringing them into contact, and moaned as her body met his, soft heat against hard steel.

He reached between them, caught his aching shaft, and eased it downwards through her slick folds, and groaned as he reached her opening and the blunt head dipped forwards, entering her.

Gods.

She clutched his shoulders, her breathless moan spurring him on, and he shook away the last of his reservations, the voice that told him he wasn't good enough for her, and pressed forwards.

She wanted him.

She had chosen him.

She believed him good enough for her even if he didn't.

He inched deeper, his breath catching as she gloved him, so tight and hot around him. She breathed hard as she held on to him, her eyes searing his face as he focused on not hurting her, aware that males did such things to females. He didn't want to be like them. He wanted his fated one to feel only pleasure.

Her hand caught the back of his neck and she pulled him towards her. Her mouth seized his, stealing his focus, sending pleasure blasting through him again that had him pressing deeper, shuddering as his cock slid into her and her heat encased the full length of him. He didn't miss the way her breath hitched, and a flicker of her pain reached him, but it was gone in a heartbeat, replaced with the same bliss that rolled through him.

And then she pressed closer.

And he slid deeper still.

Definitely enough.

Gods, it was too much.

He held her backside in his right hand, pressed her against the tree with his body and eased out of her. She moaned, and it only grew louder as he slowly thrust back in. Her lips stilled against his. He breathed against them, hot air puffing back at him as he grew accustomed to being inside her, feeling her gloving him. She was so wet, so warm, so perfect around him.

He dropped his forehead to her shoulder as he thrust, struggling to control himself when an urge to take her, to find release inside her, rose inside him. She moaned each time their hips met, her body fluttering around his, clenching him at times in a way that had him close to the edge. He wanted to tell her not to do it, but gods, it felt good when she did, when she gripped him as if she didn't want him to leave.

"Fuery," she murmured, all the pleasure he could sense in her ringing in his name, spurring him on.

She liked the feel of him inside her, stretching her.

Claiming her.

He groaned and grunted when she tightened again, body fisting his shaft, stealing his breath. He clutched her backside harder and thrust deeper, angling his hips so he could drive more of his cock into her. He wanted every inch inside her, wanted to fill her up so she would never want another.

So she would be his forever.

Marked by him.

Wanting only him.

He shuddered and gasped as her tongue stroked up his neck, and pumped her harder, unable to stop himself as primal needs flared inside him, instincts that stole control and had him wavering on the brink of doing something he couldn't take back or erase.

Something unbreakable.

Eternal.

His fangs punched long from his tingling gums and his senses zeroed in on her thundering heartbeat as he drove into her, her soft moans ringing in his ears together with the sweet rush of her blood.

He grunted and growled against her throat, gripping her harder and pumping her deeper, drinking those moans he elicited as he wrestled with himself, battling the instincts that battered him.

His mouth watered, thoughts of Shaia's blood making his fangs ache.

He wanted it.

But he couldn't take it.

Pain seared the left side of his neck, tearing a vicious grunt from his lips, and a thousand sensations bombarded him, throwing his head into a spin as his heart missed a beat and he froze, overloading and lost, struggling to comprehend what was happening.

Pleasure rolled through him, so intense it kept his mind scrambled, a combination of Shaia moving against him and something else.

Something that rocked him to his soul.

Her fangs in his throat.

She pulled them from his flesh, wrapped her lips around the wounds and sucked.

Hard.

It was over for him.

All control he had managed to claw together fled in that instant.

The feel of his blood rushing towards her, the feel of the connection blooming between them, and the emotions that coursed through it from her into him, was too much. His knees weakened beneath him and he had to lean his weight against her, pressing them both into the tree, to avoid collapsing as she drank from his vein.

And drank deep.

Her nails bit into his shoulders as she moaned and sucked harder, as if she couldn't quench her thirst for him now that she had started, as if she would never get enough of him.

He would never get enough of her.

A bright blinding flash detonated inside him as the bond formed, triggered by her taking his blood, and their hearts fell into unison, his racing to match the beat of hers. She rocked on him, reminding him what they had been doing before she had tipped his entire world off its axis, and he growled as he drove her against the tree and thrust into her, his grip on her hip fierce now as his need to claim her mounted.

She would be his.

He couldn't leave the bond incomplete, didn't have the strength to do that when he knew that she wanted it.

He would claim her.

She writhed in his arms, her instincts flaring and need skyrocketing as his blood entered her system and the bond demanded completion. Her lips left his throat and seized his, and he groaned as he tasted his own blood in the kiss. It drove him on, until the need to claim her became a fierce roar in his blood.

He needed to bite her.

He pulled back, his gaze zeroing in on her throat.

He dropped his lips to it. Parted them as he thrust harder into her.

Sense cut through the roaring in his mind, a ray of light that brought with it a flicker of control. As much as he wanted to mark her throat, he couldn't. Her parents didn't know about them yet, and he was due to leave with the legion soon. If he bit her throat, they would see it, and he didn't want to think about what they would do to Shaia while he was away, unable to protect her.

He pressed a kiss to her throat and savoured her sweet moan as he vowed he would bite her there one day.

But for now, her mating mark would have to be somewhere more private.

She growled when he pulled out of her and dropped to his knees before her, but it died on her lips when he pressed his to her left thigh. She gazed down at him, her lips painted sultry red with his blood, and moaned as she pressed her leg forwards, urging him to do it.

"Bite me," she murmured, a throaty plea that he was all too happy to fulfil.

He closed his eyes, opened his mouth and sank his fangs into her soft flesh.

Her cry echoed around the canyon, rang in his soul.

He growled as the first drop of her blood hit his tongue, as sweet as ambrosia and more addictive than any drug. He withdrew his fangs, wrapped his lips around the wound and sucked, tearing another sweet cry from Shaia. Her blood flooded his mouth, slipped hot down his throat and lit up his veins like wildfire. He groaned and shuddered, hips rocking forwards as his cock grew harder, the air cool against it.

He wanted to be inside her again, needed it with a ferocity that stole his breath.

But he couldn't tear himself away from her thigh, from her blood.

He knew the moment their bond completed, felt the link between them grow stronger and her emotions grow clearer, and heard her heartbeat fall out of sync with his, pounding faster as she writhed against him. He forced himself to pull away from her thigh and swipe the twin puncture wounds with his tongue to help them heal as he felt her need mounting, and his instincts pushed him to satisfy her.

His female needed.

He delved between her thighs, so swiftly that he stole a gasp from her as she went up on her toes and her hands flew above her head to grip the thick bark of the tree. She moaned as he briefly plundered her with his tongue, stealing a taste of her honey, unable to stop himself as his own needs rose. He needed her. All of her.

He shot to his feet, spearing her with his cock, and swallowed her moan in a kiss.

She grasped his shoulders and cried into his mouth as her body shook against his, her sheath quivering around his rigid length and growing more slick. He groaned and drove into her, his blood on fire with her release as it rolled through her and into him, and the need to give her another rushed through him.

He curled his hips, withdrawing almost all the way out of her before driving back inside, giving her every inch of him. Her moans mingled with his more animalistic grunts as his balls drew up, release rising to the base of his cock, and she kissed him. He focused on the feeling building inside her, the need he could feel spiralling beyond her control again, determined to hold back somehow and bring her to another shattering climax.

Shaia took it out of his hands when her mouth left his and she sank her fangs back into his throat.

Stars winked across his vision as release blasted through him, a thousand tiny bombs that detonated to leave him shaking as he throbbed and pulsed inside her, spilling himself. She moaned and clenched him, sending a fiercer wave of pleasure through him, and he thrust into her, wanting more. Needing to do it all over again.

She tensed in his arms.

Her nails dug into his flesh.

Her cry filled his ears.

His own hoarse shout joined it as she quivered around his cock, milking it as a hot rush of honey scalded him, and pushed him back over the edge. He clutched her to him as he spilled again, throbbing in time with her, hard fast breaths matching hers.

He wasn't sure how long he clung to her and her to him, both of them frozen in place.

Shaia moved first, pulling her nails from his flesh and sinking against him. She kissed him, freeing him too, and he wrapped his arms around her and held her, mind, heart and soul still struggling to come to grips with what they had done.

She had given herself to him.

He drew back, lifted his left hand and brushed the tangled strands of her black hair from her face as his eyes searched hers. Love shone in them, coloured with a touch of fear.

She feared losing him.

Never.

"I will come back to you, Shaia," he whispered, his voice hoarse with the raw emotion burning through him, the need to reassure her and to remain with her combining with his love for her. "When I return... I am taking you with me... because... I love you, and I will be yours forever... and you are mine now."

The colour on her cheeks darkened, and the love that shone in her eyes grew brighter, near-blinding him.

"I was always yours," she husked, the warmth and love in those words touching his heart. "I always will be."

She always would be.

Fuery opened his eyes as the dream faded, slipping from his grasp.

Her words echoed in his mind. In his heart. His blackened soul.

She had kept that promise.

He had broken his. He had left her, had travelled with Prince Vail and the legion to Valestrum, and he had never come back.

But she had waited for him.

His eyes slowly widened.

She was *still* waiting for him.

She was right there for the taking, if only he was brave enough.

His mate. His life. His light. She was still there for him.

The darkness surrounding him, gripping him, parted as that realisation went through him, cutting through it like a shaft of light to drive it back.

The inky tendrils were quick to try to seize him again, but he fought them as he pushed himself up, gritting his teeth against the inferno that swept through him in response.

Cold chased on its heels as he saw the black castle looming over him, obsidian mountains spearing the grey sky of Hell beyond it.

The scent of blood and entrails hung heavily in the stifling air.

He didn't want to look.

He wanted to go back to that dream, ached to return to a time when the darkness had been only a seed inside him, not the monster it was now. He wanted to be that male again.

Because Shaia had loved him then.

She had given herself to him.

He forced himself to lower his eyes to the carnage that surrounded him.

A ring of bodies formed around him, broken and battered, stretching at least twenty metres in all directions.

The hope that had been building flickered and died like the light inside him, and left a single thought ringing in his mind, one whose answer felt as if it would spell life or death to him.

Could Shaia ever love a monster like him?

CHAPTER 19

Pain blazed through every inch of him, but Fuery forced himself onto his feet as he shut out the grim sight of the carnage that surrounded him. When he placed weight onto his left foot, fire blazed up his bones, and he clenched his molars. Something was broken in it. He eased his weight onto his right foot, and grimaced as he commanded his armour to peel away from his hands so he could check them.

Bruises littered his right hand. A vicious black and purple mark and grotesque bump in the middle of his left hand warned that he had broken something in that too. He swallowed, drew in a breath to steel himself and pushed his right thumb against the bump.

Agony, white-hot and searing, rolled through him and he threw his head back and roared as he forced himself to continue, to push the two bones back in line so they could heal.

The darkness threatened to sweep back in to seize him but something held it back.

Shaia.

He could feel the link between them as it grew stronger and drove light back into his heart, just enough to keep the darkness at bay.

He wanted to reach for her too, but couldn't bring himself to do it when so much death surrounded him.

Death wrought by his hands.

The fight had been brutal, worse than his usual battles, and gods, it had been everything he had needed at the time.

But now?

He had emerged the victor, but it didn't feel like a victory for him.

It felt like a victory for the darkness.

He had let it consume him again, had allowed it to steal control so he could only watch, a prisoner in his own body as he had taken the lives of his marks, another large group of demon mercenaries.

He didn't remember passing out.

He only remembered the dream.

A dream that had brought light back into his soul, enough to purge the darkness from it again and give him the strength to wake, to claw himself up from the abyss once more.

Fuery lowered his gaze to his body, slowly growing aware of all the bruises beneath the tight black scales of his armour, and the cuts on his face and neck.

Gods.

He wanted to sink to his knees and remain there, wasn't sure he had the strength to move, or the will.

He had never felt so weary.

So battered and bruised, and broken.

The light that echoed inside him pulsed brighter.

Fuery obeyed it.

He turned on his heel and trudged through the battlefield, boots slipping on parts of his foes as he picked his way through them, heading towards the portal he had taken to reach the stronghold. He lost track of time as he walked, his body struggling to heal his wounds, weak from his constant fight against the darkness.

It felt as if he was going to slip into it at any moment.

Only he wouldn't come back this time.

He reached the portal near the mountains and stepped into it, and came out of the darkness in the town close to the guild hall.

Fuck, he wasn't sure he had the strength to keep fighting, to go on existing like this.

It was taking its toll now.

He was weak, constantly on the verge of collapse, a slave to the darkness, and he was afraid of where he was going.

He feared the dark path he was treading.

He reached the arched entrance of the guild hall but didn't stop walking. He kept going, following his feet.

His heart.

He needed to see Shaia.

He needed to see her, needed it in case this was the last time he came back, and in case Vail was right and she could do for him what Rosalind had done for his prince.

163

He didn't want to die, and he didn't want to become the beast all elves feared. He wanted to purge the darkness, to fight it and free himself of it at last, but he was bone-deep afraid that he wasn't strong enough.

Could Shaia give him the strength he needed? Could she give him a reason to go on, to keep fighting? Could she do for him what Rosalind had done for Vail?

Gods, he hoped that she could, because he wanted that with all of his black heart.

He wanted her back in his life, from this point forwards until the end of time.

Fuery slowly clawed himself back from the darkness as he limped through the village, tracking her scent that was ingrained in him, branded on his soul.

He ignored the innkeeper as he entered the three-storey building opposite the guild, feeling Shaia there. The male demanded to know what he wanted and Fuery drifted past him, tracking Shaia, drawn to her as if she was the light. He mounted the steps, following them as they turned, and didn't stop until a door blocked his path.

He stared at it, fear rising inside him, together with a voice that whispered to turn away, because the female whose heartbeat he could hear on the other side of the door was going to make him leave rather than welcome him with open arms.

She was going to push him away.

Because he was a monster.

That heartbeat was steady, a soothing tick in his mind, calling to his.

It remained steady even as she opened the door while he still struggled with his desire to remain and the need to leave.

Her violet eyes were soft, as if she was pleased to see him, but there was a flicker of fear in them too. "I am glad you came."

Was she?

The fear he could sense in her rose as she ran her eyes over him, and that damned voice urged him to leave now, before she could wound him.

She reached for him, and took his right hand in hers, and he could only stare at her as she pulled him towards her, into her room, and closed the door behind him.

Relief crashed through him, vanquishing his fears, and he almost sagged to his knees on the wooden floor.

Her soft smile as she rounded him kept him standing though, gave him strength and courage.

Gods, he knew he was a ghastly sight, and his sweet mate should have been horrified by his appearance.

Only she wasn't.

She lured him away from the door, her hand gentle on his, her awareness of his injuries touching him deeply, more deeply than she could ever know.

"We need to get you cleaned up."

Those words leaving her lips brought awareness with them.

Awareness that there was a large tub in front of the fire, filled with steaming water.

Awareness that Shaia wore only a long blue silk robe, tied loosely at her waist.

His pulse picked up, hammering frantically against his chest, as she released his hand and turned to face him. She flicked a glance at him, meeting his eyes for only a split-second, just long enough for him to see that she had wanted him to come to her.

She had felt his pain, had been aware of his injuries, and she had made preparations in the hope that he would come to her rather than return to the guild.

He didn't deserve such a wonderful female.

A courageous female.

If she knew of his injuries, then she knew how they had happened. She knew he had lost himself to the darkness, had probably felt the battle as it had happened, had experienced an echo of every one of his injuries through their fragile bond, and in response she had prepared to tend to those injuries.

To take care of him.

He stood mute, lost in her and the connotations of what she had done, as she stepped towards him.

"Can you remove your armour?" she whispered, no trace of nerves in her voice.

He nodded.

When he hesitated, afraid of what she would think of him if she saw him naked, saw all the bruises on his flesh, and the scars of his past battles, she offered a soft smile.

One that reassured him as much as her words.

"I only want to help you, Fuery. Please? Let me help you." She edged her hands towards him, palms up, her expression soft and soothing, easing his nerves as her words sank in.

He nodded again, and this time found the strength to issue the mental command to his armour. Her eyes tracked it as the scales swept up from his feet, the concern he could feel in her growing as she charted the black bruise on his left foot and the ones on his shins, and then the scars on his thighs, hidden among the myriad of bruises.

She gasped as his armour cleared his stomach and she saw a deep bruise on his right side, just above his hip.

Her fingers leaped to it and he trembled as they made contact with his skin, sending warmth spreading outwards from that point.

"Gods, Fuery," she bit out, a flicker of rage in her blood, anger towards the ones who had done this to him. Her eyes jumped up to meet his, her fine black eyebrows furrowing. "Does it hurt?"

He wanted to shake his head, but he had always been honest with her, open about everything, and she could feel his pain. Admitting it to her wouldn't make him weak, or vulnerable. She wasn't the enemy.

She was his mate.

He nodded.

Tears threatened to line her eyes, but she blinked them away and he could see the moment she steeled herself, drawing up her courage and refusing to give in to her fears.

His armour reached the bands around his wrists, and he grew aware that he was naked before her.

He had never been naked before her.

His pulse ticked up again, his pain forgotten as nerves swept in.

Those nerves only grew worse when Shaia untied her robe, rolled her shoulders backwards and let the satin slip from her to pool at her feet.

Gods.

She was achingly beautiful.

He tried not to stare at her soft feminine curves, at the sensual dip of her waist and the sweep of her hips, or her pert handful-sized breasts tipped with rosy nipples that peaked as she moved closer to him.

Her hand slipped into his, and he drifted with her as she led him towards the oval wooden tub. She stepped into it, and he hesitated. He wanted to be in the water with her, wanted it more than anything, but he couldn't move.

Fear kept his feet planted to the wooden floor.

He was dreaming this. It wasn't real. It couldn't be. He was a monster, but his beautiful mate was looking at him as she had all those centuries ago, when she had told him that she had always been his, and would always be his.

When she had given him forever.

"Come, Fuery," she whispered, and gently tugged on his hand.

His instincts as her fated male had him moving forwards, filled him with a need to obey his mate and do as she bid.

Because he would do anything for her.

He stepped into the tub, wincing as his broken foot hurt and body protested.

She eased into the water and lured him down to her, and he tamped down his nerves as he settled between her thighs. She gently coaxed him backwards, until his back rested against her chest and her warmth flowed into him, mingled with the heat of the water to soothe the sting of his injuries. He tensed, awareness of her sweeping through him, and he tried to keep his weight off her, afraid of hurting her.

She dipped a sponge into the water and was gentle as she washed his rigid shoulders and chest, her tenderness tearing at him and tempting him into relaxing.

Fuck.

He wanted to cry like an idiot.

"I was worried you would not come," she whispered, and he heard the pain in those words, the fear that she had experienced, and also her relief that he was here now, and was allowing her to take care of him.

He didn't deserve it.

That rang in his mind, and he did his best to ignore it and the other whispered words about him tainting her. The darkness pushed, but he pushed back, because he didn't want this to end. He wanted to stay here in her arms, feeling her loving touch, hearing her sweet voice, and pretend that the last four thousand years had never happened.

This was how he had imagined his life—their life.

Coming home to her like this.

She ran the sponge down his left arm and carefully lifted it so she could reach his hand, and was gentle and careful as she cleaned it, not jarring the broken bones. He slowly relaxed against her, letting her move him as she pleased while he savoured the feel of her against him, and absorbed her whispered words that spoke of her affection and also how she had worried for him.

When she was done with his arms and his chest, she dropped the sponge and washed his neck and his face with her fingers, taking even more care now as she dealt with cleaning the lacerations.

He sank against her while she cleaned his hair, her fingers brushing through it in a way that stirred heat in his veins, tempered with tenderness that had him closing his eyes and giving himself over to her.

She finished, and he was relieved when she didn't make him leave, when she wrapped her arms around him and held him to her. He rested the back of his head on her shoulder and pressed his temple to her right cheek.

Her soft breaths and the crackle of the fire to their left broke the silence, but he found the sounds melodic and soothing as he let all of his tension flow out of him and allowed peace to flow in.

"Who did you fight this time?" she murmured against his jaw.

"Demons," he said, because he didn't want any secrets between them.

"Demons?" She stroked her fingers across his chest. "How many?"

He sighed. "More than there should have been. More than I could count."

"A contract?" Her fingers teased his collarbones, sending a shiver through him.

He easily gave up the answer to that question. "Yes. There was only meant to be ten of them."

"Ten?" She tensed against him, sounding horrified. "Do you often take on so many foes alone?"

He shrugged. "Sometimes."

She splayed her hands out on his pectorals, and whispered softly, "Do you not work with others?"

He growled at just the thought, and the darkness in his voice surprised him. "*No*. My marks are mine."

He tensed now, fear rushing through him, and waited for her to make him leave, to kick him out for being so violent around her.

She lightly stroked her fingers lower instead, teasing the muscles of his abdomen and then lower still as she checked the deep bruise on his side. "You always were rather possessive. You never did like sharing."

He growled at that too, because she was right, and he would kill anyone who tried to take her from him.

She was his.

Darkness rose inside him, swift and deadly, poised to strike.

She skimmed her hands back up to his chest, drawing warm water up with them, and he wanted to tell her to never stop doing that.

It was bliss, and it seemed to sever the hold the darkness had on him and drive it away. Was this how Vail felt when Rosalind touched him? As if that touch was purging the darkness from his soul and allowing light to flood back in?

"You feel weak," she murmured close to his face. "Are you badly hurt?"

Fuery shook his head, because the hunger she could feel in him was a constant thing, never satisfied, and certainly never sated. He could drink forever and never assuage it.

She lifted her left hand and turned her wrist towards him.

He was quick to shake his head again.

Hurt lanced him, pain that came from her, flowed into him through their bond and ripped at his soul.

"You take blood from Hartt, do you not?" She withdrew her arm and rather than settling her hand back on his chest, where he wanted it, she gripped the edge of the tub.

There was hurt in those words too.

Fuery didn't answer her, because she obviously already knew the truth—he regularly took blood from Hartt to sustain him.

"Are you going to leave me and take blood from him?" The dark bite in her tone lashed at him, and made him realise that he had done more than merely hurt her. He had wounded her. She had never raised her voice to him before, not like this, not with so much anger and pain lacing it. She withdrew her other hand from him, and almost growled the words. "Or perhaps one of the females that regularly visit—"

"No." He tried to turn in the tub, needing to see her, but the damned thing was too small and he feared hurting her.

Gods, he was terrified of that.

It was the reason he couldn't bite her.

"I don't visit the females. I remained loyal to you, Shaia... even after I killed you." He frowned and growled in frustration. "But I didn't kill you... did I?"

He unleashed another snarl, his head hurting as he tried to remember what was real and what the darkness had placed inside him, and had made him believe so it could tighten its grip on him.

"Shh, Fuery," she whispered softly and brushed her fingers through his hair, easing him back down against her.

He sank back and focused on the light sound of her breathing, the soft way her fingers stroked him, and the gentle lapping of the water as she moved.

"It never happened," she murmured against his cheek. "I am here with you now, and you need to make yourself see and believe that."

She lifted her other hand from the water and offered her wrist again.

"I miss our bond." The water rolled down her arm and dripped from her elbow into the tub, punctuating the silence. "I need it back... as it used to be... can't you feel that in me?"

He shifted his focus to her, and it hit him hard. Her need was staggering, stealing his breath and pulling at him, commanding him to do something about it.

His female needed him.

His *mate* needed him.

He couldn't stop himself from gently taking hold of her wrist with his good hand, or stroking his thumb over the soft skin on the inside of it, his gaze boring into the veins there that throbbed and called to him. He wanted their bond stronger too. He wanted to taste her on his tongue again.

But he feared.

"I don't want to hurt you."

She shivered in response to his touch and murmured, "You won't. It will feel good."

Gods, he wanted to do it.

His mouth watered, fangs itching. He didn't want to do it because he was weak and needed blood. He craved it because he needed her.

He needed her more than anything.

He brought her wrist to his lips, kissed along it towards her forearm, and sank his fangs into her soft flesh. He waited for her to gasp, waited to feel her pain through their fragile connection.

She gasped, but it wasn't pain he sensed in her.

It was pleasure.

Pleasure that blasted through him too as her blood hit his tongue.

He wanted to devour her, to drink deep and take all of her into him, but he forced himself to be gentle, to take slow sips of the sweet blood she offered him and offer reverence in return. The backs of his eyes burned, and his lungs felt too tight, as he took her blood, felt it slide down his throat and savoured the warmth that spread outwards from his aching chest, until it reached every part of him and left none of him untouched. He felt the bones of his hand knitting back together, and the fractures in his foot heal, and even the bruises no longer stung as he drank from her, taking the life she gave him through her blood.

Fuery squeezed his eyes shut.

He didn't deserve this.

He knew it, but he couldn't stop himself from taking her blood, from stealing this moment with her, even when he feared that she would change when he was done, would push him away or be tainted by this act.

Tainted.

The thought of corrupting her, infecting her with his disease as he had Hartt, had him pulling away from her and swiping his tongue over the puncture wounds as soon as he felt his foot and hand finish healing.

He drew her arm away from his mouth and stared at the marks.

His gaze lowered to her thigh where it pressed against the outside of his, and the pale scars on it that matched the puncture wounds he had just placed on her arm.

Her mating mark.

"I'm sorry… so sorry, Shaia," he whispered, throat tight and voice scraping low as he struggled with the sudden surge of emotions that blasted through him, leaving him trembling as he remembered his dream and that moment they had shared all those years ago.

The darkness pushed, the taste of blood on his tongue bringing other memories to the surface, ones that tore at his control and had him sliding back towards the abyss. He dug his claws into the slippery slope and held on, refusing to allow the darkness to overwhelm him again, because he wanted to be lucid, needed to steal every moment he had with Shaia.

Gods, it was a struggle though.

It pushed him to his limit as he fought for the words he wanted to say to her, battled the darkness and tried to hold it back, not wanting her to see it.

"I wanted to come back." He brushed his thumb across the puncture wounds on her arm, still marvelling at the fact she had offered her blood to him, and had taken pleasure from his bite.

He hadn't hurt her.

He wished it would always be that way, that he would always be able to hold back the darkness when he was around her, but he wasn't a fool.

It was an impossible dream.

One day, that side of himself would slip the leash and he would hurt her.

He sighed and pushed back against the darkness as it snaked smoky tendrils around him and tried to pull him down, focusing on his connection to Shaia to keep the flicker of light in his soul. It was stronger now, but it was still quick to waver as the darkness continued to rise, an unstoppable tide that he felt sure would pull him under at any moment.

He needed to be away from Shaia when it happened.

He wanted to stay though, needed that more. He wanted to remain here, wrapped in her arms, her warmth against his back, and her soft breaths filling his ears as she listened to him, giving him all of her attention.

"I wanted to see your parents' faces when we announced that we were mated and that you were leaving with me." He lifted her arm to his lips and pressed them to the marks, closed his eyes and frowned as that unfulfilled desire beat inside him, returning full force.

That stolen moment with her had been Heaven to him, had given him the strength to leave her knowing that she was his, and that he would return to her, and they would begin their new life.

Together.

He released her hand, gripped the edges of the tub and turned in the water to face her, coming to rest on his knees between her thighs, a need to see her driving him to obey it.

Tears lined her stunning amethyst eyes, glittering in the light of the fire that bathed her skin in golden hues.

The need to kiss her, to erase the time they had been apart and write a new history for them swept through him, so powerful he rocked forwards, compelled to take her lips with his.

His grip on the edges of the tub tightened and he held himself back, afraid of what would happen if he surrendered to the need rising inside him, cranking his body tight as it set his blood on fire.

He was different now.

He wasn't the male he had been four thousand years ago. He felt it as he gazed upon her lush curves, and his body responded, mind filling with thoughts of taking her and making her his all over again.

He was darkness now, and his desires had grown darker with him, felt debauched as he looked at her and imagined flipping her on her front, spreading her thighs and spearing her with his cock, taking her in a hard and fast coupling as he gripped her neck, one that would end with her crying out as she shattered.

Fuery shook his head at that thought, refusing to surrender to it, afraid he would taint her.

Hurt her.

Water lapped at his thighs and his rigid cock as she moved, pulling him back to her and robbing him of his breath as she placed her hands against his chest. She gazed up into his eyes, no trace of fear in them or her feelings, only acceptance and need that echoed his own, and pulled him under her spell, just as she had forty-two centuries ago when she had triggered the bond between them.

His gaze slid down to her mouth, and then beyond it to her unmarked neck.

Gods, he had wanted to bite her there.

He *wanted* to bite her there.

CHAPTER 20

Shaia felt no fear as Fuery stared at her neck, his pupils blowing wide to devour the purple that remained in his dark irises. She could feel the conflict in him, could see it mingling with the desire in his gaze, and deep in her heart she knew how difficult this was for him.

She knew the pain that beat inside him, the fear that gripped him whenever he was around her, and she had known it for a long time.

He wore the same look he had when she had gone to him in the garden at the grand ball, when he had believed himself unworthy of her.

That tore at her heart, and it always had.

She slipped her left hand up his chest, and he tensed as she gently curled it around the nape of his neck to lure him down to her.

"I shouldn't." He tried to pull back, but she tightened her grip and refused to let him go. His eyes darted between hers, confusion and pain dancing in them now. "I am not the male you deserve."

His arms tensed, muscles rippling with strength as he attempted to push himself out of the water.

She gripped him harder, using her own limited strength to show him that she wasn't going to let him push her away, and she was going to weather those attempts to create a crevasse between them that she could see forming in his eyes.

"All I care about is that it is you with me, Fuery," she whispered, and his name on her lips seemed to work black magic on him, had his grip relaxing and the fight fading from him. Her pulse pounded, but she pushed through her nerves, and voiced the words in her heart as she held his gaze. "It is the male that I love."

His dark eyes widened.

His shock rippled through her.

Swiftly followed by disbelief and blacker feelings, ones that seemed to rouse the darkness that lived within him.

"I still love you. It never faded... and it never will." She reached up and stroked her fingers across the sharp contours of his cheek, feathering them down to his jaw, and he leaned into her touch for a heartbeat before pulling away and growling.

"I've changed though."

She brought her hand back into contact with his face again, and skimmed her fingers along his jaw to his chin.

He shuddered when she swept her thumb across his lower lip, his eyes darkening with desire again, hunger that thrilled her.

"My love for you hasn't," she whispered and thumbed his lips, and that thrill became an intense shiver as they parted to reveal his fangs. "And I can see the male I fell in love with inside you."

He turned away, but she refused to let him run. She caught his other cheek, framing his face, and forced him to look at her again. She could feel his need, his desire, and it was as fierce as her own.

"Don't run from me, Fuery. I don't want that."

He blinked and his eyes were back on hers, his dark eyebrows drawing down above them. "What do you want?"

She opened her heart, her soul, baring them both to him and not holding anything back, because he needed to know she was speaking the truth. He needed to feel the love she spoke of through their bond so he would believe it was real.

"I want you to run *to* me." She applied a little pressure to his cheeks, just enough to keep him looking at her when she could sense the battle rising inside him again, the need to shield her from the darker side of himself, the part he was ashamed of and feared.

She didn't fear it. She didn't despise it. It made him the Fuery he was now, and that was still the Fuery she loved. He wasn't the only one who had changed in their years apart. He had grown darker, and she had grown stronger.

Strong enough to take what she wanted.

She held his gaze.

"I want you."

Hartt had been right about Fuery. He could change in an instant.

One moment, he was pulling away from her, unwilling to succumb to his need and his desires. The next, his mouth was fused with hers and his arms were beneath her as he lifted her from the water and plastered her to his chest, his grip so fierce she couldn't breathe as he kissed her.

She grasped his shoulders and loosed the moan that rolled up her throat as his tongue delved between her lips, demanding entrance that she all too willingly granted him. It was warm against hers, teased her in a way that maddened her and had her desire rising to steal control of her. She writhed against him, quickly losing herself in her need and the tiny flickers of pleasure that danced through her body as she kissed him, as she tasted him and breathed him in.

Her Fuery.

The only male she had ever loved, and would ever love.

The years without him had been cold. She felt that now as she burned for him, aflame from only his kiss and the thought of what was to come. He groaned as she rubbed against him, pressing her heels into the base of the bathtub. Her slick body slid along his, his hot rigid length scalding her belly as he lowered one hand and grabbed her backside in a bruising fierce grip to hold her against him. She quivered as he skimmed his hand up to her knee and pushed it aside, and pressed between them. His hand lowered to her backside again, fingertips digging into her flesh as he ground between her thighs, rubbing his length along her cleft.

She shuddered, a moan peeling from her lips as she felt him glide between her legs, the blunt head of his heavy shaft teasing her aching nub with each stroke.

"Fuery," she husked against his lips and he growled and seized them again, his kiss harder now, claiming her mouth as he drove between her thighs.

He held her tighter, kissed her harder still, and she trembled in his strong arms.

He was so different to the gentle male she had given herself to all those centuries ago, rougher and more wicked, darker as he bent her to his will, devouring her mouth and tasting her cries, thrusting hard between her thighs.

She knew it should unsettle her, but gods, it thrilled her. It was exciting. Freeing.

It rekindled the spark he had lit in her millennia ago and this time it blazed like an inferno, one that burned away all her reservations and unchained her.

This was worth fighting for.

She was done with being told what to do. She was done with being controlled by others.

Fuery had made her stronger than that, both in life and in his apparent death. He had set her free, but she had been living in a cage since he had been gone, and it was time that she changed that. She wasn't going to let tradition or her family dictate her life for her anymore.

She wanted Fuery. She had been given a second chance with him, and she was going to take it.

She was going to fight for it, and for Fuery, because he was everything she wanted.

All that she needed.

She slipped her hand around the back of his neck, tangled her fingers in his overlong hair, and held him to her as she delved her tongue into his mouth. He groaned and shuddered, gripped her tighter and rocked more fiercely against her as she stroked the tip of her tongue over the length of his fang.

His growl rumbled through her and sent a thrill chasing over her skin, the most erotic thing she had ever heard.

She went to stroke his fang again.

He abruptly pulled back and released her, dropping her into the water. She gasped as it swept over her, hit the sides of the tub and came back at her, hitting her in the face and getting in her mouth and her eyes. She rubbed at her face as she choked, wiping the water away, and looked up at Fuery.

He stared down at her, his arms tensed and trembling as he gripped the sides of the wooden tub, and his breathing ragged, causing his bare chest to heave. His fangs were long between his parted lips.

"Fuery?" She reached for him, and he jerked backwards. She withdrew her hand as the darkness in his eyes spread to devour the violet. "What is wrong?"

Didn't he want her?

She tried to shake that thought away, but it stuck, refusing to leave her head. It tormented her as he stared at her, only darkness in his eyes, no trace of the desire that had been in them just seconds ago. Did he no longer feel the same spark he had for her all those centuries ago? Did he no longer have the same fire in him that blazed in her?

When his eyes darkened further, she risked it and probed the connection they shared. It was stronger now that he had taken her blood and she could easily feel his pain.

"Tell me what is wrong, Fuery." She wanted to reach for him again, but remained still so she didn't startle him, aware that he needed time to process whatever he was feeling and pushing him would get her nowhere.

He would bolt.

His eyes darted between hers, the violet in them gaining ground now, pushing back against the black. His heart thundered in her ears. His desire trickled through their bond, mingled with the pain.

It was strong, ran as deep as her own, but he was fighting it for some reason.

Sharp cold ran through her.

She severed the connection between them, a reaction she couldn't stop from happening as fear of feeling the darkness inside him, coating her like an oily tide, rushed through her.

Fuery looked away from her.

"I can't," he rasped, his deep voice a broken whisper that had her heart breaking for him. "I don't trust myself with you."

Shaia wanted to press him, to tell him that he could trust himself, but she bit her tongue to silence herself, aware that saying such a thing would be selfish. She wanted the pleasure he had promised her with that kiss, craved that release they had been building towards together, but she wouldn't risk Fuery to have it. So as much as she wanted to feel his hands on her again, as much as she needed him to satisfy the hunger burning in her veins, she would do as he wanted.

"We can take things slowly." She managed a smile when his gaze slid back to her, hoping to show him that she meant those words, and she wanted it. "We have all the time in the world."

His black eyebrows furrowed and he sagged on his backside in the tub opposite her, all the tension draining from him. The darkness in his eyes receded again, and when she opened their connection a little she found it was gone and only fear remained.

Fear that he needed time to overcome.

She would help him do that, little by little. She would prove to him that he could trust himself with her and he wasn't going to hurt her. She would vanquish his fear for him, because she knew that fear stemmed from his heart, from his love for her.

He had always wanted to protect her.

"With you lay with me a while at least?" She didn't have to ask twice.

He stood, scooped her up into his arms, and stepped out of the tub with her, dripping water all over the thick cloth she had put down to protect the wooden floor. When she pointed to another thick cloth she had left folded beside it, he set her down on her feet and stooped to pick it up, keeping one hand clamped around her wrist, as if he feared she might escape.

Or disappear.

She ached for him again as she realised the darkness was toying with him.

It had pushed and gained ground, and now he wasn't sure whether she was real or not. She placed her hand on his and stroked her fingers over his warm damp skin, wanting to show him that she was here with him.

He glanced up at her, and the pain she could feel through their connection faded a little as relief lit his eyes, brightening the remaining violet in them.

He loosened his grip on her, but still refused to release her, even when he carefully started to dry her off from head to toe. It was torture. She had to bite back several moans whenever he innocently brushed her nipples with the towel. When he moved around behind her to rub the cloth across her backside, she bit down on her lower lip to stifle a groan, and barely supressed a shudder as his hip brushed hers and he moved closer.

She could feel his need, sensed it rising again inside him, as his eyes burned into her as he raked them down her back to her bottom. His panted breaths cut the silence, and her heart sped to match them as she waited to see what he would do.

He skimmed his hand across her bare backside as he rounded her, and she breathed faster, pulse accelerating and desire flooding her again as he came to stand in front of her, his heavy erection jutting proudly from its nest of dark curls.

She wanted to drop her hand and stroke that rigid length of velvet-sheathed-steel, ached to rub her thumb across the dark blunt tip and elicit a moan from him, but she held herself back.

She couldn't push him.

If she pushed him, and he ended up hurting her by accident, he would despise himself and she would never be able to live with herself.

Slowly.

As painful as it was, she had to take things slowly with him.

He looked down at his cock and then averted his gaze as he teleported a pair of black trousers to his legs, covering himself. He didn't need to be ashamed that he was hard for her. She needed him. It was her need as his mate, as his female, that had him primed for her, together with his desire for her, and that was beautiful.

She picked up her blue robe, slipped it on and covered herself, hoping it would help tame her wicked thoughts.

She took hold of his hand and led him towards the bed, and he hesitated when she knelt on the pale blue covers.

She looked back at him. "We will only lay together."

Something they had never done before. There had been times before they were mated that they had lazed beside each other on the hills near her home, basking in the sunlight as they talked, or beneath the shade of a tree near the river, but they had never laid together like this—in a bed, in an intimate fashion.

She released his hand and settled herself on the bed, resting with her head on the pillows, giving him time to make a decision. It had to be his choice. He needed to be in control now. She could feel it in him.

After a tense few minutes, he pressed his right knee into the mattress, twisted and settled beside her.

She was about to risk rolling to face him when he grabbed her around the waist, hauled her against his side and wrapped his arms around her.

Shaia settled her cheek on his bare chest and listened to his heart beating steadily against her ear.

Gods, it felt good.

It struck her that this was enough for her.

If this was all she could ever have from him, it would be enough.

It felt so good being in his arms that she didn't want him to leave, even when part of her knew that he would, because he was tense against her, and she could sense the battle he waged with himself, and that trickle of fear that ran through his blood.

She didn't want to sleep, but Fuery was so warm against her, his heartbeat a melodic and soothing beat that had her eyelids feeling heavier by the second. Tiredness swept over her, the past few weeks suddenly rolling up on her and stealing her strength, and she lost her fight against it and fell asleep in Fuery's arms for the first time.

Fearing it would also be the last time.

CHAPTER 21

Fuery stood beside the double bed in the musty room, his gaze locked on the female sleeping on top of the pale blue covers. Shaia. The last few hours felt like a dream, and for once it hadn't turned into a nightmare.

She loosed a soft sigh and rolled onto her side, her right hand coming to rest on the pillow where his head had been as he had held her. *Held* her. His chest still felt warm from where her head had rested against it, his heart on fire and soul blazing from her allowing him to be so close to her, trusting him not to hurt her.

Her blue silk robe slipped as she eased onto her back again, clearing her creamy right shoulder and barely clinging to the peaks of her breasts.

His blood burned for a different reason.

Heat spread through his limbs, pooling low in his belly, and he wanted to growl at the sight of her and the need that ran through him.

He growled quietly at himself instead, chastising himself as guilt swelled inside him, shame born of the wicked thoughts that swam around his head, coaxing him into kneeling on the bed, parting her thighs and waking her by delving his tongue between her soft folds. She would cry so sweetly as he pleasured her, and then again when he took hold of her wrists, pinned them above her head on the pillow, and speared her with his cock, sinking it deep and taking her hard.

Claiming her.

He forced himself to turn his back to her as the need to act out that fantasy grew so strong that he had to fight to stop himself from going through with it.

Gods, it was a battle he wasn't sure he would win.

He wanted her.

Not just the mate in him, but the male too.

When she had offered herself to him in the bathtub, he had wanted to make love with her, to pleasure her and satisfy her.

Fear had held him back.

Fear that had been crushing at the time, and choked him now as he tried to push away thoughts of mounting the bed and feeding his cock into her so he could feel her heat scalding him, clenching him tightly as he drove into her.

The fantasy in his head took the same turn it had when he had been in the tub with her.

It twisted into a terrifying vision of him killing her.

He shoved his fingers through his overlong black hair and gritted his teeth, his lips drawing back as he fought the urges running rampant through him.

He couldn't bear it.

He didn't want to hurt her, and he didn't feel strong enough to hold back the darker side of himself that pushed him to seek violence and pain in everything he did in order to satisfy it.

The thought of inflicting his darkness on Shaia sickened him.

As much as he wanted to stay with her, needed it with every fibre of his being, he had to leave and grow stronger before he could risk being around her again.

He needed to be strong enough to hold back the darkness.

Fuery looked back over his shoulder at her as she moved again, curling up on her side, her long black hair brushing across her cheek and spilling across the pillow beneath her. Her fine eyebrows furrowed for a moment before she settled back into a deep sleep.

It struck him that he had never really tried before. He had convinced himself that he had been fighting to hold back the darkness all his life, doing all he could to stand against it, but now he could see the truth.

Those fights had been half-hearted, and he had always let the darkness win. He had wanted the oblivion.

He had coaxed and nurtured it, letting it steal more control from him and allowing it to grow stronger.

Now he needed to fight it with all of his heart, and he feared he wasn't strong enough, and he never would be.

He stared at Shaia, feeling that shake him to the very depths of his soul, the same soul that ached to find that strength because finding it was the key to being with her—his one true love—his mate.

He needed to speak with Hartt.

Fuery pulled himself away from her, treading silently across the wooden floor, and eased the door open. He glanced back at her as he closed it behind him, silently promising he would be back.

He followed the winding steps down into the main part of the inn, and issued a glare at every male present, especially the owner. The large male swallowed hard, paling a little as he polished a glass for a customer.

"Anyone goes near her, they answer to me. Understand?" He growled and eyed all the males again, making sure they got the message.

They all quickly nodded.

A couple teleported away.

Good.

The less males near his female, the less likely he was to create a bloodbath in the inn. None of the males were warriors. It would be a massacre, and Shaia would hate him for it, and he would hate himself for it too, but gods, he wouldn't be able to stop himself.

Shaia was his.

What she had said to him in the bathtub came back to him, and he grimaced as he felt the truth of it.

He always had been possessive.

But possessive wasn't a strong enough word to convey the way he felt about her. He would slay the Devil himself for her.

He stalked across the span of cobbles between the inn and the guild, a tight feeling growing in his chest with each step further he went from her. It birthed a need when he entered the guild, one that drove him to return to her. He rubbed at his bare chest and ignored the looks the males in the reception room gave him as he stormed across it to the corridor that would take him to Hartt's office.

He had to focus hard to get his senses to move from Shaia to what was ahead of him, but eventually they shifted. He scoured the room beyond the dark wooden door at the end of the black hallway as he walked towards it, and relief poured through him to ease his tension away when he sensed only Hartt inside it.

He didn't bother to knock.

He pushed the door open, strode in as Hartt's violet gaze lifted to him from the papers strewn across his ebony desk and sat down without saying a word.

"You did not return after completing the mission. I presume everything went well?" The worry Hartt felt coloured his voice so Fuery couldn't miss it.

He nodded.

Hartt looked back down at his papers. "Is Shaia well?"

There was a smile in those words. A grin. Fuery scowled at his friend, hoping to make it clear that he wasn't in the mood for teasing. Not today.

Hartt's steady gaze drifted back to him again, piercing him with a demand to know the answer to his question, and Fuery realised for the first time that Hartt was becoming attached to Shaia.

Cared about her.

He bared his fangs at that as they punched long from his gums and the darkness rose within him, slithering upwards to swamp his heart.

"You know I'm only asking as a friend, Fuery," Hartt said in a soft, calm voice, one he often used to soothe him.

Fuery managed to rein in his anger enough that he could answer. "She is fine."

Hartt nodded towards his neck. "You have injuries."

He looked away from his friend. "She took care of them."

The elf male sighed. "And now you are struggling, unsure of yourself. Why?"

It turned out Fuery couldn't speak to Hartt about it after all. Just the thought of admitting his dark desires to his friend had his mind conjuring pictures of Hartt in those positions with Shaia, and it had the hunger to bloody his claws rising inside him.

He stared at the black wall beyond Hartt, struggling with that terrible need, aware that even glancing at his friend before he was back in control would lead to him attacking him.

When Hartt moved, he closed his eyes and lowered his head, buried his face in his hands and thought about why he had come to Hartt in the first place.

To talk.

"You are afraid of hurting her," Hartt whispered, as if he was reading his thoughts—his deepest fears.

Perhaps he was. Their blood bond tied them deeply, as deeply as the one he shared with Shaia. It would be easy for Hartt to sense his fear. He wasn't exactly being guarded with his feelings. He was too tired, spread too thin, his mind leading him down paths that only wore him down even more.

He nodded.

"I thought I had killed her once..." Fuery raised his head and pushed his hands over his hair. "What if I..."

He couldn't bring himself to say it.

Hartt sighed, his expression softening. "You will not. You would never hurt her."

He wanted to believe that.

His friend leaned back in his chair, rested his hands behind his head and kicked his feet up onto his desk.

"I always thought it was my bond with you that brought you back from the darkness whenever you lost yourself in it." Hartt's violet eyes lifted to the dark wooden ceiling, and then lowered back to him as he said, "I was wrong."

Fuery frowned at that.

"I have heard the things you talk about when you are lost, oblivious to the world around you, and I have long suspected that you are the one who pieces yourself back together. My link to you only gives you a chance to do that, as does Shaia's bond with you... but it is your endless love for Shaia that gives you the strength to come back, and her love for you." Hartt dropped his feet, sat up in his chair and rested his elbows on the desk between them as he leaned towards Fuery. "It's that light she kept burning inside you all these years... the light that will save you."

Fuery could only stare at him as he felt the gravity of that.

He reached for his bond to Shaia, warmth running through him as he felt the strength of it and realised that it had survived all the centuries, had endured the darkness within him, withstanding it.

A bond that tied them deeper than either of them had known.

He was sure of it now.

Shaia had kept it alive.

Her undying love for him was the only reason he had survived so long without losing himself completely and falling into the black abyss. She had never stopped loving him, she had told him that herself. All the centuries they had been apart, she had held on to that love, and she must have been subconsciously nurturing the weak thread that linked them, keeping it alive and giving a sliver of her light to him.

His chest and lungs tightened.

The sensation he'd had before returned, stronger this time. The reason he hadn't lost himself, had never given up even when he could have embraced death, and the reason he had always come back, was his endless love for her and awareness that the bond was still there between them, tying them together, and hope that one day he would return to her.

Just as he had promised.

That hope kindled in his chest, becoming a flame that burned in his heart, bright as the light she had awoken in him when she had opened their bond again.

Hope that he could tame the darkness.

Because everything he had ever wanted and thought lost forever was back in his life, and he wanted the future they had dreamed of together.

That hope faded a little as the darkness within him pushed, snaking inky tendrils through his limbs, reminding him that they would never have the future he wanted, because he was different now.

He wasn't worthy of her.

Not as he was now.

She seemed as bright and pure as she had been as a youth, and he was tainted by darkness. Gods, the irony wasn't lost on him. He finally felt unworthy of her. Truly unworthy. He hadn't felt it back then, lowborn and nothing more than a soldier, nothing of value to his name, not like her other suitors. When her family had called him unworthy, he had fought back against them, had kept his spirit strong and refused to see himself that way. He had looked at all he was doing to better himself, and he had seen he was worthy of her. He had listened to her words, and had believed himself worthy because she had chosen him.

He felt it now though, and it wasn't even his position as an assassin or the things he did as his work that made him feel unworthy at last.

It was the darkness.

Because she was so full of light, shining so brightly it blinded him.

He wasn't worthy of her. Not as he was now.

But he wouldn't give up, would never give in. Somehow, he would make himself worthy of her again.

No matter what it took.

No matter how long it took.

He knew where he needed to start.

He pushed out of the chair and nodded at Hartt, and the male's clipped nod in return told him everything. It warned him to be careful, and wished him good luck, and asked him to come back soon.

He would.

Without looking back, he exited the office and strode through the guild building, heading back out into the town. He crossed the road to the inn, ignored the owner again as his legs swiftly carried him through it and up the stairs, taking him to where his heart needed to be.

He couldn't leave without looking upon her one last time.

He needed to see her again, to brand her face on his mind and her scent on his soul, all to give him the strength to face the darkness.

He carefully eased her door open and slipped back into her room. She slept soundly still, curled up on her side where he had left her. He silently crossed the room to her and stared down at her, absorbing her beauty, together with the fact she was real. He hadn't killed her, and he wouldn't. He would make sure of that.

He would find a way to fix himself, so he could be with her without fear.

Fuery lifted his hand to his hair and unpinned the silver clasp that held the top half of it tied back. He lowered the delicate intricate band and stared at it, remembering everything about the day she had given it to him as he brushed his thumb over the swirls and patterns raised on the ring.

She had gifted him with it before he had left her that fateful day, a token of her love for him and a memento to remind him of her on his travels, but just like her, it shone too brightly for him to look at right now.

One day, he would be worthy of her again.

He was going to fight to make it happen.

Until then, until he felt worthy of her love, he didn't deserve to wear the clasp she had given him.

He set it down on the blue pillow beside her hand, and whispered, "Keep it safe for me. I will be back for it. I will be back for you."

He hoped.

He leaned over, drew down a deep breath of her sweet scent, and pressed a kiss to her forehead, and then to her lips. She stirred, kissing him back for a brief agonising moment that tore at his will to leave before she sank back to sleep.

Fuery straightened, tied the top section of his overlong blue-black hair back with a leather thong, and stared at her.

More than ever, he needed to know how Vail did it. He needed to know how he was coming back from the darkness. He hadn't believed it possible before, but he needed to believe it was possible now.

He turned away from Shaia, determination in his stride as he left the inn and the guild behind, his eyes fixed on the other end of the town and his destination.

A portal that would take him to the mortal world.

To his prince.

CHAPTER 22

The pretty thatched cottage looked just as Fuery remembered, always in a perpetual state of summer or possibly spring, with blood red roses blooming against the creamy stone walls of the one-and-a-half storey building and threatening to creep high enough to start clambering over the reeds that formed the roof. His gaze followed the line of the roof as it undulated in sweeping curves over each window on the upper floor. Smoke curled lazily from the chimney, drifting high into the clear blue sky as it turned towards evening.

He drew down a deep breath and waited for his nerves to dispel, using the sight of the cottage and the flowers that bloomed in a hundred colours in its walled garden to soothe him. Nature. Pure, beautiful, nature. It calmed him as it always did, even though she bared her fangs at him if he tried to connect with her. He still loved her, still felt the deep draw to her that all elves did.

Even the tainted.

Those she despised.

Gods, he missed the connection to nature, one he now felt he had squandered, had never really appreciated until it had been taken from him by the darkness.

How many elves treated her the same way as he had, thinking that connection to her would always be there within them when they needed it to drive back the sliver of darkness all of his kind held inside their hearts?

How many elves now felt the same way as he did, as if he had been a fool, had treated nature with little respect and none of the reverence she deserved, and now she was gone, he would do anything to have her back in his life?

His black heart said the elf that lived in this magical cottage in the mortal world, surrounded by nature and held deep in her embrace knew his pain, suffered as he did.

No. Not as he did.

Vail still possessed a strong bond with nature.

One that had a vile snake hissing in Fuery's heart, and a need to turn on his heel and leave blasting through him.

He ignored them and marched forwards along the narrow country lane, soaking in the birdsong and the deep quiet of this remote part of England, his eyes roaming the distant green hills, and the verdant forests, and then drifting back to the colourful garden of the cottage.

He could see why his prince lived here.

Felt sure that if he was to spend only a few days here that it would do him some good, would drive back the darkness and perhaps even help him form the fragile beginnings of a new bond with nature. He could make it work. He had felt the benefit of visiting this place had been waning, but perhaps he had been drawing away from it, refusing to allow it to flow into him in order to stop hope from building inside him, hope that had been liable to destroy him when the darkness crushed it.

But now Shaia was in his life again, and with her she had brought a flicker of light, and he wanted to get better. For her. So he could be with her. He wanted to embrace that light and use it to drive out the darkness. He wanted to forge a new connection with nature and embrace her again, was no longer afraid to hope.

He reached the sun-bleached arched wooden gate that intersected the low sandstone wall and stopped with his hand on it. Magic hummed in the air, penetrated his skin and sank deep into his bones. Magic laced with nature.

It was that magic that had the flowers blooming out of season, and the trees to the left and right of the cottage ripe with fruit. He stilled and absorbed that magic as he watched bees flit from flower to flower, buzzing gently as they raced to gather nectar before the sun set. A bird dipped and bobbed in the air as it flew past, another chasing it through the hollyhocks and the poppies, disturbing the bees as they ambled around the lavender. The second bird twittered and chirped, and Fuery soaked it all in, sighed as it eased his nerves and steadied his racing heart.

He was welcome here.

He could feel it in his bones, deep in his troubled soul.

In this place, and only this place, nature opened her arms to him.

He pressed down on the rusted metal lever and lifted the latch on the gate, and eased it open. It creaked, and the air seemed to still, everything suddenly stopping.

The air shimmered in front of him.

A male appeared there, tight armour covering him from head to toe, the black scales flowing over his muscles and rising up to form a helmet that flared back into spikes like a crown and dipped to a point above his nose.

His violet eyes were bright, flashing with a need for violence that dulled as the male recognised him and he eased back onto his heels, the tension draining from his shoulders.

"Fuery," Prince Vail whispered, a note of warmth in his voice that spoke to Fuery and told him that the male was pleased to see him.

His helmet disappeared, the scales filtering back down into the rest of his armour, clearing his wild blue-black hair and revealing his handsome face.

The door of the cottage burst open and Rosalind came bounding out, her knee-length black dress flapping around her thighs and her wavy ash blonde hair bouncing with each step. When she spotted him, she ground to a halt, bent over and pressed her hands to her knees, breathing hard.

She glanced up at him, her blue eyes sparkling.

"I thought you were an intruder." She turned her gaze from him to her mate and scowled. "You bloody scared the shit out of me disappearing like that."

Fuery looked between them, and his eyes slowly widened as he noticed that Rosalind's dress was on backwards. Heat bloomed on his cheeks, and his mind swiftly filled with images of Shaia standing before him, naked and bared to him, desire flashing in her eyes and need flaring in his blood. Her need.

"I can come back," he muttered, and went to turn away, shame sweeping through him as he pushed the fantasy of Shaia away and was faced with a very rosy-cheeked Rosalind and caught Vail staring at her with hunger in his eyes, a need to continue what they had started before he had disturbed them.

"Not at all." Rosalind looked down at herself, a flash of horror crossing her face as she realised her dress was on the wrong way around.

She fixed it with a wave of her hand, and Vail scowled for a different reason as the hum of magic in the air grew stronger. She cast a watchful glance at her mate. He scrubbed a hand over his tousled hair, huffed and began pacing, his tension flowing through the air the magic tainted.

When his pacing grew more intense, she went to him, and stopped him by slipping her hand into his. He looked down at them, his eyes glassy, distant, and then up at her face.

She smiled softly. "We have a guest."

He glanced Fuery's way, and his violet eyes widened, and then he blinked and they cleared, growing sharp again. "Sorry. The magic…"

Fuery shook his head, telling his prince not to apologise. He understood, and knew he would probably react the same way, the darkness inside him pushing, if he had suffered the things Vail had.

If he had known all those centuries ago, when Vail had attacked his own men outside the town of Valestrum, the reason behind it all, he would have helped him. He should have known. He should have helped him. He had been Vail's second in command, but he had been unaware of the male's pain, had been blind and hadn't seen the witch they had found and taken care of hadn't been Vail's fated one, but an imposter, a dark witch bent on casting a spell on him in order to seize his kingdom and set herself up as queen of the elves.

Gods, he couldn't imagine, didn't want to imagine, the horrible things Vail had endured as her slave.

Fuery killed because it was his job, and he had chosen it.

Vail had killed because Kordula had commanded him to do it, using him against his will. She had forced him to fight his own beloved brother, and he had been under her spell for four thousand years.

It was little wonder Vail despised magic.

But he was growing used to it, learning to control his darkness around it.

In the short time Fuery had been visiting Vail, the male had made great progress, could now endure Rosalind using basic spells in his presence without losing himself to his darker urges.

"Would you like tea?" Rosalind offered him a kind smile as she laced her fingers with Vail's, and Fuery shook his head. "Some fruit juice then?"

He couldn't remember the last time he had eaten, so he nodded, grateful for her kindness.

"I'll bring it out to you." She turned away, but Vail kept hold of her hand, stopping her.

She looked back at her mate, her blue eyes soft with affection and understanding, and returned to him. Fuery tried to look away, but he couldn't as she lifted her free hand and cupped Vail's cheek. The male leaned into it, his eyes closing, and eyebrows dipping low above the elegant slope of his nose.

The petite witch tiptoed, and Vail seemed to know what she wanted because he dropped his head for her. She brushed a kiss across his lips and whispered something, voice so low even Fuery's heightened hearing couldn't pick it up, and then rocked back onto her heels. She smiled Fuery's way again, and then squeezed Vail's hand.

Vail released her this time, and she stepped away from him. His violet gaze tracked her as she walked back towards the house, and lingered on the door as she disappeared from view, and Fuery could sense his desire to follow her and take her up on whatever promise she had whispered to him.

He turned towards Fuery instead and nodded towards the winding golden gravel path to Fuery's right, the one that would take him to the back of the house where they always passed his visits.

Vail led the way, his armour disappearing as he walked, replaced with black leather trousers, heavy boots and a thick dark violet jumper that looked out of place on him.

When Fuery continued to stare at him as he followed him towards the rear of the cottage, Vail looked over his shoulder and shrugged.

"It is Rosalind's idea. She believes it makes me look more… approachable."

Fuery could see that, but the mortal clothing still didn't suit his prince. It was strange seeing him in anything other than formal clothing of tunic, tight trousers and riding boots, or his armour.

He looked down at his own armour, and focused on his body and his link to everything he owned. He called a pair of black trousers, and his boots, but couldn't bring himself to call his tunic. Instead, he materialised a dark shirt that Hartt had given him, and let the tails hang loose over his trousers.

Vail ducked beneath the washing line that spanned the gap between two apple trees in the huge rear garden of the cottage, and continued deeper into the orchard, following the grass as it began to sweep down towards the valley below them.

Fuery stilled and looked down at his feet, at the very spot he had appeared before Vail while he had been lost to the darkness. His memories of that day were still fragmented, patched together by things Hartt had told him that had been relayed to him by Vail and Rosalind when his friend had finally found him.

"Do you still suffer the blackouts?" he whispered to his feet.

Vail's booted ones appeared in view. "Yes… but they are rare now. As I learn to control the darkness again, I learn to sense them coming and I can prevent them… sometimes."

That gave Fuery hope.

"I hate them." Admitting that lifted an invisible weight from his shoulders—from his chest.

He swallowed hard, gathered his courage, and lifted his eyes to meet Vail's violet ones, and an ache started in his heart, born of a desire to have eyes like that again. When was the last time he had looked in the mirror and seen more violet than black in his irises? Shaia had spoken of his eyes, had been shocked by the sight of them, and he wanted them to look as she remembered, wanted the violet back and those flecks of lilac she had mentioned.

"Do you think I... I... could learn too?" His eyes leaped between Vail's as he waited desperately for the male to answer him.

His prince sighed, clapped a hand down on his right shoulder, and squeezed it, no trace of a lie in his eyes as he spoke. "Of course."

He released the breath he hadn't realised he was holding and followed Vail as the male turned away and strode into the orchard. The trees were heavy with fruit but also blossoms, the leaves rustling as a gentle breeze blew through them, stirring the scent of their blooms. He breathed deep of it, drew it down into him together with the scent of the grass he crushed beneath his boots, and the earth beyond it, and the sunshine that bathed his skin.

Vail seated himself on the rickety sun-bleached wooden bench beneath one of the trees, his amethyst gaze fixed on the valley and his noble profile to Fuery. When he patted the spot beside him, Fuery took it. He gathered his courage again, and leaned back against the broad trunk of the single oak tree in the garden, and waited.

Waited.

But nature didn't bare her fangs at him.

The expected pain of being rejected by her didn't come.

He felt only peace.

As if she reached for him, wrapping him in her gentle embrace and welcoming him home.

Because of the light Shaia had awoken in him?

"You are different today." Vail's deep voice rolled over him just as he closed his eyes and he opened them again and looked to his right, to his prince. The male glanced at him and then set his eyes on the distance again. "Not in a bad way. In a good way. You feel..."

"Lighter?" Fuery offered, because it was the only word he could find to describe how he had felt since Shaia had come back into his life.

Vail nodded. "The last time I saw you, you were unwell... sick in mind and body... but now you seem a little better. What happened?"

Fuery sighed and closed his eyes, sank deeper into nature's tentative embrace, well aware it was in part thanks to the male next to him and his unbreakable connection to her. It bled over into him when he was this close to Vail, as if everything the male came into contact with, or even just remained near for a period of time, was touched by her grace too.

"Shaia," he whispered, and sensed Vail's gaze come to land on him. He sought the words, struggling to find them as he mulled over everything and found he wasn't sure where to begin. Hartt had told him once when he had been fighting for the words that it was easier to begin at the start. So he did. "She is my fated one. We mated before…"

Vail tensed and said what he couldn't. "Valestrum."

Fuery nodded and opened his eyes, checking his prince's ones for any speck of black, afraid he had stirred the darkness in him with his careless words.

Vail managed a smile, although it was tight and he struggled to hold it. "I remember I sensed a difference in you back then too… you felt happier… lighter. I did not know where the change had come from, but it must have been from your mating. I know this because mating with Little Wild Rose changed me too."

Little Wild Rose was Vail's term of endearment for Rosalind, one that spoke of his deep love for her.

Fuery wanted to know more about it, about how Rosalind had changed Vail, but he feared it at the same time. He wanted to nurture the hope Shaia had brought back to life inside him, believing it possible to reverse the damage he had done to himself, but if he discovered that it wasn't, that hope might crush him when it died.

He stared at Vail, studying him and forcing himself to see the truth—Vail was even less darker now than the last time they had met like this.

If it was his bond with Rosalind taking away that darkness and allowing light back in, then there might be hope for him too.

Fuery saw the truth in that hope when Rosalind rounded the tree, a silver tray gripped in front of her, two tall glasses of golden juice on it. She smiled at her mate, and Vail's eyes brightened, the light in him shining through them for Fuery to witness, and he could feel the darkness receding in him too, driven out by his love for the witch.

Vail rose and took the tray from Rosalind, and she thanked him with another smile. He pressed his side close to hers, lowered his head and nuzzled her fair hair before pressing a soft kiss to her brow, one she leaned into as her eyes slipped shut.

Her cheeks grew rosy again as she opened her eyes and looked at Fuery, and she cleared her throat.

Vail huffed and stepped back. "You do not need to be so embarrassed around Fuery, Little Wild Rose… he too has a mate."

Her blue eyes widened. "You do?"

He nodded. "I thought I had killed her, but she is alive."

Rosalind looked as if she wanted to probe into that, but merely smiled and glanced at her mate. "If you need anything else, you know where to find me."

Vail nodded, balanced the tray on one hand and swept his other arm around her waist, hauling her up to him so quickly that she gasped, her hands flying to press against his chest. He swallowed the gasp in a brief, fierce kiss that had her blushing as he released her and had Fuery imagining Shaia in his arms like that, her lips on his and her hands against his chest.

The witch scurried away, Vail's eyes tracking her, never leaving her as they darkened with need. They cleared when the door to the house closed in the distance, and he sighed, set the tray down on the bench where he had been sitting, and patted the grass.

Evidently pleased with what he found, he sat on the ground and lifted one of the glasses from the tray.

He sipped it, grimaced and shuddered. "Little Wild Rose thinks it is funny to slip grapefruit juice into her smoothies. She does it to tease me."

Fuery eyed the concoction he had been in the middle of reaching for, his hand frozen near the glass on the silver tray. "Is it dangerous?"

He wasn't familiar with grapefruits. They sounded harmless enough.

Vail pulled a face.

"Only if you drink half a carton without taking a breath." His prince shrugged stiffly when Fuery looked from the glass to him. "I was thirsty and did not read the label. I was not aware it was a sharp citrus fruit. Rosalind happened upon me when I was choking on it."

His mate had a strange sense of humour.

"Now she slips it into my drinks just to watch me react to the sourness."

Fuery cautiously lifted the glass to his lips and sniffed. Vail was right, and there was a sharp bitter note hidden among the sweeter ones. He was familiar with some of them. Mango. Pineapple. Banana. Vail's mate certainly liked the more exotic and sunny fruits.

He sipped it.

The sweetness was pleasant, and he couldn't see what Vail had a problem with.

And then his mouth dried out and his eyes watered, his right one developing a vicious tic as a thousand tiny needles stabbed his senses.

Dear gods.

He set the drink back down and glared at it.

Vail sighed. "It will pass. I believe she does something with a spell to make the first sip hit as if you had swallowed an entire sour grapefruit."

As if to prove his point, his prince sipped the drink again, and this time he didn't grimace at all. He even smiled.

Which Fuery found amazing. Not because the drink was no longer toxic, but because Vail had mentioned Rosalind using a spell—magic—on the concoction and he was still willing to drink it, and there was no sign of the darkness pushing inside him.

During his second visit, Vail had explained that being around magic had an adverse effect on him, driving him into the waiting arms of darkness, and he found it hard to control his blacker urges around Rosalind when she was using it.

Now, barely weeks later, he could tolerate small spells and even trusted her to place them on his drinks and still consumed them.

What magic was she working on Vail?

He must have asked it aloud, because Vail looked up at him.

"She calls it exposure therapy." Vail swirled the golden liquid around in his glass, his eyes on it now. "She creates a safe environment, one where I know I am in no danger, and will use a small spell, just enough magic to make me feel it."

It sounded fascinating.

Vail set his glass down, leaned back and splayed his hands out on the grass behind him, propping himself up. "Each time she will make the magic a stronger spell, allowing me to grow used to the feel of it, and to overcome my fear that I will be the target of the spell."

That sounded dangerous.

"But what if you react?" Fuery took another sip of his drink, waited for the sourness to hit him, and was pleasantly surprised when it didn't.

Vail tipped his head back and stared up at the sky as it began to change colour, becoming threaded with gold and pink. "I am in control at all times. If I feel the darkness rising, if it becomes too much and I remember things, I tell her to stop and we stop."

His prince's darkening eyes and the tension that radiated from him said that sometimes they weren't quick enough to stop the memories from seizing him together with the darkness. Sometimes, the darkness won.

Would such a thing work for him?

What was it he feared?

He stared at the distance, watching the trees sway and a deer cross a meadow as he searched his feelings while thinking about Shaia.

"I fear killing her," he whispered and felt Vail look at him. "How do you overcome that?"

He lowered his gaze to meet Vail's, needing to find an answer in them.

Vail's expression turned sympathetic, his eyes softening as his lips twitched into a slight smile. "I have the same fear. I hurt Rosalind once... more than once... but she is strong, both of body and of heart, and she forgave me... and gave me as good as she got."

"Shaia is strong." Fuery felt that in his heart, knew that if he were to lose himself, she would be able to defend herself, might even be able to defeat him. It didn't stop him from fearing the worst though. "But I do not want to hurt her... I do not want her to see me like that."

Vail sighed. "I did not either. I expected Little Wild Rose to turn her back on me when she saw the darkness in me... my other side. She surprised me by embracing it instead, by embracing me... by loving all of me."

Shaia's words came back to Fuery, echoing in his head and in his heart, her voice in his mind telling him that he might have changed, but her love for him hadn't, and she still loved him, because he was still the same male inside.

He had felt the truth in her words when he had been holding her in his arms, watching her sleep, trusting him to protect her and not hurt her. He hadn't hurt her. The thought hadn't even crossed his mind, and he hadn't feared it happening either.

What if he could use the same sort of therapy as Vail was undergoing?

But how?

How did he overcome the fear of killing her?

Vail feared magic because it made him feel he was about to be controlled, forced to do things against his will, and the darkness within him responded in order to protect him.

Being exposed to magic allowed Vail to overcome that fear, seeing that he wasn't going to be controlled whenever he felt it around him.

Fuery feared the darkness consuming him and waking to find he had hurt Shaia. Killed her.

He wasn't sure there was a therapy that could fix that, not without placing her in grave danger, exposing her to his darkest side. He wanted to overcome the fear, but he couldn't risk her, would die if he came around to find he had killed her. He wanted to be with her, but part of him felt it would be better for her if he never saw her again.

It would be hell for him though.

Living his life, aware that she was out there, would destroy him.

Vail's hand came to rest on his knee, drawing him back to the world, and he looked down at it and then up into the male's eyes.

"Sit a while with me?" Vail gestured to the grass, and Fuery did as he bid, easing down onto it.

The moment he placed his hand down to prop himself up, the blades of the grass tickling his fingers, calm swept through him, easing his fears and scattering the black clouds in his heart and his mind.

"Better?" Vail said, and Fuery nodded. "Do you see how the light can chase back the darkness?"

It struck him that he had been losing himself, sinking into the dark abyss, and just touching nature had been enough to shatter the hold the darkness had been gaining on him.

"Shaia woke it in me," he murmured and brushed his fingers over the long blades of grass, feeling their coolness on his skin as warmth in his heart as he savoured the connection to nature that had been denied him for so many years he had lost count. "I thought I would never feel this again."

The part of him that wanted to destroy all hope in an effort to protect himself whispered that it was only Vail's strong connection to nature that was allowing him to feel her now without her baring her fangs at him.

Vail seemed to read his mind. "It is not me. There is light inside you, Fuery. Light born of love. Endless. Unbreakable. The darkness can try, no doubt despises it and wants it gone, but it will not smother it."

The darkness was trying to do just that. Before Shaia had awoken the light inside him, the darkness had come and gone, leaving him free of it from time to time, brief moments of respite from its torment.

Now, it was a constant thing. He could feel it lurking in the background, always there, as if it refused to leave him now there was light in him again.

Because it feared losing its hold on him.

That hit him like a thunderbolt.

He feared the darkness, but the darkness feared the light. It feared Shaia and her love for him, and the light that grew a little brighter inside him whenever he was with her. Vail had said he was different now, and he felt that deep in his soul. Since Shaia had walked back into his life, softer feelings had been trickling back into his heart, ones he hadn't experienced since the darkness had taken hold of him. Ones that tempered the violence and his black hunger to inflict pain, and experience it, and to shed blood and revel in it.

Was it possible that simply being around Shaia would be enough to help him ease the grip the darkness had on him?

When he looked to Vail, that question balanced on his lips, he found the male staring at the cottage with darkness in his eyes. Black spots coloured his irises as his lips peeled back off his fangs and his pointed ears flared against his wild short blue-black hair.

Fuery focused and stilled as he sensed the magic, but it didn't feel like Rosalind's.

It felt darker.

Vail shot to his feet and his armour swept over him as his clothing disappeared, the tiny black scales covering him from toe to neck, and forming sharp serrated claws over his fingers.

The magic humming in the air disappeared, together with the second heartbeat Fuery had just locked on to in the house.

His ears twitched as a door opened, and he sensed Rosalind approaching.

The darkness in Vail's eyes only grew as he narrowed them on her.

She stopped just short of him, huffed and planted her hands on her hips. "He knows you hate him, you know?"

"Who knows?" Fuery looked from Vail to Rosalind.

She sighed, let her hands slip from her waist and her shoulders slumped. "An old friend... Atticus Darcy. He's a witch. Vail made it very clear the first time he visited that he wasn't welcome."

"The male is a damned lothario." Vail flexed his claws and scowled at the cottage, as if the male was still there. "He hardly has the appearance of a witch. Am I to sit idly by while he seduces you out of my grasp?"

Rosalind's eyebrows rose. "Lothario? Where did you learn that word?"

"The television." A flicker of unease crossed Vail's face. "It is the correct usage of the term, is it not? He strikes me as a male determined to seduce females."

"Well... yes... that is the right definition... and I don't want to know what sort of TV you've been watching to learn it... but... hang on." Her eyes narrowed on Vail. "What do you mean he doesn't have the appearance of a witch?"

Vail looked away from her now, fascinated by his feet. "He is too handsome."

She huffed, and bit out, "So witches are meant to be ugly?"

His eyes shot up to meet hers and he took a step towards her, his right hand lifting to reach for her as his eyebrows furrowed. "No... I... you are beautiful... and you know that is not what I meant, and it is not my fault I do not like the male. It is his fault. He looked at you."

She frowned at him, her lips settling in a mulish line. "He has eyes... that tends to happen when people have eyes!"

"Not like that. He *looked* at you." Vail ran a pointed and lustful glance up and down her, as if to illustrate the way the witch had looked at Rosalind.

She turned her gaze towards Fuery, clearly seeking his support.

He held his hands up. "I would have killed him if he had looked at my mate like that."

Her eyes brightened and she leaped on the change of subject like a fiend possessed. "You thought you had killed her?"

He nodded, weathered Vail's growl of displeasure as the male glared at him for allowing his mate to divert the course of their conversation, and said, "I think the darkness muddled things. Even when she came to the guild to find me, I thought her a ghost, an apparition sent to torture me with my sins. Sometimes, I still believe I have killed her."

Vail slumped back onto the grass, crossed his legs and grumbled, "It happens."

"She thought I was dead too." Fuery picked at the grass, idly plucking a few stems, and wove them together as he talked. "When I became tainted—"

He cut himself off as Vail tensed.

Rosalind was swift to sit beside her mate, her hands gliding over his stiff shoulders, massaging them as she whispered sweet things to him. The darkness in the male's eyes slowly receded, but the hurt lingered, pain that Fuery had caused with his careless words.

"I am sorry," Vail whispered. "It is my fault."

Fuery shook his head. "The darkness was always there in me. We were trained to use it, and I allowed it to take hold of me like that."

He leaned towards Vail, placed his hand on the male's leather-clad knee, and waited for him to look at him before continuing.

"I hold nothing against you, my prince. You did what you had to do in order to save the lives of everyone else in the kingdom, including my Shaia."

"Pretty name," Rosalind murmured softly as she rubbed at her mate's shoulders, kneading the tension away. "I bet she's a looker."

Vail tilted his head towards her, his amethyst eyes clearing as they sought her. "No one is as beautiful as you."

She pushed his shoulder, jerking him forwards, and grinned. "Charmer."

Fuery wanted to say that Shaia was even more beautiful than Rosalind, but he liked being alive now that she was back in his life and was sure Vail would kill him if he dared to voice that opinion.

Rosalind settled beside her mate, her left side leaning into him as she pulled her knees up to her chest. Vail slipped his arm around her and pulled her closer still, his fingertips pressing into her arm as he clutched her. Blotches of black still marred his eyes, a sign that he was still thinking about the male Rosalind had been meeting with at the cottage.

Fuery made a mental note to look into Atticus Darcy and see about eliminating him.

"Hartt believes my bond with Shaia might have been holding back the darkness all this time, stopping it from taking me completely and bringing me back." He inspected the braid of grass, plucked a few more stems, and began weaving them into the others to extend its length.

"It is possible," Vail said, a thoughtful edge to his eyes as he frowned. "My bond with Rosalind does much the same. Even when she is away from me, I am affected by it."

Fuery sighed and lowered the braided grass into his lap as he thought about Shaia, and the hope in his heart threatened to shatter. "There is blood on my hands though. I am not the male I once was, and though she says she still loves me, I know I am changed. I'm no longer noble or good, and I'm not sure she will be able to say she loves me if she witnessed the things I did... the person I become. How can she love a monster?"

The heavy silence that descended on the orchard pressed down on him.

Rosalind broke it before the weight of it became too much.

"If Shaia loves you... truly loves you... then she loves all of you. The things you have done will not stand in the way of that love. She will understand and she will still want to be with you." The witch brushed dirt off her knee and fixed him with a soft look, one filled with warmth and overflowing with understanding. "You say she came to you at the guild?"

He nodded.

She smiled. "Then she knew you are an assassin, Fuery. She knew the things you did and yet she still came to you... she still wants to be with you."

He had never thought of it like that.

Hartt had told him that she had travelled the free realm looking for him, had visited several guilds in the course of her search, and she must have learned of his reputation in that time, and yet she had still come to find him.

She had stayed when she had.

Even when Hartt had turned her away, she had refused to leave, had remained close to the guild.

For his sake.

Because she wanted to be with him.

"If anything," Rosalind said, pulling him back to her, "she will want to be with you more, because she will want to help you, as I have helped this heavy-handed somewhat-grumpy and hellaciously-jealous man beside me."

Vail's eyebrows knit together as she spoke about him and then his expression softened as he smiled and corrected her. "As you *continue* to help me."

Fuery reached for the connection between him and Shaia, needing to feel her, growing aware of the vast distance between them as he watched Vail and Rosalind, and the witch's words sank in. The link was weak, but he could feel her, and warmth spread through him, feeding the hope in his heart.

Hope that whispered that Rosalind was right.

Shaia had come to him knowing of his past, knowing what he was, and she had remained. She had taken care of him when he had come to her, hadn't pushed him away or looked at him with disgust in her eyes. She had embraced him.

She had still wanted him.

Even when he had been thinking dark things, wicked things.

Things he had thought would horrify his delicate female.

The desire he had sensed in her had only grown stronger. She had responded to him so beautifully, but he had failed to see it at the time, had been convinced she wouldn't want him if he was unable to control his passion for her and became rough with her.

Gods, he had been so blinded by fear that when he had been kissing her, gripping her so fiercely, drowning in the urge to take her in a frenzied outpouring of his need, he had mistaken her excitement for his own. She hadn't been shocked or horrified by him using his strength on her, trying to bend her to his will and dominate her.

She had been thrilled.

He needed to return to her, needed to see if she was still willing to embrace him like that, accepting all of him.

Loving all of him.

Because he was sure being with her in that way, both of them made vulnerable and trusting each other, was the key to overcoming his fear of hurting her.

The link between them flared.

Fear swamped it.

Not his.

He shot to his feet and black stilted smoke stuttered over his body as the desperate urge to teleport rushed through him.

"Shaia."

CHAPTER 23

Shaia paced the banks of the river, the soil soft beneath her boots and the gentle sound of running water soothing her. Her heart thumped at a fast pace against her ribs, refusing to settle. She gazed at her footprints as they merged together, marking the passing of time and revealing how long she had been waiting. She clenched and unfurled her fingers, shook them in an effort to expel her nerves, and turned, walking back the other way.

She lifted her head, glancing at the water that flowed around the bend in the stream and glittered in the light from the portal. It wetted the rocks on the other side, where a cliff rose high to shelter this small part of the elf kingdom.

Was he not coming?

He was coming. She was sure of it. He hadn't missed one of their meetings yet. She had time and could wait for him. Her family thought she was visiting one of her friends and didn't expect her back for hours yet.

Perhaps she had the wrong place?

She shook her head at that. She had followed his instructions to the letter, and this place, with the cliff on one side and a thick forest on the other, matched his description of the one where he had asked her to meet him this time.

Maybe he had been detained.

"Sorry I am late."

Shaia gasped and turned, her heart lodging in her throat and trembling there. A warm, teasing smile tugged at his firm lips and sparkled in his amethyst eyes, causing the flecks of lilac in them to brighten.

"Lost in thoughts of me?" he husked, a wicked and tempting note in his voice that had her quivering and caused heat to ignite inside her.

It spread as she looked him over, taking in his crisp black tunic and matching trousers, and his perfectly polished riding boots. The uniform hugged his lithe figure, leaving little to her imagination.

Her imagination still did a very fine job of picturing him as he had been that day years ago by the stream when he had come to her shirtless and fresh from sparring.

His eyes darkened, his pupils devouring the violet as he stared at her, and she stretched with her senses, pinning them on him. Desire. She could feel it beating inside him just as it beat inside her, pounding in her veins, filling her mind with images of them entwined in an intimate fashion.

Her body tingled, the heat pooling lower, at the apex of her thighs, as she recalled the way his hand had felt against her flesh, how he had given her pleasure that had left her shaking, her strength stripped from her.

"Shaia," he croaked and a pleading look flitted across his handsome sculpted face as his black eyebrows pinched. "You're killing me."

She tamped down her wicked thoughts, brought her body back under control and breathed through it to expel her need, not wanting to torment him when they had made a promise to wait until he was in a position to speak with her parents before they did anything intimate again.

It was sheer torture.

He had awoken something in her and she couldn't put it back to sleep. Whenever she was in his presence, her body came alive, need spiralling through her that robbed her of her breath and had her trembling for him, aching to have his hands on her again.

A pained growl left his lips, his face twisting in agony, and he paced away from her. He stopped a few metres away, his back to her, and remained there for long minutes that felt like hours as he wrestled with himself and she fought her desire, struggling to bring it back under control so she could be with him.

She didn't want him to leave.

He had done so once, the need to touch her becoming too much for him.

When he finally turned back to face her, he was calm again, no trace of desire in his eyes. She held hers back, reminding herself that it was best they waited, even if waiting was killing her.

He went to a large smooth flat rock that was half on the bank and half in the river, stripped off his boots, rolled up his trousers, and sat on it with his feet in the water. He stared down at them, watching the clear water rushing over them, and then looked over his shoulder at her and held his hand out to her.

She went to him, peered at his feet and up at the sky, and made a decision. It wasn't ladylike of her, and her family would be horrified if they saw her, but she didn't care. It was hot today, the air humid, and though she had chosen her lightest summer dress, a pale lilac one that fitted well enough that she could forgo a corset, she needed to cool down.

She unlaced her boots, placed them beside his on the dirt, and then stepped onto the rock. It was warm beneath her soles, but cooled as she neared the river and Fuery.

He looked up at her and offered his hand. She slipped hers into it and allowed him to help her as she neared the edge of the rock and sat down, taking care not to slip on the damp stone. When she was settled, he released her, and she sighed as she hitched her dress up a little and sank her feet into the water.

"Gods," she whispered as she instantly cooled and flames licked at her cheeks as her eyes widened and leaped to Fuery.

He didn't seem to care that she had cursed, or that it was very unladylike of her. His eyes remained locked on her hands. Not her hands. He was staring at her legs.

"It'll break soon," he muttered, his voice distant, as if he wasn't quite with her. "It's almost harvest time."

"Harvest time?" She frowned at that. There were a lot of different harvests, so which one was he speaking of? Which one did he know about, and intimately by the way he suddenly blinked and looked at her, a flicker of shock in his eyes and something else.

Embarrassment.

He had no reason to be ashamed around her.

She didn't care about his lineage.

She did care about learning more about him though, and this seemed like the perfect opportunity. He hadn't told her of his family, had kept so much to himself, and now she could see it was because he thought she would react like her mother and be horrified by whatever upbringing he'd had.

"Are your family farmers?" She meant that as a gentle prompt, one designed to ease him into talking to her about them, but he clammed up and turned his cheek to her. While she enjoyed taking in his noble profile, she much preferred him talking to her. "Millers? The millers in my village are one of the nicest families I know. Their son recently joined the legions."

"Farmers," he muttered beneath his breath and glanced at her out of the corner of his eye.

Gauging her reaction?

She smiled at him and smoothed the layers of her dress as she arranged them so they wouldn't fall into the water and she no longer needed to hold them. "So... at this time of year... they would be farming... um... some sort of grain?"

He nodded and relaxed a notch. "They farm and mill wheat and barley that we sell to the demons for their brews and bread. Our land is close to the border with the First Realm. It is a beautiful place, a quiet place, but I did not want to live my life that way. I wanted something different for myself."

Adventure. It was there in his eyes as they sparkled at her, a trickle of excitement running through their tentative connection.

"So you enlisted in the army." She looked from him to the sky, and wondered what adventure was out there for her.

"My family always spoke of me learning how to farm, how I would join their business and become like them... because that was what my father had done, and his father before him." He sighed and lay back on the flat rock.

Shaia looked down at him as he folded his arms beneath his head and stared at the sky, his words striking a chord in her.

She hadn't thought it possible for them to be similar in any way, but they were more similar than she could have imagined even in her wildest dreams.

"Your mood changed." His violet eyes slid down to her and narrowed, curiosity shining in them. "Why?"

Fear trickled through her veins.

He sat up, planted his hands behind him on the rock, and frowned at her. "What is it?"

She couldn't find the courage to tell him while she was looking into his eyes so she dropped them to the patch of grey stone between them, studying the lichens as she found the words.

"I feel the same way as you," she whispered, and gathered the strength to put more force behind her voice as she told herself that it was Fuery beside her, and if anyone in this world would understand, and not judge her harshly, it was him. "I know I shouldn't. The tradition that binds me is more powerful than any that bound you."

She started as his hand suddenly pressed against her right cheek, his skin warm against hers, and he brushed his fingers down to her jaw and lifted it, making her look at him.

His eyes were soft with understanding, warm with affection, and she stared into them, losing herself in them a little.

"I know it is difficult for females. You are expected to do as you are told, to follow the path your family set out for you, and gods... Shaia... that is not right." He growled the last few words, including her name, the force behind them thrilling her as she spotted his emerging fangs between his lips and felt a ripple of his anger roll through her. "You shouldn't be treated in such a manner. You are strong, and you know your mind, and you should be free to do as you please, as a male is... I understand why you feel the traditions that bind you are so hard to break free from... but know I am here for you, and I will not allow some foolish, outdated view of how females should behave to stand between us."

Heat bloomed on her face.

"Do not be ashamed or shy away from the things you want, allowing others to dictate your life for you." He swept his thumb across her cheek, his soft gaze imploring her to listen to him. "You are strong, beautiful, and I will do all in my power to give you the freedom you desire, and to make you see that you have a right to stand at my side as my equal."

He lowered his hand from her face and she gasped as a dagger appeared in it, the short flat black blade reflecting the light.

He eased onto his feet, caught her wrist and pulled her onto hers. He pressed the dagger into her free hand, forcing her to curl her fingers around the curved leather-bound hilt.

She couldn't believe it. She had asked him to train her, but he had been reluctant and hadn't agreed to it, so she had accepted that he wouldn't train her.

"I will start right now, by teaching you how to fight."

Those words swam in Shaia's head as she rose from the dream, a sigh escaping her as she remembered how adamant he had been about that.

His attitude towards females had been so refreshing. He hadn't believed she should be docile and gentle, or kept from things like fighting. He had wanted her to be able to protect herself, not reliant on males to do that for her.

Gods, it had been wonderful. Freeing. He had made her stronger, both physically and of heart, stoking her desire to live her life the way she had wanted it and not be bound by the rules of society.

She called the dagger to her hand and studied it, watching the way the light of the lamps reflected off the gleaming black metal surface of the blade. She had kept it sharp, had taken good care of it, and had always kept it with her.

She had continued to practice everything he had taught her in his lessons, shutting herself away in her rooms in her family's home and using the excuse that she was studying more feminine and acceptable things such as needlecraft in order to avoid questions about why she had locked the doors and didn't want to be disturbed.

It wasn't the only weapon she owned either.

During a trip to a large town with her family, she had snuck away under the pretence of purchasing fabric for her dresses and had found a store selling weaponry. She had bought another dagger, this one made of silver metal mined in the dragon realms, and had concealed it in a bundle of fabric to keep it hidden from her parents.

It was nothing like the blade Fuery had given her though.

A dagger he had confessed he'd had made as a gift for her.

It must have cost him a lot of coin.

When she had bought the silver blade, she had inquired about elven metal, and the male in the store had blanched and muttered that such finery was hard to come by and he had never been able to afford such a weapon for his store. Not only that, but the kingdom had strict control over the metal, not allowing any unsanctioned purchases and limiting distribution to only a handful of smiths who worked for the palace.

It was special. Unique. Hers.

She twisted it towards the light and frowned as she spotted something on the pillow beside hers in the reflection.

Her heart sank.

She lowered the dagger, rose onto her knees on the mattress and stared at the silver clasp on the pale blue pillow.

She had given it to him as a memento to take with him during his long journeys, a symbol of her love for him. He had tried to refuse it, stating that such finery didn't suit him, but she had insisted and eventually he had accepted it.

Shaia picked it up. It was cold on her palm, had been there some time. That cold seemed to leach into her, flowing from her hand up her arm to sink into her heart.

Was he telling her to give up on him?

She wouldn't do it.

They had been apart for four thousand years, but she had never stopped loving him, and she knew that deep inside him, he loved her too. He needed her as much as she needed him.

Perhaps more so.

She wouldn't allow his past to stand between them and the future they had always wanted. She would find a way to make him see that the feelings in her heart were true, and constant, and unbreakable, and nothing he did could change them. She loved him, all of him, both the dark and the light.

She teleported her dagger away from her, sending it back to her small home, and shuffled to the edge of the bed. She slipped out of her robe, and into her tan trousers, grey tunic and leather boots, and pocketed the clasp as she strode towards the door of her room at the inn.

It creaked as she opened it, and the sound of it slamming behind her echoed through the still building. She didn't stop to ponder the hour, instead hurried down the steps to the ground floor and out into the street, crossing it swiftly to the guild. She pushed the arched wooden door open and strode along the elegant hallway, and across the reception room, heading for the door in the far right corner.

A male stepped into her path and she bared her fangs at him on a growl, only realising after threatening him that he was massive, a wall of muscle and menace that radiated danger.

He looked as if he might back off, but then he seized her wrist.

His mistake.

She called her blade to her hand and had it pressed to his throat before he could move, a combination of adrenaline and fear controlling her as it screamed at her to fight and protect herself.

"Fuery taught you well." Hartt's deep voice rolled over the room, and the large brunet male slid dark eyes his way. "Unhand her."

The assassin huffed and pushed her wrist away from him as he released it, the force of it shaking her balance so her blade came away from his throat, leaving her wide open.

"Not that well," he grumbled and stomped away from them, brushing his unruly brown waves back from his face as he stalked towards the exit.

"Do not mind Klay. I think he lost whatever manners he had back in Archangel's cells." Hartt issued a troubled look in the big male's direction and the worry remained in it as he shifted it to her. "Fuery isn't here."

"Do you know where he is?"

He shook his head, sighed and scrubbed a hand over his face, drawing his lower lip down as it passed over it, and then rubbed at his jaw, his expression shifting towards thoughtful.

"I told him my theory that it isn't only my bond with him that has kept him from losing himself all these years. It was yours too. You are the reason he has always fought back against the darkness, even when he believed you dead. You are the reason he is still alive now." He gestured towards the black couches, but she shook her head, too on edge to sit when she needed to find Fuery. "I think it was… is… your love for him that has kept a glimmer of light in his soul despite the darkness."

A glimmer of light she had apparently caused to grow when she had reconnected with him through their bond.

"It shocked him a little." Hartt's sharp amethyst eyes gained a worried edge that showed in his voice. "He left and I presumed it was to return to you, but then he... he cannot normally teleport, not unless he is desperate..."

But he had teleported away from the guild, and now Hartt wasn't sure where he had gone.

Where would her love go?

She wracked her brain and her heart, searching for the answer to that question, needing to know it because she needed to find him. He needed her now more than ever. She believed that Hartt was right, and love had kept Fuery from slipping into the black abyss, giving him a reason to live, but it wasn't only her love for him that had kept him going.

It was his love for her too.

A love that she knew was eternal and unbreakable.

It was the promise he had made to her, vowing he would always protect her.

Hartt's theory had shocked him though. Because he was finding it difficult to believe that she still loved him?

She had felt his fear when they had been together, knew it stemmed from the darkness that lived within him and the thought she might witness it, that it might drive her away.

Or he might hurt her because of it.

Fears that were unfounded, and ones she was determined to erase for him.

If only she could find him.

"He will come back."

She didn't heed Hartt's words, because she wasn't going to wait. Not anymore. She was done with waiting. She was going to find Fuery and bring him home. She *needed* to find him.

Where had he gone?

She closed her eyes and thought about everything Hartt had told her, and all that she felt, and tried to think in the way Fuery would be. He would look for a place where he could think, where he could gather himself and somehow come to terms with the things Hartt had told him—things he probably knew in his heart were true. He would look for somewhere that soothed him, a spot that would help him clear his mind and seek the answers to the question that plagued him the most—the one he had revealed to her in her room.

Could he trust himself with her?

Her eyes popped open as a place came to her.

"I know where he is."

She teleported before Hartt could respond, landing on the soft rich dirt that lined the bank of the river as it curved in a sweeping bend, hugging the cliff on the other side and embracing the woods on the one where she stood. The sound of it cut through the still cool night air, bouncing off the steep rock face.

Her knees weakened as her strength faltered, the teleport draining her more than she had anticipated. She swiped the back of her hand across her damp brow and breathed slowly, attempting to settle her heart. Giving Fuery her blood had left her weaker than she had thought. She reached out in front of her, towards the rough trunk of the nearest tree, needing support while she caught her breath.

The soft click of a branch snapping came from behind her.

Shaia whirled to face that direction, heart lifting as she sought Fuery.

A trio of males stared at her, all of them dressed in black clothing that made them blend into the darkness and long cloaks with the hoods drawn over their heads. Warm light from the small fire they had been sitting around chased across their faces as they each moved a step closer to her, revealing violet eyes. Elves. She breathed a little easier, sure she had shocked them as much as they had surprised her.

They were probably merchants, stopping for the night to rest.

She glanced around their makeshift camp, her gaze slowing and heart beginning a hard thump against her ribs when she didn't find any goods, cart or horses nearby.

The tallest of the three stepped towards her, leaving his place to the right of the fire.

He raised his hand to his mouth, his eyes dark as they locked on her.

"I did not mean to disturb—" She flinched as the right side of her neck stung and her hand darted up to it.

Feathers brushed her fingertips.

Numbing warmth spread through her from that point, clouding her mind, and she staggered backwards as her legs gave out, her muscles turning liquid beneath her skin. She twisted and hit the trunk of the tree behind her, tried to grip it and find the strength to run as fear rushed in her blood, stealing more of it from her.

Fuery.

She panicked and reached for him through their bond, using her grip on the tree to strengthen her connection to nature and their link.

The tree wobbled in her vision and the light that had flowed into her as her connection to Fuery had opened wavered and died, and darkness swept in to replace it.

She sagged against the tree, her limbs heavy as she struggled to lift her hand, her breath sawing from her lips in shallow pants and sweat rolling down her spine beneath her tunic. She needed to reach it. Gods, she needed to feel it. Her trembling worsened and she grunted as she forced her limbs to work and kept reaching upwards, little by little. She needed the comfort now more than ever.

She sighed in relief as her fingertips brushed familiar lines and curves, initials that Fuery had carved on this tree to symbolise their love and eternally mark it for all to see. Initials she had reinforced with the dagger he had given her each year on the anniversary of their mating, ensuring they remained, and had uttered a prayer for him, asking nature and the gods to take care of her love.

Tears filled her eyes.

She sank to her knees, her hand slipping from the initials to fall into her lap, and her cheek resting against the rough bark.

Darkness swirled around her, and she tried to push it back, but it was too strong, easily devouring her and pulling her down into it.

Words swam in her mind in unfamiliar male voices as she wavered on the brink of oblivion.

"The lord will be pleased."

Five words that chilled her and she knew with a cold sort of certainty who had sent them.

Eirwyn.

CHAPTER 24

Fuery had thought himself crazy before. How mistaken he had been. He was going out of his fucking mind as he leaped into yet another messed up teleport that took him from Vail's orchard to the guild, landing him in a shaking heap in the middle of the reception room. He staggered onto his feet, pain branded on his bones, burning like wildfire as Shaia's fear consumed him.

And then disappeared.

Cold swept through him, a chilling numbness that tore at the fragile tethers of his sanity and had the darkness surging, roaring to the fore again together with a crushing need to find her as he stumbled across the black stone floor towards the male he could sense moving swiftly towards him.

Hartt appeared at the end of the corridor just as Fuery's legs gave out, a strange combination of fear, grief and sheer agony boiling inside him, pulling him apart.

Ripping his heart out of his chest.

"Shaia," he breathed, and it seemed it was all he needed to say.

Hartt rushed to him, skidding to his knees before him and gripping his shoulders to help him up into a sitting position. "What happened to her?"

"Where?" he bit out, wrestling with the darkness, desperate to hold it back and retain his sanity, his tentative grip on this world.

He needed to find her.

He couldn't let the darkness consume him now.

Wouldn't.

He would fight it with everything he had, would vanquish it somehow this time, because Shaia's life depended on it. He felt sure of it. She was in danger. In pain. Fearing for her life.

He reached through their bond, focused on it and growled through his fangs when he felt nothing.

The darkness surged again, writhed like a living thing inside him, as wild as the rest of him, as if it too needed to find her, couldn't live another second without her. Impossible. It despised her light. He could feel it as he focused, the way it boiled with fury, antagonised by the seed of light Shaia had placed in him. It whispered to him, poisonous words about giving in, surrendering and forgetting everything.

It didn't want him to find Shaia. It wanted him to give her up and continue down the dark path he had been treading before she had come back into his life.

He refused to do such a thing.

Shaia was his light. His love. For her, he would do anything.

Even use the darkness and embrace it again.

It was that need that was dragging it to the surface, a desperate need for strength and power that called on it and had him battling to recall his training so he could mould it into a weapon he could use to save her.

Hartt's eyes leaped between his and he swallowed hard. "She came to find you. I did not know where you had gone, and when I told her that, she believed that she knew where to find you. Fuery... she teleported before I could stop her. I'm sorry..."

Fuery shook his head, gritted his teeth and growled again.

It wasn't Hartt's fault.

While he might have held it against the male just days ago, might have lost his grip on the darkness and attacked him for failing to protect his mate in his stead, allowing her to head out alone, he only blamed himself now.

Was only furious with himself.

He had been the one to leave her, not considering how upset she would be or what actions she might take as her need of him drove her to find him. He had been a fucking idiot, and now he had to live with what he had done.

He had to fix it.

"I was with Prince Vail," he breathed and eased back, his hands shaking against his knees as he gripped them and tried to hold himself together, fighting to master the darkness and harness it. It was difficult when he danced on the cusp of madness, fear gripping him tightly, giving the darkness a strong hold on him too. He shook his head again. "She could not have known... does not know that place."

"So where would she go?" Hartt squeezed his shoulders and his voice dropped lower, laced with the same desperation that flowed in his own blood. "Think, Fuery... where?"

The buzzing in his skull was too loud, drowning out his thoughts as he ran over everything that had happened, tried to piece together how she would have felt and where that would have taken her.

When he found no answer, he lifted his head and stared into Hartt's eyes, desperately searching for one in them.

Hartt's dark eyebrows dipped and he dropped his gaze to Fuery's chest, looking straight through it, a thousand thoughts flittering across his eyes as his lips pulled into a grim line.

"I told her what I told you," his friend whispered. "I mentioned you were shocked by it... and that I felt you teleport, and how rare that is for you."

Because his powers were messed up, but his last teleport had felt more stable. He had felt in control, at least to a degree. He had been desperate, the key behind his ability to teleport working, but it had felt easier to call that power this time and open his portal.

Because of Shaia?

Because of the light that was growing inside him each second they were together?

He cursed as he considered where she might have gone.

"The elf kingdom." He didn't want to think about her there, back within her family's grasp.

They would try to take her from him again.

He was damned if he was going to let it happen this time. Shaia wanted to be his, wanted to break free of the ties that bound her, the shackles of tradition, and she had been doing just that. He had felt how happy she had been to be away from the elf kingdom, to see a new place, and to be with him in it.

She had been free.

Unchained at last and able to seek the adventure she had always craved, without scorn or condemnation.

He pushed onto his feet and snarled as rage poured through him, determination that had his darkness growing stronger to swirl in his veins and blaze in his heart.

He would set her free again.

He would give her the life she wanted, would guide her in this new world and stand at her side through it all.

Power flowed through him, and the inky cold black swallowed him, rushing over the obsidian scales of his armour as it covered him from neck to toe. When the darkness dissipated, the gentle rustling of leaves reached his ears together with the steady babbling of the river. The scent of cool earth and water filled his senses and he breathed deep of it.

Stilled.

Shaia.

He caught her sweet scent and growled as he smelled others too.

Males.

He flicked his eyes open.

They settled straight on the tree where he had carved their initials after they had mated, and had vowed to always love her, to always be there for her.

To always protect her.

His eyes rapidly adjusted to the darkness and the world around him brightened to reveal the trunk of the tree and those initials, and the river that swept around the bend beyond it. His gaze dropped from their initials to the dirt at the roots of the tree and narrowed. It was scuffed. Disturbed.

His eyes drifted over the scene and then leaped back to a single point.

Something was there in the dirt beside one of the roots.

He stormed towards it, crouched when he reached the tree and snarled through his fangs as they emerged.

A dart.

The fury that had already been boiling in his veins was nothing compared with the red rage that descended on him, sweeping through him to burn every other emotion away. He snatched the fallen dart from the ground, seizing a fistful of earth with it, and growled as he shot to his feet. He uncurled his fist and stared at the dart, breathing hard as he wrestled with the black need to run, to tear apart this fucking kingdom to find his mate.

He closed his eyes and sucked down breath after breath in an attempt to steady himself. Rushing would get him nowhere. He needed to uncover as much information about what had happened as he could and remain rational if he was going to find Shaia.

Or as rational as he could be with his blood thundering, burning hot in his veins, and a fierce desperate need to find his beautiful mate driving him wild.

The darkness surged again, comforting him with the feel of its power flowing through him, strength that he was going to unleash on the bastards who had stolen his love from him.

He calmly brushed the dirt from around the dart, plucked it from his palm and lifted it to his nose, his entire body trembling with the force of his anger as he waged war against it.

Information. He needed information. A direction.

Something to go on.

He closed his eyes and sniffed the point of the dart.

It smelled sweet. Sickly sweet.

He took another breath and focused to calm his mind so he could determine which drug had laced the dart. He was familiar with many that could be used on such a weapon, although he had never stooped to using such a tool in his work.

He opened his eyes as it hit him, and relief poured through him, washing some of his anger away and restoring a sliver of hope.

It was a drug meant to render someone unconscious.

Shaia was alive.

The reason he couldn't feel her through their bond was because she was still out cold.

He couldn't bide his time and wait for her to come around though. He couldn't stand still and do nothing. He needed to act, would go mad if he didn't.

He scanned the ground around him and the tree, and growled as he saw footprints and two long grooves.

As if someone had been dragged across the earth.

Where had they taken Shaia?

His eyes followed the tracks from the tree and past him. He turned on his heel, vision growing sharper as he picked out the footprints in the low light. They led to a darker patch of earth. Someone had lit a fire there. His focus leaped to the logs scattered around the clearing as he walked towards the ring of scorched dirt. Whoever they were, they had tried to cover their tracks.

Tried and failed.

He crouched as he picked out a clear footprint and fingered it. Boots. Not army issue. He found another print nearby. Different to the one near him. This male had worn a boot with a heel. He spotted another clear set of prints and moved to it. The style of boot matched the first print. He measured them with his hand, huffed, and then scoured the camp to see if there were any more.

Three males had been here.

Shaia wouldn't have stood a chance against them.

His face twisted in a dark snarl as he thought about his beautiful female fighting for her life and he consoled himself by looking back at the tree, at the place she had reached before the males had darted her. She hadn't fought. Her footprints were few, starting at a point between the fire and the tree, and heading towards the trunk of it where she had passed out.

Had the males been waiting here to ambush her?

He scanned the camp again, the relief he had felt dissipating as he thought about where they might have taken her.

What they might do to her.

Fury rose again, a black and terrible rage that poured through his veins like acid and ink, pushing him to find her now before anything could happen to her.

His heart hitched as his eyes fell on the long grooves in the dirt.

His fingers curled into tight fists at his sides.

He would find her. He would protect her.

He would kill whoever had taken her.

The scuff marks led past the camp, into the thick woods that swathed the hill on this side of the river.

Heading towards the village.

The fury that had been building inside him rose to a violent boil as a possible location hit him.

It would be just like her family to do such a thing, hiring mercenaries to take his mate from him, attempting to push him out of her life again or convince her to do as they bid and wed a male of high standing.

They had never liked him.

It went both ways.

He hated them.

They were going to pay for what they had done. Shaia was his, and he wouldn't leave without her. She wanted to be with him, and she would be. He would set her free and they would be together.

Forever.

He focused on his body, on his portal, and growled when it flickered over him and then faded. His breath sawed from his lips as he shook, his head spinning from the exertion of attempting to teleport again. Too much. He wasn't used to using the ability anymore, and he had already teleported twice in the past hour, and a third time before that to reach Vail's home.

It wasn't going to stop him though.

He might not have the strength to teleport, but he still had enough left to reach Shaia.

He kicked off, throwing up dust as he sprinted from the clearing and into the woods. Branches whipped his armour and lashed at his face as he crashed through the trees, heading up the hill. Startled animals broke cover in all directions, fleeing deeper into the woods as he sped past them.

The trees thinned ahead.

He didn't slow as he crashed through them and out into the meadow. He pushed himself harder, sprinting faster, driving himself past his limit as his muscles burned. He couldn't slow. Not until Shaia was back in his arms.

He raced across the dark lands, down into the valley where a pale streak snaking between the hills marked the road into the village.

The burning in his muscles grew fiercer, but he kept pushing, kept running, refusing to give in even as fatigue swept through him and had his head turning. Sweat trickled down his spine beneath his skin-tight armour and crawled over his scalp. He shoved his hand over his long hair, slicking it back from his face as a cool breeze swept down the side of the hill and over him.

His boots skidded as he hit the road and he kicked right. His right hand touched the pale dirt and then he was running again, long strides devouring the distance between him and the village. His heart lightened as he spotted the windmills towering on the hills above the village, and then golden lights that marked the houses.

"I'm coming, Shaia," he breathed and pushed harder, his body screaming in protest but his heart driving him to go faster still.

Shaia needed him.

He reached the village and caught the curious looks on a few of the faces of those out on the streets as he blazed a trail through it, following the road to the square and then taking the left fork as it split into two.

He was close now.

He hit the final hill, his legs burning, thousands of flaming needles piercing his muscles and bones with each stride. When he reached the top of it, and the elegant large stone two-storey grey stone house came into view, golden light illuminating several of the ground floor windows, relief mingled with hope eased the ache in his heart but stoked his rage so it burned white-hot.

Her family would pay for taking her from him.

Fuery bolted down the hill, making fast work of the distance between him and the house, and didn't stop when he reached the door. He dipped his right shoulder and barged through it, splintering the wood and tearing a startled shriek from a female on the other side.

The servant dropped her tray. It clattered on the polished stone floor, the sound loud in the double-height vestibule, clashing with that of crystal smashing as the goblets that had been poised on it hit the ground and shattered.

"Elys!" A high female voice snapped.

Fuery's head whipped towards the source of it and he called his black katana to his right hand.

The owner of that voice stormed out of the room to his left, her black-blue hair neatly swept up and held in thick twisted curls and her deep violet dress cinched at her waist with a corset of fine filigreed gold.

The maid bowed her head, quickly stooped and began gathering the broken crystal.

The older female's gaze slowly shifted towards Fuery.

Widened.

"Aylen." Her voice trembled as she took him in, enormous violet eyes dropping to the blade he clutched.

The male she had summoned appeared behind her, his dark green tunic with fine gold embroidery on the two long panels in front of his thighs a rich contrast to her dress. His violet eyes went equally as wide on seeing Fuery and he paled a little.

"What have you done with her?" Fuery snarled and advanced on them.

The maid stopped her work and stared at him, and then her mistress as the older female signalled to her with her left hand. He paid no attention to the servant as she quickly left the room, keeping his focus fixed on the couple in front of him.

Shaia's parents.

His fingers flexed around the hilt of his sword and fire burned in his heart, blazed in his soul as their cruel words echoed in his mind, every vicious thing they had ever said about him battering him as he stared at them and fought the urge to cut them down.

The darkness pushed him to do it. Life would be easier without them. Shaia would be his. No one would try to take her from him ever again.

Gods, he wanted that.

He wanted to cut them down and watch them bleed. He wanted to be the last thing they saw. He wanted to make them pay for hurting him, denying him.

He would move Heaven, Earth and Hell to save Shaia. Would do anything, no matter the cost. He would kill, sacrifice others, or himself. Whatever was necessary, so long as Shaia lived and was free again.

"Monster," her mother spat.

Fuery growled at her and tried to deny the pain that stabbed through his chest on hearing that word, on seeing the contempt in her eyes, and the disgust.

He was well aware of his appearance.

Darkness reigned in his eyes, and he was sure his pupils were on the verge of turning elliptical, and his irises in danger of gaining a crimson glow.

But he didn't care.

All that mattered was Shaia, and if he had to condemn himself to the abyss in order to save her, then he would do it.

"Where is she?" he bit out, and advanced another step.

Aylen's hand came down on the female's shoulder. "What is it to you?"

He growled as pain suddenly filled him, colliding with fear that stole his breath and had his knees weakening beneath him.

"Shaia," he breathed and clutched at his chest with his left hand, digging sharp claws in as he struggled to breathe and tamp down the raw agony flowing through him. He snarled and lifted his black eyes to Aylen. "Tell me what you've done with her. I know it was you... you set a band of mercenaries on your own damned daughter!"

Gods, the pain.

He swallowed against it and gritted his teeth. It felt as if someone was pulling him apart, piece by agonising piece. He needed to find her. He needed to take away her pain and her fear, before it destroyed him.

Before it destroyed her.

"I will fucking end you both if you do not give her back!" he roared, and the couple flinched in unison, her mother backing into her father.

Her eyes filled with tears. "What do you mean... mercenaries?"

He refused to believe the worry that shone in her violet gaze as she turned her cheek to him and gazed up at her male. He refused to believe the fear that reflected in Aylen's eyes as he wrapped one arm around her and tucked her closer to him.

"Do not listen to him, Sarea. I am sure Shaia is fine, at home where she belongs." The male rubbed his hand against her shoulder, and Fuery didn't miss the way she tensed and glanced at him.

She was hiding something.

He focused on her, a monumental feat considering his mood was rapidly degenerating and the darkness rising, consuming more of him by the second and filling his mind with beautiful images of bloodying his blade and painting the walls of this house crimson.

It took all of his effort, but he managed to lock his senses on her and he growled as he felt something from her.

Fear.

Not fear for her daughter, nor fear of what he might do to her.

Fear born of nerves that told him that he was right and she was hiding something and she feared him finding out what it was.

"Our servant will be at the castle by now, and they will bring a legion back with them." Aylen's words had no effect on Fuery.

"Fuck the soldiers," he snarled and delighted in the horror that crossed their faces. "The kingdom could send one hundred legions and I still wouldn't leave... not until you tell me what you did with Shaia. You know where she is."

He readied his blade and advanced another step, the thought of battling soldiers sending him sinking deeper into the darkness and conjuring a need to feel pain and deal blows, to tear flesh and shatter bone. Gods, he needed it. He needed to fight. He needed to taste blood on his tongue. Needed to kill.

He froze when he sensed the air shimmer behind him.

Braced himself for the coming battle.

Turned as his foes appeared, prepared to kill them all.

His eyes landed on two males.

One with dishevelled finger-length blue-black hair that brushed the collar of his obsidian armour, and one with neatly-trimmed short hair that was swept back from his face and matched the colour of his fine tailored tunic that had elegant scrollwork edging the two sides where they joined in the centre of his torso and flowed down to his knees.

Fuery's eyes instantly dropped to his own boots.

Prince Loren.

"What is happening?" The prince took a hard step forwards, radiating anger that had Fuery fighting to find his voice so he could answer him.

Loren's eyes shifted away from him as Aylen spoke.

"This creature intends to attack us."

Loren was silent and the air in the room grew heavy around Fuery as he battled with himself, memories of a time long past tormenting him, a collision of the handful of moments he had been in Prince Loren's presence that took him from the day he had enlisted in the army to a night recently when he had gone with Hartt to rescue Harbin, one of their assassins, from the cells of Archangel, a mortal hunter organisation.

He had crossed paths with Prince Loren twice that night, and had discovered that Prince Vail was alive.

He tensed as Loren's gaze came back to rest on him.

"I was speaking to Commander Fuery."

His eyes leaped to the male, and then to his left, to the one his prince had brought with him. Bleu. They had been close once, millennia ago. He had taken Bleu under his wing and had trained him, helped him ascend through the ranks of the legion, partly because he had known the male hailed from the same village as Shaia and partly because he had liked the spunky youth and his attitude towards life—one that had said he could achieve whatever he wanted as long as he worked hard enough.

Bleu nodded, offering silent encouragement that Fuery seized with both hands.

He couldn't bring himself to meet Prince Loren's gaze though, not when his eyes were near-black and he was finding it impossible to bring his darkness under control. The need to find Shaia, the pain and fear he could feel through their bond, kept the darkness boiling in his veins, whispering tempting words in his mind about cutting down anyone who stood in his way.

He needed to reach her.

Losing himself to the darkness in the presence of Prince Loren would be a grave mistake though, one that might end with the male calling in a death squad to deal with him, so he kept fighting it, chanting calming things in his mind to drive it back.

Until he needed it again.

He would unleash it then, would let it all out and not hold back.

He would kill whoever had hurt Shaia.

"Shaia," he started and swallowed hard as he pictured her, thought about how frightened she must have been when the males had attacked her, and how afraid she was now as she waited for him to save her. "She returned here believing she could find me, but I was with... your brother."

Prince Loren's gaze grew more intense, piercing his face, and he could almost sense the male's need to ask about his kin.

"When I came to the kingdom, I found a dart and signs of a fight. Three males have her. Three I am convinced were hired by these people. Sarea knows where she is and will not tell me." He growled as the need to find Shaia blasted through him again, shaking the hold he had on his darker urges. "They mean to keep her from me... when I know she wants to be with me."

He risked a glance at Prince Loren.

The male's clear violet eyes grew stormy and he turned them on the couple behind Fuery. "Is it true you meant to keep Commander Fuery from Shaia?"

"She is to mate with a male more worthy of her. One she is promised to," Sarea snapped.

Fuery saw red.

He turned on his heel and snarled at her through his fangs as her fear suddenly made sense. She was afraid he would find Shaia before the male who had hired the mercenaries could force her to wed him.

Loren's hand on his shoulder held him back.

He looked across at the male as he passed him.

The male's black eyebrows dipped low over stormy eyes, ones that flashed with lightning as he directed his anger at the couple.

"Do you believe the rank of commander, a rank not bestowed lightly and one earned rather than inherited, is not a worthy rank to possess?" The air in the room seemed to darken as Prince Loren halted before Shaia's parents and fear flitted across both of their faces.

Bleu growled in a low voice, "Weigh your answer carefully."

Sarea's mouth flapped open and closed. Aylen rubbed his hand across the back of his neck and looked at anything other than Prince Loren, him or Bleu.

Fuery haemorrhaged patience so fast he thought he might pass out, so he opened his mouth to demand the bastards tell him what had happened to Shaia and where she was now.

Loren stunned him into silence, and almost knocked Shaia's parents on their backsides, when he spoke.

"Why do you mean to keep your daughter from her mate of forty-two centuries?"

He knew?

Fuery whipped his gaze to Loren and stared at the back of his head as he remained facing her family.

"I am aware of your shock," Loren said. "I met Shaia at the palace some days ago and learned of her situation when she sought advice from me about her bond."

She must have gone to speak with Bleu and had somehow ended up talking to Prince Loren instead, asking him about why she had believed Fuery dead and why he had thought he had killed her, and why they had both been unaware of their bond, believing it gone when it had still been alive inside them, tying them together.

Aylen and Sarea looked from Loren to him.

"It is true," he said, somehow managing to keep the darkness from his voice as the pressing need to find Shaia battered him. He clawed back patience, aware that if he could hold on a little longer, there was a chance they might break and tell him where to find her. "I am bound to Shaia and have been for four thousand two hundred years. We sealed our bond the night before I left for the borders of the free realm with the legion. She is mine, and I am hers."

"So the matter seems rather resolved to me." Prince Loren's tone brooked no argument as he released Fuery's shoulder. "Commander Fuery has every right to know where his blood-bonded mate is being held... against her will."

Sarea paled and looked as if she might have slumped to the floor had Aylen not tightened his hold on her.

"We were not aware," Aylen said, his voice steady despite the fear Fuery could see in his eyes and smell on him. "Neither were we aware of any plan to capture her. Eirwyn was distraught when she went missing. He might have…"

Fuery cut him off with a snarl. "Eirwyn?"

The bastard was the son of the late Commander Andon who had taken Fuery under his wing. Eirwyn had always despised him, jealous of the attention his father had given him. He had been a scrawny youth the last time Fuery had seen him at his family's mansion, before his father had died in a war with the Fourth King of the demons. More than once, he had made his feelings about Fuery clear.

And more than once, he had mentioned taking Shaia as his bride when he was older.

Fuery was fucking damned if that was going to happen.

"I know the place." Bleu grabbed his arm before he could move an inch and darkness descended, cold that chased over his skin and seemed to seep through the tiny gaps between the scales of his armour.

He shuddered as he landed outside the grand mansion on the other side of the village with Bleu and Prince Loren, and rubbed his hands over his arms.

"Is my brother well?" Loren had barely appeared before he asked that, his violet eyes bright with a need to know the answer to his question.

Fuery wanted to growl, wanted to snarl and tell the male that he was here to fight, to reclaim his mate and free her, not make idle talk, but he bit his tongue and found a shred of civility that the darkness hadn't managed to eradicate yet.

"He is well. Better than I. He has been helping me." When Fuery glanced at Bleu, he saw relief in the male's eyes.

He remembered Bleu being there in Vail and Rosalind's garden the first time he had gone to see his prince. He had needed to see Vail, and had been drawn to him and hadn't been able to hold himself back from going to him. To this day, he still wasn't sure how he had known where to find Vail. The darkness that always came over him on the anniversary of the day Vail had turned on his legion and made himself into an enemy of the kingdom was strong and often left him unaware of the things he did.

It had been that day that had brought him back to Vail, centuries after they had parted on the very same day.

"You seem a little better too." Was that relief he could hear in Bleu's voice?

He didn't dare believe it, but when he looked into the male's eyes, he saw it there. He nodded and turned away, feeling awkward as both males scrutinised him, as if they were trying to chart how deep his darkness ran now so they could see if he was any better the next time their paths crossed.

It seemed Vail wasn't the only one who wanted to see it was possible to come back from the darkness.

He faced the door of the mansion and blew out his breath.

While he had been making progress towards the light again thanks to Prince Vail and Shaia, he was about to take a huge step away from it.

It would be worth it though.

Gods, it would be worth it.

He lifted his boot and kicked the door open, and stormed into the mansion as Loren muttered behind him.

"He could have knocked."

Bleu grunted. "Would you knock if he had Olivia?"

"I would tear the fucking building apart stone by stone," Loren growled and prowled into the mansion behind Fuery.

It was as if Loren had read his mind. Fuery's dark eyes scoured the unlit vestibule of the mansion, his ears twitching as he strained to hear anyone so much as breathing in it. His heart laboured as he fought the urge to begin ripping everything apart, destroying all that Eirwyn held dear in an effort to draw the bastard out of hiding.

He could hear the fucker's heart beating in the distance above him.

Drawing closer.

A light appeared at the top of the balcony that ran around all four sides of the vestibule, the candle flickering in the darkness, illuminating a male's face.

Eirwyn.

Fuery bared his fangs on a low growl. "What have you done with her?"

Eirwyn tilted his chin up and glared down at him. "Done with who?"

"Don't fucking test me." Fuery took a hard step towards the arrogant male, hungry with a need to wipe the imperious look away by gripping his long hair and pummelling his face with his fist.

Bleu moved up to stand beside him, and Fuery shot him a glare, daring him to try to hold him back and stop him.

Eirwyn casually leaned over the elegant wooden balustrade, resting his right elbow on it and causing his ponytail to fall over his left shoulder to brush his bare chest. "Commander Bleu. It is a surprise to see you again. I assume you have come to escort this male away?"

Bleu rolled his shoulders in an easy shrug. "Probably not. Depends on how things go. If you tell him what you've done with his mate, then I might stop him from killing you."

"His mate?" Eirwyn's left eyebrow rose.

"Shaia," Fuery bit out. "What have you done with Shaia? I know you think she is promised to you. You cannot have her, because she is mine and has always been mine. She is my mate."

"Ludicrous," Eirwyn scoffed, and then his eyes slowly widened as Loren stepped out from beneath the balcony, coming into the sphere of the candlelight.

"I assure you, it is the truth. If you know where Shaia is, it would be wise to tell us." Prince Loren stared the male down, and a flicker of nerves began to show in his eyes.

Fuery locked onto them as he scoured the building with his senses, searching it for a sign of Shaia. Only four heartbeats came to him, and he growled when he couldn't scent her in the mansion either.

Or on Eirwyn.

Either the male hadn't been in contact with her, or he had scrubbed himself clean after he had, erasing any trace of her scent.

Eirwyn gathered himself and calmly straightened, turned to his right and slowly descended the stairs. Fuery tracked him, keeping a close eye on him, refusing to let him get the jump on him. He turned slowly as the male rounded the curve in the staircase, shifting so his back was to the entrance and Loren. Eirwyn stopped on the bottom step, his face fixed in a concerned expression that didn't fool Fuery.

"What happened to Shaia?" He leaned right and rested the candle on the flat top of the broad pillar at the bottom of the banisters. "I swear, I have not seen her. She disappeared weeks ago and her parents have been frantic. I have been frantic."

Lies.

Eirwyn knew where she was.

He might not have seen her yet, but he knew what had happened to her. Fuery could see it in the bastard's eyes as the male tried hard to hide it from him. The smugness shone through though, eclipsing the fake worry for brief flickers, revealing it to Fuery. He knew where Shaia was, and couldn't contain his elation, his excitement at taking her from Fuery and having something he wanted.

Prince Loren moving snapped Fuery out of thoughts of tearing into the male and slowly clawing through his chest until the male gave up her location or died.

"We will find her, Fuery," Loren whispered, his deep voice smooth and calm, comforting him as it swept through him and pushed the darkness out enough that he could scrape together a modicum of control over it. The male approached him, and stopped close to him, genuine concern in his clear eyes, mingled with hope and determination. "You can use your bond with her to locate her. It is stronger now, yes?"

He nodded. It was, but he didn't dare hope he could use it to find her. He could feel her pain and her fear, but the desperate need to find her had his darkness at the helm, and it was drowning out the light inside him.

"Focus on your bond," Loren murmured. "Close your eyes and focus on Shaia and the connection that links you together."

He did as instructed and felt Eirwyn move. Bleu was between them in a heartbeat, blocking the male's path to him.

"Focus." Loren placed his hand against the back of Fuery's neck.

Darkness surged through him in response and Fuery turned and knocked his hand away. "Don't."

As much as he wanted Prince Loren to use his connection to nature to aide him with locating Shaia, he couldn't let him do it. He didn't want to taint the male, and he knew the prince would feel the darkness in him, would be affected by it. Vail would never forgive him if he passed this terrible disease to his beloved brother.

Loren nodded. "Very well. I shall not."

When the male lowered his hand, Fuery closed his eyes again and tried to focus. The roar in his mind and in his veins was too loud though, the darkness writhing and wild with a need to shed blood, break bone and carve flesh. He frowned and pushed, attempting to focus through it, and felt a glimmer of Shaia's pain, saw a flash of the red ribbon that connected them, and then it was gone.

The darkness was too strong, denying him as it fought against the light his bond with Shaia created in him, clouding their link so he couldn't find her.

Fuery flicked his eyes open and settled them on Eirwyn.

Centuries of life as an assassin had taught him to read people.

The male knew where Shaia was.

Centuries of life as an assassin had taught him to see all the possible moves a mark would make and pick the one they would choose and use it to his advantage.

The male would meet with the mercenaries to take his prize from them.

When it happened, Fuery would be there, ready to strike.

Right now, he needed to give Eirwyn a reason to believe he would no longer be a threat to him and he could meet with the mercenaries without interference and claim his bride.

On a roar, he launched at Eirwyn, managing to rake his claws down the male's bare chest before Bleu tackled him as predicted, taking him down in a tangle of limbs and pinning him to the cold stone floor.

Eirwyn spluttered, his face red with rage. "Imprison that animal."

Loren looked as if he didn't want to do it.

Hope fled Fuery's heart.

Bleu eased back and looked down at him, and Fuery shifted his gaze to him. The moment their eyes locked, Bleu began wrestling with him, jostling him as he grabbed Fuery's wrists and moved them, making it appear as if he was fighting him.

"Calm down," Bleu snarled and his eyes widened, just a brief flash of white around his irises as he gave Fuery a pointed look and raised his voice again. "I said calm down!"

Realisation swept through Fuery like a blinding sunrise.

He growled and fought Bleu's hold, managed to break one arm free of his grip and slammed his fist into the male's face, knocking him sideways.

Bleu scowled at him as blood pooled at the corner of his lips. "You left me no choice. It's the cells for you."

He teleported.

Fuery dropped into the darkness with him, and landed in the courtyard of the castle with Bleu still astride him.

Prince Loren appeared a second later. "What in the gods' names is going on?"

Bleu rose onto his feet, grabbed Fuery's wrist and pulled him onto his. "You had better be right about this... because Eirwyn's brother is one of my subordinates and I don't want to have to explain to Leif that we were hunting his brother if it turns out you're wrong. He'll give me hell for years."

The way he said that made it sound as if Leif would be supportive of their actions if it turned out he was right though.

Leif sounded like his father, Andon, noble and courageous, a male who did the right thing and followed the law to the letter in order to maintain the reputation of their family and avoid tarnishing their name.

"The male hired the mercenaries." Fuery dusted himself down, hands trembling as he used the small task as something to focus on so he could gather himself and push back against the darkness. Losing his shit in the middle of the castle courtyard would be a death sentence. While Prince Loren seemed fine with the tainted, most of the occupants of the castle were not and they would call for his head. "I'm sure of it. He despises me because his father had a soft spot for me and he wants to take what is mine. He knew I had feelings for Shaia, and told me several times that he was going to wed her. He wanted to spite me."

Loren looked to Bleu.

Bleu shrugged. "It sounds reasonable. I met him once with Shaia when I was taking Taryn to meet my parents. Taryn remarked that the male had the same look in his eyes that she gets whenever she sees treasure. Having seen the way her brother looked at the sword, I can see what she meant. It was a little too possessive, and not in a good way. Eirwyn thinks that Shaia will achieve him something, and I'm guessing it's power. It's always fucking power with these nobles."

A passing well-dressed male scowled at Bleu. Bleu shot him a black look that challenged him to say something. The male huffed, turned his nose up and kept walking.

Fuery had to agree with Bleu.

"Whenever Eirwyn had spoken of marrying Shaia, he had said nothing about love and everything about what it would gain him." A fact Fuery wanted to growl over, because Shaia deserved to be loved, cherished, not treated as a possession. "He wants power, standing, and taking Shaia as his bride would gain him that. She is the sole heir in her family's bloodline. With no male to inherit it, marrying her would pass that power on to him, and would help him ascend in rank."

Loren let out a low groan. "Nobles."

It sounded strange coming from a prince.

"The thought he would use someone to bring himself one step closer to me is... well..." Loren trailed off and looked to Bleu.

"Fucking sickening?" Bleu offered, a half smile dancing on his lips. "We could dispatch a legion to deal with him. Leif might want to head it and deal with his brother before the male can tarnish their precious name."

"No." Fuery gripped Bleu's arm and shook his head. "I will deal with him. If you go in now, we might never find Shaia. I can't... I need to find her."

Bleu nodded, and Loren followed suit.

"You have a plan?" Loren said, concern flickering in his eyes, warning Fuery that if it didn't sound like a good one, the male might send a legion after all.

This time, Fuery nodded.

"Now that he thinks you're going to lock me up and I'm no longer a threat, he will go to them." He held the prince's gaze, hiding nothing from him as the darkness surged in response to the thought of what was to come. "He will lead me right to her."

And then Fuery was going to kill him.

CHAPTER 25

It wasn't anywhere she knew.

Shaia kept her eyes almost closed, feigning unconsciousness as she took in her new surroundings. A fortress, but a forgotten one. The walls were broken in places, the pale grey stone crumbling to ashes and entire blocks fallen from their places, as if dragons had ravaged it or perhaps just the passing of time.

She squinted up at the dark sky, finding no trace of amber from the Devil's fires.

The colour of the stone and the sky told her one thing.

She was still in the elf kingdom.

Watery sounds warbled in her ears and no matter how hard she tried to focus on them to turn them into words, her head refused to clear enough for it to happen. Her vision wobbled as she lay on her side on the cold ground, staring across the courtyard of the ancient fortress, past the bright glow of a fire to her left and the dark ring of a walled well to her right, to the arrow slit in the far wall.

She ached to look out of that narrow gap and see familiar lands so she would know where she was in the kingdom and could tell whether the males were taking her back to the village or not.

She didn't remember there being a fortress like this one close to her home.

But why would the males take her further from Eirwyn if they had been hired by him to find her?

Part of her had expected to wake to find herself already in his company, trapped in his home, a slave to the male she had foolishly thought would give her some freedom.

Gods, she had been an idiot to go along with her family's plans. She could see that now. She had been desperate though, worn down and lonely, and had truly believed that with Eirwyn she could continue to tend to a garden and pass her time in peace, rarely bothered by him and her parents.

Heavy thuds sounded close to her and her skin crawled as she felt eyes on her, and then the male moved on, saying something to the others.

Shaia stared at that slit in the wall opposite her.

She wanted to be home.

She focused, willing her portal, calling it to the surface so she could return to the place that had become that home.

Fuery.

Nothing happened.

Was it the drug? It still tainted her blood, making her head fuzzy.

She went to lift her hands to rub at that head.

Her wrists were so heavy she could barely shift them across the stones, and when she did, a distorted sort of scraping sound reached her ears.

She slowly opened her eyes all the way and looked down at her wrists.

Shackles.

They were thick, the metal dark and worn in places, speaking of years of use.

Enchanted.

Many species in Hell and the mortal world could teleport, or had powers that might prove dangerous to a band of mercenaries. They had used a witch to place a powerful spell on the cuffs. A spell that rendered her powers useless to her.

The same spell her parents had once dared to use on her.

A spell Eirwyn would no doubt employ too.

Everyone wanted to lock her in a cage and make her do what they wanted.

Well, she was done with it.

She was done with everyone trying to run her life, as if they knew what was best for her, as if she was a possession that should do as they bid and obey them without question.

She was done with everything.

Fuery had lit a fire in her forty-two centuries ago, and it had dwindled to a bare spark in their time apart, so much so that she had almost forgotten it had existed, but now it burned inside her again.

Blazed hotter than ever.

It was a furnace that fuelled her, had her formulating a plan as the three males who had taken her captive laughed around the fire and spoke with each other, their words becoming clearer as the haze of the drug began to lift, allowing her to catch words. Coin. Slave. Beautiful. Auction. Lordship. Waste.

They meant to threaten Eirwyn in order to get more money for her, painting a picture that they would sell her on the black market for more if he didn't give them what they wanted.

A life spent at Eirwyn's mercy was preferable to one where she was kept in chains and bought by whatever sick sort of person attended the slave markets.

But neither was going to happen.

She was going to escape.

She was going to be free again. Free to live her life the way she wanted, as the female Fuery had awoken in her, one that made her feel alive.

These males weren't going to sell her to a slaver, and Eirwyn wasn't going to take her. Neither were an option for her, because both would threaten the future she wanted—one with Fuery at her side.

He would come for her, and slavers ran in large troupes, filled with powerful demons and immortals, and Eirwyn had connections to commanders at the palace and would call a legion to protect him.

She couldn't let Fuery fight for her, because if that happened, he would lose—not the battle against a paltry legion of elf warriors or a small army of immortals and demons, but the battle against his darkness.

That much violence would be his end, and she knew in her heart that neither her nor Hartt would be able to bring him back.

Gods, it would be a vicious enough blow if he discovered what had happened to her.

His need as her ki'aro would drive him to find her and would tear him apart as it did it, filling his mind with all the terrible things that could be happening to her.

She had to get back to him before he discovered she had been captured.

Shaia tilted her head and eyed the three males around the small fire, their conversation growing clearer still as her vision stopped fluctuating between sharp and fuzzy. The drug. She swore she could feel it leaving her system, and her strength returning with it.

"It will not be long now," the largest of the males, the one who had darted her, rumbled and swirled a pewter mug of something around in his hand, his eyes on it.

"I still think we would make more for her if we took her to the free realm. They pay a pretty price for pretty elves there." This one sounded younger than the others, and she singled him out as the slimmest of the group, a male who stood a good few inches shorter than his companions.

His black cloak swamped his slender figure, wrapped tight around him with one arm while his other hand rested on the sword strapped to his waist.

Weapons.

She was going to need some if she was going to escape. She doubted she had the skills to take theirs from them, which meant she was going to need to get enough of her powers back to be able to teleport a blade to her.

When her parents had held her captive in her room using a spell that had stopped her from teleporting out, she had eventually been able to teleport items to her, things she owned.

She focused on her hands, and on the blade Fuery had given her. Her fingers tingled and she felt the link between her and the dagger open, and her heart soared.

It plummeted a moment later when the link wavered and died, leaving her empty-handed.

Shaia cursed the shackles.

They were inhibiting her powers more than she had anticipated. If she wanted her blade, she was going to have to convince one of the males to remove the cuffs from her wrists. It was a long shot. They would laugh at her if she asked them to do such a thing.

She studied the shackles in secret, trying to keep her movements to a minimum so the males didn't notice, and smiled to herself when she found the same inscription carved into both.

Two separate spells.

If she convinced them to remove one of her cuffs, it might be enough to allow her to bring a blade to her. She just had to hope that one cuff would be enough to stop her from teleporting, so the males would think it would be safe to unlock one of them and wouldn't suspect anything.

It was a risk though.

To convince them, she was going to have to play a dangerous game.

One of them had called her beautiful.

She was going to have to play on that.

She moaned for effect as she pushed herself up, catching the males' attentions. The youngest's gaze followed her every move as she raised her hands, her eyes widening as she looked at her cuffs, and then brushed her long wavy hair from her face as best she could.

The third male, one whose face she hadn't caught yet, nudged the younger male forwards. "Go check on her."

He nodded, rounded the fire under the watchful gaze of the leader of the group, and approached her.

Shaia rubbed her hands over her drab tunic and pulled a face as she spotted a tear in the material, and then skimmed her fingers over her hands.

"What happened?" she whispered, her eyes enormous as she lifted them to the male as he halted before her and eased into a crouch. "Am I a prisoner?"

He shook his head, only enough that it moved beneath his hood, as if he didn't want his companions to see it, and spoke in a low, quiet voice. "We are waiting for your intended."

Intended.

She wanted to growl at that.

She held it back and looked herself over again, paying close attention to her dirty hands and then lifting them to her face. "I must look awful."

He shook his head again, his eyes brightening as he ran them over her, as if he couldn't stop himself. His pupils blew wide, devouring the violet of his irises, as she pushed her tangled hair behind her ear to reveal the pointed tip and accidentally brushed it with her fingers.

Her whole body shook in response, fear rising to get the better of her for a brief heartbeat of time before she managed to squash it. She was strong. She could do this. It was the only way to get free before Fuery discovered she was gone and foolishly came after her, placing himself in grave danger.

She could do this to spare him.

Save him.

She slowly lowered her hands to her chest and looked there at the dirt that coated her exposed collarbones.

"I need to wash."

Those words leaving her lips snagged the male's focus away from her breasts and had his eyes shooting up to meet hers.

Her eyebrows furrowed. "I am a mess, I know it. I need to bathe."

"No." The leader didn't even look at her.

She switched her focus to him.

His square jaw set hard, the muscle in it popping, and he stared at the fire. He was going to be difficult to convince. She had almost won the younger male over, but now he was looking at his leader, the flare of desire in his eyes fading. Damn it.

What else had they mentioned that she could use to her advantage?

Coin.

She gestured to her body, drawing the young one's focus back to it, pulling him under her spell again as she spoke to his leader.

"I am sure Eirwyn will be inclined to pay more for my return if I was presentable. *Perfect.*" She tugged at the chest of her tunic. "He will hardly recognise me like this."

The older male didn't move, didn't even glance at her.

She had to convince him.

Her eyes widened as it hit her.

She fingered the rip in her tunic.

"He might hold you responsible for my appearance." She held her smile inside when the male finally looked at her. "If he believes you have harmed me in any way…"

"Just get her clean," the male barked. "If only to shut her up. *Females*."

The younger elf was quick to grasp her left arm and haul her onto her feet.

He led her away from the other two males, beyond the sphere of the light of the fire, into the shadows, and stopped at the wall of the well. It ran at waist-height to her around the deep pit.

"Undress," he muttered as he released her and shoved the wooden pail over the edge, letting it plummet into the well.

It took a long time to hit the water.

The sound echoed up to her as she bent and removed her boots. She set them aside and slowed as she felt the male's eyes come to rest on her as he hauled the bucket back up, his actions slowing as he followed every move her hands made. She pretended she hadn't noticed him as she carefully removed her trousers, tugging them down her legs, her hands shaking a little as she revealed her thighs to him.

The feel of his gaze on her grew more intense as she reached her calves and stepped out of them.

He set the bucket down on the thick wall of the well, the sharp sound of it startling her into looking at him. Her eyes leaped to his, her breath coming faster as adrenaline surged and fear began to rise again, slipping beyond her control.

He jerked his chin towards her top.

Shaia sucked down a secret breath, hoping to still the nerves that raged out of control the moment she thought about doing as he bid. It did nothing to calm them. Her fingers trembled as she gripped the hem of her tunic and went to lift it.

She lowered it again and looked at the male.

"The shackles." She held her hands out to him. "I cannot remove my tunic while I wear them."

He eyed them and growled. "Not going to happen. They stay on."

"But…" She made a show of trying to remove her tunic while wearing them, flashing her undergarments and her belly before screwing her face up in frustration and letting the material drop again. "It is impossible. Just one. I will not be able to go anywhere, will I?"

He dumbly shook his head, his eyes still locked on her stomach, pupils so wide there was barely a sliver of violet in them.

She backed off when he advanced on her, and tensed when her bottom hit the wall of the well and he crowded her, his thighs brushing hers as he took hold of her wrists. His hands were cold on her bare forearms, sending a chill through her together with the way he pressed against her.

She wanted to break free of him but found the strength to stand her ground and bear it as he intentionally rubbed against her as he leaned to one side to pull a set of steels from his pocket. He unwrapped the leather holder, taking his time about it, his hips pressing close to hers, groin rubbing her thigh. She swallowed and held her trembling hands out to him, and breathed through her fear as he took hold of her right wrist and began to work on the shackle.

When it was free of the cuff, he snatched it in a bruising grip before she could move a millimetre. "Behave yourself."

His eyes lowered to her chest and he remained pressed close to her as he pocketed his set of steels. His tongue poked out, traced over his lips to wet them, and she could almost feel his hunger as it rose within him.

"Let's get this off you then." He lowered his hand, flattened his palm against her hip and coursed it up over her stomach and breasts, heading towards the collar of the tunic.

Shaia closed her eyes and struggled to focus as fear swamped her, born of both what he was doing and what she was about to do.

Sickness brewed in her stomach, turning it over and over. The male could easily kill her. She had to do it though. It was her only choice.

It was him or her.

She focused on her shackled left hand where it hung limp beside her, close to the male's hip, and it tingled as the connection between her and her blade opened. The link was stronger than before and she put all of her strength into calling the dagger to her hand.

The male gripped the neck of her tunic and yanked hard, pulling her towards him as the material tore.

Bitter disappointment flashed in his eyes as he saw the bandages binding her breasts.

The blade materialised in her hand.

She drove it hard into his side and swiftly covered his mouth with her free hand, muffling his cry.

He went down hard, taking her with him, and she closed her eyes as she pulled the blade free of his flesh, the wet sucking sound and the resistance turning her stomach, and plunged it down into his chest with all of her strength, punching through his ribs and into his heart.

He instantly stilled beneath her.

She sagged against him, breathing hard, her hands shaking violently where they gripped the hilt of the dagger.

"Bitch!" the second male snarled.

Shaia snapped her head up, her eyes locking straight on his as he shot to his feet beside the fire, and the leader rose beside him.

She eased back into a crouch, pulling the blade free as she went, and eyed them both.

Her heart steadied.

The trembling stopped.

It was them or her.

She couldn't back down now, she couldn't let fear overcome her. She had to fight.

She had to fight for the future she wanted with Fuery.

CHAPTER 26

Eirwyn wasn't difficult to track through the darkness.

Wherever the male was heading, he was unfamiliar with it, forced to travel on foot for the most part, with only short teleports to the furthest point he could see helping him gain ground on Fuery.

The male was slower on foot than he was though, so Fuery caught up with him whenever he teleported, easily closing the distance between them again.

He had taken to sprinting after his last teleport, covering ground at speed that was probably impressive for him, but felt like a jog to Fuery. The male had led a soft life if he couldn't sprint at a speed even the most junior members of the army could manage.

Fuery spotted trees ahead, flanking a hill, and mountains beyond them. It looked like the border with the First Realm of the demons, but might be the one that skirted the Second Realm. Whichever one it was, it was too close to demons for Fuery's liking and no place for his mate.

The First and Second Realms had been peaceful for centuries, but demons were demons, and Fuery didn't trust any of them.

They craved war, hungered for violence and bloodshed nearly as fiercely as he did.

With that thought, the darkness pushed inside him, running through his veins like a black tide to fill his mind with pleasing images of diverting course and attacking Eirwyn. He grunted and gritted his teeth as he fought back against that need, telling himself on repeat that he needed Eirwyn alive to lead him to Shaia.

Then he would kill him.

Once she was safe.

He hit the trees and sprinted into them, steps silent as he leaped fallen branches and twisted around broad trunks, his eyes never straying from his prey.

Eirwyn began to slow.

Either he was tiring, or they were nearing the meeting point.

Fuery slowed too, easing into a casual jog as he breathed in a controlled manner to bring his heartrate back down, a contrast to the puffing and panting male out in the field to his left.

The distance between them was narrow enough that Fuery could see him clearly in the dim light, but far enough that the male wouldn't sense him.

Was utterly unaware of the wraith that shadowed his every step.

He grinned and licked his fangs as the darkness inside him purred in approval of that thought and the fact he was enjoying stalking the hapless bastard and would soon be claiming his head.

And his heart.

His fingers twitched, sharp black claws itching to sink deep into his chest and rip that still-beating organ from his chest.

Gods.

He wanted that.

Hungered for it.

Even the part of him Shaia had brought back to life, a softer part he had expected to put up some sort of fight against the idea, wanted it. Craved it.

The male had dared to take his ki'ara from him.

The male would pay.

In blood.

Eirwyn began to walk.

Fuery looked ahead of them.

The trees obscured his vision, and it was difficult to make anything out in the pre-dawn light, but he was sure something was there.

A tiny flicker of gold.

He squinted and focused harder as he moved closer to the edge of the trees, removing them from his field of vision.

A fire.

As he focused on it, he saw the shadow of a building.

Fuery kicked off, running towards it, his every instinct driving him to reach it before Eirwyn and take back his mate. He needed to see her, had to know she was unharmed and safe, and take her away from this hellish place before anything could happen to her.

Needed it.

Needed her.

The scent of blood hit him.

Distant. Elf.

His knees almost gave out. He stumbled but remained upright, cold rushing through his blood as he struggled to focus through the roar in his head that demanded he reach Shaia now.

Her fear flooded the link, together with pain that crippled him, scraped out his insides and left him raw.

Shaia.

He focused as Loren had taught him, trying to picture Shaia so he could see where she was and teleport straight to her, but again nothing happened.

He still hadn't regained his strength. He was lucky he had managed to teleport so many times in the last day. His powers were becoming more reliable, but he had a long way to go before he could depend on them.

He bit out every curse he knew as he pushed forwards, running towards the ancient fortress as quickly as he could manage.

His senses reached outwards even as they delved inwards, connecting him to Shaia on all levels as he closed the distance between them. She was afraid. Hurting. Not just emotionally. There was physical pain there too, wounds that began to burn on his own arms and torso as he growled and strengthened the connection between them, wanting her to feel that he was coming.

He was coming for her.

The walls of the fortress loomed ahead of him and he sprinted up a fallen section of it, leaping from huge stone to stone.

As he reached the top of it, his eyes leaped straight to Shaia.

A male closed in on her, his blade lunging towards her, and she stumbled backwards, brandishing the dagger he had given her in trembling hands, her violet eyes wide with the fear he could feel in her.

He roared and kicked off, heart hammering against his ribs and fear closing his throat as he willed himself to reach her in time.

Darkness swept over him.

He collided with Shaia, knocking her backwards, and growled as white-hot pain erupted in his right side.

Shaia's beautiful eyes widened further, tears shining in them as she sat on the dirty ground and stared up at him, her face ashen and blood streaked over her cheek and chest.

His blood.

He slowly looked down at the point of the black blade sticking out of his side, punched clean through his armour. Blood rolled down to the tip and dripped to the earth, and formed a thick cascade down his thigh.

Fuery frowned.

Calmly took hold of the blade and pushed it back, not feeling the pain as it slid through his flesh, and not stopping when the tip disappeared back into his side. He pushed it deeper, sticking his fingers into the wound, hearing Shaia's pained gasp and barely registering the way her hand flew to her own side as the pain he didn't feel burned inside her.

The darkness devoured it in him.

Used it as fuel for the fire that blazed within him.

A black fire that consumed him.

He pulled his fingers free, reached behind him and gripped the blade again, easing it out of his flesh.

When it pulled free, he turned slowly to face the large male.

The elf's eyes were on the blade and Fuery's hand where he still gripped it, as wide as Shaia's had been.

"Leave," he ground out, and the male blinked, but Fuery wasn't talking to him. He turned his head slightly to his left, so he could see Shaia in the corner of his vision as he kept his eyes on the male. "Leave!"

"No," she said, such force behind that single word that it shook him.

He growled at her, cast the male's sword away from him and shoved his free hand forwards, hitting the male in the centre of his chest with the flat of his palm and sending him sailing through the air.

Buying her time.

"Leave. Now." He turned on a pinhead to face her and froze when he saw the fear in her eyes, written across every line of her beautiful face.

Her clothes were in tatters, her lean legs exposed and only flimsy dark undergarments covering her hips, and the bandages around her chest were covered in his blood, together with her torn grey tunic.

He gripped his side to stop the flow of blood and eased to his knees in front of her, softening his tone as he reached his other hand out to her and gently brushed her tangled hair from her dirty cheeks. "Teleport out of here. I will be right behind you."

"I-I…" She held her hands up between them. "I cannot."

He growled when he spotted the thick metal shackle around her left wrist.

"Run then. Just get—" He grunted as someone slammed into his back, sending him face first into the ground, and growled as he bucked up, shoving the male off him. "Run."

Shaia scrambled backwards, looked as if she might obey him, and then her hand knocked her dagger and she looked down at it. He willed her not to do it as he grappled with the male who had stabbed him, but her fingers closed around the curved hilt of the black dagger and she rose onto her feet before him, transforming before his eyes.

Into a breathtaking warrior.

Resolve shone in her eyes, and although her fear still ran in his blood, she stood firm, facing her opponents.

The second male, this one of lighter build, finished checking the fallen one by the well and eased onto his feet. Fuery shoved the heavier male off him and landed a hard blow to his face, cracking bone and sending blood streaming over his lips. He pushed away from the male and called his own blade to his hand as he moved into the path between the second male and Shaia.

The heavier male found his feet and his blade again, and flanked him as the second male drew his sword.

Fuery breathed hard, wrestling with the darkness as it rose within him, swept through him and carried away all of his pain, replacing it with a cold sort of numbness that he embraced as he allowed his darkest urges, his blackest needs, to fill him and seize control.

He needed the strength his darkness gave him.

He needed to protect Shaia.

The heavier male lunged for him, and Fuery blocked his attack, the sound of their swords clashing ringing through the still night air. He growled and shoved forwards, knocking the male back, and grinned as the male struck him with his fist, slamming it into his right cheek.

He savoured the brief flash of pain and the taste of blood on his tongue.

Just as he was going to savour tearing this male apart piece by piece.

Heat bloomed in his side, a dull ache that throbbed and pulsed, pushing through the numbness. He growled and lifted his foot and kicked hard, shoving it into the male's stomach and knocking him back. As the male staggered across the stones, fighting for balance, Fuery dropped his gaze to his side.

Blood.

It streamed over the scales of his armour, shining in the light of the fire.

He grimaced, lips pulling back off his bloodied fangs as he touched the wound. He was losing blood faster than his body could heal, but it wouldn't be a problem. Not yet. He had time to deal with these bastards and Eirwyn, and then he would feed to kickstart his healing process.

He had time.

He wavered on his feet and growled as a wave of fire rolled through him, fiercer than before.

Not his pain.

He whipped towards Shaia.

She grunted as she dodged the other male's blade, just as he had taught her, using her smaller size and her speed to her advantage, and growled as she sliced across the male's side, cutting through his black tunic.

The scent of blood grew thicker in the air.

Not only the male's.

She staggered a little and pressed her hand to her right arm.

Blood trickled from between her fingers.

"Shaia!" His left boot skidded as he kicked off in her direction, and he grunted, the air rushing from his lungs as his opponent tackled him from behind, sending him slamming into the ground beneath his weight.

Fuery could only stare as she desperately blocked another blow, her dagger no match for the male's sword, and it glanced off the blade.

Time seemed to slow as the sword cut down her chest, leaving a long red gash between her breasts as she screamed.

Her pain flooded him.

The darkness rushed in behind it and he clung to the slim thread of light inside him that connected him to Shaia as the black abyss yawned before him.

But it wasn't enough to save him.

The light flickered, slipped through his fingers, and died.

Darkness devoured him.

CHAPTER 27

Shaia felt it the moment Fuery snapped.

Icy cold swept through their fragile link, a dark tide that crashed over her and rocked her, battering her as their connection wavered and she fought to keep it open. Alive.

It was her fault.

She should have run when he had told her to, but she had known his words had been meant to soothe her, not a lie but not the truth either. He had wanted her to leave, and had said the one thing he had believed would make her do it—that he would be right behind her.

When he had intended to stay and punish those who had taken her from him.

The sight of him injured and the knowledge he was going to fight rather than come with her, had filled her with a need to stay. He was her mate. Her ki'aro.

Her love.

She couldn't just leave him to fight alone.

But as his eyes blackened, his pupils began to transform into vertical slits, and a flicker of red licked around them, she knew she had made a terrible mistake.

He roared and moved faster than she could track, savagely attacking the male who had tackled him to the ground. She flinched away as he gripped the male's sword arm and brutally yanked backwards, the sound of breaking bone turning her stomach. The male screamed, the sound garbled as his face screwed up and he tried to break free of Fuery's unrelenting grip.

The male nearest to her immediately went to his companion's aid, swinging hard with his sword the moment he was within reach.

Fuery snapped violet eyes up to him and bared his bloodied fangs as he blocked the male's blade with his own, and the relief that poured through her on seeing the red that had been in them gone was short lived.

It flickered again, a corona of fire that turned her blood cold.

The tales of the lost were true.

They did lose all of their light and become shadows of their former selves, gaining the scarlet eyes of a vampire, a species born of the tainted the elves had left behind in the mortal world millennia ago.

Only the lost became monsters, a slave to their bloodlust, no longer conscious of the atrocities they committed, driven only by an unquenchable thirst that consumed them.

Fuery roared as he shoved upwards, springing to his feet and into the male, knocking him backwards. He growled and pressed the flat of his free hand against his blade, driving it against the male's chest.

The male teleported.

Her mate turned on another low snarl, his black eyes scanning the darkness for his foe.

When they settled on her, she gritted her teeth and risked moving, reaching for him. Pain blazed through her, robbing her of her breath as she desperately clutched the deep wound across her chest with her other arm.

Fuery's eyes narrowed on her.

On her wound.

She felt the rage in his blood, the darkness as it drove him, flooded their link and spilled into her.

"Fuery, no," she whispered, trying to keep his focus on her face and not her wound—on her feelings and desires, not her pain.

She wanted him to come to her, wanted him to leave with her, now before it was too late for him.

He growled, the sound vicious and more beast than the elf she loved, and was gone in a flash, appearing behind the male with the broken arm.

She grimaced and looked away as he attacked with his claws, her stomach rebelling as the scent of blood in the air grew thicker and the male cried out again.

She had to do something.

Pain tore through her as she moved and she bit back the cry that burned up her throat and somehow managed to get onto her knees. Her hand shook as she gripped her thigh, breathing hard to bring the pain back to a manageable level so her head would stop spinning. Her stomach turned again, the warm wetness of the blood that covered her chest and her arm making her want to vomit.

Boots appeared before her.

Not Fuery's.

She tipped her head back, her eyes watering as she struggled to breathe through the agony tearing her apart.

The second male.

He glared down at her and raised his sword.

She pitied him.

A clawed hand closed around the front of his throat from behind and savagely snapped his head up as it dragged him backwards, away from her. He bellowed in agony as Fuery raked those claws down his back as he spun the male away from him. The male arched forwards as he staggered across the stones to land on his knees near the other male.

Her eyes landed on the prone elf.

Blood glistened in a pool beneath him, spreading outwards across the packed dirt, still seeping from the lacerations that covered his face and body. Blank eyes stared straight at her.

Dead.

The male was dead.

"Fuery," she whispered, and he looked over his shoulder at her. Fire. It blazed in his eyes. Burned right through her. She shook her head. "Do not."

The injured male foolishly moved.

Fuery snapped back to face him and her heart lunged into her throat, propelling her onto her feet. She cried out as white-hot fire seared her chest but didn't stop. She grabbed Fuery's arm and pulled him back, refusing to let him kill the other male.

It would be too much for him.

He turned on her, flashing his fangs, and pulled his arm free of her grip. She sagged to her knees again, despair flowing through her as she realised he was already too far gone, slipped into the black abyss.

No.

She shook away her fear, refusing to succumb to it and lose hope.

She could still help him.

She glared at the damned shackle around her wrist. If she could get it off, she might have enough strength left to teleport. She only needed one shot.

Fuery needed Hartt.

He needed help.

She could get it for him.

She moved onto her knees and slowly crawled across the flagstones towards the well, and the male she had killed. Fuery's snarls rang in her ears, his pain echoing on her body as he fought and the darkness pushing at their link, trying to seep into her. She held it back, refusing to let it overcome her too, but also refusing to close her connection to Fuery.

She was his light.

He needed her.

The darkness had him, but she wouldn't give up on him. As long as she could hold the connection between them open, she would. As long as she could steal even a drop of his pain to help him, she would. She wouldn't give up. Never. Not until she drew her final breath.

She reached the dead male and slumped beside him, fighting to catch her breath.

Fuery moved like a wraith in the darkness, toying with the poor male, making him turn this way and that, his sword cutting through the air in desperate strikes that hit nothing. His fear flowed over her, tainting the air together with the heavy odour of blood.

Her mate stopped behind the male and grinned as he shoved his hand forwards, driving his claws deep into the male's side, ripping a scream from him.

She had to stop him before it was too late.

She mustered her strength, lifted her hand and searched the young male she had killed for his set of steels. When she found them, she sank back against his legs. Her hand shook as she opened the leather wrapped around them and she grimaced as she lowered her other arm away from her chest, relieving the pressure on her wound.

Her vision wobbled as she pulled out each steel and tried them, wriggling them in the lock, her frustration mounting as she failed to get any of them to work.

A bellow sounded.

Then silence.

She stilled, her strength flowing from her as she fought for breath and battled the pain.

Fuery grunted as his knees hit the ground beside the male he had just killed, breathing hard and fast, his chest heaving as he stared straight ahead, the flare of crimson around his eyes bright in the darkness.

But it was fading.

She wanted to cry as violet began to emerge again.

The need to reach him had her finding her feet and he looked at her. Her beautiful warrior. Blood and dirt covered his face, and rips in his armour revealed deep lacerations that she could feel echoing on her body through their bond. He needed her.

She staggered towards him.

A wall of black appeared in front of her and she bumped into it.

Slowly tilted her head back.

"*No,*" she breathed.

"It is time to come home." Eirwyn grabbed her right wrist in a bruising grip. "It is time to end this foolish behaviour."

She tried to twist free of his hold, but he only tightened it and she cried out as pain seared her bones and they felt as if they might break.

She called her dagger to her left hand and grunted as she swiped at him, cutting him across his right shoulder before he could block the blow.

He glared down at her, his violet eyes brightening as his pointed ears flared back against his ponytail, and growled as he caught her wrist and twisted it. She cried out and dropped the dagger.

He pressed forwards, into her, and snarled, "I can see I will have to keep you locked away until the day of the ceremony. You are the key to my future happiness after all... the key to gaining power and a position in the council that advises the prince's elders."

Shaia spat in his face. "I am not an object you can use as you please!"

He backhanded her and she dropped to the dirt, her ears ringing as pain swamped her and his grip on her right wrist growing tighter as he held her arm above her head.

Fuery's vicious growl cut through the sound.

"Take your fucking hands off her."

Eirwyn slowly turned to look at him, a smile curving his lips. "Come and get her."

Her eyes widened as something hit her.

He was trying to drive Fuery into the darkness, was going to play on his need as her mate to protect her and use it against him.

If Fuery became truly lost, or better yet dead, then his claim on her would end and Eirwyn would be able to claim her. Prince Loren wouldn't be able to condemn Eirwyn for taking her under his wing, giving her a shoulder to cry on and a place to call home.

"Do not do it, Fuery." She shook her head. "He is playing you. Go to Hartt and get help."

Fuery staggered onto his feet and bared his fangs at Eirwyn, and despair mingled with desperation swept through her. He wasn't listening.

Her heart bled for him as he swayed on his feet and she looked at him, her beautiful warrior all torn up and on the verge of collapse, his armour in ruins and blood covering him, but still refusing to give up.

Still fighting for her.

Eirwyn's smile turned cold. "It was not difficult to lure you here. Honestly, I wonder why you were ever given the rank of commander. You clearly lack the necessary intelligence."

Fuery snarled at that. "Because I *earned* it… and was not given it… and you were the fool for setting a trap so far from help… one that easily became my trap for you."

Eirwyn's face darkened. "No… all you did was spare me having to waste my coin to take back what is mine."

Fuery was gone when she blinked, appearing right in front of Eirwyn. Eirwyn teleported and landed behind Fuery, and her mate growled as a blast of telekinesis hit him in the back and sent him flying over her head. She squeaked and ducked, and flinched as he hit the wall on the other side of the fortress.

She scrambled for her dagger, snatched it up and roared as she sprang to her feet, mustering all of her strength as she launched at Eirwyn. He backhanded her again, sending her down hard, and her grip on her dagger loosened. It spun away from her.

Landing at Eirwyn's feet.

He looked down at it, casually bent and scooped it up. He weighed it in his palm and grinned as his gaze slid back to Fuery as her mate found his feet again.

"Fitting you die by a blade you gave her… it was such a shame that you attacked her and she had to defend herself like that." Eirwyn's slow smile as he closed his fingers around the hilt of the dagger chilled her blood.

"You dare." She tried to get onto her feet, but her legs gave out and she grunted as she landed on her knees, her entire body trembling as pain burned across her chest.

He slid her a black look that told her to be quiet and kicked off.

Fuery was gone before he could reach him, disappeared in stilted black lines. The moment he reappeared near her, he went flying again, spinning through the air.

Eirwyn chuckled where he stood with his hand outstretched, his palm facing her mate. "You really are predictable."

Her link to Fuery grew increasingly agitated, the darkness in it growing stronger as he picked himself up again, and she knew with chilling certainty that he was falling into it.

Losing himself again.

She couldn't let it happen.

She growled and found her feet, staggered across the courtyard of the fortress towards Eirwyn, and gritted her teeth as she held her right hand out towards him and pushed it forwards, hurling a blast of telekinesis at him.

He barely rocked on his heels.

She cursed in the elf tongue, the rattle of the chain between the manacles still attached to her other hand mocking her.

Eirwyn appeared before her, gripped her by her throat and hauled her up to him. "You continue to resist me and I will have to punish you."

She raised her knee and landed a hard blow between his legs.

He grunted and dropped her, doubled over and then growled as he lifted his head and fixed her with a black look.

She didn't have a chance to evade his blow.

The dagger cut across her stomach.

She looked down, dazedly watching the line of crimson that appeared in its wake just above her navel, and then shrieked as he hit her with a blast of telekinesis, sending her rocketing across the courtyard.

Her back hit the wall of the well and the air burst from her lungs.

She felt it the second the darkness consumed Fuery and he was lost to her.

The link between them flooded with darkness, oily and smothering, and then it was gone.

Leaving her empty.

"No," she wheezed, and tried to move but she didn't have the strength as the shallow cut across her stomach burned fiercely.

She refused to believe it was gone again. It was still there. She struggled to focus on it as Fuery roared and hurled himself at Eirwyn, his black sword clashing with the one the male had taken from the ground. He was faster now, his eyes burning crimson as he teleported in bursts of jagged black smoke, but Eirwyn blocked him at every turn, faster still.

Fuery.

She growled as Eirwyn managed to land a blow, his sword piercing Fuery's shoulder and tearing a grunt from his bloodied lips. Fuery gripped the blade and shoved forwards, knocking Eirwyn back, and attacked again.

She tried to tear her eyes away from the battle so she could focus on restoring the connection between them, but it was impossible. She could only stare with her heart in her throat, a timid thing on the verge of breaking as Fuery fought with every last drop of his strength, taking blow after blow as he sought an opening. He whirled beneath Eirwyn's sword to land on his knees and growled as he thrust forwards with his own blade.

Her heart almost stopped, breath hitching as she watched, waiting for it to hit.

Eirwyn swept his blade up in a swift arc, knocking it against Fuery's, and her mate's katana sailed through the air.

Fuery growled and looked in the direction it had gone as it clattered across the stones.

Eirwyn grinned and raised his sword.

Shaia roared, willed her portal and moved the moment the dagger whipped into her hand, hurling it point over end at his back.

It struck.

Bounced hilt-first off his shoulders and dropped to the flagstones behind him.

He slowly turned to look over his shoulder at her, his face a black mask of fury that promised pain.

He brought his blade down, aimed at Fuery's throat as her mate fought to stand.

"Fuery!" She couldn't watch.

Fuery threw himself forwards, rolled and snatched the dagger as he came onto his feet behind Eirwyn, and roared as he plunged it deep into the male's neck. Blood burst from beneath the guard, spraying everywhere. Eirwyn's face froze in a look of disbelief and horror, and she couldn't drag her eyes away from his as the light left them.

When it had slowed to a trickle, Fuery released Eirwyn and watched him slump to the ground, no trace of emotion on his bloodstained face. He eased into a crouch, resting on his haunches, and prodded him, rocking him back and forth, as if checking whether he was going to spring back to life.

It struck her that he wanted him to.

Like a feline with its prey, he couldn't understand that he had killed the male, was confused that the fight was suddenly over, and disappointed.

Something else struck her as his face slowly set in a scowl and he began shoving Eirwyn's body harder, as if that would bring his foe back to life, and then started to rain blows down on the dead male's chest, ripping at it with his claws.

His bloodlust wasn't sated. It needed more.

"Fuery," she whispered, desperate to stop him and unable to watch him ripping into the body in such a savage, brutal way. "It's over."

He stilled, tilted his head slightly towards her, his overlong wild blue-black hair concealing his face from her, and then rose fluidly onto his feet, twisting and coming to face her in one sweeping move.

It wasn't over.

She could see it in his crimson eyes as they landed on her.

She could feel it in her soul as he advanced on her and she witnessed the hunger in him.

He wasn't sated.

He needed more and she was the only one left alive.

The only one who could satisfy that hunger that ruled him.

The need for blood and violence.

A need for death.

CHAPTER 28

Shaia stood her ground on trembling legs as Fuery prowled towards her, his hunger beating in her blood together with a terrible weight of darkness that pressed down on her. She weathered that darkness, holding their fragile connection open as it began to form again, hoping her light would reach him and free him of its grip. Hope that felt as fragile as their bond to her, liable to shatter and fade at any moment, and take the last of her strength with it.

"Fuery," she whispered, keeping her voice soft and light, free of the fear that ran in her veins.

He wouldn't hurt her.

He wouldn't.

His crimson eyes narrowed on her face, and then lowered to her throat.

Her pulse ticked up, a staccato rhythm that sent a trickle of panic flowing through her and jacked her fear up another notch, until her legs felt like rubber beneath her.

She reached a hand out to him, and he halted and growled at it, his expression turning wary as he eyed it, as if she was going to lash out at him.

Only if he gave her no choice.

"Listen to my voice, Fuery." She swallowed her pounding heart and forced herself to remain where she was as his eyes snapped back up to her face and he snarled, flashing enormous fangs at her.

She wasn't going to be cowed by him.

She was strong, and he had taught her to fight well. If he became a threat to her, she would fight him. Even with the shackle binding her left wrist, she had the strength to call her dagger to her hand.

But gods, she didn't want it to come to that.

"It is me, Fuery... your Shaia. Your mate."

He paused again, his dirty face softened and he stared at her blankly, and she could see she was reaching him.

The relief that went through her had her lowering her guard as her hope blazed brighter.

Fuery was suddenly in front of her, his clawed fingers closing over her upper arms, pinning them to her sides, and his eyes on her throat.

She struggled against him, adrenaline rushing through her as she tried to get her arms free. "Fuery, no!"

Because he had thought he had killed her once, and it had torn him apart for centuries. If he killed her for real, it would destroy him, and the darkness would finally devour him before he could end himself, transforming him into a mindless monster who knew only an endless thirst for blood.

She managed to get her hands between them and went to shove.

Tremendous pain rolled through their link, stealing her breath and making her still as it battered her. Gods, he was hurting. He needed her.

He opened his mouth to speak as his corrupted eyes sought hers.

He went flying off her.

Shaia blinked as he suddenly sailed through the air to land hard on the grey flagstones of the fortress courtyard and tumble across them, grunting as he slammed into the wall and dust rained down on him.

"Fuck, Shaia… are you alright?" Hartt's deep voice rolled over her from behind, a breathless note to it that spoke of exertion. "I got here as quickly as I could but tracking Fuery through his implant is difficult at the best of times."

She wasn't sure what an implant was, but part of her was glad to hear his voice and feel his presence. Not because he had saved her from Fuery, but because he might be able to save Fuery.

Before she could look at him, Fuery rushed past her in a blur and barrelled into him, his roar echoing around the broken walls of the fortress. Hartt grunted and she turned in time to see Fuery ploughing him into the low wall of the well.

"Fuery!" She managed two steps towards him before he halted her in her tracks.

He looked over his shoulder as he gripped Hartt by his throat, both hands closed tightly around it as he bent the male backwards over the well, in danger of sending him plummeting into it.

Gods.

The sheer rage, the raw fury in his eyes stopped her dead.

It drummed in her blood too.

Told her everything she needed to know.

He thought Hartt was going to take her from him, he feared that he was going to lose his mate, and it was giving the darkness a firmer hold over him, allowing it to drag him down into the abyss.

"Hartt, don't—" She winced as Fuery flew off him, tumbled across the flagstones past her and rolled onto his feet.

Her mate shook his head, his shoulder-length black hair a tangled mess as thick hanks of it fell down from the thong he had tied it with at the back of his head. He hunkered down and growled as he bared his fangs at Hartt.

"You're making him worse," she bit out and Hartt spared her a glance.

She winced again as Fuery slammed into him, using the opening she had given him, and Hartt hit the well again. He shoved the flat of his palm against Fuery's chin, pushing his head back as they wrestled with each other.

"Calm the fuck down," Hartt snapped and for a moment, Fuery eased off, but then Hartt made the mistake of looking at her.

Fuery grabbed him by his throat and banged his head against the thick wall of the well.

Hartt snarled and teleported, and she gasped as Fuery almost toppled into the well, barely catching himself at the last second. He pushed both hands against the wall and spun to face Hartt where he had reappeared beside her.

"Gods, stop coming near me!" She shoved him too, and he growled at her as an affronted look flickered across his face.

"I came here to help you," Hartt barked.

She knew that, but Fuery didn't. All he could see was her dressed in nothing but her undergarments and a ruined, open tunic, and another male trying to defend her.

Shaia grimaced as Fuery hit him hard in the gut with his right shoulder, lifting his feet off the ground.

The hunger that raged in their bond grew stronger.

Awareness rolled through her as her brain caught up and she watched Fuery as he fought Hartt, dodging every attempt the male made to grab hold of him and flashing fangs at every turn.

The pain she had felt through their bond was responsible for Fuery's hunger and the need that was driving him. It wasn't pain born of the darkness, but it was pain that gave the darkness a stronger hold on him and was pulling him down into the abyss.

He hadn't wanted to hurt her when he had turned on her.

He had wanted her blood.

His need to heal was driving him, his instincts hijacking control, a desire to survive that she was familiar with because it burned in her too.

She catalogued his injuries and focused on their bond and a trick she had heard mates could use. Her eyes widened as his injuries burned on her body, pain blazing in long lines over her chest, legs, and arms, and she gasped.

Fuery stilled and looked at her.

"No," he growled, deep voice like rolling thunder, and turned towards her.

Hartt tackled him from behind, taking him down face-first onto the hard ground.

Fuery snarled, elbowed Hartt in the face and twisted beneath him as the male shifted his weight to one side. Before Hartt could defend, Fuery was on top of him, his fangs buried deep in the male's throat.

The relief that went through Fuery was swift and had her head spinning a little as she sagged to her knees.

Her mouth watered as she watched Fuery, her own need for blood rising to the fore as the echoes of his injuries faded, leaving her aware of her own again. She pressed one hand to the long slash across her chest and the other against the shallow cut across her stomach. Both were still bleeding in places and her fangs ached, descending as she watched her mate feed.

Hartt muttered words beneath his breath.

Fuery reared back from him, his hands flying to his head. He gripped it hard as he roared and shoved off Hartt, staggering a few steps before collapsing to his knees.

She looked between her mate and Hartt as the male lay on the flagstones, breathing hard, staring at the lightening sky.

He was pale, too pale, his skin ashen and lips drained of colour, and when he slid a look at her, his eyes sent a chill skating over her skin.

Black blotches tainted his violet irises.

She looked to Fuery.

The crimson was gone from his eyes.

Because Hartt had somehow taken some of the darkness from him.

"It isn't over," Hartt husked as he rolled onto his side and struggled to sit up. "I have never seen Fuery this bad."

She mustered her strength and crawled across the flagstones to Hartt, and reached out to grasp his shoulders to help him.

Fuery snarled.

The bond flared back to life inside her, warning her away from the other male.

She eased her hand away from Hartt and looked at Fuery.

He knelt on the ground, staring through dull empty eyes at the flagstones, his body motionless, as if he was trapped inside his own body somehow.

"The darkness is too strong this time." Hartt moved beside her, finally easing onto his knees, and sagged forwards as he gripped them and breathed hard. "I have done all I can through our bond and the spell."

"Spell?" Her gaze whipped back to him.

He nodded. "A blood bond with Fuery was never enough. I thought it would be... but when I almost lost Fuery the first time, I realised I needed a stronger power over him."

She stared into Hartt's eyes, at the darkness swirling there. "This spell allows you to steal some of the darkness from Fuery and take it into you. You are tainting yourself. Why?"

Hartt gave a stiff shrug, and she thought he wouldn't answer her, but then he looked across at his friend and sighed, a softness entering his eyes that spoke of love and something more.

"I owe Fuery a lot... a life debt... the sort that is impossible to repay. He saved me once, and so I do what I can to save him... because I owe him."

It was very noble, but also extremely dangerous. Hartt's line of work placed him in enough danger of becoming tainted without him taking on Fuery's darkness too.

How tainted was he?

Fuery suddenly collapsed.

She was by his side in an instant, rolling him onto his back so his head rested on her knees. He stared at the sky above her, his black eyes glassy, and her heart hitched as his pupils began to contract and turn elliptical again.

Hartt stopped beside her, his eyes on Fuery and his tone sombre as he spoke.

"It's your turn now. I can't save Fuery this time. Only you have that power."

CHAPTER 29

Endless darkness stretched around him and he drowned in it, let it roll over him and pull him apart as it put him together, embraced him and smothered him. Black needs shot through him, and he revelled in them and the pleasure that blazed at just the thought of indulging them.

The coppery sweet taste of blood on his tongue was thick, swirled in his senses and made his gut clench with a need for more. Delicious. Intoxicating. It was everything he needed, all that he desired. It filled him up, but left him empty at the same time, craving more. Eternally.

He drifted in the black abyss, that craving creating a driving urge for blood, transforming him into a slave for it. An addict. He clung to that need as fiercely as the part of him that lingered and refused to die, a part that didn't want to give in to his hunger for blood, clung to something else.

Something he couldn't see or describe, a feeling that beat within him that made no sense, because he was part of the darkness now.

Why would he ever want to step into the light?

But that dreadful light beckoned him, tried to pierce the veil of night with each fresh wave of blood on his tongue, slowly cracking a hole in the void around him to allow pale gold to filter in and blind him.

A sound rolled through the black.

A growl.

Followed by a whispered word.

A word that held such emotion, such force, that it shook him to his soul.

Fuery.

It echoed in his mind in the voice of an angel, and the light grew stronger, flickering brighter in the darkness. He snarled and pushed back against it, afraid the vile light would steal the darkness away. The darkness was his home, his lover, his sanctuary.

His everything.

He sank back into it and the light faded.

Fuery.

The voice came again in a blinding flash of lightning that revealed nightmarish creatures formed of stilted black ribbons of smoke. They skittered into the shadows, chittering at each other, the sound combining into a rolling boom of thunder in his ears before dropping to silence as the light faded again. He felt the creatures roam closer, edging nearer to him. Sensed their intent.

Growled as a need to fight them arrowed through him.

The sweet taste of blood on his tongue grew stronger still, and he moaned as he drank it down, savoured it and let the warmth of it flow through him to chase the cold away again.

Fuery.

The lightning struck again and the inky creatures bared sharp fangs, their talons poised to seize his ankles and wrists as the blinding white illuminated them. Red eyes flashed as they hunkered down on all fours, their pointed ears flaring back against the jagged sides of their heads. One hissed at the light, and the others joined it.

Fire began to burn in his blood.

Heat that gave way to wretched icy cold as the light flickered and faded once more.

Red eyes moved in the darkness, blazing like fire, and he growled as a pair appeared above him. Cold hands pressed down on his shoulders, talons digging into his flesh, but no cry left his lips as the pain burned through him, stealing away the last of the warmth.

The creature snarled and pushed him downwards, and the ground beneath him became thick black liquid that seeped over his ankles and hands, and sucked him down, pulling him deeper into it.

"Fuery!"

Her sweet voice struck like lightning once more, revealing the creature perched on his chest.

He stared into its crimson eyes and saw a shadow of himself in them, in its twisted form that began to distort to take on his appearance. The black beast bared pointed teeth at him, wide lips peeling back off them, stretching almost to the lobes of its ears, and weight pressed down on him, cracking his ribs, compressing his lungs. Pushing him deeper into the darkness trying to swallow him.

"Drink, my love."

The taste of blood on his tongue grew thicker, stronger still, and it swept through him like a blazing trail of wildfire, of light so pure it stung his eyes and he couldn't contain it. The creature growled as its skin began to fracture, and the light shone through, chasing back the darkness.

He looked down at his own body as he struggled to pull his limbs free of the black tar. That same light poured from him, glowed from the cracks between each tiny scale of his armour.

The darkness around him began to shift as the creature balanced on his chest scrambled off him and tried to flee into the shadows. The light grew brighter still, and he squinted against it, trying to see the darkness that was his home.

No. It wasn't his home.

His home was this light that bathed him in warmth, in love he could feel all the way to his bones, and called him back to it with every sweet drop of her blood.

The creature let out a pained screech as that thought struck him and lit up the land, and green rolled outwards from beneath him, a thousand blooms springing to life from the long grass, and blue devoured the black above him.

With one last hiss in his direction, the black wraith disappeared into the shadows.

Gone for now.

But not forever.

He could feel it inside him, writhing and furious, battering the cage the light created and desperate to escape it, to drive that light back out of him.

"Fuery?" A soft hand stroked his cheek, smearing wetness across it.

Gods, he wanted to consume the owner of that voice, wanted to devour all of her and take her into him so she would never leave him again.

The taste of her blood on his tongue was Heaven.

Like dew and lavender.

"Come back to me."

He obeyed that command, opening his eyes and looking up at the female who leaned over him, upside down in his vision. Her violet eyes were bright with unshed tears, filled with love that stole his breath and made him feel unworthy of her, but blessed at the same time.

Her smile wobbled on worry-reddened lips as she lowered her head and he closed his eyes as she pressed a kiss to his brow and he felt her relief go through his blood.

Together with her fear.

"You scared me," she whispered, her lips brushing his skin, and there were a thousand things that he wanted to tell her, some about where he had been that he knew would scare her, and some about the way he felt about her, but he couldn't find his voice as she pulled her wrist away from his lips and wrapped her arms around him.

Home.

This was home.

Light rushed through him as he opened himself to her, and the darkness writhed harder, desperate to escape its touch.

He relaxed into her embrace, not fighting the light this time, letting it flow into him from her, savouring it as sweetly as he had savoured the blood she had given him.

He raised his hands above him and wrapped his arms around her as best he could, holding her to him. Gods, it felt good to hold her, to feel her in his arms and know she was safe.

He frowned as he focused on her.

Cold chased the warmth away.

She was weak.

The cold became numbing ice as he gripped her shoulders and eased her back, and saw how pale she was. He shifted onto his knees and frowned at the angry red marks on her exposed midriff and legs that had joined her own injuries, and growled at the way the long gash across her chest wept crimson.

She had harmed herself by taking on some of his injuries, and while he was thankful she had because it had helped him come back from the darkness, he couldn't stop the anger from boiling through his veins.

"I will get her blood." Hartt disappeared before Fuery could even look at him, leaving him alone with Shaia.

She shook beneath his hands.

"You... I... gods... Shaia. You shouldn't have." He looked her over, cataloguing every injury that had been his, and thankful that she had left the deepest of his injuries alone for him to bear.

He cursed himself.

His mate had hurt herself for his sake and had then endangered herself further by giving him blood to help him heal his other injuries.

Sweet fucking gods, he didn't deserve her.

"You are my mate, Fuery... I would take on ten times as many injuries and give you ten times as much blood if it meant saving you." She tried to smile, but her lips barely twitched and her eyes gained a dull edge that terrified him. "I just need to rest."

No, what she needed was blood.

Hartt had gone for some, but he couldn't wait. He feared he would lose her if he did.

He stared into her eyes, another fear taking hold of him as she shook in his arms.

What if he tainted her with his blood?

He shook that fear away, refusing to allow it to sink its claws into him and stop him. His blood didn't contain the darkness that still infested him. That was held in his soul, his to bear. Giving her blood wouldn't harm her.

But it would help her.

He wouldn't let any of his fears hold him back anymore.

Because he knew in his black soul, in his dark heart, that he would never hurt Shaia.

Even in the grip of the darkness, lost in the black abyss, he hadn't hurt her. He had bitten her, had wanted to devour her, but his love for her and his instincts as her mate had held him back and stopped him from harming her.

"I'm sorry I scared you," he whispered and cupped her cheeks, making her look at him as fear began to get the better of him again—fear of losing her. "I would never have hurt you. I lost control because—"

"You are my ki'aro," she murmured and smiled softly as her eyes held his, all of her love shining in them, "and other males threatened me."

He nodded. "I wanted your blood... and that was all I wanted from you. I was never going to hurt you."

She gave a subtle dip of her chin. "I know... I know, Fuery. You needed blood, my blood... that of your mate. It was wrong of me to fear you, even for a second. I am sorry... I should have trusted you."

Fuery shook his head and let her see in his eyes and feel through their bond that her words had touched him, had reached the deepest part of him, and soothed the side that was still afraid of hurting her.

She raised a trembling hand and brushed her thumb across his lip, her gaze distant as she stared at his mouth.

Her irises brightened.

He felt the need go through her, hunger that echoed in his own body in response.

"I need your blood now," she whispered throatily. "Will you give it to me?"

CHAPTER 30

Shaia felt the fear that went through Fuery as he stared at her, conflict reigning in his eyes as the black finally began to abate, leaving a ring of violet around his wide pupils. She waited, on fire with the need blazing in her soul, a need that had ignited the moment he had sunk his fangs into her arm and taken the first sip of her blood.

It wasn't only the toll of taking on some of his smaller injuries and giving him blood that had her hungry with a need of him though. Part of her ached to taste him again, to have his powerful blood on her tongue, sliding down her throat once more. That part of her mingled with the weakness infesting her, and had her eyes dropping to his throat as her hunger raged fiercer in her veins.

Her hands shook, muscles weak as she thought about blood, craved the taste of him and the strength that would come with it. Gods, she needed to feel that flowing into her to chase away the cold numbness that had seeped into her bones. Fear ran like an undercurrent through her body, whispering words to her that froze her soul and made it stronger.

She was weak.

She needed to feed.

She needed his blood.

Her mate's blood.

She looked down at the deep slash across her chest and the dark scarlet that had soaked into the bandages across her breasts. Beads of crimson dotted the line, trembling on the brink of falling as she shook with the force of her hunger and her need to survive.

She needed blood.

Was this how Fuery had felt?

She hadn't considered the consequences of giving Fuery her blood, hadn't noticed herself weakening as he had taken it in long deep draughts.

Now she was consumed by a need for blood, couldn't think of anything else as she stared at Fuery, waiting to hear his answer. The hunger grew ravenous, pushing at her and goading her to take what he wouldn't give her, and she wriggled in his grip, unaware of what she was doing as she fought his hold, her eyes fixed on the pulse ticking in his throat.

"Do not hate me," he whispered hoarsely, voice thick with the emotions that suddenly swept through her, stealing her breath so she couldn't answer him.

Never.

His grip loosened, and the part of her that wanted to press him to tell her his fears was crushed by the overwhelming need to sink her fangs into his flesh.

She lunged and struck hard on the left side of his throat as his armour cleared away from it.

Her hands seized his shoulders, fingertips pressing into his muscles as she collided with him.

He didn't resist.

He welcomed her, cradled her gently in his arms as he banded them around her, and she tried to be gentle with him in return.

The first taste of him had heat boiling through her veins and a single thought singing in her mind, born of the fear she could feel in their bond and knew came from him.

He wasn't darkness.

He was light that filled her until she was fit to burst, sent her soaring skyward as she desperately pulled on his strong blood that tasted of earth and spice, an absolute ambrosia to her.

She couldn't stop herself from biting him harder, desperate for more of him as she lost herself in his rich taste and the strength that immediately swept through her veins, sending her head spinning.

He was beautiful as he accepted her savagery, embracing her rather than pushing her away. He grunted with each bite, each fierce pull on his blood, but hissed too, bursts of pleasure that left his lips and had shame sweeping through him in the wake of each one, tinged with fear.

Gods, he didn't need to be ashamed.

She was lit up too, on fire with need even in her wounded state. She was as coiled tight as he was, the taste of his blood drugging her, sending a warm delicious haze through her that had her melting in his strong arms.

He cradled her, tenderly palming the nape of her neck and holding her to him as he whispered, "You are my forever... my reason for existing... my life... my heart."

Sweet gods, she loved this male.

Loved him so much she felt she might die in his arms right that second.

She fought her instincts and the hunger running rampant in her veins, and managed to slow her drinking.

A strained groan left his lips.

His fear spiked.

She smoothed her hands over his shoulders, slipped them beneath his arms and then wrapped her arms around him, pressing her palms against his back as she settled herself astride his thighs. The hunger that raged in her began to ease, transforming into a different need as she sucked on the wounds on his throat, taking sips of blood from him, and her head cleared enough that she could pinpoint his feelings in their bond.

She grew aware of something, and it broke her heart.

She needed to be gentle with him, as gentle as he was being with her, because he was fragile, broken in a way. She could see it now and it undid her, had sorrow sweeping through her in response, together with a need to hold on to him and never let go.

He drew her closer and murmured, "I am sorry... I am sorry I did this to you. I should not have."

That tore at her and she wrenched herself away from him, passion flaring hot in her veins, a need to tell him that he was wrong that only grew stronger as she caught the pain in his eyes.

He thought the sorrow he had felt in her was for herself, because she drank from him.

Because he believed he could taint her.

She cupped his sculpted dirty cheeks in her trembling palms. "I am not sorry. What you felt in me, Fuery... it's because of what you have been through... how you have suffered... and I was not there for you. I have been living my life oblivious to your pain, your suffering. Gods... I am a monster for that."

"No," he croaked and shook his head, his dark eyebrows furrowing as he fiercely gathered her to him, his grip bruising. Desperate. "I am the monster. You must see that now."

Shaia looked at him when he pushed her back, the link between them wide open, and his face hiding nothing from her, baring all of himself to her.

"All I can see is the male I thought I had lost," she whispered and brushed her thumbs across his cheeks as he tried to look away from her, keeping his gaze on her. "I see you, Fuery, and I want a second chance at the life we should have had."

He closed his eyes and tilted his face away from her. "I'm not the male I was back then."

"I know that." She feathered her fingers lower and caressed his strong jaw. "I'm not the same either… and I won't let you slip through my grasp again. I am done being everything society expects of me or my family want for me. I know my mind, and I know my heart… and it belongs to you, Fuery."

He slowly opened his eyes and looked at her, his expression softening as the darkness faded from it and their bond relayed his feelings to her, easing her fear and lightening her heart as she felt that he believed her.

She focused as she drew her right hand away from his face and he looked down at it just as the silver clasp he had returned to her appeared in it.

He didn't stop her as she gathered the top half of his hair and closed the clasp over it.

Her hand lingered on it, her body pressed close to his and his breath washing over her face as he stared at her.

"It was a token of my love, Fuery… and that love is the same today as it was all those centuries ago." She swept her hand down his hair to the nape of his neck and shook her head. "No… that is not true… that love is stronger now. It grows stronger every day, and nothing will stop that. I love you… now and forever… all of you."

He growled and gathered her to him, one hand pressing hard between her shoulder blades and the other fiercely gripping her nape as his mouth descended on hers.

She relaxed into him, holding him to her as she kissed him back, savouring the desperate way his lips moved across hers, as if he couldn't get enough of her.

She had missed this.

But she would never have to miss it again.

Their love had stood the test of time, and they would triumph over whatever lay ahead of them too, and would seize that future they wanted together.

Someone cleared their throat.

"Guess you don't really need this now."

Fuery growled at Hartt as his lips broke away from hers and he gathered her closer still, concealing her body by pressing it hard against his.

"I thought as much, so I brought this too." Hartt held her cloak out to her.

Fuery was quick to snatch it and wrap it around her as Hartt turned his back to give her some privacy. Her mate's motions slowed as he looked down at her chest and the dark pink line darting across it, and she felt the fear go through him again. She clutched his hands and squeezed them, bringing him back to her before the darkness could take hold.

"I'll be sure to keep out of trouble from now on." She smiled when he lifted his beautiful eyes, filled with worry and love for her, and settled them on hers.

He nodded, his relief flowing through their bond and shifting into another emotion as his eyes darkened. "I will protect you... I will never let anything happen to you. Never again. I swear that."

She wrapped her arms around him and sealed that promise with a kiss, making her own at the same time, swearing that she would do the same for him. She would always be there for him, to take care of him, to help him in whatever way she could, and if he ever needed her, she had a dagger and knew how to use it.

And perhaps he could teach her how to use a katana too.

The sour look on his face when she pulled back said that he knew her thoughts and it wasn't going to happen.

She would just have to change his mind.

She fingered his chest, running the pads of them over the small scales of his armour and the patches of exposed skin where it had been cut with an elven blade.

The heat that began to blaze in his eyes said that he wouldn't take much convincing.

Hartt cleared his throat again.

Fuery tugged at her cloak, holding the side of it nearest Hartt in a way that concealed her body from the elf's gaze, and looked at his friend.

"Thank you for being here for her," he said, and then added, "and for me."

Hartt scrubbed a hand around the back of his neck. "No problem. Just... tell me where you're going next time so I can help. You don't have to fight all your battles alone, Fuery."

Her mate seemed to consider that as he looked between Hartt and her as she finished fastening her tunic as best she could and called her trousers to her, covering her legs.

He nodded.

Hartt held a metal canister out to him. "Now, both of you drink this, or I get elf medicine."

The face Fuery pulled and the flicker of fear that went through him warned her that elf medicine was not something she wanted to try.

He snatched the canister, unscrewed the cap and shoved it towards her. "Drink."

She wanted to refuse and make him drink first, but took the container and lifted it to her lips. The blood was cold and tasted sharp, and she shuddered as it slipped down her throat.

"You get used to it." Fuery looked around as she sipped the blood, dark eyes scouring the fortress, and when they stopped on something, he snapped his fingers and pointed to it.

Hartt tossed him a scowl. "I'm not your dog."

But he went to fetch whatever it was Fuery wanted anyway, grumbling the whole time. Fuery's eyes drifted back to her, darkening as he watched her drinking the blood and his hands slipped beneath her cloak to palm her backside where it rested on his legs.

His left hand suddenly shot up beside his head and he glared at Hartt. She lowered the canister from her lips and frowned as Fuery uncurled his hand and revealed the set of steels Hartt had launched at him.

She watched as he nimbly unlocked her remaining cuff, took the set of shackles and eyed them, and then half-smiled as they disappeared together with the steels. He looked quite pleased as he lifted his eyes to meet hers and took the canister from her.

"It's expensive to get shackles impregnated with such a powerful spell," he said it casually and then began drinking.

"They could probably hold a dragon," Hartt chimed in and Fuery nodded enthusiastically. "You know my bond with you means we get to share them."

Fuery scowled at that. "Some things I don't share."

Hartt's expression remained unreadable as he folded his arms across his chest.

Fuery tossed the canister over his shoulder.

Shaia didn't get it until he wrapped his arms around her, gathered her to him and growled low in his throat.

Hartt grinned and waved his hand through the air. "I was kidding. She's not my type."

A slow smile curved Fuery's lips. "You mean, elf and female? I thought that *was* your type?"

Hartt glared at him. "Pushing your luck now. I don't have to teleport your arse home."

Shaia wanted to mention that she could probably teleport Fuery back to the guild but held her tongue. This was clearly a standard threat between Hartt and Fuery, in what seemed to be a rather strange but normal round of banter. She had a lot to learn about this new world she was stepping into, one where a procured set of shackles was met with excitement and glee. But then, she supposed finding a set of shackles that could hold a dragon might come in handy for an assassin, and could just save their life.

That had her feeling as enthusiastic about them.

Fuery gripped her waist and helped her onto her feet, setting her down in front of him.

She gasped as he swung her up into his arms a moment later, cradling her against his chest with one arm around her back and the other under her knees, and she wrapped her arms around his neck.

He stared at her, his black-to-violet eyes beautiful in a way in the morning light as they shone at her, showing her all of his feelings.

"Ready to go?" Hartt said and placed his hand on Fuery's arm.

Shaia nodded and smiled as she spoke the words in her heart and stared into Fuery's widening eyes.

"Let's go home."

CHAPTER 31

Fuery prowled back and forth along the grassy bank, his eyes never leaving his foe as he wrestled with the darkness that pulsed in his veins, blazed in his blood. He growled and pivoted on his heel, swiftly turning to pace back the way he had come. His muscles coiled tight beneath his black armour, the pale sunlight catching the tiny scales and making iridescent colours ripple over them.

He breathed through his nerves, vanquished his fear, would let nothing stand in his way as he mastered the darkness, pulling back on the reins to force it to yield to him.

He had been training for over two weeks for this mission, had been mentally preparing himself the past day, and now it was time.

The broad wooden door of the elegant pale stone mansion slowly opened.

His heartbeat jacked up, hammering in his throat, and he curled his fingers into fists at his sides as he turned towards the two-storey building and bravely strode forwards, through the open gate that intersected the stone wall and into the grand garden that suited the house it embraced.

Shaia appeared from the shadows, stopping on the doorstep, looking radiant in a pale lilac dress and a wrought silver corset that hugged her torso, arcing beneath her breasts to push them upwards and cinching in her waist.

This was it.

He blew out his breath, tipped his chin up and marched towards her.

His nerve faltered as her mother appeared behind her and he spotted her father lingering in the vestibule.

Shaia said something, her sweet smile capturing his black heart and easing his nerves as she turned from her mother and came to face him. She held her hand out to him and he went to her, couldn't stop his feet from carrying him towards her to close the distance between them. He needed to touch her. He needed to hold her.

It consumed him, drove him onwards despite his fears and the insidious words whispering at the back of his mind, born of his past.

He lifted his hand when he neared her, wanting to slip it into hers and clutch it, but hesitated when eyes landed on him. It was only for a heartbeat before he conquered the fear that had birthed it, but it was a hesitation nonetheless.

The feel of Shaia's soft warm hand in his drove all fear out of his heart and the way she slipped her fingers between his to lock their palms together eased his nerves.

"You remember Fuery." Her tone was matter of fact, bright despite the anger he could feel in her.

His little viper.

He had worried about bringing her to the guild when she had announced it was their home now, hadn't been able to sleep a wink the first two nights, forever on alert and waiting for something terrible to happen, something that would drive her away from such a dangerous place. He had imagined it all, tormenting himself with visions of her being harassed by the other assassins, or harmed by them.

But on the third day of her being there, when he had been called to Hartt's office and had left her unattended for the first time, she had shown him that he had no reason to worry about her.

His worst fear had come true, and one of the newer assassins had dared to block her path when she had been coming to find him, trapping her in the corridor and speaking disgusting things to her.

He had felt her fear go through him.

Had burst from Hartt's office.

But by the time he had reached her, she had laid the wolf shifter out on his back and had been poised on top of him, her dagger pressed against his throat and her other hand fiercely gripping the male's hair, pulling at it as she growled at him, flashing fangs in warning.

Gods, he had been hard in an instant.

His gorgeous, surprising little viper.

She had a mean streak in her, one that stole his heart.

He had helped her stand, had kicked the wolf's arse until he had been little more than a whimpering, apologising mess on the floor, and had then started her training.

She was a natural.

Even Hartt was impressed with the skill she displayed at such an early stage in her training with sword and spear.

Fuery had warned his friend that she wasn't going to become their first female assassin.

Although he wasn't sure how long he could stick to his guns on that one.

The thought of Shaia coming with him on missions was appealing, always there when he needed her calming touch, or hungered for her.

Her gaze landed on him during a lull in her conversation with her parents, and he burned as an electric sizzle chased over his skin, cranking his muscles even tighter.

He slid his eyes to land on her, breathed harder as he spotted the unmistakable flicker of desire and need in her violet ones and felt it ripple through their connection.

Oh gods, yes, he could imagine taking her on missions with him. It would be glorious.

She would watch his back, and he would tear apart any foe who tried to reach hers.

"Fuery?" she whispered and subtly widened her eyes as she jerked her head a little towards her parents.

He shook his wicked thoughts away and focused on his mission.

They had decided to continue where they had left off all those centuries ago, starting with telling her parents they were mated and she was leaving with him. That had been her idea. Her parents already knew she was his fated one, and they were bound, and that had been enough for him, but it hadn't been enough for her.

So here he was.

Trying to play nice to appease her.

Because despite the things her family had done to her, they were still her family, and for some reason he couldn't fathom, she loved them and wanted to remain in touch with them. This was important to her, and so it was important to him.

But he was only going to let her visit once every decade and he was coming with her when it happened. He wouldn't put it past her parents to attempt to find a way to take her from him and hand her over to a noble male of their choosing.

"Shaia is mine," he growled, a little harsher and more possessive than anticipated, and weathered her glare that told him he was doing this wrong. He cleared his throat and told himself again to play nice. "Your daughter is my ki'ara, and we are bound. She is no longer your pawn or your possession to do with as you please. She is mine now, and I will protect her by any means necessary."

A little harsh again judging by how Shaia sighed emphatically.

"Very well," Sarea muttered and barely spared him a glance before she turned and swept imperiously away from them, disappearing into the house.

Fuery half-expected Aylen to do the same.

The male surprised him by coming forwards and extending a hand to him.

He eyed it.

Shaia nudged him in the ribs.

He sighed, released her hand and clasped the one the male offered.

"Hurt her, and I will hunt you down like the tainted beast you are," Aylen growled.

Fuery grinned, flashing his emerging fangs, and gripped the male's hand harder, squeezing his bones. "You wouldn't see me coming."

Shaia placed one hand on his arm and her other on her father's and broke them apart. "No one is killing the other one today. This was meant to be a happy occasion, Father."

Aylen looked at her, a sombre edge to his expression. "You love him?"

She nodded. "I love him, and I have loved only him, and I will love only him. Even if he hadn't been my fated one, I would have loved him... because he is my soul mate... my one true mate."

The older male sighed. "Very well. I have seen the error of our ways with you, Shaia, and although your mother would never say it, I do believe she is happy for you. Seeing you in this visit, seeing how happy you are, has made us both realise that this is what is best for you."

Tears lined her eyes, and Fuery wanted to growl at the male for upsetting her, even when he knew they were tears of happiness, because her family weren't such utter bastards after all. His desire to rip them to pieces to make them pay for everything they had put her through faded a little.

Just a little.

If they ever upset her again, they would have him to deal with, and as he had told Aylen.

They wouldn't see him coming.

He did growl when Aylen pulled her into an embrace.

"Visit any time," he whispered, all sweet and nice as he glared at Fuery over her shoulder.

Fuery glared right back at him, making it clear that if she did come to visit, she wouldn't be alone. He wasn't going to risk them using a spell to lock her in her room or attempt to palm her off onto another male.

He snagged her arm and pulled her away from the male.

She came willingly, only sighing a little at him as she turned away from her family home and followed him along the path to the gate. When they reached it, she slipped her hand into his and he looked down at them. She gave his a squeeze, one that reassured him that she wasn't going anywhere.

She was his now.

She always had been.

"Did you mean that?" he muttered as he strode up the hill towards the woods, avoiding the path that would have taken them towards the village.

"With all my heart, Fuery," she whispered, her voice soft and warm, bringing light to his dark heart and chasing the storm from it, leaving it clear again.

He looked across at her and saw in her eyes, felt in their bond, that she had meant every word.

She would have loved him even if he hadn't been her fated one.

Soul mate.

He fidgeted with his tunic a little as it appeared on his body to replace his armour, adjusting it with his free hand, and couldn't find the courage to look at her as he found his voice.

"I would have loved you too," he murmured and refused to look at her as her eyes lifted and burned into his profile. "You are my true mate... the other half of my soul."

"Fuery." She had her arms around his neck and her lips on his before he could react, and all he could do was catch hold of her and drown in her kiss as she poured her love and her light into him, filling him up until he feared he might burst.

He gathered her against him, clinging to her as their hearts beat in unison and her feelings flowed into him, echoing his own.

"Gods, I love you," he whispered against her lips and clutched her to him, aware he was probably holding her too tightly but unable to stop himself.

He needed more of her.

All of her.

The world around him dropped away and another replaced it, the tall trees rustling in the evening breeze and the river behind him babbling as it coursed around the rocks and ran over the boulders in the bend.

Not his doing.

Shaia breathed hard in his arms, the exertion of teleporting him taking its toll on her, and he wanted to scold her for taxing herself by doing such a thing, but he couldn't find the will to be angry with her.

Not when she had brought him to this place.

Their place.

He set her down and walked to the tree, his boots sinking into the soft sandy earth on the bank of the river. He stroked his fingers over the marks on the trunk, remembering that day forty-two centuries ago, when he had made them to commemorate their mating. The marks were deep now, as if someone had returned frequently to carve them into the fresh layer of bark, stopping the tree from repairing them.

His heart warmed as he lingered with his fingers on them, aware that it had been Shaia's doing. She had come back to this place and had kept their love alive here.

"Fuery," Shaia whispered, voice drenched with the desire that suddenly flared in their bond, rushing through him.

He slowly turned to face her, his heart beginning a thumping rhythm against his ribs as his eyes landed on her where she stood on the earth, her nimble fingers unlacing the silver ribbon that held her corset closed over her chest and her eyes dark with need.

Need of him.

He growled as he raked his eyes over her, taking in the way her dress dipped low in a sweeping curve across her chest and her corset arced beneath her breasts, pushing them up to form a tantalising flash of cleavage. Her nipples beaded beneath the ruched lilac fabric as he stared at her breasts, his mouth going dry as he thought about tugging that barrier down to reveal them.

She gasped as he closed the distance between them in a flash and did just that, hooking his thumbs into the sides of her neckline to pull the material down and free her breasts. He dropped his hands to her backside, lifted her up his body and seized her left nipple, tugging it between his lips. She moaned, the sound sweet torture in the evening air, and arched backwards, pushing her breasts up, as her hands clasped his shoulders.

He groaned as she slid one hand over his back and buried it in his hair, twisting the black strands around it as she held him to her.

Gods, he needed her.

He could barely breathe as he suckled her nipple, his cock so hard in his trousers that it ached and he couldn't stop himself from forcing her hips against his and grinding against her.

He fought to hold on to some restraint as he thumbed her other nipple and drank in her moans, feasted on the desire and need that raged hot inside her, driving him to satisfy her.

Shaia shattered it when she spoke.

"I want you to mark my neck." Her breathless, eager words were followed by a flash of embarrassment that coloured her cheeks as he suddenly jerked back and looked at her face.

She worried her lower lip with her teeth in a way that made him imagine doing that for her, and his eyes dropped to them, shock over what she had said fading away as he stared at them.

Her embarrassment faded too, and when she spoke this time there was force behind her words, a determination that said she had made up her mind and nothing would change it.

"Mate with me, Fuery... as we should be mated... as we wanted all those years ago."

She searched his eyes as he lifted them to meet hers, a flicker of something in them that their bond relayed to him.

She didn't need to fear he would refuse her.

He wanted it as much as she did.

Possibly more.

He showed her by gripping the nape of her neck, dragging her up to him and kissing her hard, thrusting his tongue between her lips to tangle it with hers. He moaned as she met him, pushed for dominance and teased his fangs with the tip of her tongue, sending a hot shiver down his spine. He tortured her back, ripping a low sweet groan from her as he tongued her fangs, teasing them into dropping.

She growled and cranked things up a notch in response, waging war on his restraint again as she made fast work of the buttons of his tunic and shoved it open. Her palms scalded his bare chest, sending another electric shiver over his skin that shot downwards and had his cock jerking against the confines of his trousers.

Gods.

When her hands drifted downwards, nails raking over his stomach, he couldn't stop himself.

He growled, spun her in his arms to face away from him and palmed her breasts as he drew her back against his front and devoured her neck with wet kisses and gentle nips, drawing droplets of blood that only sent him soaring higher as they hit his tongue and exploded on it, filling all of his senses with her.

She rocked back against him, her need ratcheting up as swiftly as his was, her movements jerky and as desperate as his own, calling to his instincts as her mate.

As her male.

He caught her cheek with his left hand as he rolled her nipple between his fingers and forced her head around so he could kiss her again. She groaned into his mouth as hers found it, her kiss so fierce that it stole his breath. She raised her left arm above her head, cupped the back of his neck and held him to her as she lowered her other hand to his hip and pressed back against him.

He shuddered and rocked against her buttocks, trembling as he thrust his aching erection between them, gliding up and down, his heart pounding as he imagined being inside her and feeling her wet heat gripping him as he sank his fangs into her neck.

He dropped his right hand, skimming it over her breasts and down her corset to her hips, and pulled her skirts up, bundling them at her waist. She tore another groan from his lips as she released his hip and helped him, parting the material for him and baring herself.

He wanted to see her, wanted to taste her honey on his lips and drink from her.

Fuery swept her up into his arms, kicked off and swallowed her gasp in another fierce kiss as her back hit the broad trunk of the tree where they had first made love. He had wanted to taste her then, but hadn't been able to hold back, had barely taken a sip before need of her had consumed him.

This time, he would do it.

He dropped her to her feet, and fell to his knees before her. She trembled as he skimmed his hands up her calves to her knees, and then higher, lifting the layers of lilac fabric to reveal her as he caressed her thighs. She caught her skirts and raised them, held them against her stomach as he stared at her, drinking his fill of her.

Her neat thatch of dark curls glistened with her need, tempting him.

He growled as she inched her thighs apart.

Siren.

He couldn't stop himself from grabbing her hips, spinning her away from him and dragging her backside towards him, forcing her to bare herself to him.

She groaned as she gripped the tree to stop herself from falling and he swallowed as she stood bent over before him, her pert backside high in the air, her sweet core bared to him.

Fuery trembled as he eased towards her, running his hands up the backs of her thighs and dipping them inwards as they neared her plush petals. She moaned and quivered beneath his touch, her anticipation running hot in his blood, the need he had stoked by exposing her like this, passion and desire that robbed him of his breath and drove him onwards.

He ran his thumbs up her folds and she trembled harder, her breath coming faster. He dipped his head and brushed his tongue over the delicate bead that was tensed and crying out for his attention, and groaned as his first taste of her filled his senses. Honey, lavender and dew. He wanted to drink all of her, ached to feast on her and hear her cry over and over again as she came for him.

He growled and stroked his tongue up her, lapping up her honey and shuddering in time with her. He couldn't get enough of her. He growled and grasped her hip in his right hand, holding her immobile as he lost control, each stroke of his tongue harder than the last as he devoured her, each moan that issued from her lips tearing another fragile piece of his restraint from him. She shook in his hand, against his tongue, his name falling from her lips as a breathless chant as he swept his tongue between her petals, devouring her.

When he dropped his mouth to her bead and suckled it, she barked out a moan and jerked against him, and his cock ached in response. He rubbed at it, unable to stop himself as it demanded attention, heavy with need that had his balls tight and throbbing.

He had the laces of his trousers opened and his cock in his hand before he was aware of what he was doing, need driving him to take the edge off before it pushed him over it, beyond the point of no return.

Shaia moaned and rocked against his tongue, and a new need rose inside him as he swirled it around her slick opening.

He wanted to feel her.

Her gasp was sweet music to his ears as he released her hip, stroked his fingers over her backside and eased one inside her. She tensed at the invasion, and then relaxed and began rocking on him, a wanton and wild thing that had his breath coming faster and his hand moving on his cock, stroking it in time with each thrust of his finger into her.

She was so wet, so hot, so ready for him.

"Fuery," she whispered, a seductive plea that he answered.

He rose to his feet behind her, twisted her to face him and lifted her. Her legs wrapped around his waist as he pinned her to the tree, entering her in a single deep thrust that buried his cock to the hilt inside her heat. She groaned, grasped the back of his neck and kissed him hard. He grunted and curled his hips, driving into her, trying to hold back and be gentle with her even as he knew it was a fight he wouldn't win this time.

He would make love to her later, as gently and beautifully as she deserved.

Right now, he needed her.

He needed to mate with her.

She clung to him as she kissed him, welcoming his deep thrusts, moaning each time their hips met and he filled her. He swallowed those moans, devoured them as fiercely as he devoured her lips as she rocked against him, writhing in his arms, her breasts brushing against his chest with each of his thrusts that drove her up the tree.

Her nails dug into his neck, the brief flicker of pain only stoking his need hotter.

He growled and kissed her harder as he claimed her hips, holding her in place as he drove into her with long, measured thrusts, making her feel every inch of his cock and feeling every inch of her as she flexed around him.

His fangs ached, his mind swimming with her request, one that now drummed in his blood as a need that demanded he sate it, a hunger that had existed inside him since they had first mated in this spot and one he had left unfulfilled.

Until now.

This time, he would bite her throat as he had wanted to back then.

He would mark her as his mate for all to see.

He shuddered and drove deeper as she feathered her fingers over his lobes, anticipation making him tremble as he willed her on, ached to feel her stroking higher. She obeyed, her delicate fingertips following the curve of his ears.

It was game over when they reached the pointed tips.

Fire swept through him, had him shaking against her as it blazed a path from the sensitive tips of his ears to his groin and burned all restraint away. He snarled, tore his mouth away from hers and sank his fangs hard into her throat.

She cried out, the sound echoing in the darkness, carrying for miles on the still air, and jerked against him, her body going as tight as a bowstring as she clutched him. He growled into her throat as her blood hit his tongue and thrust deep and hard, his fingers digging into her backside as he drove his cock into her, propelling her over the edge.

Her body gave a fierce kick against his, another cry left her lips and then she quivered around him, her core throbbing madly around his length and heat scalding him. He grunted and joined her, release boiling up his shaft and sending his legs trembling as he clung to her with one hand and the tree with the other to stop himself from falling, aware of what came next.

He wasn't sure he could take it.

Her breath washed over his throat.

Her fangs pierced his flesh.

The entire universe detonated.

Stars flashed across his eyes and his head twirled, growing hazy as a second release swept through him and he felt it go through her. The intensity of it had his knees giving out and he managed to gather enough of his wits to twist his body beneath hers so she landed on him, safe from harm.

She moaned and sucked, sending wave after wave of fire through his veins, and along his cock, each pulse of it stealing a little more of his awareness and sending him a little deeper into a blissful haze where he drifted with her, lost and found at the same time.

Home.

At some point, he managed to convince himself to release her throat. He swept his tongue over the marks and savoured the last few drops of her blood as warmth flowed through him, filling every inch of him and leaving no part untouched.

Gods, he loved her.

His beautiful mate.

She slowed her drinking and he shuddered as she stroked her tongue over the marks on his throat, threatening to reignite his desire with each one.

When she settled against him, he drifted with her in his arms, floating somewhere above the world, aware but unaware of it at the same time. He wasn't sure how long they remained that way, but when he finally opened his eyes again, she was watching him, a beautiful soft look on her face that spoke of her love for him.

He brushed her wavy hair behind her ears, getting his own back a little as he caressed their tips and tore a soft gasp from her, and sighed as he looked at her.

She smiled and rolled off him, and he covered himself as she adjusted her dress and rested against him. He wrapped his arms around her, holding her as she pressed her cheek to his chest, and looked up at the sky as it began to lighten.

It was beautiful as it changed colour, dark blue becoming threaded with ribbons of gold and pink, and he wasn't sure he had ever seen it this way before.

It felt fresh and new, vibrant and breathtaking, so colourful.

His life had been darkness for so long that he had forgotten such colours existed.

He looked down at Shaia in his arms and silently thanked her for giving them back to him, together with the sliver of light he could feel in his soul.

She shifted so she could see him, and his eyes dropped to the marks on her throat.

His marks.

He lifted his hand and brushed his fingers across them, still a little hazy as he studied them. "You are mine now."

She whispered, "I was always yours, and I always will be."

His eyes widened and leaped to hers.

She remembered.

She had said those exact words to him in this very place four thousand years ago.

The heart in his chest that had been cold for so long melted at that, warmed and even burned, his love for her blazing in it like an eternal flame.

Gods, he was blessed to have her.

She was the reason he had never lost himself to the darkness and the reason Hartt was always able to bring him back.

Her love for him had kept him strong even when he had reached his breaking point, had given him light even in his darkest hour, and his love for her had kept him coming back.

For her.

He held her to him, pressed a kiss to her lips, and whispered against them, "I was always yours too, and I always will be."

Love burned in his heart, and he felt it burn in hers too.

Love that had set them both free, releasing him from the bonds of darkness and her from the shackles of society.

Now they could begin the forever they had always dreamed of together.

Unchained by that forbidden love.

The End

ABOUT THE AUTHOR

Felicity Heaton is a New York Times and USA Today best-selling author who writes passionate paranormal romance books. In her books she creates detailed worlds, twisting plots, mind-blowing action, intense emotion and heart-stopping romances with leading men that vary from dark deadly vampires to sexy shape-shifters and wicked werewolves, to sinful angels and hot demons!

If you're a fan of paranormal romance authors Lara Adrian, J R Ward, Sherrilyn Kenyon, Kresley Cole, Gena Showalter, Larissa Ione and Christine Feehan then you will enjoy her books too.

If you love your angels a little dark and wicked, her best-selling Her Angel romance series is for you. If you like strong, powerful, and dark vampires then try the Vampires Realm romance series or any of her stand alone vampire romance books. If you're looking for vampire romances that are sinful, passionate and erotic then try her London Vampires romance series. Or if you like hot-blooded alpha heroes who will let nothing stand in the way of them claiming their destined woman then try her Eternal Mates series. It's packed with sexy heroes in a world populated by elves, vampires, fae, demons, shifters, and more. If sexy Greek gods with incredible powers battling to save our world and their home in the Underworld are more your thing, then be sure to step into the world of Guardians of Hades.

If you have enjoyed this story, please take a moment to contact the author at **author@felicityheaton.com** or to post a review of the book online

Connect with Felicity:
Website – http://www.felicityheaton.com
Blog – http://www.felicityheaton.com/blog/
Twitter – http://twitter.com/felicityheaton
Facebook – http://www.facebook.com/felicityheaton
Goodreads – http://www.goodreads.com/felicityheaton
Mailing List – http://www.felicityheaton.com/newsletter.php

FIND OUT MORE ABOUT HER BOOKS AT:
http://www.felicityheaton.com

Made in the USA
Columbia, SC
10 October 2023

24259123R00174